REDACTED WEAPON

BOOK ELEVEN OF RISE OF THE PEACEMAKERS

Kevin Ikenberry & Kevin Steverson

Seventh Seal Press
Coinjock, NC

Chris Kennedy/Seventh Seal Press
1097 Waterlily Rd.
Coinjock, NC 27923
https://chriskennedypublishing.com/

Cover Art by Ricky Ryan.
Cover Design by Brenda Mihalko.

Ordering Information:
Quantity sales. Special discounts are available on quantity purchases by corporations, associations, and others. For details, contact the "Special Sales Department" at the address above.

Redacted Weapon/Kevin Ikenberry & Kevin Steverson -- 1st ed.
ISBN: 978-1648553165

Kevin Ikenberry:

For My Girls.

Kevin Steverson:

For my family...My very large family.

Chapter One

Twelve standard months after the ending of Harbinger

Indonesia

Earth

"I ever tell you how much I hate stakeouts?" Larth licked cold fish stick breading off his digits. He sat to Jyrall's left, finishing the last of his meal, while Jyrall kept the watch.

"Every five minutes for the last two days," Jyrall rumbled without taking his eyes from the warehouse across the dingy alley. For the first time in fifteen months, they had a viable lead on Hatfield and Kr'et'Socae. All they needed was a little activity to confirm their suspicions. Activity on any front would be a blessing. The Peacemaker Guild hadn't responded to much of anything, and as the leads dried up, their attitudes had soured. They needed action, and it finally appeared they were about to see some. A rolling steel door that hadn't opened in days began to move, and a thin sliver of light spread across the asphalt below. Jyrall stood, retrieved his weapon from the small table, and slipped it into the holster without taking his eyes from the window. Six shadows moved in the night outside.

"What is it?" Larth sat forward. His whiskers twitched as he dusted crumbs from his tactical vest.

"Wake up the boys. It's time."

"We're already here, Jyrall," Keaton drawled from the doorway separating their resting quarters from the darkened observation room. His brother, Ricky, stood next to him and covered a yawn with the back of one paw.

"Them sumbitches finally come back?" Ricky asked, as pointedly as ever.

"Yeah." Larth secured his trademark pistols in crossed holsters. "You ready with those toys of yours?"

"Toys? Like hell." Ricky grinned. "Frank and Stein are powered up and ready in their hiding spots."

"I've got comms in the area set to go down thirty seconds from whenever you tell me to engage," Keaton replied.

"You sure we shouldn't call the Misfits?" Larth asked.

"No. They're underground for a reason. This is up to us. I think we can handle it."

Once again, they were on mission, and everything felt right. They'd taken on their identities as smugglers and ne'er-do-wells for the job. Given how good they were, Jyrall couldn't help but wonder if they were enjoying the fall.

One-Eyed Varkell and Switch, together again. Jyrall blinked the thoughts away, but the doubts about their duty lingered.

"We do this just like we planned. Identify our target, scare and scatter the rest, and I'll secure the target for questioning," Jyrall replied. "Get into your positions and be ready. Larth? You're the go signal."

"Already on my way out," Larth said. He stepped through a small hatch cut into a corner of the room and was gone.

Ricky and Keaton retreated into their quarters and down the hidden stairs there. Jyrall padded to the opposite corner to Larth's exit and climbed up a steel rung ladder to the roof access. They'd carefully greased it to avoid noise, and it swung open silently and rested against the roof as Jyrall emerged into the humid Indonesian night.

Earth was, by far, Jyrall's least favorite planet he'd ever visited for longer than a few days. Deep cover operations often took place in locales both unforgiving and uncomfortable. Palopo, located on the western side of the long, natural harbor on the Indonesian island of Sulawesi, was both—but for different reasons than Jyrall and Larth had expected. Home to a major commercial starport, Sulawesi's towns either catered to intergalactic shipping or to intergalactic crime syndicates. Were it not for the support of the Intergalactic Haulers, widely recognized as the transportation industry leader, Jyrall would have had trouble separating the shipping companies from criminals. The movement of goods served as a viable opportunity for the laundering of funds received through less than honorable circumstances. Of that, Jyrall was certain there was no difference at all. Then again, honor no longer appeared to exist in large quantities.

Jyrall moved silently into the shadows and made his way toward the target. He felt anxiety and excitement for the first time in almost two years. They'd trained and simmed as many missions as they could alongside the Kin, but it wasn't the same. Nor was it the same without the Blue Ridge Kin in support. His mind flashed to Cora McCoy. They'd grown close over the last few years. Aside from Larth, she was the best friend he'd ever had. They'd been away from Krifay for three months and out of communication from necessity. He'd give…

Stop it, pup. You can address your feelings later. Get the target.

Dreel's voice was clear, even though his mentor was now long dead. He'd died at the hands of Kr'et'Socae, and there wasn't a moment Jyrall didn't pray the rogue Enforcer would put up enough of a fight that he'd be justified in killing him.

He forced himself to relax. After a moment, Jyrall took a long, deep breath through his nose and sifted through the various scents on the wind. The one he wanted to find was there. Nothing stank like the fear scent of the Zeewie. He'd known a few in their class at the Peacemaker Academy. From the moment they'd arrived, the peculiar aroma had filtered through the quadrangle between the Hall of Heroes and the Administrative Center. Most of the Besquith found the aroma too pungent to do much of anything other than laugh for the first several hours. The upperclassmen acting as drill instructors had tried to contain the Besquith laughter, but it'd been too much. One scared Zeewie could clear a room, but *twenty-three* of them?

"*In position*," Larth reported. He'd moved to the dark alley far west of the open doors. He was prepared to make his move, one Jyrall wasn't exactly sure of. Simply walking up to the six bodyguards and opening fire wasn't much of a strategy.

"Boys?"

"*Almost there*," Keaton whispered. The brothers had moved from their overwatch building across the rooftops to the adjacent building to the east. From there, they planned to move north and cover the tight alley immediately behind the target location—their most likely avenue of escape if Larth managed to cut them off. If they made it to the alley, Ricky and Keaton would channel them into the alley where Frank and Stein waited. The target, and any surviving bodyguards, would have no choice but to surrender. There was no reason to think his partner wouldn't kill all the guards in the attack, though.

There were times Larth scared him.

"*Set,*" Keaton replied.

About twenty seconds later, as Jyrall reached his own vantage point and readied to cover the unexpected arrival of reinforcements from Boesak some thirty kilometers south, he heard Ricky's drawl.

"*Rarin' to go.*"

Jyrall glanced at his slate. Any hope he'd had for guidance or instruction from the Peacemaker Guild died at that moment. They were truly on their own. If the overzealous Humans on Earth blew their cover, they might never be able to close the gap to Hatfield and Kr'et'Socae. A seed of doubt long planted in his subconscious spoke up again.

We should have called the Misfits for support.

And you didn't, pup. Accept the responsibility and complete the mission.

Jyrall settled into his position and drew his sidearm. "Set. You're go, Switch."

"*Meep, meep,*" Larth said, deadpan. While meant to be funny, there was little amusing about where they'd been for the last two years, and they still had light years to go.

Much too young to feel this damned old. Jyrall heard Ricky's incessant country music playlist in his head, but the line of the song stuck with him because it fit. He couldn't stop to think about the future, though. Even with an earworm attempting to take his focus away from the task at hand, Jyrall knew what had to be done. He swung his eyes back to the alley where Larth would approach. Too tight for any type of vehicle aside from an aircycle, it was a perfect approach path for Larth. With Frank and Stein covering the rear, and Jyrall monitoring the dockyard entrance 300 meters away, the target wasn't going anywhere. Even if they managed to get past Larth and attempt to flee, Ricky had wired the entrance gates with enough C4 to cause a tsunami—or so he said.

"*Fifty meters*," Larth whispered. "*You ready for the fun part boys? Because here comes the fun part.*"

* * *

Larth drew his dual Llama MicroMax .380 1911 pistols and flexed his digits around the grips. He moved slowly, rolling his feet from the heel forward to minimize the sound of his steps. He could hear the low, terse voices of his targets. Eyes fixed on the door and the shaft of light spilling across the opening of the alley ahead, he concentrated on the voices.

"We move soon. Yes?"

That's a Lumar. If there's one, there's usually a—

"Yes. Boss say soon."

And there we go.

"You two! Focus outside. Sweep the perimeter," another voice growled.

Definitely a Don't Care Bear. Fuckin' Oogar, man.

Larth grinned. He'd likely found the security team's leader, though. An Oogar and two Lumar. Odds suggested another Oogar and a couple of faster, smaller beings would round out the detail. Zuparti? No, that would be too easy. He would've smelled them by now. Same with MinSha and Jivool. Larth kept wondering as he closed the distance, but he made no radio call. Instead, he picked up his pace slightly and walked up to the door and into the light. The two Lumar appeared stunned, which gave him enough time to raise both pistols and put two rounds in the center of each heavy forehead. As they fell, he danced between them and saw the two

Oogar—*I was right!*—in the distance behind two well-armed K'kng in heavy body armor. Each of their hands held weapons trained in his direction. They opened fire.

Shit!

Larth darted low in front of the target's limousine, a sleek electric Viscount utility vehicle, and kept himself masked from the two foot soldiers.

"I've got two down here, Varkell. Four to go," he said into the radio before emerging from cover to fire at the K'kng on the right. Of course, the damned thing was experienced enough and fast enough to get out of the way.

"*You need me?*"

"Not yet," Larth replied as he moved to fire on the left K'kng. He holstered the left pistol and grabbed a flashbang from his vest. With one paw, he released the safety and activated the device before throwing it toward the K'kng. Larth mashed his eyes closed just before detonation.

WHAMM!

Disoriented, the K'kng sprayed their fire harmlessly over his head. Larth came up with both pistols. He took the K'kng on the left first. The hard-headed asshole took three shots to down. He turned to the second K'kng and caught a glimpse of the armored thug ducking out the rear door toward the Oogar and their target.

"Phase two," Larth called as he vaulted onto the Viscount and ran up the sloping hood toward the door. "Ready, boys!"

Larth leapt from the rear of the Viscount and backed into the wall nearest the door. He dumped the magazines and reloaded in a blur. The target and his remaining minions had stepped into the alley, but nothing was happening.

"Boys?"

There was no response.

Dammit!

Larth took a deep breath and turned into the doorframe with his weapons up. The rear door to the alley sat ajar. They'd moved outside, but where were those damned—

"Drones!" one of the Oogar roared. A fusillade of gunfire erupted outside, and Larth grinned. As soon as it started, the coordinated fire stopped. He whirled into the door and saw the two Oogar sprawled on the alley floor. The Zeewie whirled and locked eyes with Larth before it turned and sprinted down a tiny alley leading toward the water. An avenue of escape they hadn't believed capable of being used, but the little bastard disappeared into it.

"He's moving north!" Larth started after him.

"*Y'all relax; I got this,*" Ricky replied over the channel. Larth looked up to the rooftop where Ricky had been stationed with his rifle. A shadow moved and sprinted to the north. Larth watched him as long as he could before the shadow leapt into the night and down into the tight alleyway.

There was a high-pitched scream and then nothing.

A flutter of movement from behind alarmed Larth, and he spun around with his weapons up, but a familiar shape filled the doorway of the target's garage.

"Have you searched them? Or the vehicle?"

Larth shook his head and holstered his pistols at the same time. "Not yet. What're you hoping to find?"

"Hope is not a method," Jyrall rumbled. "Any shred of information we can gather from their slates, their pattern of life, or their trash matters."

Larth recognized the quote from one of their instructors at the Academy, but he couldn't remember who anymore. Nor did it seem to matter. Everything was wrong. The guild he'd wanted to serve was in disarray. He'd tried, successfully, to block his concerns and doubts from rising by focusing on their mission. While they'd been passively gathering data and doing odd smuggling jobs undercover, Larth realized he felt less and less connected to his role as a Peacemaker and, shockingly, less connected to his best friend.

"We're not going to find anything in their trash, Snarlyface."

"We don't know that until we try." Jyrall glanced at him. "Complete the mission."

Oh, here we go again.

Instead of biting back the next thought in his head, Larth said, "Don't bring them into this. Or her."

Jyrall froze and his eye narrowed. "I'm not bringing anyone into this. We have a job to do and a mission to complete. Don't make anything about this personal."

Larth sighed. "Trying not to. Just seems like everything is against us."

"Us." Jyrall grinned. "As long as there *is* an us, everything will be against us except our friends and allies. Take solace there, Little Buddy."

The nickname never failed to fluster Larth, who snorted a laugh. "Fine. We'll search 'em. Here comes Keaton."

The Pushtal emerged from the shadows carrying the sniper rifle at the ready. "Y'all heard from Ricky?"

"Figured he'd let us know if he needed anything." Larth pointed at Frank and Stein in the alley. "Those things worked like a charm this time."

Keaton grinned. "Ricky Shit needs to be tested thoroughly, but when you care enough to use the very best, it'll do."

"Well said." Jyrall moved toward one of the Oogar guards and knelt to grab its wrist slate when he froze. His head came up in alarm. He blinked several times and turned to glare down the dark alley.

"You okay?" Larth asked. Even as the words left his mouth, his senses flared. "Oh, hell no."

Keaton gasped. "What the fuck is that *smell?*"

From the darkness, the figure of Ricky McCoy emerged. The Zeewie known as Tzegelo lay draped over the Pushtal's left shoulder. His right arm came up to his face and attempted to wedge his muzzle into the crook of his arm. He stopped suddenly, grabbed for one knee with his free hand, and hunched over retching.

"God damn mother fuckin—" He stood, shifted the Zeewie, and made his way forward. "Just… just tell me one damned thing."

Larth saw Jyrall not even trying to hide his amusement. His partner said, "What is it, Ricky? What's the problem?"

"Problem?" Ricky almost fell down with another abdominal spasm. Larth risked a glance at Keaton to find the other twin had removed a portable gas/vapor mask from his vest and placed it over his nose and mouth. Keaton still appeared on the edge of nausea and was barely holding it together.

"Y'all cain't smell this?" Ricky knelt on the ground and somewhat gently laid Tzegelo at Jyrall's feet. As soon as he'd done so, Ricky retched again and scrambled away from the Zeewie. Keaton's effort to contain his own discomfort failed. As both the McCoys dry-heaved, Larth caught Jyrall's eye. The Besquith winked at him.

"What's wrong with you two?" Larth asked as he stepped forward to search Tzegelo's clothing. "Did he gas you?"

The boys didn't immediately respond. Larth tried not to cough, and his eyes watered from the smell. No matter how used to the Zeewie fear scent a Peacemaker got—and they'd been trained with it numerous times—its potency remained without question or equal.

Ricky looked incredulously at Larth. "Look, man, I didn't do nothing. This lil' fucker ran away, and I jumped in front of him to scare him. I heard a *pop* as he fainted dead to the ground, and next thing I know—"

Ricky retched again, and Larth finally let out the cough he'd been holding and turned away. He looked at Jyrall, who stood with his big hands on his hips, shaking his head in disgust.

"Zeewie are deathly afraid of Pushtal," Jyrall said. "When confronted with a fight-or-flight situation, they'll run. In extreme cases, they'll faint and release a natural pheromone designed to drive a potential predator away until they can recover and run again."

"So, he's gonna run again?" Keaton coughed.

"If we let him." Jyrall walked over to the Zeewie and rolled him over to get a look at his face. "He's going to be out for a couple hours. Let's get him back to *Night Moves* and be on our way."

"Aw, hell naw," Ricky protested. "What if he does that on the ship? We ain't got no place to go!"

Larth tapped his vest. "We'll sedate him just enough so he won't."

"And if he does?" Keaton asked.

"Gonna space the lil' fucker. There. I said it. Don't make me do it, either," Ricky growled. "What's he got that's so special anyway?"

"Other than a commercial transport ride to Prestone in six hours?" Larth asked.

Jyrall raised a hand. Dangling from his claws was a tiny, clear bag filled with red diamond dust. On the bag, clearly visible in the light from the open garage access door, Larth read "Parmick Mines."

The Besquith turned and grinned savagely at Larth, who returned it. They had their Zeewie. He grinned at Ricky and Keaton. "Jackpot, boys. Jackpot."

"Let's get a move on," Larth said. "I don't like sitting out here like this. Grab the Zeewie, Ricky."

"He's out for days?" Ricky asked. "All because of me? Hell, that's some Ricky Shit right there, ain't it?"

*****

Chapter Two

Blue Ridge Kin Headquarters

Krifay

Colonel Cora McCoy leaned back in her chair and threw her boots up on her desk. She put her hands behind her head and stared at the ceiling of her small office. She ran the numbers again in her mind. The cost was of no concern; her mercenary company, the Blue Ridge Kin, had plenty of credits in several accounts and financial institutes, split deliberately in case there was an issue with one. She also kept actual hard credit on hand, locked in safes here in her headquarters and on each ship.

"They're not the brightest individuals to ever put on a uniform, that's for sure," she said. "Still, they come highly recommended by someone Jyrall trusts. Another Lumar. A Peacemaker, no less, by the name of Millzak."

"True," Colonel Pete Brentale agreed. "Nowadays, it's hard to know who you can trust. If Jyrall has no problems with a recommendation from Peacemaker Millzak, even if it was made a year ago, I sure don't have a problem with it."

"Well, Keaton checked it out," Cora said as she dropped her boots to the floor and leaned forward. "The recommendation isn't forged. Tivlang has been carrying it with him since he and the others left the Trindlark System. Before Jyrall and Larth left, we spoke about it."

"Yeah. Can't blame them for looking into a group of Lumar and Jivool hiring on and working the docks together. It was strange."

"From mining to the fishing industry," Cora said. She grinned. "Well, seafood storage anyway. The seven of them worked the warehouses."

"Is it a recommendation for mercenary work?" Pete asked.

"No," Cora explained. "It's a general 'these are trustworthy hard workers who helped out a Peacemaker when they weren't obligated to' kind of recommendation. Jyrall said, from what he knows of Millzak and those who knew him in the past, if Millzak says someone is honest and trustworthy, they are. Period."

"What makes them want to join a mercenary company?" Pete wondered. "Besides the obvious. Credits."

"I don't know," Cora admitted. "Tivlang says Millzak told him it seemed things were changing, and he might have to pick a side. He's not the brightest, as I said, but he seems to like the side where races work together and not against each other. That's why he and the others applied to join the Kin."

"We are growing both our units," Pete said. "I'd take them if they asked to join the Barnstormers… though I don't know how I'd train them to fly a powered glider. Like I said, if Jyrall didn't have a problem with them due to a recommendation, I sure don't."

He stood to leave. "I haven't known the Peacemakers and their crew as long as you, nor do I have the level of friendship you have, but I know I'd trust them with everything I have, up to and including my life and the lives of my company. They've earned it."

Cora stood to see him out. "That they did, more than once. I'll go talk to them and offer contracts. See you at our meeting tomorrow."

* * *

"Lieutenant Rhineder will be your platoon leader," Cora explained. "All the infantry soldiers fall under him when we're on contract."

"Yes, ma'am," Tivlang said. "What is infantry?"

"Nails." Rhineder looked back and forth between his commander and the seven-foot-tall Lumar standing slightly ahead of three other big Lumar and three Jivool. It didn't escape him that the Jivool stood a head or more taller than the Jivool who were already part of Blue Ridge Kin.

"You have *got* to be shitting me," First Sergeant Figgle exclaimed. He stood beside Cora.

"They come from a mining background, Top," Cora explained, "not a mercenary one."

"I..." First Sergeant Figgle closed his mouth. Cora knew he didn't want to protest her decision in front of the troops. He might be a Goka, but he'd studied the Human mannerisms of non-commissioned officers. He knew better, even if much of what he'd learned from was entertainment films more than a century old.

"It means you'll fight with handheld weapons, not operate CASPers," Cora explained.

"Yes, ma'am," Tivlang said. A wide grin spread across his face. "Fight with hands and hold weapons. Not get inside big war machine."

May giggled and elbowed Nileah. The unit's XO shook her head and held it in.

"Major Sevier and I have to leave for the day," Cora said. "We'll be attending the meeting with Colonel Brentale concerning the final plans for the defense of Krifay, should it be needed."

She turned to May. "Captain Bolton and Lieutenant Rhineder will put together a training plan for you seven. It won't be actual Basic Training, but I expect you'll learn a lot in a hurry."

"Ma'am?" Figgle asked. "If I may. I think it's a good idea for the officers to plan, but the actual training needs to be handled by an NCOor two."

"What do you have in mind?" Cora asked.

First Sergeant Figgle rubbed two of his small pincers together. "Sergeant Squarlik and Corporal Bweenkit."

"Makes sense," Nails agreed. "Squarlik is ready to be a squad leader. It'll be good to give him more responsibility than the sniper duties."

"It'll keep them busy," Figgle added. "Both of them have been around that specialist from the Barnstormers too much lately. What's his name?"

"Haney," May said. "Specialist Haney."

"That's the sonofabitch," Figgle said.

"You need to let that go, Top," Cora advised.

"He had Bweenkit yelling about being a pirate while he was under the influence of pain meds," Figgle protested.

"He did have an eye shot out," May said.

"Just because he wears an eye patch does *not* mean he is a damn pirate," Figgle countered, "and he meant one of those in the entertainment videos with the hats… not an actual pirate attacking cargo freighters in sketchy systems and mining colonies."

A voice spoke from behind the group. "Did someone say hat? Hat, that is? I have several in the most delightful colors. Delightful, don't you know."

"Mister Stew," First Sergeant Figgle said without turning around. If he'd had actual Human-like teeth, he'd have said it through clenched ones. "If you don't move out and draw fire, I swear to the blazing stars, I'm going…"

"Top," Cora warned. She looked over her shoulder.

The pilot and recently promoted warrant officer was wearing a blinding outfit consisting of a teal- and yellow-ruffled long-sleeved flight suit. A floppy purple hat was cocked sideways with a pink feather in it. Cora wondered if it was one of his own.

Sometimes she wondered if allowing the two avian race Miderall the leeway to create their own uniform instead of the standard color of muted gray and black camouflage all the other members of the Blue Ridge Kin wore had been a good decision.

"We'll let those appointed over the new squad make the decisions, Chief. Sergeant Squarlik will let you know if you're needed for the crash-course training the new recruits will receive—quick ship exits and the like."

"Yes, ma'am," Stew said. He shrugged and walked back toward his fellow pilots, a Miderall like himself, and two SleSha.

* * *

Planetary Administration Offices
Snapper Isle, Krifay

Cora and Nileah stepped into the conference room and looked around. Pete and his executive officer were already seated on the far side. They walked around the table and joined them. Seated were the planet administrator, the head of the planet's law enforcement and customs, two representatives from the fishing industry, and two officers of the planet's unofficial reserve forces. Peacemaker Zetchek, a Zuparti, was the last to join them.

Walton Burlif called the meeting to order, and they ceased talking among themselves to listen to the administrator.

"Now that we've all had a few days to consider the various proposals, I'd like us to come to a consensus and work toward the goal." Heads nodded all around.

He continued, "Now, I don't profess to be an expert on defense, especially planetary defense. You all know I come from a fishing background. That's all I've ever known. The reason it's not hard to govern this planet is because many of its inhabitants come from the same. I like to think we all have some good old common sense."

"The unwritten 'laws of the sea,'" agreed Norman Rayner, the CEO of the largest seafood export company on the planet. "Man Overboard—or any other race for that matter—means we all stop whatever we're doing and rush to the site. Mayday is a cry none should ever take lightly."

"That is an unusual way to say it, but I concur," the Peacemaker said. "My observations have shown that the Human saying of 'do unto others' holds sway on this planet. It's refreshing, to say the least."

"With that being said," the planet administrator continued, "I'd like to bring the proposal that makes the most sense—to me anyway—up for vote. All in favor of Brentale's Barnstormers and the Blue Ridge Kin mercenary companies heading up the defense, say 'Aye.'"

Everyone spoke. "All opposed?" No one spoke. "Like I said, common sense. We'll leave it to the professionals to put together a plan. Colonel Brentale, do you and Colonel McCoy have any preliminary plans we can get started on? I've already got the lure ready to cast, as far as catching a large portion of reserve credit from the yearly budget."

"We do," Pete said. "It'll involve our ships, our troops, some of the corporation's ships… and ships of the floating kind. It'll also include the law enforcement and volunteer reserve forces. That a few retirees still have CASPers is a bonus."

"Well, the floor is yours," Walter said.

* * *

Blue Ridge Kin Headquarters

"Get up off the floor," Bweenkit said. "Let me show you what I did, step by step."

The large Jivool stood up and rubbed his backside. "I would like to know, Corporal. I've never been thrown that way. Not even by Tivlang when we wrestle."

"Being able to disarm and subdue an opponent when fighting in close proximity is very important," Squarlik said, his voice serious.

"It's nearly as important as being able to send accurate rounds downrange." He was quoting something he'd heard Nails Rhineder say.

"I understand," Private Mooknol said, still rubbing the sore spot.

"What's 'downrange?'" Private Tivlang asked.

First Sergeant Figgle made an attempt to shake his head at the Lumar. It didn't come off well, as it was a Human gesture, and not one natural to a Goka.

"Squarlik! You shit-birds better get this squad squared away," Figgle said. "I need to go check on the supplies those four technicians are loading on the ship. It'll be in orbit tomorrow morning. I want to see what kind of stuff Specialist Conner is trying to sneak on board."

As the first sergeant walked by Nails, he mumbled, "Not that I'll catch her with half of whatever she procured."

"Sergeant Squarlik," Tivlang asked, his voice deadly serious, "did First Sergeant just insult you? You said we're family in this squad. Kin. I understand what kin is now. I cannot let an insult pass against family. Where did he go?" He punched two of his fists into their opposite hands.

Nails stepped in front of the big Lumar. "Hold on, Private. Top just talks that way. He doesn't mean to actually insult members of the unit. We're all kin in this unit. Sometimes family does that. We just don't let anyone outside of us do it."

"Yes, sir," Tivlang said. "I think I understand."

"Besides," Squarlik said, "if you thought Bweenkit could toss you about, you don't want to have a go with the first sergeant."

Tivlang scratched his chin with a lower hand. "But… he is smaller than I am, and he is older than you two. I can tell, even if he is Goka."

"Old?" Nails asked. "Since when does that matter?"

"Old means slow," Tivlang explained. "I can wrestle one who is slow and win."

Bweenkit looked at Squarlik. Squarlik looked at Bweenkit. They both slowly turned to Lieutenant Rhineder. Nails grinned and ran a hand across his close-cropped gray flattop.

Ten minutes later, Tivlang was sitting against the wall, nursing his upper shoulder and his chin. "I think I should listen to what First Sergeant says and not talk. Just listen and learn. Learning is hard, but I will try." He looked up into Corporal Bweenkit's one good eye. "I don't like fighting old ones anymore. Can we do more weapons training instead?"

* * *

"Conner!" Figgle yelled. "What the hell is in this case?"

"Personal stuff, First Sergeant," Specialist Conner answered. She blew a puff of air upward to move a strand of long red hair from near her eye.

The first sergeant attempted to squint his eyes. It didn't work. For a brief moment, he considered ordering her to show him, but thought better of it. He probably didn't want to know what was in it.

Private Sreet, one of the Maki technicians, stopped and watched the senior NCO of the unit walk away. He turned to Conner. "Isn't that the box with the shock plugs?"

"Yeah, but he doesn't need to know Haney traded them to me. I had to give up a copy of a music file for them."

"A what?"

"Music. Keaton secured a file of every song by a band well over a hundred years old. A band called Molly Hatchet."

"Something that old for little shock plugs?"

"They may be little, but they'll knock a grown man to his knees. Ricky made them."

"What did Haney trade for them?" the Maki asked as he tried to keep it straight.

"A 10mm socket," Conner answered. "Very rare."

"This is all really confusing."

"What is?" the red-haired woman asked. "Trading?'

"Mafia business," Sreet said.

Specialist Conner gave the young Maki a look any race would understand. Sreet apologized, said he never asked, and moved off quickly. As a lower enlisted, she knew he knew about the E4 Mafia, he just wasn't of sufficient rank nor accepted into it to be able bring up the subject. And in the open, no less. She took note of the discrepancy for later consideration once the Maki made the rank of E4.

* * *

Up front in the operations center of the ship, Stew turned to Monty. "See! She *is* a member of the E4 Mafia! The rumors are true. True, I say. I would wager she's a Made Woman, Made, that is."

Monty reached over and turned the video and sound feed off to the cargo hold. "Are you insane? Insane, I ask? Do you want our pay to get messed up? Paid as a private with no time in the company? Company, don't you know!"

"I—"

"No!" Monty insisted. "You know nothing of that conversation. Nothing. You'll cause your hats to disappear from your berth, traded for a handful of Human chewing gum or something of the like. Chewing gum, I say!"

Stew's eyes widened at the thought of his precious hats going missing, swallowed up into the E4 Mafia's never-ending trade cycle. "I didn't see or hear anything."

He didn't repeat any of what he said. He was now nervous.

* * *

Barnstormers' Headquarters

Cora looked at the map and nodded. "Looks good to me, Pete. If the maintenance is halfway decent on their CASPers, the reserve forces should be able to cover both those big islands until we can send in the reactionary force. I doubt that'll be where anyone lands to stage from, but it's a solid plan."

"I thought so," Pete said. "Customs and law enforcement should be able to handle the smaller areas. We'll be able to get to and deploy quickly with our insertion ships. We drop the ramp and come out swinging."

"We should have plenty of warning as we rotate our ships to keep watch on the system long before anyone enters the atmosphere," Cora said. "Stockpiling ammunition and supplies, including rockets for our CASPers in hidden caches, is going to be a game changer, too. Whoever chooses to invade—if anyone does—is going to be limited to what they bring with them."

"Yeah," Pete agreed. "I can tell you from experience what it's like to have to count every round."

"Agreed," Cora said. "It sucks."

"Yeah, there was this one mission where—"

He didn't get to finish his sentence as his computer chimed with an incoming call. "That's funny," Pete said. "Very few have this link. Mike, you, the Peacemakers.

"Barnstormers' HQ, Colonel Brentale," Pete said as he answered. He waved Cora around to see who it was.

"Colonels," Peacemaker Zetcheck greeted them. "I have news. News I would prefer to speak to you about in person, as you Humans say."

"Is that an invasion?" Cora asked quickly.

"That's… a complicated question, is it not?" Zetcheck answered.

"We're here," Pete said, "and will be as we finalize small details. Come on over. I'll have a cold one waiting for you."

The two commanding officers continued with the final planning of the defense of Krifay. There were many things to consider. Everything from orbit to ground defenses had to be finalized. The planet didn't have a fleet of warships to defend the space between entry points to the planet itself, so whatever happened in atmosphere and below had to be accounted for… or at least considered.

Forty minutes later, the Peacemaker arrived. He nodded and sighed before he frowned.

"The Crusaders are coming, and there's nothing I can do to stop them."

* * * * *

Chapter Three

Prestone
Freh Region

As a young mercenary, Smith had learned to smell opportunity. He'd ascended through the ranks of three separate mercenary companies before he'd signed on with his last company, Talmore's Ridgerunners. He hadn't trusted the lot of them. Most of them were related in some way or another, and their whole "blood over anything" mentality infuriated him on a regular basis.

When Colonel Talmore had bought the farm on Naar, he'd leapt into command, and his first order of business had been to break up as many of the familial units as possible. Granted, the high casualty rates the Ridgerunners had taken on that final mission had accomplished most of that for him, but his message to the rest of them was simple. Family had no place in warfare. Closeness might have some advantages in combat, but as the contracts dwindled and became more competitive, those relationships challenged what little command presence he had.

Getting rid of Cora McCoy and her band of harpies—a nickname he'd taken great pride in belatedly giving them—had been the best decision he'd made. With them gone, he'd been able to wrangle more risky contracts with higher payouts. The tight cadre of Humans from northern Georgia and western North Carolina had either died or left the unit in droves. He'd filled their spots with the cheapest and roughest mercenaries he could find. Business was good, until another opportunity came along—one even Smith couldn't resist.

The Crusaders offered higher payouts, better equipment at wholesale prices, and the legal backing of the Peacemaker Guild. With the death of Guild Master Rsach, though, the moral compass of the guild swung wildly toward the nigh-impossible goal of making peace throughout the galaxy. Crusader units swept onto planets, established martial law in the name of the guild, and quelled any and all disturbances. Regular business activities were allowed to continue—for a fee. Their protection schemes gave the Crusaders an almost impenetrable legal shield. When he couldn't believe business could be any better, word had come from the guild's new leadership that Crusader units could capture credits and valuable items as necessary to quell potential disruptors of the peace. They'd been given license to steal. Smith, and his newly rechristened Templars, had taken the guidance like their ancestors had and enjoyed leaving little of value in their wake.

Crusader Prime had specifically ordered Smith to Prestone because of his ability to see opportunity. Prestone had enjoyed a reputation before the Omega War as the galactic equivalent of Las Vegas on Earth—an oasis of gambling and debauchery. Prestone was deemed mostly inhabitable, save for certain areas of three continents. Only two of them were populated because of the presence of thousands of species of dangerous flora. Among them were new species of life, but none with any sort of intelligent behaviors. As such, the developers of Prestone were more than happy to leave it alone, save for the occasional high-end survival experiences they sold. Smith didn't care about "the most dangerous place in the galaxy." He knew Prime saw something happening on Prestone, where the Crusaders didn't have to worry about making the peace, but where they could make credits. Lots of credits.

"*Aircraft squawking as* Templar One*, this is Prestone Control. Welcome to our airspace. Please declare your intentions for vector to your destination.*" The emotionless voice came through in perfect Standard English, though his communications equipment identified the voice as a Jeha.

Smith waved off his communications operator and leaned forward in his seat. The return of gravity as the dropship settled into the upper reaches of Prestone's thick atmosphere felt good after the hyperspace transit, and stretching helped. "Prestone Control, this is Lieutenant Colonel Trevor Smith in command of the Templars. We're here on a classified mission from Crusader Prime and request vectors to meet with our contact, Mr. Hatfield, who should be expecting us."

The response was immediate and promising. "Templar One*, welcome to Prestone, Lieutenant Colonel Smith. Mr. Hatfield is expecting you. From your current position, assume a heading of 164 degrees and maintain flight level 30 and your current airspeed for 12,000 kilometers until you're contacted by Limerick Arrival and Departure for direct vectors. May fortune find you during your stay. Prestone Control, out.*"

Smith turned to the command pilot, Lieutenant Hantleman, who had rightly anticipated his question. "Sir, at present speed, we'll be within the Limerick airspace in roughly four and a half hours."

"Excellent. I'm going down to the bays for PCCs and PCIs. Notify me when we're in range."

"Yes, sir," Hantleman responded without taking his eyes off the distant curving horizon of Prestone. At their 30,000 kilometer altitude, there wasn't much atmospheric resistance on the dropship's control surfaces. Handling a vehicle at hypersonic speeds took impressive control, and the Crusaders made sure to hire the best pilots from Earth. With their deep pockets, they could afford the absolute best. Hantleman was no exception.

Smith made his way out of the cockpit as Lieutenant Grissom, the copilot, dropped into the seat he'd just vacated. He reached the round hatch and descended the ladder toward the upper of the dropship's two main decks. The first stop on his journey to the bays, where his Templars should be deeply involved in pre-combat checks and inspections, was his quarters. The return of gravity meant he could shower for the first time in a couple of weeks. While the flight crew wouldn't have had time to formulate an opinion of his appearance, his troops needed to see him cleaned up and in a fresh uniform. Leadership required respect, and nothing accomplished that better, in his mind, than setting the standard.

Once he was clean, he pulled on the Crusaders' official uniform. Taken from the dress white uniforms of ancient Earth militaries, primarily that of the United States, the pressed pants and white jacket were nowhere near as heavy as their wool ancestors. Given the climate near Limerick, he'd appreciate not sweating heavily. Adorned with gold brocade and epaulets, the uniform gave him the appearance of having a much higher rank than lieutenant colonel, which was his intention. Crusader Prime cared little for the dress uniforms in the conduct of official business, but Smith was dependent on the illusion. This Hatfield character needed to know who he was dealing with, even if the Crusaders and the Peacemaker Guild appeared to know little about *him.*

Official files had little more than his surname, Hatfield, and a highly redacted list of charges for crimes from a host of planets over the last twenty years. Hatfield was Human, believed to be from the North American continent, and less than forty years old. His birthplace and date were unknown. The more Smith read, the more befuddled he became. The Peacemakers, and the Crusaders by default, had complete records on almost all criminals. Why was Hatfield's record incomplete?

Smith considered the problem as he stood before the mirror, touching up his uniform. The most likely explanation was that the Peacemaker Guild's new leadership had redacted the file purposefully. Hatfield was connected to suspicious dealings on Parmick, a fight at Hope Station, and a handful of black-market dealings on Earth. Whatever those incidents had in common, they'd been enough to convince Crusader Prime that Hatfield needed both watching and more proper motivation. But what if the truth was different?

Smith shook his head and said softly to himself, "No, that's not all. Gotta find the advantage. That's why you're here."

He nodded to himself and smiled at his reflection before donning the stern façade of a commander. He wanted the troops to see he was prepared and ready for whatever they'd find. He'd reward them with liberty—the chance for some time off to sample the local delights—while he decided what their mission would be and how to use them best. When recalled, they would have their weapons and equipment at the ready. He knew the promise of liberty would drive them faster than he could, but a Crusader commander needed to push his forces to the brink at all times. Once rewarded, they would return ready for the mission. All he had to do was keep them in line and properly motivate them.

"Time for a little strategic chicken shit," he said. The grin on his face appeared perfectly evil, and that satisfied him. He was ready to face them and give them both what they wanted and what they needed. Part of that was chicken shit. He'd learned the term from his very first platoon sergeant, Hockley. When Hockley wasn't enforcing strategic chicken shit on his troopers, he'd hum calliope music. When Smith had taken over the platoon, he'd asked Hockley why he did it.

"Simple, Lieutenant." Hockley had never said "sir" during their time together. He'd addressed Smith by his rank with a hefty measure of disdain. "If I inspect a rifle and it's perfectly clean, the soldier has shown they can clean a rifle; that should be the standard. Trouble is, perfection is unattainable. I push them harder on the little things that don't mean anything in garrison. When we're training or on a mission, I want them to do what they're told. When they pull out the shit that doesn't matter, that's when I start humming. They shut their traps and get down to business. So should you."

Pre-combat checks and inspections had the stated goal of preparing a unit for action. In reality, his Templars were always ready for action. They were a highly functional weapon system in their own right. All he had to do was point them at a situation and turn them loose. They knew what to accomplish, and the rules of engagement were always in their favor. No one in their right mind would stand up to the Crusaders.

"With great power comes the responsibility to forcefully apply it," Smith quoted Prime's guidance to him verbatim. "The peace will be made in our image. One planet at a time."

* * *

Halfway down the lone straight section of the Rue d'Amour stood the Omni. The combination casino, resort, and racing complex dominated more than three full kilometers of prime roadway real estate in the heart of Limerick. To Smith's eyes, the Omni seemed undoubtedly Human in its design. A conglomeration of various landmarks from Earth seemed built to cater to the tourists who'd long ago given up on seeing the actual Earth for all the chaos therein.

Over a hundred structures replicated sites like the Great Pyramid, the famous skyscrapers of New York, and all manner of smaller buildings, from the Sydney Opera House to a reproduction of the ancient Globe Theatre. The sight of a massive artificial lake containing a replica of Chicago's famous Navy Pier, something he hadn't seen in more than two decades, almost cracked Smith's carefully constructed stoic veneer with a smile.

The Blevin security detail wouldn't have cared. Their attention remained rightly outside the three-vehicle motorcade. While Smith worried about notoriety, he soon learned the local custom, especially for powerful and popular visitors, entailed such accommodations.

Powerful. He rolled the word around in his mind for the millionth time in the last two years. The rise of the Peacemaker Guild, specifically because of the founding and deployment of the Crusaders, had given him all the power he could have ever imagined. He was fourth in the line of succession for commander of the Crusaders, and his task force had pacified more than twelve planets in those two years, earning multiple commendations from the guild master. But Prime wanted him to do what he did best—find opportunities. That sometimes meant applying his power forcefully. As the more familiar façades of New Vegas appeared, the motorcade turned into a Roman-themed monstrosity, which broke his veneer with a wild thought.

Emperor. I like the sound of that.

The motorcade slowed, and the security detail deployed and opened the door so he could disembark. Scores of beings of all species milled about the area, but none of them paid attention to him or the detail, and he knew why. They were used to seeing powerful and popular beings. His appearance was nothing new to them, even if they didn't understand what the Crusaders were.

We'll change that the first chance we get.

A Human male with longish blond hair slicked back from his tanned face smiled and made his way down the red-carpeted stairs. He wore a beige suit over a dark shirt with a mandarin collar and what appeared to be a cummerbund. In his left hand was a large brown cigar, trailing smoke. Smith wrinkled his nose in disapproval but stepped forward to greet the man.

"Colonel Smith?" the man drawled.

Spare me from another redneck.

Smith forced a smile onto his face. "Mister Hatfield?"

"All my life. How 'bout you?" They shook hands firmly, and Hatfield patted Smith on the upper arm with his free hand. "Welcome to the Omni, Colonel. I'm awfully glad you're here."

"Oh?" Smith asked. "Why would that be? Prestone isn't in need of the Crusaders, is it?"

Hatfield puffed once on the cigar. "'Course not. That's not why you're here. Y'all asked to come to Prestone. I can only assume you have need of the particular… amenities Prestone can provide for your organization."

Smith had to laugh. It was a genuine response. Hatfield might sound like a dumb hillbilly, but he'd clearly seen the reasoning behind Prime's request. The Crusaders had abilities far beyond their original intention, and being able to properly secure their holdings—in the form of properly laundered credits—was paramount in this new phase. More goods and valuables of all types flowed into the Crusaders' coffers on a daily basis. They'd need a place to store it while attempting to move it, and there was no better place in the galaxy to do so than Prestone. Everything found its way through the system, and the Peacemakers had never had cause to step in, because, on this planet, contracts didn't matter. Only credits mattered.

Money talks. Let's see how fluent you are, Mister Hatfield.

"I'm certain Crusader Prime had such capabilities in mind." Smith nodded. "Is there someplace we can talk?"

Hatfield grinned. "Hell, yes. Matter of fact, you're just in time for the main event. If you'll follow me?"

They moved through gilded doors into the casino. Familiar and unfamiliar table games dominated the center of the space. Slot machines dotted the walls amongst the vendors selling alcohol, all manner of drugs and paraphernalia, and food. They turned right and seemed to be following signs for the racing complex when he saw a bank of video slot machines themed as the Peacemakers. One of the images was of Jessica Francis staring into the distance with her hands on her hips. News must not have traveled this—

Oh, Justicemakers: The New Breed. Not *Francis.*

But that actress is cute.

Hatfield turned toward him, the cigar clenched in his teeth. "Colonel? Is everything good?"

"Yes. Something caught my eye."

"Ah." Hatfield grinned. "That happens 'round here. I was askin' if you liked racin'. We got all types here—for the Humans, we've got greyhounds and horses. Lots of species like watching them, but we're looking to expand our repertoire, so to speak. I think we've found something special, and we're gonna debut it today."

His curiosity piqued, Smith followed Hatfield rather than asking any of the numerous questions that came to mind. Casinos, as his father had described them, existed to separate fools from their money. Where their money went was something he'd always wanted to know. Then again, he'd never seen a casino mogul who didn't appear to have a shit ton of money. With his custom suit and smelly cigar, Hatfield looked the part, but already, Smith could see his potential angles. There were ways he could manipulate this man. All he needed to do was figure out which ones to use. All he needed was an opportunity.

The Omni Racing Complex encompassed the south side of the casino. A greyhound race had just ended. The dogs were collected, and their mechanical rabbit quarry retracted. Several hovercarts driven by enthusiastic Jeha groomed the surface—what Smith thought was dirt—for the next race. The arena itself matched the track's oval shape. Smith guessed the track was around eight hundred meters in length, as it looked bigger than the countless ovals he'd run physical fitness assessments around in his youth. One side of the arena was open to the southern sky. Prestone's star warmed the grandstands pleasantly in the late afternoon.

On the edges of the stands were seats and grassy areas open to the lower paying customers. Near the center of the stands, immediately opposite the finish line, were boxed seats complete with waitstaff serving food and drinks. Above them were enclosed seats in a club level and an elevated seating area much like the ones on the edges. All the seats were filled with enthusiastic spectators.

"Next race in ten minutes. This will be the final session of the day—our Omni main event," a public address announcer called. "Betting closes on the main event in five minutes."

Hatfield made his way down the center staircase to the boxed seating area. An Oogar wearing a tuxedo, or his species equivalent thereof, opened the gate. Hatfield turned and gestured to Smith. "The colonel is with me, Brusk."

The Oogar nodded silently as they passed into a private box containing two richly-appointed chairs. As Hatfield sat in the one on the left, a uniformed Veetch placed a whiskey on the rocks on the table next to him.

"Much obliged, Qada." Hatfield smiled and gestured for Smith to sit. "What would you like to drink? We have everything in the galaxy."

"I'll have a seltzer, please," Smith replied. The Crusaders followed old military protocols, and drinking wasn't allowed on duty. As much as their official business hadn't been convened, it was best to remain neutral in word and deed. He almost changed his order to a beer but decided against it.

Hatfield appeared to cover a laugh with a cough and sat back against his seat. "I'm really glad you made it in time to see this, Colonel. We're about to blow the roof off this place."

Smith wanted to bring up that the racing arena had no roof, but his curiosity overrode his sarcasm. "So, what other kinds of racing do you have here?"

"All kinds. We race greyhounds, horses, and all kinds of exotic game animals from across the galaxy. We host sporting events for all species. The track can be expanded to three levels with a length of about 2,000 meters, and it can handle hoverboards and aircycles. It's busy eighteen hours a day, every day of the Prestone year—all 634 days." Hatfield grinned. "And before you ask, we grossed almost a billion credits last year."

Smith felt his eyebrows rise despite his attempt to control them. "A billion?"

Hatfield nodded. "That's just from the racing we've already done. I think we have some growth potential."

Growth potential. Now you have my interest.

His drink was delivered, and Smith caught sight of a parade of GenSha waving glowing prods at ten lizard-like beings he'd never seen before. Each stood about a meter high, with long, lean legs over a powerful body. Their limbs had wide, clawed feet, which he assumed were webbed, based on their amphibian features. Their heads were wide and triangular in shape, with a protuberance of skin behind their angled jaws. They slowly moved toward the starting boxes. More than one had to be prodded. He heard the crackle of flesh, and the lizard-things screeched and scrambled forward clumsily. A murmur went through the crowd.

Smith turned, expecting to see concern on Hatfield's face. These creatures didn't appear capable of walking fast, much less racing. The blond-haired man sipped his drink and puffed on his cigar with a smile on his face.

He knows something we don't.

Smith sipped his water and watched the unfolding scene. "Okay, Mister Hatfield. I've never seen those creatures before. What are they?"

"Agamydi." Hatfield turned to him. "They're native to Prestone in the Southern Hemisphere. One of the continents nobody messes with—well, most of the time. You ever been to Australia? They're kinda like them frilled lizards they got Down Under."

"I have to say, they don't look fast enough to race anything."

"Looks can be deceiving, Colonel." Hatfield chuckled and watched as the Agamydi were shepherded toward the starting boxes. One by one, with the press of a prod to their hides, they loaded silently, almost forlornly, into the boxes. There was a tiny slit in the boxes facing the opening straightaway. Smith saw the lizard-things moving but couldn't see their faces.

A Human in a tuxedo appeared near the finish line and raised a trumpet to her lips. The traditional bugle call to racing sounded, and the crowd roared its approval.

"It's time for the main event. The racers are loaded for a one lap race," the announcer called. "All bets are now off. Prepare the quarry!"

For the first time, Smith noticed the fence along the infield had a track installed. Of course it would—they raced greyhounds. *It must hold a rabbit or something…*

A shimmering, golden figure appeared from a box on the raised track. There was a thunderous bellow from the track. The change in the Agamydi startled the audience. The docile creatures howled and charged headlong into the front of their boxes. Where they hadn't looked outside the slits at all before, now their black eyes blazed in rage.

What the hell?

A buzzer sounded, and the effigy shot down the straightaway just as the starting boxes opened. The Agamydi shot forward much faster than anything Smith had ever seen. He gasped along with the ten thousand other patrons in the arena as they reached full speed.

"Holy shit," he said. "They're *fast*!"

"Cheetah speed. Maybe a lil' bit more." Hatfield laughed as the crowd shot to its feet to watch the first turn. The pack of Agamydi clustered near the fence and almost fell over themselves as they attempted to catch the effigy.

Hatfield touched a button, and a screen between their chairs came to life. "Watch this. Get yourself a better view."

The static image changed to follow the Agamydi. In front of them, the dirt track opened into a wide expanse of water, bridged only by a thin plank. The crowd groaned.

"Now approaching the Pool of Death! Remember, the water is five meters deep, and ten meters across. The place where big bets go to die!" the announcer called.

The Agamydi approached as a sprinting, snarling mass. None of them went for the bridge in the center of the track. Smith sat forward with his eyes fixed on the screen. He held his breath as they reached the pool and—

They ran across the surface of the water.

Smith shot to his feet. The crowd roared its approval so loudly, he barely heard the announcer call for mid-race parlays. Seemingly everyone around them reached for the betting terminals.

"Second obstacle. The Wall!"

The crowd roared as the Agamydi never broke stride down the backstretch toward a rising four-meter-tall wall. Almost as one, they leapt to the top of the wall and down again before resuming their all-out chase. The crowd roared again as one of the Agamydi opened up a small lead.

"One more obstacle." Hatfield giggled. "This is gonna be *fun*."

"It's time for the Fires of Hades!" the announcer roared, and what appeared to be a line of flamethrowers came to life. "We'll see which of our racers wants the prize!"

Smith turned to Hatfield. "They're not going to run through that." *Are they?*

"Watch."

His stomach tightened as the Agamydi indeed raced into, and then through, the flames. Many of them smoked and smoldered as they charged after the effigy. As they rounded the final turn and entered the straightaway, Smith saw a large, armored vehicle parked along the inner fence line. The Agamydi roared down the stretch and neared the effigy. At the finish line, the leader edged further ahead of the others and leapt for the effigy just as they reached the truck. With a roar followed by a sickening *smack*, the Agamydi sped through the vehicle's open rear doors and into what appeared to be large cushions. The effigy disappeared into its receiver, and the truck's doors slammed shut violently. The truck revved and the muffled, ear-splitting roars of the Agamydi reverberated almost as loud as the tumultuous crowd.

Hatfield stood and applauded. Smith shook his head and joined in the applause. "I've never seen anything like that!"

Hatfield tapped on a wrist slate. "New one-race betting record. A little over six million credits in our bank. Just wait until we add this to the rotation on a regular basis. Bettors are gonna lose their minds."

"Are they hurt? The fire?"

Hatfield shrugged. "A little. They can take it. If we lengthen the race to two laps, it might kill 'em. If that's the case, I'm gonna need to get more of them."

Smith nodded. *Opportunity.* "And the effigy? Statue? Whatever they were chasing; what is it?"

"No idea, but it's gotta mean something to them based on the reaction it gets." Hatfield met his eyes with a wicked smile on his face. "Might be worth something."

"Valuable, huh?" Smith smiled in return. "What else have they got?"

* * * * *

Chapter Four

Parigi Spaceport
Sulawesi, Indonesia

The Zeewie wasn't knocked out for days. Within ten minutes of moving from the ambush site to the spaceport, Tzegelo had woken up in the back of their skiff and demanded release from his restraints and blindfold. Leaving the McCoys in the driving compartment, Jyrall and Larth were more than happy to agree. Larth waited until Jyrall was positioned directly in front of the Zeewie before yanking off the blindfold. The Zeewie blinked, let out a small "eep" of shock, and then composed itself. Larth was impressed. Either the Zeewie was braver than its entire species, or whatever experiences it had lived through had toughened it. He'd bet on the latter.

A Zeewie who's a stone-cold criminal. Who'd a thunk it? Same folks who believe Peacemakers aren't crazy, too.

"Your name is Tzegelo?" Jyrall asked. His voice was low like a distant rumble of thunder. "Is that right?"

Larth stepped around as the Zeewie locked eyes with Jyrall. In a high-pitched voice tinged with a distinct Human accent, Tzegelo said, "Yeah, and just who the fuck are you? Why the fuck are you in my car?"

Jyrall rumbled, "My name is Varkell. This is Switch. I want some information, and you're going to give it to me."

"Oh I am, am I?" Tzegelo grinned. "There's nothing you can—"

"My Pushtal friends are in the front of this vehicle and will pull over when I tell them to," Jyrall said slowly. "They'll eat you without question. I'm giving you the chance to walk away unscathed. Your choice."

Tzegelo seemed to consider it. "Pull over."

"You want them to eat you?" Larth blurted. "That's not too smart—"

"Not to eat me," Tzegelo replied. "I get motion sickness when I'm not driving the fucking car, and I'm not feeling good, okay? Let me get some fresh air, and we'll have a chat. You gotta have something I want, too, Varkell."

Ah, yes. The standard line. And right now, Jyrall is gonna say—

"You recognized my name; I saw that in your earlier reaction. Perhaps we do have business together." Jyrall grunted. "Hatfield."

"Who?" The Zeewie appeared to belch. "Never heard of him."

"I said Hatfield." Jyrall leaned close. "Where is he?"

"Why?"

"So, you do know him?" Larth asked.

The Zeewie glared at him. "Of course I do. Same as you. Guy was a pretty decent fence at one point. Could sell anything we brought him. Then he started buying up stuff a couple of years back. He's running a casino on Prestone, or so I heard. Owes me five million credits I ain't ever gonna get back."

"Why not?" Jyrall asked.

Tzegelo belched again and licked his lips. The difference in his coat, once shiny and now dull, indicated he was indeed sick. "He's surrounded by a fucking *army*. Nobody's gonna get close to him."

"We will," Larth said. "You're going to tell us everything about his army, Tzegelo, or I'm gonna enjoy watching our friends tear your guts out."

"Yeah." He belched again and then retched. Nothing came out. "Yeah, sure. Just stop the car."

Jyrall turned to him. "Have them pull over in a defensible position, but remain in the vehicle. Let's do what we can to make sure our business is peaceful."

"You sure about this?" Larth asked. Giving an enemy a potential avenue of escape wasn't smart, but if Zeewie vomit smelled anything like their fear scent, he wanted no parted of it.

Jyrall nodded solemnly. "Our friend looks ill."

Larth tapped his earpiece, and Ricky drawled, "Yeah, boss?"

"Pull over, but stay in the vehicle."

"What in the hell for?"

Larth growled. "You heard me."

"Okay, but if this ain't a goddamned recipe for disaster—"

Larth terminated the connection as the vehicle slowed and stopped. Jyrall opened one wide, gull-winged door and stepped outside. Larth motioned for the Zeewie to do the same with the intention of keeping him between them, but realized he needed to undo Tzegelo's ankle restraints. He leaned forward and disengaged the magnetic locking mechanism, and the Zeewie quickly shot past him. Larth whirled, expecting the little bastard to flee, but he saw Tzegelo barely make it out the car's door before vomiting all over the asphalt.

"Eww," Larth said. The Zeewie stood with its front paws on it knees by the side of the road. Larth stood by Jyrall. "Good call."

Jyrall nodded but said nothing. After a minute, while the Zeewie retched two more times, each with smaller results, he knelt down by Tzegelo. "You ready to tell me what I want to know?"

"I told you. He's on Prestone. Runs a casino. They're running all sorts of ops through that place, and he's got a security detail better than anything I've ever seen." Tzegelo wiped his mouth with the back of one paw and turned to Jyrall. "And you're the infamous One-Eyed Varkell. Smuggler extraordinaire, right?"

Jyrall nodded. "That's right."

"What do you want with Hatfield?"

"Deal gone wrong. I want my credits."

Tzegelo laughed and straightened. "I don't think so. Hatfield wasn't in charge of anything. He was the fence. The fixer. You needed something done, he did it. You're lying, Varkell."

Larth stepped in between them. "Listen here, you little shit. Our business with Hatfield is none of your fucking business. He did us wrong, and we want our—"

"Revenge." Tzegelo laughed. "This isn't about credits. It's about revenge. Just who do the two of you think you are? You're not gonna waltz onto Prestone and take him down. Even the fucking Peacemakers couldn't do that."

Larth drew a breath for another verbal tirade but stopped. Sirens wailed in the distance. They were getting closer by the second. He glanced at the ground, in the widening pool of Tzegelo's stomach contents, and saw a small gray cylinder glinting in the low light from the street.

Beacon. Emergency. Indigestible. One Each. Activates when exposed to the environment. Often used as a panic device.

Larth looked over his shoulder. "Beacon!"

Jyrall's mouth opened. "He's moving!"

The Zeewie took off in the most ludicrous direction possible—*though* the oncoming traffic of the hyperway adjacent to where they'd stopped. Larth gave chase.

Damn, he's fast.

Tzegelo leapt over the retaining wall separating the off ramps from the hyperway and disappeared. A second later, Larth heard the squeal of breaks and the bark of rubber tires attempting to gain purchase on the roadway. To make matters worse, it started to rain.

Larth followed the Zeewie's path up the wall. At the top of the concrete divider, he saw the hyperway's traffic stopped. To his left was an accident blocking all six lanes of the expressway. To his right, sprinting into the night, was Tzegelo.

Larth stood and prepared to jump, but paused. His hands flew to his pistols. He drew the right one and leveled it on the fleeing Zeewie.

Night-night.

Larth pulled the trigger, and a half second later, the Zeewie pitched forward onto the asphalt. In the distance, red and blue lights descended on the accident and toward the off ramp where Jyrall and the boys remained.

Tzegelo lay still. Larth wanted to sprint over and make sure the little bastard was dead, but he was also sure he'd nailed the little bastard in the back of the head.

Won't be getting up from that.

His earpiece crackled. "*Is he dead?*"

"I think so."

Jyrall rumbled, "*Come down. We can wait for the authorities to show up and—*"

"No," Larth interrupted. "We need to go. Now."

"What?" Jyrall said loud enough Larth heard him without the earpiece. "All we have to do is explain—"

Larth turned and stared at his friend on the ground some thirty meters below. "We're not Peacemakers right now, Jyrall."

"We're *undercover.*"

"And if we expose ourselves now, we can forget Hatfield and Kr'et'Socae." Larth climbed down as fast as his arms and legs would take him. "We need to go. Now."

Jyrall didn't respond. When Larth dropped the last five meters to the ground, he saw Jyrall entering the car. Lights from law enforcement vehicles reflected off the nearby buildings. Larth sprinted and dove into the gull-winged car as Ricky stomped the accelerator panel. He executed a 180-degree turn under the hyperway and rocketed down a thoroughfare leading toward the water and the spaceport beyond.

Larth looked at Jyrall. "That's the right decision, partner."

Jyrall shook his head but said nothing. He tapped on his slate for a moment and leaned forward to rap on the window separating the driver's compartment from the passenger. Keaton opened the window.

"Yeah, boss?"

"Power up the ship. We're going to Krifay. I'll send a message and give them at least an hour's notice before we get there. We're going to need to move fast if that Zeewie isn't dead."

Larth bristled. "He's dead. I put him down with a round in the back of his skull."

"And we don't know that," Jyrall growled. "Either way, dead or alive, word is going to get out."

Larth shook his head. "We don't even know how connected Tzegelo was to Hatfield. He just knew where he was, right? They weren't best friends or anything."

"I said we don't know that." Jyrall sighed. "We know where he is, and we know we're going to need help to get him. That's our priority right now. We have to assume Hatfield will hear about this before we get there. A few hours could make all the difference, Larth."

Larth took a breath and held it for a few seconds. Jyrall was right. They couldn't be sure of anything anymore.

"Ship is powering up," Keaton replied. "I've requested clearance. I have all the emergency services comms in the area down. We just have to get to the spaceport in one piece. The navicomp in this bucket says we'll be there in nine minutes."

"Y'all wanna bet I can't get there faster?" Ricky asked with a laugh.

Nobody replied. Larth swallowed and looked at Jyrall. "I can't believe you let him drive."

"Keaton is plugged into the net and needs to—"

"Still," Larth interrupted and reached for a seatbelt. "You better strap in, 'cause Ricky's not gonna touch the brakes, Snarlyface."

"Straightenin' them hills!" Ricky yelled.

"That's not how the song goes!" Larth dug his claws into the nearest handrest and closed his eyes as Ricky stomped on the accelerator, and they rocketed into the night. "I thought we said never again!"

"YEEHAAAWW!" Ricky yelled from the driver's seat.

* * * * *

Chapter Five

Brentale's Barnstormers Headquarters

Krifay

"What?" Cora asked. She stared with her mouth open, her head tilted sideways and slightly down.

"The Crusaders. Here?" Pete asked. "Why *here*? There are no issues here. There are planets and systems with far more problems than the inhabitants of Krifay would even consider entertaining."

"I fear that's precisely the reason," Zetchek said. "Perhaps Krifay is on a priority list because it's too quiet."

"Like that's a bad thing," Cora said.

"Whatever the actual reason, they're coming, and I've been recalled to Kleve."

"Great." Cora shook her head and sat down. "Just great."

"There's more," Zetchek said. "The planetary security mission has been canceled by the guild."

"What?" Pete exclaimed. "We've put a lot of work into this. Time, resources, credit expenditure. They can't just cancel it!"

"They can, and they have, my friend. The instructions invited no discussion. It was, as you say here on Krifay, cut and dried."

"Damn," Pete said. He slammed his hand onto his desk. "This is bullshit!"

Zetchek, though a Zuparti, didn't flinch, a credit to his training and discipline as a Peacemaker. Neither he nor any other Zuparti living had the lone trait that made Larth unique among his kind. Larth was truly fearless and, as such, thought to be insane by Zuparti standards.

"I understand your frustration," Zetchek said. He raised his hands chest high, palms up. "I'm not pleased with the decision, either. I've expressed my concerns, but they've fallen on deaf hearing orifices."

"This is my home," Pete declared. He looked toward Cora. "Our home. The residents of Krifay should be the ones in charge of its defense, not some power-mad, shitty leader like Crusader Prime and his flunkies. Everything we know about them, what Cora's witnessed… this is not good. Not good at all."

"What about everything we've already done?" Cora asked. "We have half the emergency defense budget left, since we're just now getting the shipments in through the Slow Killers' network of arms trade."

"Yeah," Pete said. "It's all under the radar and bought through back channels, but I did give my word on the future deals."

"Perhaps your friends and the dealers will understand, given the circumstances," Zetchek suggested. "These are unusual times, to be certain."

Zetchek found himself a chair and climbed up on it, his feet dangling. "I'll say this. Reading between the lines and studying the recent past concerning the Crusaders… Prime will demand full control of any defense budget. The Crusaders will deplete it quickly, billing for everything from routine maintenance to feeding his troops. He will also insist the budget continue to be funded at current levels."

"It's a damn racket," Cora declared.

"Extortion," Pete confirmed. "Call it anything you want, it still boils down to extortion."

Zetchek leaned back in his chair, crossed a leg over his knee, interlaced his fingers behind his head, and stared at the ceiling. "Unless…"

Cora and Pete waited while the Peacemaker thought. A grin slowly spread across the Zuparti's face—what could only be described as a grin by a Human, that is. Their facial features weren't like a Human's, but the look was universal.

He sat forward. "Now, I can't presume to tell you what to do in this situation. I have, after all, been ordered to inform all involved that the mission here is canceled. I have also been recalled to Kleve and must prepare to leave."

He paused. "Therefore, I won't be able to continue monitoring the budget—what might be left and what might have already been spoken for. As a matter of fact, when asked, I'll honestly be able to say I have no idea what's left, nor will I know if the entire budget has been dispensed, or done away with completely, absorbed back into the planetary budget for normal governing."

Cora glanced at Pete. The look on his face said he knew she had an idea. She turned back to the Peacemaker, who was walking back and forth with his paws clasped behind his back as he spoke.

"I would absolutely not know if more weapons, equipment, rations, or ammunition have been secreted away. I simply couldn't, as I'll spend my time on another island preparing to leave. So, I'll say my goodbyes to the two of you now. I have several others here on Krifay I need to say goodbye to. I must let the planet administrator know the Crusaders will arrive in sixty days. There's no need to let you two know this, as you are no longer part of the aforementioned canceled mission."

* * *

Planetary Administrative Offices

"There," the planet administrator said. "All the funds have been dispersed to pay for your unit's 'protection' for the last year. The emergency budget will now be closed, and the files… lost in the system. I have a meeting scheduled for the first of next week with all interested parties. The notification went out face to face. No traceable messages were sent. From there, it will disseminate, and all the volunteer reserve forces will know. We have sixty days to set this up. Well, not set up anything. You know what I mean. Hide it all."

"We're working on it," Pete assured him. He and Cora left the unscheduled meeting for another planned that afternoon.

* * *

Blue Ridge

Thirty minutes later, Cora and Pete were in the cargo hold of the *Blue Ridge*. The ramp was up, and the only ones on board the ship with them were the officers of both companies, the two senior enlisted—First Sergeant Figgle and Sergeant First Class Wilson—and two others.

Figgle glared at the two others. He spoke sideways without turning to Cora. "Are you sure about this, ma'am? *Really* sure?"

"I am, Top," she answered. "Pete—Colonel Brentale—and I agree. If anyone knows where we can secure everything we plan to hide away, it's these two."

Specialist Tony Haney brushed his longer-than-regulation bangs back over his head. He could have used a little more product to keep it there, but he hadn't planned on being the focus of this many officers and senior NCO types. He wouldn't be here now if Fiona hadn't called him direct and asked him. His leaders would never have been able to reach, much less locate him. It was a day off, and he'd had plans to get in some gliding off the cliffs on the other side of Snapper Isle.

He glanced at her to get a read of her thoughts. She gave him a slight nod, so he answered the question. "Well, ma'am, the short answer is yes. There are several locations that'll serve the purpose. If Conner or I don't know of them, we know folks who do. Well, I say folks… several aren't Human, but I trust them."

"He's talking about places besides the ones already planned for," Conner added. "The lofts, attics, cellars, and spots you already have designated for ammunition storage are fine. Obviously, not all of them will be discovered. What he's talking about is on a much larger scale."

Conner turned to Haney. "You might as well tell them, Tony. It's not like you'll get to use it now that the Crusaders are coming."

Haney looked at Pete. "Sir, what I'm about to tell you is… well, it's some secret shit. I'd like immunity first."

"What?" SFC Wilson demanded. "What do you mean, immunity?"

Pete raised a hand, ending her tirade before it could begin. He looked back to the man. "This isn't a legal issue, Specialist Haney."

"Some of it could be," Haney countered. "Anyway, I'm giving up some good shit here, and I don't want to catch hell for it once I do."

"I see. All right, you have my word. No repercussions. Not from anyone in the unit."

"Or my company," Cora added. She stared directly at First Sergeant Figgle.

"What about the local authorities?" Haney asked. "Never mind. I'm sure you can handle that, sir."

He took a deep breath, and then, with a glance once again to Conner, he said, "I have a cave. A limestone cave, on property I now own. The only way to get to it is to dive beside the cliff and come in through the sea. You need a rebreather or a great set of lungs, though."

"A cave?" Cora asked.

"Yes, ma'am," Haney answered. "A big one. Once you come up out of the water onto its sandy beach, it rises up at least fifty feet to the roof. It's about thirty yards wide and goes back about a football field, give or take."

"Who knows about this cave?" Pete asked.

"No one besides Conner. I was diving for spiny lobster near there and found it. I followed the cave until I was on dry land. The pool I came up in was smooth as glass. The entrance is well below the water line, so the tide doesn't affect it."

"You say you own the property?" Cora asked. "Did you buy it once you found it, or did you find it after you bought it?"

"Buy?" Haney asked. "I didn't buy it, ma'am. I traded a refurbished houseboat for it after I discovered the cave. A nice one. Fifty-footer. The man who owned it wanted to retire to some of the smaller islands where there are even fewer people than around here."

"So, you bought the houseboat, then?"

"No, ma'am. I traded a tri-hulled catamaran I got for a four-engine cigar boat. I acquired that for two rebuilt hovercraft and a case of underwater explosives. Both of the hovercraft needed engine work, so I had a guy fix them for a double person glider I had… in storage. Now, I got those hovercraft for a dozen grenades, three rifles, a pistol, and some rounds. Those, um, *found* their way into my duffle bag when we emptied the gate before taking it apart."

"Is that why you asked for immunity?" Pete asked. He shook his head.

"No, sir," Haney answered. "That kind of trading isn't unusual. I need immunity for the power I'm not paying for and possibly other things."

"Power?" Figgle asked. "What do you need power for in a huge cave?"

"I have it all lit up. There's a spot near a wall with a shack. It has a bunk and some other stuff if I need to rack out. The ventilation fans need power; they suck up a lot of energy. There are big fans in the cave pulling and returning air up through a shaft I have running to a new shed on my property that looks like an old shed with a wall caved in. Gotta have clean air, you know."

He shrugged. "Anyway, the fans are in the cave, and not on the surface, so they can't be detected by sight or with scanners, since they run constantly. The power cables are insulated with some stuff that's supposed to render them undetectable. I was going to have Ricky and Keaton check it out to be sure, but I think it's good to go."

"Power? Air circulation? Just what were you planning on doing? Moving into it?" Cora asked.

"No, ma'am. I have a nice shack on my land. I just want to use it to store things. You know… stuff."

"Do I even want to know?" Pete asked.

"Probably not, sir," SFC Wilson said. "Rumor has it he's the local fence."

"Yeah?" He turned back to Haney.

Haney explained, "Sir, I may get a good deal on some things from time to time. I don't ask where it comes from. I just trade for it or buy it with the profits from something else I traded for or acquired."

It was quiet as everyone digested the fact that Specialist Haney had a… a lair.

"Who told you I was the local fence, Sergeant?" Haney asked. "I got something for his ass. Running his mouth. Who was it?"

"Us senior NCOs have our sources. Don't worry about it. The secret is safe," Wilson answered.

Haney turned back to Cora. "To answer your original question, Colonel McCoy, yes. I know of several places to hide CASPers and other large equipment. I know of two other caves on different islands. Now those, at least two other people know about. The guys who told me about them."

"Do they have hidden entrances underwater?"

"No, ma'am, but you can't see the caves unless you're on the water close to them."

Cora said, "Well, let's go. Take me to it." She turned to Pete. "I'll leave it up to you and Mike at the bar to talk to those who have old CASPers and any other weapons and equipment we don't want the Crusaders knowing about. They'll probably want to confiscate it all, anyway."

"We have a lot of work to do," Nileah said.

"And only sixty days to do it in," May added. "All to store enough stuff so we can fend for ourselves if we need to run those dang Crusaders off."

"Or die trying," Nails added. "Or die trying."

* * *

A week later, Cora stood on the deck of a large trawler and watched a combination surface ship and submersible pull a large, sealed container underwater.

"There goes another one," she remarked.

"Yeah," Nileah said. "That one has two Mk 5s in it belonging to a couple of old timers from the village on the far side. Sreet says they're still in decent shape."

"Their owners are still in good shape, too. The island life keeps you healthy, I guess." Cora sighed. "I hope they never have to climb into them. If it comes to that, lives will be lost."

"I know," Nileah assured her. "We all know. Even the two retired mercs know. There are folks who ain't never been mercenaries, just fishermen and women, who've turned over weapons and such for us to safekeep. They know the deal, too."

"Some things are worth fighting for," Pete said, "no matter the cost."

"That reminds me," Cora said. "I received a message today. At least I think it is. It came in three parts, along with some other messages from back home in the mountains. From some of my kin. Anyway, the boys are coming back. Whatever they were working on is either over or they're between stuff."

"I thought they were deep undercover," Pete said. "Do you trust the source of the message?"

"Oh, yeah," Cora said. "All the right code words were used… in the right places. It's legit. Jyrall, Larth, and my cousins are coming home."

"I wonder how long they'll be here?" Nileah asked. "Peacemaker Zetchek was recalled. They might be, too."

"Lord, I hope not," Cora said.

* * * * *

Chapter Six

The Farm
Vicinity of Caney, Kansas
Earth

The first surprise for Araceli Cignes was the breadth of the Intergalactic Haulers' facility at what had once been known as the Independence Regional Airport. Now dubbed Eastern Kansas Spaceport and featuring a hangar complex brightly identified as the "Dawg Pound," the facility rivaled larger spaceports on the outskirts of Houston and Atlanta.

Haulers' lifters were parked side-by-side on the tarmac, manned by a flurry of workers moving enclosed cargo capsules in and out. Smaller regional transports, which looked to be repainted *Columbia*-class tactical dropships, seemed to launch every few minutes, bound for destinations in all directions. There was no mistaking that the Haulers were back in business.

Her second surprise was more personal. When the jet taxied up to the Fixed Base Operations hangar, a driverless auto car waited. There was nothing else. While operational security was imperative in her time on Earth, she'd at least expected someone to meet her. She collected her bags and thanked the flight crew before approaching the autocar. The cargo compartment and a passenger door popped open, and she placed her bags inside, triggered the lid to close, and stepped inside.

The autocar failed to provide any answers. One of the earliest models of purely autonomous transportation, the vehicle was clean and smelled nice, but there was no interactive technology onboard. The refreshments cabinet remained closed. Araceli shrugged and sat back against the cushions. She had a water bottle and some food in her backpack on the seat next to her, as well as her sidearm if things went really crazy.

The autocar left the spaceport and accelerated into the sunset. She peered out the windows and watched the farmland rush past. While she'd overflown the Farm a few times, they hadn't actually resumed operations there until now. During the last year, the Misfits had spread out again for fear of discovery and blended into their surroundings. For Araceli, she'd worked for a produce company in southern Arizona, managing shipments of citrus products, while conducting the occasional intelligence-gathering mission for the Haulers. She'd been all over the world, including four months in western Australia, as they tracked down information on all manner of requirements. Action had been nonexistent, but with the call to report to the Farm, she expected that to change quickly.

The autocar decelerated at the intersection of a dirt road and the wide asphalt. After turning left, the quiet ride of the autocar became an unsettling, constant shimmy. Everything in the car rattled in four directions at once as the vehicle accelerated to the same speed it had traveled on the highway. Araceli looked behind the car and saw a massive cloud of dust rising and moving off with the breeze. Her teeth chattered, and she carefully tightened her seatbelt. There was no relief. After two minutes, her eyes and head ached.

"Slow down," she said, hoping the autocar would hear her and adjust. All she could hear was the vibration of the car as it raced down the dirt and gravel. There was no response. "I said, slow down!"

The car responded by slowing only a fraction. Araceli yelled again, "Reduce speed by 50 percent."

The autocar slowed and turned onto another dirt road. She expected it to speed up, but the car maintained its slower speed on the winding road before turning at a white painted gate into what she recognized as the Farm. It took a moment for the gate to open. As the car rolled through, Araceli looked for security forces or guards. There was nothing.

We can't just… not need it out here, can we?

Something's wrong.

The Farm had all the appearances of being a working dairy farm. There was a farmhouse with its lone porch light shining in the rising darkness. Beyond it were several outbuildings tucked between a maze of pastures and access ways. To her right, corn grew in nearly perfect rows as far as she could see. It looked to be about her height, so it wasn't ready for harvest. The car stopped in front of the farmhouse. The doors opened, and she heard the cargo compartment do the same.

"You have reached your destination. Please disembark the vehicle. Thank you."

Araceli gathered her backpack and stepped out into the warm evening air. By the time she'd collected her bags from the cargo compartment, she'd slapped two mosquitoes biting her exposed legs. Frowning at having worn shorts, Araceli walked up to the farmhouse and reached for the doorknob. It didn't turn. She knocked three times and waited. There was no response. She set her bags down and moved to the nearest window. She couldn't see a thing. The windows appeared to be coated with security mesh.

The autocar roared to life, tore down the driveway, and went through the gate. Araceli watched it for a moment before looking at her wrist slate. Maybe she'd missed something in her instructions? She tapped the screen, and it came to life, but there was no connection. Everything was down, and a warning box illuminated.

Jamming present.

Araceli shrugged off her backpack and withdrew her weapon. The .40 caliber Smith and Wesson wasn't as powerful as the .45s Tara and Jessica carried, but it fit her hand, and she was comfortable with it. Carefully and quietly, she worked the action to chamber a round. With good trigger and muzzle discipline, finger off the trigger and the weapon pointed at the ground, Araceli worked her way around the farmhouse. She didn't call out or engage a light from her slate. Instead, she let her eyes and ears adjust as Quin'taa had taught her on Snowmass.

The farmhouse yielded no clues or other entrances. She moved to the first outbuilding, a lean-to housing two combines and a smaller enclosed tractor, but nothing else. The second outbuilding was similar, but held a bevy of smaller personal vehicles as well as a menagerie of other equipment, including two canoes.

Darkness was almost total as she moved toward a large Quonset-hut-like structure next to a pasture filled with black and white cattle. They stared at her. A few made mooing sounds, but they stood still. If they knew she was there, somebody else would. The hair on the back of her neck stood on end as she made her way to the wide opening of the hut. She stepped inside and smelled gasoline and freshly cut grass. Shadows made seeing anything further than a few meters away impossible. In the center of the doorway, about two meters inside the hut, she stopped. Through the soles of her low-cut boots, Araceli felt a hum. She knelt and brushed at the dirt near her feet. Under a few centimeters of dirt was a cold steel surface that thrummed beneath her fingers. What was under—

"Eighty-six seconds. A new record," a low voice rumbled deep from the shadows to her left. Araceli squared on the unseen target but didn't raise her weapon.

"Told you she'd find it faster than you!" Another voice laughed. This one she recognized.

"She didn't wander around outside for five minutes like you did, Homer." The voice was Quin'taa's, and Araceli put her pistol on safe and lowered it completely.

Homer laughed. "Have you even *smelled* all the stuff outside? It's like heaven, Q."

A low light turned on above them as Quin'taa and Homer approached. Araceli leapt into the Oogar's arms for a tight embrace before doing the same to the Pushtal. "I missed you guys *so much*."

Homer shrugged. "Of course you did. Look at this handsome face and tell me you—"

The Oogar punched him in the shoulder. "We missed you, too, Little Sister. Welcome home."

CLANG!

The floor moved and began descending. She glanced at Homer, who grinned at her. "Why wouldn't a bunch of misfits and criminals have a lair?"

"We call it an Operations Center." Quin'taa frowned. "Perhaps you've heard of something serious in the last year, Homer?"

"Your Mom."

Quin'taa whirled on the Pushtal and raised a mighty paw toward his face. "I told you that's not funny, Homer."

Araceli giggled and slapped her hand over her mouth. She couldn't conceal her smile, however.

"What? You can't have me working off-world with kids for a year and not expect my humor to improve." Homer grinned. He looked at Araceli. "I worked at the Center for Galactic Experiences for a while as a training liaison."

"Think camp counselor." Quin'taa lowered his paw. "His humor devolved to a new level as a result. Everything now is poop jokes and innuendo."

"In *your* end, doe." Araceli winked at Homer, and the three of them laughed together.

Quin'taa laid a hand on her shoulder. "It is good to have you home. For all of us to be together."

The elevator lurched to a stop. From the light on the wall, Araceli knew her back was to whatever opening there was, and she quickly turned to see Tara Mason standing in the door with her hands on her hips. Her artificial legs were different from the pair she'd worn in Arizona. If anything, they appeared more natural, even in their skin tone. Tara looked none the worse for wear. Her hair was tied back into a ponytail, and she looked like she'd just finished a workout in her Nebraska Athletics shirt and black shorts. She grinned at Araceli and opened her arms.

"Welcome home, Araceli."

Araceli embraced her friend and mentor tightly. "I've missed you all. I've been ready for this for a long time."

"I know, Little Sister."

Araceli flushed. Hearing her nickname from Quin'taa and the others was one thing. For Tara to say it really touched her heart. After the loss of Victoria Bravo and the death of her immediate family, the Misfits were truly all she had.

Tara released her just enough to grab her shoulders. "Let's get you settled."

"Sounds great."

Tara glanced over her shoulder at Quin'taa and Homer. "You guys collect Araceli's bags and update security up top. We'll meet in half an hour in the wardroom."

"Got it, Boss," Homer replied. The elevator lurched upward, and Araceli smiled at her friends before walking at Tara's side.

"Anything new from Bull?"

Ace Tomato Company had once been a shell company. In a great twist, Bull had actually purchased the Arizona company where Araceli had worked. "No. They're still monitoring the situation. If Jessica left Khatash, we'd know."

"Is she alive?"

Araceli nodded. "Tirr said she survived the fight, but given the planet, I don't know beyond that. Anything from Jackson?"

"He's recovered pretty well, but he and the Cajuns are laying low. They're doing good business with Hope Station and the Haulers now." Tara smiled. "I should really check up on him, though."

"Anything from the boys?" Araceli asked. They'd taken to calling Jyrall, Larth, and the McCoy twins "the boys" as shorthand. She loved the ring the nickname had for the curious band of brothers. "Bull suspects they might be on Earth."

"We think that, too. They've been here twice in the last eighteen months, chasing down leads. If they need us, they'll call."

Araceli looked at her friend for a long second. "Is it really safe for us to be together like this?"

"We're not separating again, if that's what you're asking." Tara took a breath. "With the Haulers compound by the spaceport, and in two of the nearby towns, people here think we're part of the security detail so they leave us alone. On the other side of the pasture and field you saw on the way in? All the land in all directions is owned by Snowman. We'll know if anyone comes looking for us, and it's better that we're together if they do."

"*They* meaning the Crusaders," Araceli said, and Tara nodded. "Snowman told Bull he doesn't expect them to move on any of us until Jessica resurfaces. It's been more than a year, though. Should we be worried?"

Tara shook her head. "No. She'll move when she's ready. Now that we're together again, we'll get ready in case the boys need us here on Earth, or elsewhere. When they make their move, we'll be in support of them. That was our mission. Now, there'll be time for questions and plans. Let's get you moved into your suite, and then I'll give you the grand tour. Everyone else is dying to see you."

Araceli took in the wide, well-lit corridors. "How big is this place? And did you say 'suite?'"

Tara grinned. "Yeah. We have more than 200,000 square feet down here, not including the hangar. Snowman did us good, Little Sister. Welcome to Misfit HQ."

* * *

Vicinity of Bean Station, Tennessee

Earth

Raley Reilly woke with a start. For the last week, give or take, her sleep had been restless and filled with strange, disconnected dreams of her childhood and her father. Now twenty, and almost four full years after his death, Raley had come to realize she *wasn't* past his death. While not in her nature, or her training, to grieve, his death and the circumstances therein caused her uncertainty. Uncertainty, for a mercenary, was a death sentence. Her…

What was Kr'et'Socae? Her mentor? Her teacher? Her… friend?

Raley didn't know. But she knew he was correct in his assessment that she needed to be over her father before they could effectively recruit a company for her to lead in the pursuit of credits.

Meanwhile, the rest of her training had progressed well. An expert marksman and able to handle herself in a fight, she'd spent much of the last six months working with planning and tactics between her more challenging physical workouts. She felt she was ready, yet at the same time, she believed Kr'et'Socae.

He didn't seem like such a terrible being to Raley. Over the last two years, they'd rebuilt or improved almost every aspect of the forgotten training complex. From a new dock in the private lake cove to the rifle range and barracks facilities for up to 500 mercenaries, they'd done it together, with more than a little cost—part of which the Equiri had fronted without question or debate. They'd only discussed the future in fits and spurts, most of those related to two requirements of Raley.

The first was that she complete a bevy of physical and tactical challenges under his direct instruction. She'd done so. At times she'd hated him and called him the drill sergeant from Hell. He'd snarled at her and kept pushing. He'd also pushed her academic studies, including enrolling her simultaneously in an undergraduate and graduate program in Mercenary's Studies through Duke University's Department of Offplanet Studies. Classes were held over the AetherNet, which meant she could continue both aspects of training at the same time. Raley wasn't sure that was a highlight of their arrangement, but she'd excelled. Short of a few on-campus sessions in the next few months, she was on track to graduate with honors.

Daddy would've been proud.

She saw his face clearly for the first time in months behind her closed eyes. They were touring the company flagship, the *Satisfaction.* He'd shown her his cabin and bunk. She was eight, maybe nine. Her favorite part of the room was that the bunk folded down out of the wall.

"How does it do that?"

He'd smiled at her. "You just have to have the right key, Rae."

Raley opened her eyes and sat up. Daylight touched the eastern sky outside, but the sun was far from rising. She glanced at her slate but decided not to activate it. Instead, she felt a familiar anxiousness in her body—one that needed release. She dressed quickly, tugging on a black one-piece swimsuit and then a shirt and shorts over it. Raley walked to the door of her cabin and looked out over the wide clearing between it and what had once been the dining facility, but was now Kr'et'Socae's quarters. She saw no lights in the windows. By the door, she grabbed a swim cap and her goggles, slipped her feet into thin rubber sandals, and grabbed a bottle of water from the porch cooler. She headed off to the lake.

Most mornings, she played music from her slate into waterproof earbuds. Without her slate and the earbuds, she listened to the sounds of the dawn around her. A few birds called, but most were quiet. Insects buzzed to life—mainly crickets. A fine blanket of mist rolled amongst the tall grass as she made her way out of the clearing and into the forest. The path was wide enough for two vehicles to pass abreast, but Raley walked down one side. Blood flowing now as she walked fast, she felt the barest hint of a breeze as she emerged from the forested trail into the clearing by the lake. There, the air was cooler, and it prickled her skin. As she walked, Rae tucked her hair into the latex swim cap and pulled it tight and low over her ears. On the dock, she passed her two boats—a speedboat named *Big Money* and a pontoon boat named *Killin' Time*. She peeled off her shirt and stepped out of her shorts before pulling on her goggles. With a deep breath, Raley dove into the still lake.

The cool water shocked her for a millisecond as she submerged and resurfaced. She pulled in a deep breath of air and swam toward the buoy line at the edge of the cove 800 meters away. She settled into a rhythm, breathing every other arm stroke, and thought through the images she'd seen in her dreams and memories. There had to be a reason. There had to be something—

* * *

Daddy never really could sing. He loved to try. Sounded more like a cat in heat than a singer, but there he was, singing away, while beating out the dent in that old Mk 6 CASPer he worked for years to recover. Humming the same few bars of a song—the intro wasn't it? Then singing under his breath as he worked until he'd stand up straight, belt out the chorus of whatever he was singing in his head, and grab another beer.

Those same few bars. All the time.

"Satisfaction" by The Rolling Stones. That's what it was.

Now, I'm humming them.

Daddy was so happy when he purchased the ship. The smile on his face was the best she'd ever seen on his constantly haggard face. He'd showered and shaved and been sober for a whole week before picking up the cruiser and bringing her home.

My first dropship ride up to orbit. Daddy laughing when I got spacesick and then giving me the meds with a soda and astronaut pizza.

Spending the night in the cabin.

Damn, he loved the Satisfaction.

His face crystallized in her mind. He was smiling at her ten-year-old self.

"Check out the bunks, Rae. I mean, look at this. I pull this down, and there's a king-sized bed with restraints. We can have a campout. Wouldn't that be fun?"

She saw herself point up at the underside of the bunk strapped against the bulkhead. "What's that box-shaped cutout?"

He grinned at her. "Our little secret, my sharp-eyed little princess."

"Secret?"

"Yeah." He dug into his coveralls and pulled out a container shaped the same as the rectangular space, and made seemingly from the same material. "For this."

"What is it?"

He hummed the song's opening bars again and sang the words, except he added a line the Stones hadn't. "And I've got the key."

* * *

Her hand touched the buoy marking the edge of her private cove, and Raley popped up and treaded water for a moment. She breathed fast, and her heart pumped hard, but she was shaking from shock and realization.

"I have to go to Weqq."

Fragments of thoughts and memories crashed together in her mind. She reached out and held onto the buoy as a fresh set of tears flowed from her eyes. She hadn't cried over her father's death since the day she'd heard the news. He would have wanted her to keep it short, she'd told herself, and she'd turned off the waterworks. Now, they came, because, despite all the things she'd done and trained for, she'd almost forgotten something important. Something her father had wanted her to know. All she had to do was go find it.

Kr'et'Socae won't like this.

She spat in the water. *Fuck him. This is my daddy, and something I have to go and see. What's in that bunk leg might be important.*

She heard the Equiri in her mind. *"It's not going to bring your father back, Raley."*

Raley spun in the water and glared in the general direction of Kr'et'Socae's bunk. In her mind, she stared him down with the idea in her head. She rehearsed the line aloud. "I'm going to Weqq. Either you're coming with me, or you're gonna get out of my way."

* * *

"I think that's an excellent idea," Kr'et'Socae replied. "This may help you achieve closure with your father's death, which will only accelerate your training.

Anything that gets you ready for the future is worth pursuing. I'll arrange transportation and escort. Weqq is a protected world, meaning the Peacemakers or their ilk may be present."

"We'll deal with them," Raley replied. "I have the title to the *Satisfaction.* I can claim ownership anytime I want."

He nodded. "Impressive. Did your father's lawyer tell you that?"

"No, it was on my last test in Merc 402." Raley smiled. "When do we leave?"

"I'll need a week," Kr'et'Socae replied. "It's two jumps from Earth. Can you afford to miss your schoolwork?"

Raley frowned. He was like a father in a lot of annoying ways.

"I'll handle that. Just get us to Weqq."

*****

Chapter Seven

Night Moves
Hyperspace

As the effects of transition faded, Larth opened his eyes and looked around the cockpit. The McCoy brothers sat at their consoles, hands off the controls, and their bodies pushing against the harnesses as microgravity took hold. Ricky glanced at Keaton, who returned the look. Both of them drew a long breath and sighed. Larth resisted doing the same. The rush of the strike and the frantic dash to the ship were over, but his body hadn't fully adjusted. Now, after thrusting hard out of Earth's gravity well before shunting into hyperspace, all he could do was relax. For 170 hours, there was nothing else he could do. He turned to Jyrall, who was staring straight ahead, almost without blinking.

"Snarlyface?" Larth asked.

The big Besquith didn't stir. Instead, he glanced down into his lap at his hands.

"Jyrall?" Larth called a little louder. "You okay?"

"I'm okay." Jyrall nodded once and then looked up at his partner. "Just wondering something. What the fuck are we doing?"

Larth squinted at him. "Completing our mission. Doing what Rsach told us to do."

"The late guild master told us to find Kr'et'Socae," Jyrall growled. "We've been fucking around for two years, and when we get our first real lead, we lose him, and you gun him down. We couldn't even prove he was dead, Larth. What's the difference between what we did and a band of feral Oogar or a swarm of KzSha? We acted outside the law."

"What did you want to do? Wait to hear from the guild? They haven't called in two years. They don't care about us!" Larth yelled. His anger boiled up and over. "We can't sit around and wait for guidance anymore. We can't piddle around with passive intelligence anymore. If Hatfield really is on Prestone, we've got to go in there and take him down."

Jyrall shrugged. "Can we do it alone? No. We can't. We have to have assistance. We have to do this in a Peacemaker way, Larth."

"You think we haven't been?" Larth crossed his arms across his chest.

"I think we've enjoyed the fall."

Larth drew a breath to respond, but the weight of Jyrall's words hit him squarely between the eyes. They'd fallen into their undercover roles so easily. The mission had brought out the best in them, and they'd been able to uphold the law and do their official duties. But now, with time and distance against them, maybe they *had* enjoyed the fall. Would they be able to turn back to the guild and uphold their office?

Do we even want to?

The Peacemaker Guild lay in complete disarray. Across the galaxy, regional barracks commanders used to controlling operations in their sectors deferred to the guild master's office. The Council and the High Council, the representative bodies of the guild, hadn't met in two years. The Crusaders, once the guild master's idea to help augment the Peacemakers' thin line of defense, were now policing planets and entire sectors without direct influence from the guild itself. Individual Peacemakers sat unused and forgotten in most regions. The reports of the Kahraman returning from the Fourth Arm had had little noticeable effect on the current workings of the galaxy. Most planets hadn't seen a Peacemaker in more than a standard Earth year.

Larth met Jyrall's eyes. "You think we're not Peacemakers anymore."

"I don't know what a Peacemaker *is* anymore." Jyrall sighed heavily and reached for his harness.

"What do you want to do?"

"Besides go to Kleve and demand a meeting with the new guild master and Counselor?" Jyrall laughed. "Yes, I know that would be a suicide mission, Larth. Even you would have to agree there. I want *guidance*. I want someone to tell me what to do."

Larth nodded but didn't say anything. He glanced at Keaton and Ricky. Keaton wasn't looking at either of them, but Ricky sat with his arms crossed and a half-smile on his face. "What?"

"Y'all cain't expect people to tell ya what to do all the time," Ricky said. "Time's a-coming when ya gotta get it done, no matter what."

Larth found himself nodding along. He snorted and smiled up at Jyrall.

Jyrall smiled as well. "In the Academy, they say when in charge…"

"Take charge," Larth finished. "The guild's not going to call, Buddy."

"I know," Jyrall said quietly. He rolled his head on his neck and stretched. Larth heard a dull *pop* across the ship's bridge. "We've notified the Kin and the Barnstormers. They'll have about forty minutes of prep time before we arrive in the system. We'll rendezvous with them."

"Best case scenario, how fast can they be ready to move?" Keaton asked.

"Depends on the package we take," Jyrall conceded. "Did you get all the information on Prestone?"

Keaton laughed. "Man, there's *petabytes* of information on Prestone. I've got as much as I could gather. I'll start going through it soon. I did see that Hatfield is the primary owner of the Omni."

"What's that?" Larth asked.

"Casino, resort, and racing complex in the area they call New Vegas," Keaton said. "Supposedly designed with Humans in mind. Clearly, he's wanting to establish it as a new tourist destination. Place has a little bit of everything."

"Then start with everything you can get there. When we emerge at Krifay, tap every source you can." Jyrall undid his harness and let himself float free of the seat.

Keaton leaned forward. "Should I get in touch with Lucille?"

Larth raised his brows. "You think that's necessary?"

"I don't see how it could hurt," Keaton said. "I realize we haven't really seen Lucille in a while now, but she's got passive systems out there listening, especially at the gates. She's a collector—that's one of her tools. She's like a multi-tool, man."

Jyrall actually laughed. Larth couldn't help seeing that as a good sign. "She'd likely take offense at that, Keaton."

"What are you thinking, Snarlyface?" Larth asked.

"Start figuring out what to do and how to do it?" Jyrall grinned. "That, but first things first. We've got bigger fish to fry—so to speak."

"Hell, yes!" Ricky blurted. "Anybody else hungry?"

"Not yet," Jyrall said. "We can eat in a bit. Larth? I need you and Keaton to get the hose."

Keaton recoiled. "The hose?"

Jyrall raised a big hand and pointed a clawed digit at Ricky. "He stinks."

Keaton grinned. "I'll get that big bag of powdered sugar, too."

"Hey!" Ricky unsnapped his harness and pushed off his console to fly toward the hatch. "That shit ain't funny!"

"It's the best thing there is for Zeewie fear stink." Larth held up his paws in a shrugging gesture. "It's that or we use the hydrogen peroxide and risk bleaching your fur."

"I ain't doin' that shit again!" Ricky yelped.

Jyrall cocked his head. "Wait. Again?"

Ricky disappeared through the hatch faster than Larth had ever seen him move in microgravity. Keaton was laughing. Larth stared at Jyrall. "I sense a story here."

Keaton nodded and took several breaths to control his laughter. "We were ten or eleven, and went to a summer camp, while Pops ran a quick hop for a couple of weeks. All the boys—the Human ones—were trying to bleach their hair. The lifeguards, in particular, were all over this trend and using lemon juice and all these things to bleach their hair. Ricky being Ricky, he told them none of that stuff was gonna work worth a shit if they didn't change their formula. He took a bunch of shit and made this stuff nobody believed was gonna do a thing. So, dumbass lathers up his head with it."

"I told 'em that shit was gonna work. I proved it, too!" Ricky said from the hatch.

"You looked like a dandelion for a week!" Keaton laughed.

"A what?"

Keaton and Ricky started talking at once, but Larth was already tapping on his slate. When the image came up, he guffawed.

"Holy shit! Are you serious?"

Jyrall stared at him. "What? Show me."

Larth turned the screen around and heard Jyrall snort once and then again, then he laughed in earnest. Great, belly-shaking laughter erupted from his maw. Larth couldn't remember when he'd ever seen his friend laugh so hard.

Jyrall caught his breath and turned to Larth. "No powdered sugar. This time."

"Very damned funny, Jyrall."

Jyrall pointed at him. "I'm serious. I want to clean up, and you damned sure need to take a bath, Ricky. I will not have this ship stinking all the way to Krifay."

Ricky disappeared again. Jyrall turned to Larth.

"We're Peacemakers, Little Buddy. It's time we act like it again, even while we're falling."

Larth nodded. "I think I know what you mean."

Keaton gaped at both of them. "What do you mean? What am I missing?"

"Movie night?" Larth asked Jyrall.

The big Besquith grinned. "Movie night."

* * *

The Farm
Vicinity of Caney, Kansas

The reunion took Araceli's breath away. After meeting with Jessica Francis at Davis-Monthan's boneyard, the Misfits had scattered again to their hiding places. Intelligence estimates changed, and Jyrall and Larth's pursuit of Kr'et'Socae had come to a standstill for more than a year. Seeing her old friends and teammates, especially with the knowledge they were together again for the duration, thrilled Araceli. Since leaving Victoria Bravo, Araceli had felt useless and bored, doing anything other than piloting a CASPer. She'd used the CASPer-like loaders at the tomato company to get better with her footwork and coordination, but she couldn't wait to get back in the cockpit.

And then she walked into the main hangar complex. Two familiar CASPers stood in their maintenance racks. Maarg and Gnrra sat at terminals connected to the mechs. The TriRusk turned toward her and waved. Gnrra did the same. Araceli jogged across the deck and quickly embraced both before stepping back and looking up at her CASPer.

"You guys painted her."

Maarg chuckled. "Bull's team did. Gave Thumper a full maintenance check out and upgraded pretty much all its sensors and command systems. New MAC. More efficient jump jets. They did a number on it—not just the black and red paint. I think it's pretty."

"She looks *incredible*." Araceli glanced from Thumper to Deathangel, which looked as sleek as ever. There was no visible damage from its last engagement. The memory of Tara lying in her CASPer with her legs severed angered Araceli to the point she had to force herself to take a deep breath and let it out slowly. Her hatred for the man who'd tried to kill Tara nearly burned a hole in her chest.

I'm going to take Crusader Prime down; I swear it. Even if it's the last thing I do. Nobody hurts my family like that. Never again.

"They're ready for operations," Tara said.

Araceli jumped. She hadn't heard Tara approach. "How do you do that?"

"I'm going to teach you," Tara replied. She looked to Maarg and Gnrra. "Are we ready?"

"We've made the transition from the ops center to Deathangel with Thumper as the secondary carrier," Gnrra said. Seeing him as part of the team made Araceli proud of their little unit.

We're all equals. That's pretty cool.

Tara looked at her. "I didn't show you something in the command center because I wanted to make sure everything worked as Lucille said it would. She's solely with Jessica now, but she's done a few things to help us gather intelligence from as much of the Galactic Union as we can while helping us do our business, too."

"She copied herself?"

"Not quite," Maarg replied. "I'll send you the after action reports for what Jessica and Lucille encountered at Uluru when they rescued Snowman. There was an SI present in the network by the name of Minerva. We think it's tied to the Science Guild like Counselor's tied to the Peacemaker Guild. When Lucille entered the network, Minerva withdrew completely. Jessica realized Lucille was even more special than we thought."

"And," Tara continued, "Lucille realized we needed something to help us without giving herself away, so she created Nike."

<<Hello, Araceli Cignes. It's nice to meet you.>> The voice was quite different from Lucille's measured contralto. Nike's voice was pitched slightly higher, and Lucille's somewhat measured diction was gone. Nike sounded even more like a real person—someone Araceli's age, even. <<Tara, upload to Deathangel and Thumper is complete. Both CASPers are 100 percent operational at this time.>>

Tara raised her eyebrows at Araceli as if she knew the younger woman had a question in mind. Araceli nodded. "Nike, are you an AI or an SI?"

<<You're seeking a definitive term when there is none, Araceli Cignes. I'm a hybrid, like my mother, Lucille.>>

Araceli's brow furrowed and she realized the entire team was waiting for her reaction. *What am I missing?*

Oh, shit!

"You said 'I' and you called Lucille your 'mother!'" Araceli gasped. "You don't consider yourself either an AI or an SI at all."

<<I'm a hybrid, yes,>> Nike replied. << I'm nowhere as capable as my mother. My limitations are strictly C5ISRC based.>>

"C5ISRC?" Araceli shook her head. "What's that?"

"Computers, communications, command-and-control, and CASPers." Tara smiled. "That's the C5. ISR is the same as ever—intelligence, surveillance, and reconnaissance, and the final C is coordination. Nike isn't Lucille, Araceli. She's built on a similar construct, but will only integrate with our internal systems. If we're hacked, she'll self-destruct. Nike can't connect to GalNet or anything else. She's a closed loop for us."

Araceli nodded. "That makes sense. But how do you integrate ISR, Nike? You'd have to connect to certain sources."

<<You're correct, Araceli Cignes,>> Nike replied. <<I'll integrate ISR from each of you and your sensors and weapon systems. For external intelligence, I process packets left for each of you in encrypted mail and messaging.>>

"But in the case of emergency, you can make contact and—"

<<No. I'll self-destruct and reload from here in the command center.>>

Araceli studied Tara's expectant face for a moment. "She's integrating us, providing information, and clearing messages received to our slates, but isn't capable of connection? That doesn't sound possible."

"Receive only," Tara said. "Lucille advised us this was the way to go until she can operate freely."

"Which we don't know, because Jessica's still missing," Araceli finished.

Tara shook her head. "I have it on good authority she's on Khatash, but until she surfaces on her own, that's the party line—so to speak."

"Got it," Araceli said. "It's nice to meet you, too, Nike, Goddess of Victory. I like it. Please just call me Araceli or Little Sister." She saw Quin'taa and Homer beam at her, and she flushed. "It's good to be home."

Tara nodded. "It's good we're together again. It's time we get to business. Nike? What's the latest update?"

<<Activating workstation screens for relay. Transferring broadcast from antenna four.>>

The monitor turned, and the speaker snapped to life.

"…authorities have been unable to identify the deceased. The Zeewie was found on the median of the 180 Expressway north of Sinjai. Cause of death was a single gunshot wound to the head. Police are searching for another alien, possibly a Zuparti, believed to have been involved in the mysterious death."

Tara frowned. "'Believed to have been a Zuparti.'"

<<Intelligence packet received. Classified source. Believed deceased Zeewie is known as Tzegelo, who is a known associate of Hatfield. Scans of the deceased's slate indicates Hatfield is on the planet Prestone.>>

"Prestone?" Homer asked. "That place is a cesspool."

"It's like New Vegas," Maarg replied looking at Araceli, "only worse. Everything truly has its price on Prestone. The whole planet is nothing but debauchery."

"I love it already," Quin'taa rumbled, smiling. "Nike? How far away is Prestone?"

<<Three standard jumps.>>

Tara stroked her chin. "They'll go to Krifay and get the Kin. They're going to need fire support."

<<Confidence is high for that course of action, yes.>>

"Then it's time to recall Carter and Mata. We'll need *Mako 15* to get us and the gear to orbit," Tara said. "Maarg? Get in touch with

Reecha at the Carpet Factory and hitch us a ride to Prestone. Everybody else, grab some food, and let's get moving. We can chat more tonight once travel is arranged."

"So much for enjoying my suite." Araceli laughed. "I've been living in pretty spartan quarters for the last little bit. Was looking forward to a bath in that jacuzzi."

Tara grinned and turned to Maarg. "Get us at least one jump on a Class A freighter."

"That's gonna cost us."

Tara shook her head. "It'll be worth it. Might as well have some comfort for part of the ride. Three jumps. Three weeks. Lots of time to train and shake off the rust, everybody."

Homer laughed. "Speak for yourself, Boss. Quin'taa says he can take you any day of the—"

Quin'taa slapped a massive hand over Homer's mouth. "Can't we leave him home?"

Gnrra laughed. "He'll wreck my nice clean headquarters."

"Maarg?" Tara asked. "Bill Intergalactic Haulers for our transport and recall *Mako 15*."

"Done. Snowman sends: 'Good luck and keep us informed.' *Mako 15* ETA is eight hours and fifty-two minutes."

Araceli turned to Tara. "That was fast."

Tara shook her head. "Fast? Honey, we're just getting started."

* * * * *

Chapter Eight

Krifay

Staff Sergeant Jerund stepped back and rubbed his chin. He looked over and down at the Maki standing beside him. "You think so?"

"Yes, Sergeant," Corporal Kylont said. "Don't let its looks deceive you. I ran the diagnostics myself. That… is a Mk 4, 5, *and* 6. Well, mostly a 6, but you know."

"And it works?"

"For the most part, Sergeant. There are bypasses, of course. Some extra armor bolted on. Anderson moved it over here for him. It's ugly, but it works."

Jerund shook his head and sighed. "It's on you, Corporal. Get it loaded. I'll go talk to him."

Jerund walked over to an older man sitting on a bench on the dock. The man was tossing pieces of bread into the water, while small fish caused the water to swirl as they fed. When he saw Jerund approaching, the man put the rest into a chest pocket in his waders.

"Sir?" Jerund said.

"Sir!" the man said, surprised. He started to stand. "You watch your mouth. I might be a little long in the tooth, but a fella's not gonna call me an officer and walk away from it. Hell, I worked for a living for a lot of years."

"Whoa!" Jerund said, raising his hands, palms out. "I didn't mean anything by it. I was born and raised in Northeast Georgia. My daddy would tan my hide if I didn't show respect to anyone older than me."

The old man settled down. "Well, that's different." He stared off. "I knew a few boys from the South. They were the same way. It was always please and thank you from those two; it didn't matter who they were talking to. Both of them threatened to whup my ass one night because I got a little smart with a waitress and didn't tip her in this dive we ate at." He grinned, showing more wrinkles on his weather-worn face. "They were serious, too."

"Can't say I blame 'em," Jerund admitted. "My mama worked at a place called the Universal Joint for a lot of years. Tips kept food on our table while my daddy turned wrenches in a small shop to pay the rest of the bills."

The old man nodded. "Most of my family were clammers. Some had a couple lobster boats. I grew up on the end of Long Island. And not in those fancy neighborhoods, mind you."

"And you?" Jerund prodded.

"Me? I took my VOWS as soon as I was able. There was no way I was going to work my ass off like my father, uncles, and cousins. Not on a beach, in the bay, or on a boat. Got off that island, and off the planet, you could say. Bounced around a few units through the years. Saved a few credits. Ended up here… clamming and setting a few lobster traps." He looked up and squinted one eye, causing even more wrinkles around it to form. "Go figure."

"I hear ya. It all comes back around, I reckon. I turn wrenches like my daddy did, these days."

"You a pilot, too?" the old man asked. "I saw you looking at my baby like you knew what you were doing, both inside and out."

"Yes, sir, I do."

"Which outfit?"

"The Barnstormers."

The old man nodded. "I figured. Pete Brentale is a good man. I've known his family for years. Sure miss his aunt and uncle. Haven't seen their boy in a while now. Young Giles was always a little different. Always digging in the dirt. The boy never cared much for the merc life or going out to sea."

"I heard he's doing all right these days," Jerund said.

"Who is?" a voice asked behind him.

Jerund turned to see Lisalle walk over from the barge the man's CASPer was being loaded onto.

"Hey! How was it?" he asked.

"It weren't bad," Lisalle said. "It was smooth all the way there and back." She smiled at the old man. "Who's yer friend, Jimmy-Ray?"

Jerund turned and said, "Sir, I'm sorry. I don't know your name."

The old man stood up. "Travis. Travis Gannon. You can call me Yankee; my friends in the units did. I'm just an old master sergeant who's past his prime."

"This is Lisalle Jones," Jerund said. He put his arm around Lisalle as she stepped closer. "I'm Jimmy-Ray Jerund."

"Ma'am, if you don't mind me saying, you've got to be the prettiest captain I ever saw." He looked at Jerund and said, "You need to hold on tight to her every chance you get. One day you'll blink, and you'll be holding her hand in a hospital room somewhere, making promises you might have to break once she's gone."

"Promises?" Jerund asked, taken aback a little by the tears in the man's eyes.

"I swore I would never climb inside the old girl and fight again." The old man looked at his war machine swinging slightly as it was moved over to the deck of the barge.

He wiped his eyes with his sleeve. "I can't keep that promise. My Emma loved this world. Loved it almost as much as she loved me. I can't sit back and watch when it comes time to defend it. I just can't."

"I'm sorry for your loss," Jerund said, "but we may all have to fight for it."

Lisalle stepped over and gave the man a hug. "Colonel McCoy may find a way so's we don't need to come out of them caves swinging. But… if we do—if *you* do—I think your Emma would understand. She would want you to."

The old man nodded. "Yeah. I think you're right. Especially if those Crusaders are as bad as everything I'm hearing."

"They are," Jerund said. "They are."

* * *

Night Moves
Krifay System

"And we're back!" Larth exclaimed. He shook his head a few times. "I'm headed back for a snack. Anybody want anything?"

"I'm coming," Ricky said. "Ain't no way I'm letting you get in there and eat the last of them fish sticks."

"No, thank you very much," Jyrall groaned. "I don't know how you two can eat after a transition."

"It's only fish sticks," Larth explained. "It's not like we're going to get a bowl of spicy fish stew."

"Hot. Spicy. Fish. Stew," Ricky intoned as he tried hard to suppress a grin, while Larth covered his mouth to hold back giggles.

Jyrall covered his mouth and groaned again.

"Hey!" Keaton said. "You two shut up before you make him puke. What in the hell is wrong with y'all?"

Ricky kicked off a bulkhead and disappeared through the hatch. "Last one there ain't gettin' a damn thang!"

"Wait! What?" Larth exclaimed. "No fair!" He reached for a hand grip to chase Ricky down.

"Sorry, Boss," Keaton said. He glanced sideways to be sure Jyrall didn't actually throw up.

Jyrall sighed. "I should be used to it by now."

"It's not like either one of them are ever going to change," Keaton said.

"No, I don't suppose they will."

"It ain't a bad thing."

"No. It's not."

* * *

Starport Tarmac
Snapper Isle
Krifay

"This is not a good thang," Ricky declared. "Why in the hell did we have to set down this far away from the Kin Headquarters? Hell, we coulda parked over at the Barnstormers' AO."

"That's what the message said," Keaton explained again. "Cora has her reasons."

"True," Jyrall said. He adjusted his eyepatch. The deciphered message had also told them to stay in character as One-Eyed Varkell and crew.

"Hey, Snarlyface," Larth said. "Not that I mind being Switch, 'cause I look good in this vest, but I thought we were coming home to relax for a couple days before we leave again. This doesn't seem relaxing."

"I'm sure the reason will reveal itself soon," Jyrall said. "See, that's Sergeant Squarlik in the hovercraft coming to pick us up."

"Well, at least we don't have to walk all the way over there," Ricky said. He adjusted the rifle slung across his back, barrel down.

The hovercraft slowed and swung around gently. Squarlik waved with several of his limbs. "Would you like a ride?"

"Squarlik!" Ricky said, taking his rifle off his back. "I see yer still totin' that .50 cal. How you been? How's yer mom and 'em?"

"I—what?" the Goka stammered.

"He means how're you doing, how's the family?" Jyrall interpreted. He was understanding more and more of the accent and slang Ricky used.

"Oh. Fine, I think. My new squad is coming along nicely. Bweenkit has them on the range today."

The four of them settled into the vehicle, and Squarlik smoothly accelerated. "I'm glad you came back before they arrived," he said.

"Who?" Jyrall asked. He felt his senses tingle, and his fur rippled involuntarily down his back. He soon found out.

* * *

"I agree," Jyrall said. "We need to stay out of sight as much as possible. I don't think our disguises will work this time. I'm sure the Crusaders know about them."

"I figured it couldn't hurt," Cora said.

"Say, where's Keaton?" May asked.

"I had Squarlik take him back to the ship so he could bring up another identity for it," Jyrall answered. "It won't take him long to enact it."

"So, your contract's no good?" Larth asked. "That sucks."

"Yeah," Cora agreed. "It's not so much the credits. It's the fact those damn Crusaders are coming here to supposedly 'protect' the planet. I've seen them in action. They don't *protect* anything but their own agenda."

"Why would the Peacemaker Guild force the planet's administration to cancel our contract?" May asked. "It don't make no sense."

"A lot of decisions and directives coming from the guild make no sense," Jyrall said.

* * *

A week later, the Crusaders landed on Krifay. They immediately enforced a curfew at night. Squads walked around on patrol, fully armed. Demands for accommodations were made. Several prominent citizens were forced out of waterfront homes and other desirable neighborhoods.

The few times Jyrall ventured out in public, he had the feeling the locals were being intimidated for no reason. The few who protested publicly were arrested. Business owners were forced to pay squad leaders out of pocket for "protection." The oppression was as bad as any he'd seen on the entertainment videos Ricky and Larth loved to watch.

Twice he almost exploded out of character when he saw women spoken to in a way that would have caused Ricky to leap onto the offender with the intention of killing him on the spot. Businesses shuttered rather than pay the protection fees. He spent nights pacing, wondering if he should even ask Cora and the Kin for help. They were needed here in case it all boiled over. Prestone wouldn't wait. He knew he couldn't rely on indecisiveness for much longer.

As usual, Jyrall couldn't sleep. Returning to gravity always threw off his ability to sleep for a couple of days. He had plenty of options to assist, both medicinal and trusty breathing techniques, at his disposal. Instead of using them, he opted to get up, sit in the great room of his quarters, and read a book.

While his instructors at the Academy, and even his intermediate teacher during his schooling as a pup, would disagree, Jyrall actually believed Human literature was far more than pure, simple entertainment. Sure, there were millions of works that fit that description, but there were some beautiful, classic works in the Human catalog, and Jyrall had enjoyed reading them. His study had taken him through a broad swath of Human history, and he'd noticed how significant events and shifts in culture had taken literature into varied, if somewhat chaotic, directions.

Jyrall padded across the room and collected the dog-eared copy of *The Sun Also Rises* he'd borrowed from Cora—one of her favorite books—and continued to read. He lost himself in the book within minutes, so much so that he flinched when he heard his name.

"Peacemaker Jyrall."

Jyrall stared across the room, where a familiar Depik sat, watching him with bright eyes. "Honored Tsan. I wasn't aware you were here."

"I arrived on one of the Crusaders' ships. They have terrible security practices because they believe all their enemies are Humans. Traveling undetected was far easier than I imagined when I started the journey." Tsan cocked her head to one side. "I bring you news, Jyrall. We found Hatfield."

"He's on Prestone." Jyrall smiled. "We found that out from one of his stooges on Earth. Given what's going on here, we'll take care of the Kin and the Barnstormers before we head there—"

"No."

Jyrall blinked at the Depik's matter-of-fact challenge. "Why?"

"Taking care of your friends is important, and no one understands that more than I do. Hatfield is not merely involved in illegitimate businesses and criminal activities, he is also subverting a sentient species of aliens on the planet. One we've known about for many hundreds of years. One who does not deserve the hell that Human is putting them through for his own profit."

"Profit? How?"

"Racing. They are fast creatures, the Agamydi, when provoked. He is doing so for entertainment value and allowing citizens to bet on their races. Profit margins for him are extremely high, and he's paying winnings with the Parmick credits," Tsan said. "Money laundering, as the Humans say."

"I see." Jyrall set the book down and leaned forward. "This is confirmed?"

"Yes." Tsan slow blinked. "I trust you'll figure out a plan, Peacemaker Jyrall."

Jyrall shook his head but said nothing.

"You are uncomfortable with your title?" Tsan asked. "Why?"

"Our guild is in disarray. Our leadership is doing things with severe consequences to innocent civilians across the galaxy." Jyrall stared at Tsan. "I feel dishonored to be a Peacemaker, Tsan."

"Then stand against your guild, Jyrall. Perhaps that is your destiny."

Tsan disappeared into quintessence and was gone. Jyrall sat for a long time, staring at the spot where she'd been. His book lay forgotten as did his attempt to sleep. There was simply far too much on his mind for either, and nary a solution in reach. He would talk to Cora as soon as Krifay's star rose in the east. He needed far more than her counsel.

* * *

"Cora, we need to talk," Jyrall said. He paused. The look on Cora's face was confusing.

"I was just coming to find you. We need to talk," she said.

"You first," Jyrall insisted.

"Well," she said, "I just got off a call with Pete. It seems we—meaning the Blue Ridge Kin and the Barnstormers—have to leave the system, or face a 10,000 credit a day fine for disturbing the peace."

"What?"

"That's what they called it," she answered. "Our presence here is causing the locals to be 'kind of uppity' to the Crusaders."

"So, you're being forced to leave."

"It looks like it. For now."

A door slammed open across the bay of the hanger. Four Crusaders strode toward them. "Peacemaker Jyrall. You and Peacemaker Larth have been summoned. You're to depart within seventy-two hours."

"Seventy-two hours?" Jyrall asked, his voice low. He didn't like the threatening manner of the man in front of him. His base instincts crept forward, and he wanted to silence him. He forced the thought from his mind.

"Seventy-two hours," the man said. He turned to Cora. "Your decision?"

"We ain't going anywhere," Cora said. She folded her arms.

"I see. Well, you'll be fined accordingly. We'll ensure your guild is informed of the fines, and they will be paid, one way or another."

The thought came back to Jyrall. The man was threatening Cora. *Threatening!*

"I think you'll find it in your best interest to leave this building now," Jyrall said. A slight growl followed his words. All four men stepped back a pace. Jyrall smelled their fear.

They turned and left. Before he went out the door, the same officer said, "This isn't over."

"Well, that didn't go well," Cora said. "Bastards."

They were being forced to leave Krifay, all of them. Jyrall asked the question that had caused him to seek Cora in the first place. "Cora, I have to go to Prestone. Me, Larth, the brothers—we have to go. We could use the Kin on this mission. I could use them. I could use *you*." The last came out strained. He' surprised himself with it.

"You're not answering the summons?" Cora asked.

Jyrall was conflicted. "No—Yes. I don't know." He saw his surfboard leaning against the wall. On a whim, he grabbed it and headed toward the door.

"Hey," Cora said. "You know a storm's a-coming. This ain't the time to go surfing."

Jyrall kept going. He heard her call out, "I'm with you, Jyrall. When you figure out what to do, I'll be there with you."

* * *

Reortia

15,023km Southwest of Limerick, Prestone

"L*ionheart, Archangel One.*"

From his seat aboard the dropship *Ivanhoe*, Smith surveyed his tactical analysis board and found the icons for his Archangels. The six Mk 7 CASPers were his contribution to Hatfield's security forces platoon and occupied two firing positions about a kilometer away from their objective. Hatfield's forces were ready to move, but he'd sensed the reluctance of his pilots, even before the call.

They had to cross a kilometer of deep swamp to reach the swell of ground housing the targeted Agamydi village. Given the double canopy of the scraggly trees overhead, the CASPers' jump jets wouldn't have their normal range. Depending on the depth of the swamp, and whatever might lurk below the surface of the still black water, reaching the objective would be difficult. But that wasn't his problem.

"Go, One," he replied.

"Negative visual contact with security forces. Too much fog at the objective. Target obscured. We're on thermals. Over."

Smith blinked. Hatfield's forces had pushed off in their shallow-bottomed boats and would be closing on the objective. They should have been in visual range even with the CASPers using their infrared sensors. "You can't see them with thermals, One?"

"Negative, sir."

Smith's slate buzzed. He tapped the connection, and Hatfield drawled in his ears, *"Have your CASPers change to dark mode on their thermals, and they'll pick up the boats. Something in the vapor throws off the white-hot settings."*

"Thanks," Smith said. Flushed with embarrassment for not thinking of the solution himself, he tapped the external comms. "Archangel One, Lionheart. Switch to dark mode and report confirmation. Over."

"Lionheart, Archangel One, we're good. Preparing to move."

His slate buzzed again, and Hatfield whispered, *"Final approach. Be ready to turn them boys loose and hold the perimeter."*

I know what I agreed to do.

"We'll be there. The minute you hit the shore, they'll jump in and hold. What are we holding against?"

Hatfield laughed. *"You're holding the door closed, mainly. We don't want any of the good ones to get away."*

"Good ones?"

"Adult males and females, mainly. Them females are harder for us to get race ready, but they's just as fast." Hatfield paused but left the radio transmit switch keyed. *"Fifty meters. Get ready."*

In the background, Smith heard the constant noise of the swamp. Insects of all sizes and shapes buzzed around the cameras and sensors. Bird-things called and swooped between the moss-covered trees. His position on the dropship suited him. Being in a CASPer wouldn't have been so bad, but he'd done the infantry bullshit with the Ridgerunners and was fine leaving it to someone else. Staying inside, and in control, was everything.

"*Eyes on*," a low voice whispered into the channel.

The target materialized out of the thick, daylight fog. No more than a meter above the still, black water, the small knoll appeared crammed with trees and brush. As the security force closed the distance, Smith could see earthworks between the trees made of mud and driftwood. The walls rose a few meters above the exposed, muddy ground and appeared solid. These weren't the haphazard intricacies of a beaver dam or some other natural type of structure. A degree of engineering was at play. To get the mud and wood to rise, and hold, took ingenuity. There was a definite architecture here that was defensive in nature.

Almost as if—

"*Breach Team. Go!*" Hatfield commanded from his boat on the far side of the objective. They'd close in when the work was complete. Smith watched a K'kng lurch to the bow of the boat and heave a large breaching satchel at the earthen wall. The canvas-clad device impacted the wall and detonated instantly.

Smith clicked his transmit button. "Archangels, go."

A separate Tri-V feed changed to the external cameras on Archangel One, Major Sciortino. As Smith had thought, the low jump angle and the thick overhead cover proved to be a challenge. Sciortino was an excellent pilot, however, and he managed to bound off a thick, low branch and engage his jets a second time before landing softly on the knoll outside the established perimeter. There was something about the target Smith didn't like. Something was out of place and—

"*Shit!*"

An indicator on the screen identified the voice as coming from Archangel 2. The screen instantly changed, and Smith saw the CAS-Per falling toward the surface of the water and submerging. The mech found bottom and jumped up quickly. As it broke through the surface, Smith heard its pilot mutter, "*Good thing it's not too deep.*"

"*Shut up, 2,*" Sciortino said. "*Angels, report set.*"

"*Three, set.*"

"*Four, set.*"

"*Five, set.*"

"*Zero, set.*"

"*Two, set.*"

Smith tapped the screen. Archangel 2's pilot was Sergeant Avery. *You're going to pay for that mistake.* Discipline might not work anymore, but taking away your credits does wonders.

"*Lionheart, Angel 1. Set and providing security.*"

"Acknowledged," Smith replied and snapped his camera feed over to Hatfield's command-and-control linkage. There were three channels available, and Smith chose that of Sergeant Tren, one of the Jivool squad leaders. He could've chosen the action commander, the Gtandan known as Rorkr, but Smith declined. Listening to Rorkr undoubtedly talking nonstop to Hatfield, and vice versa, wasn't what he wanted to hear. His first impression of the Gtandan was unsatisfactory, despite the forces themselves being among the most competent he'd seen since the Ridgerunners themselves.

The camera mounted on Tren's helmet provided Smith's view as the Jivool entered the Agamydi enclave. He turned up the volume and routed the image to the full complement of curved monitors at his station.

Almost as good as being there. No bugs, either.

The security team, led by four K'kng and three Jivool, moved quickly between a series of randomly spaced, round structures. The mud huts, as Smith immediately called them, gave up a host of Agamydi. The young and old were left alone. The able males and females were the targets of the lead element. They worked together, brandishing electrified prods, and pushed the Agamydi toward the Lumar, who efficiently captured and pushed them out through the wall breach and into the boat. The older aliens hissed and clawed at the forces, but none came within a dangerous distance.

A flurry of communications came in, and Smith struggled to follow it. Something about resistance. Something about herding the targets. Something about… There were too many voices on the command net. Smith checked the settings and realized he was listening to all communications from every headset on the ground. He filtered all out but Tren's, and the situation cleared. Tren moved through the village toward the breach.

"Recovery team, move out. Get those things aboard and make a second run. There's plenty of room."

The Lumar and K'kng heaved the restraint bags in their arms and moved. The boat rocked from side to side as the K'kng lumbered aboard with their captives and set them roughly near the stern. The Lumar, unsure of the boat's movements, paused on the centerline, blocking the way.

"Come on," one of the K'kng said. When the Lumar didn't move, the large male K'kng launched itself over the side toward the shallow water at the knoll's edge. There was a large splash on the far side of the boat. A few seconds passed before Smith distinctly heard the K'kng scream.

"*Lionheart, Angel 4. There's something in the water!*"

"Where's the K'kng?" Smith asked.

"*Gone! The water off the knoll is really deep!*"

Smith watched as Tren vaulted into the boat and ran to the starboard gunwale. Below him, the black water roiled toward stillness.

Tren called, "*Kru? Kru, where are you?*"

There was no response.

When Tren looked up, Smith could see Angel 4 turned toward the water and scanning as he'd ordered them to do. Angel 4 raised an arm. "There!"

Tren turned, and Smith caught sight of something large and extremely fast cutting through the water. Through Tren's headset, he heard a rising sound, like a trumpet of sirens rising from the compound.

"*What's the status?*" Smith heard Rorkr snort into the comms channel.

"*They're crying and screaming,*" the other Jivool squad leader, Dseck, replied.

"*Contact, my ten o'clock!*" Angel 0 said from the far side of the knoll. "*Jesus, that's huge!*"

The Agamydi's pitch and volume rose. Smith turned down the transmit volume from Tren's headset, but the awful sound wouldn't stop. When Tren didn't move from the boat, Smith gave in and changed the channel to Rorkr as the Gtandan lumbered through the breach into a full-fledged riot. The Agamydi charged the security team. Smith didn't know who fired first, but facing the threat, his troops did as expected. Agamydi fell over each other.

"*Cease fire! Cease—*" Rorkr called, but it was too late. The forces unloaded on the weaponless aliens.

"*Hey, Lionheart. Have your boys help put them things down. We'll search and burn the village when we're done. One of them huts has their stash,*" Hatfield said. Smith hesitated. The Agamydi weren't wild and feral. There was intelligence in their engineering. There was something there he couldn't identify, but it seemed wrong.

"*Lionheart, Angel 1. Contact my position. I've got something large. Looks to be a whitish green. No. Scratch that. I have multiples. One moving toward Angel 2 at this time.*"

Smith reached for the camera controls and switched to Angel 2 just as something large and eerily similar to a saltwater crocodile from Earth came up out of the water and snatched the Mk 8 CASPer off the knoll in its powerful jaws. All feeds from Angel 2 went out seconds later. Smith reached for the radio.

"Archangels, engage and destroy all targets, inside the enclave and out. If it moves, kill it." He tapped over to the frequency he shared with Hatfield as the CASPers turned their fire onto the helpless Agamydi. "You better know what you're talking about, Hatfield. There better be something of value in there."

"*We got a dozen new racers, Smith. I guarantee I can pay you more in three days time than you earned in the last two years.*" Hatfield laughed. "*Welcome to our little game, Colonel. I trust you'll take your payment in credits?*"

* * * * *

Chapter Nine

Krifay

"Hey," Cora called as she paddled toward him. "What's wrong?"

Jyrall wiped at his wet fur and adjusted his seat on the board. He hadn't been out on a board in a stormy ocean for quite some time. The angry feel of the waves matched the rising anger in his heart. None of this was fair. The Crusaders had made a mockery of the Peacemaker Guild. Everything he'd ever wanted to do now seemed far away and dreamlike. There was nothing he wanted to do but crush them and—

"Jyrall?" Cora was there looking up at him, her dark eyes wide and concerned. She reached up and touched the side of his face with one hand. "Honey, talk to me?"

He shook his head before slapping angrily at the water. There was nothing to say. His throat tightened, and he tried to form the words, but his tongue lay dormant in his mouth, and a fog filled his brain. In his frustration, he was afraid, and the realization crept through his entire body. His hands gripped the sides of the surfboard tight enough, he imagined tearing it into chunks. That would feel good. A release. A—

"Was it something I said?"

"No," he managed to choke out. "I know you'll be right there, Cora."

She paddled alongside, grabbed his hand, and squeezed. "I'm right here. I'm not going anywhere, Snarlyface."

He laughed, and the tension eased. The feel of her hand on his warmed him, and the anger eased with every heartbeat. "There's no way this should be able to work, Cora."

She smiled at him and brushed a lock of dark hair away from her face. "You think I don't know that?"

Jyrall nodded. "My gamma didn't prepare me for this. I mean, we have this connection at a level I can't describe. You finish my thoughts. I understand you inherently. I can't understand it—especially because there isn't an… um… physical aspect."

He drew in a ragged breath, frustrated, but Cora only smiled. "We have a connection, honey. It's as much security and finding a kindred spirit as it is trust and love. I'm sweet on you."

"I don't understand."

Cora laughed. "Ask Ricky."

"Forgive me, but he's the last source of relationship advice I want."

They laughed for a moment and bobbed on the boards. The waves were stronger. More urgent. Amplitude rising and surging toward the shore with a power he hadn't felt in months. He stared over his shoulder at the oncoming sets, and beyond to where sky met sea. The words formed, and he let them come. "I've always been about answers, Cora. I wanted to be a Peacemaker because I wanted to get, and give, answers. Solutions. I wanted to be part of something finite. Now? With everything like it is? There aren't any answers, anywhere I turn. We have missions, yes, but those aren't outcomes or solutions. They raise more undefinable questions. And now, on top of that, I realize I have feelings for you. There are no answers there, either. We have a connection, but we can't physically mate or anything like that. I mean, physically, you repulse me."

"Gee, thanks," Cora said. Before he could defend himself, she punched his shoulder playfully. "It's okay, Jyrall. I know what you mean."

"You do?"

"I wouldn't have said it otherwise." Cora patted his arm. "I have feelings for you. That's what being sweet on you means. I love you, but in a way that's not just friends—"

"And not mates." Jyrall nodded and looked at her. The angst in his heart grew still. Her words rang through every part of his being in a way he'd never thought he'd experience. There would never be another Cora McCoy. "I… I love you, Cora. I don't know what the answers are to the questions that poses, and that's okay. I know there doesn't have to be an answer for now."

"Do you trust me?" Cora asked.

"Yes."

"Then we just go with it. There might not be an answer, Jyrall. You're my best friend, and I love you like that, and more. It's okay for two beings to love each other without being mates." Cora smiled, and he found himself returning it.

"I feel the same, Cora. I just don't like not having answers."

"Maybe we're asking the wrong questions," Cora replied. She looked away, but he could see her face betraying her thoughts. Those thoughts weren't about him, though. They were deeper and more troubling. "This whole situation bothers me. Why are the Crusaders coming here, except to take whatever they want? You know I can't let them do that."

"I know, Cora. But I wouldn't have asked for your help at Prestone if I didn't think we'd need it."

"I know, Honey. You want us to back you up, and we'll be there. But I'm afraid of what's going to happen to Krifay. I can't help but think them bastards are gonna wreck everything here. This is my home now."

"Our home," Jyrall said. As the words left his mouth, he knew them to be true. Krifay was the only place he'd ever felt at ease and relaxed. A large portion of that was due to the pretty Human at his side. He believed he knew her well. They were cut from the same cloth, so to speak. "You have a plan, don't you?"

Cora flushed. "Yeah, I do. You'll think it's crazy."

"Tell me." Jyrall grinned as a gentle rain started to fall.

"Once we're done at Prestone, we're coming back here. We've prepped a number of caches and supply depots. That crazy bastard Haney has a series of caves out on the coast."

She paused. "Maybe crazy is a bit harsh. He belongs to an organization formed long before there was even a computer available to everyone on Earth. They… procure things in ways that defy explanation. They also, unofficially, handle things among the lower enlisted troops, kind of 'in house.' It is, or I should say *was*, within the branches of the US military, but not a part of it. It's spread into mercenary companies. They seem to recognize a like individual when they meet and defer leadership to those known as Made Men or Made Women. It's hard to explain, because the first rule of it is: You don't talk about it."

"Then again," Jyrall suggested, "him being a member of an organization not spoken of or not, crazy might accurately describe Specialist Haney. He did fly a powered glider through the passageways of a gate."

Cora grinned. "He did, didn't he? That's the thing about those considered 'made' by their peers. They're exceptional troops. They know their jobs, and many of the jobs around them, including those above their pay grade. They could climb the ranks to serious leadership positions. They prefer not to. Occasionally, they aren't given a choice, and become senior NCOs."

She spoke almost to herself. "The E4 Mafia. Most think it's a myth." She ran a hand through her wet hair. "Trust me. It's not."

She continued, "Anyway, he provided a place to store equipment along with some things already hidden that may come in handy later. We've stockpiled a bunch of stuff there. With that plus what we have in orbit, we should be okay." Cora drew a breath. "Just so you know, this isn't just something I want to do."

Jyrall squinted. "I assumed the Kin were okay with this plan."

"They are," Cora said. "This is the Phoenix Initiative, Jyrall. We're a mercenary unit, and the guild says we need to clean things up and get back to business. We, along with Pete's company, had a contract here to protect the citizens and businesses, and that's been taken away from both of us by the Peacemaker Guild. You, Larth, and Jessica are the only Peacemakers I know. I just want to make sure you're okay with us chasing them off Krifay."

Jyrall turned his face up into the strengthening rainfall. "I am, Cora. I've doubted being a Peacemaker since all this went down. I'll support you and the Kin in everything you do, as long as you follow the prescribed laws of the Union. That's my charter as a Peacemaker. It doesn't say my enemy can't be part of my own guild."

"Well, there's one answer." She grinned at him. "Once we're done, and we head back here, though, I need to know something. Let's say you get a lead on Kr'et'Socae from Hatfield. Are you going to drop everything and go after him? Your mission is—"

"Not important if my friends and my loved ones are in harm's way," Jyrall growled. "We'll find him, Cora. It's a matter of time and heart."

The gentle rain turned cold and fell in great drops, smacking the ocean around them. He saw Cora shiver on her board and wrap her arms around her stomach. "Brrr. I think a storm's comin'."

Jyrall didn't reply. He felt it, too.

* * *

Omni Racing Complex
Prestone

Had Smith not seen the first Agamydi race in the Omni's arena, he'd have assumed the circus atmosphere to be normal. Hatfield had somehow constructed more bleachers near the ends of the main stadium complex, and he'd added more seating and standing areas along the track's infield as well. All told, he thought there were at least 60,000 seats, and every single one of them was full. The Agamydi would be the last race of the session, and after two hours of high-stakes racing and a list of drink specials as long as Smith's arm, the crowd would be in a frenzy—just as they'd hoped. Hatfield believed a single day betting record haul was in the works for them. All the Agamydi had to do was deliver.

Two days had passed since the operation on Reortia. While a search of the Agamydi village hadn't delivered any real treasure or another gold effigy of any type, it had delivered fresh racers to the arena. For Hatfield, that was all that mattered. While Smith's concerns that they were attacking a sentient—if not completely civilized—species bothered him, the possibility of making credits and furthering opportunities for both himself and the Crusaders overrode his doubts. Especially as he made his way down the main stairwell into the arena toward his seats.

How Hatfield had done it, Smith didn't know, but everyone seemed to know who he was. Exuberant cheers greeted him. Aliens of all the species he knew, and some he didn't, slapped him on the back and offered thanks and congratulations in equal measure. By the time he reached the box seat entrance, his back hurt as much as his face did from smiling. Effused, he tried to put his commander face on, but failed as he looked up into the happy face of the Oogar named Brusk.

"Welcome back, Colonel Smith. You know the way?" The Oogar gestured toward Hatfield's opulent seats in the center of the section.

"Thanks," Smith said. He climbed the small stairs and opened the gate. Hatfield stood to one side, speaking over the rail with several opulently-dressed aliens. They were quite the menagerie, and Smith recognized they were the "high rollers" in the Omni trying to get more information for their bets. Smith had never gambled before, save for tossing an idle bill or two into a slot machine. He considered their conversation for a moment and decided he didn't want to partake.

Qala, the Veetch server, appeared with a seltzer water on ice and set it next to his chair. Before he could thank her, she was gone. Smith smiled to himself. Being taken care of was, indeed, quite a thrill.

He sat in the comfortable chair and perused the running odds. Surprising himself, he picked up the tablet and selected a simple wager—the number of racers who would complete the course. Given all six had finished the previous race, that had the lowest odds. The second lowest, however, was three of six. Smith selected it at two-to-one odds and placed a 5 credit bet.

Almost instantly, a Jeha appeared at his side. "Your bet, Colonel Smith."

Smith reached into his coat for his UACC and handed it over casually.

"Thank you, sir. Best of luck to you," the Jeha said before inserting the card into a reader. There was a beep and a green light. The Jeha handed the card back and disappeared from the box as fast as he'd appeared.

Really excellent service. Smith took a sip of his water and relaxed into the chair. Movement caught his eye as the Agamydi racers and their handlers appeared on the straightway. The crowd roared in approval as the bugler appeared, and the call to racing sounded. The noise far exceeded anything Smith had ever experienced.

His conversation ended, Hatfield made his way over. "A little wager, Colonel Smith?"

Smith nodded at the racers. "I had a feeling you'd put males and females on the course together."

Hatfield grinned. "We'll see how vicious this gets. Them females might be larger and look slower, but I've gotta good feelin' about 'em."

"We'll see," Smith replied.

"Cigar?" Hatfield extended a case toward him.

"No, thanks." Smith couldn't stand them. Most smelled like burning cowshit, and tobacco in general was disgusting.

"How about some champagne, then?" Hatfield grinned, undeterred.

"What are we celebrating?"

"Credits," Hatfield said around the cigar clenched in his teeth.

"Maybe after the race."

The first of the Agamydi were loaded into the starting boxes. Hatfield tapped his slate, and the private booth screen turned to the running odds and a report of bets placed. The tallies were over fifty million credits. And rising.

"That's… stunning," Smith managed to say.

"Just watch," Hatfield said. He tapped a series of controls, and the crowd gasped. The track rose and twisted. Smith immediately realized the race would be double its previous length. The markers for obstacles increased as well.

"More difficult and longer," Smith noted.

"More fun." Hatfield laughed and pointed at the tally indicator. Bets were over fifty-five million credits and rising.

"Last call for wagers! Last call for wagers!" the announcer bellowed over the ecstatic crowd.

The Agamydi were finally loaded, and the effigy rose up along the track. He'd expected the racers to bellow and roar, but he hadn't expected the boxes themselves to shake from the impacts as the aliens charged the gates. A crescendo of noise rose from the crowd, loud enough that Smith barely heard the bell releasing the racers. A smaller male darted into the lead, with the pack of five close on its heels.

The crowd rose to their feet, as did Smith. A larger female accelerated up behind the male. Without breaking stride, she swiped a clawed hand at the other's legs and took it down. The male rolled in a frantic cloud of dirt, and the pack charged over it and closed on the first obstacle.

Smith watched the fallen male for a moment. It didn't move.

By the time the pack reached the wall, another male was down. The remaining four leapt over the wall almost without touching it and raced toward a wider pool of water. As Smith expected, the Agamydi darted across the surface without sinking, despite its length. At full speed, he imagined they would be capable of running atop the surface for as long as they maintained that speed.

Incredible.

As the pack raced up the track curving skyward, a manufactured ditch full of stakes waited. All of them jumped the ditch with little effort and then charged headlong into the flame obstacle. Smoking and howling, they emerged and ran up the second straightway toward a series of pedestals before the track descended to the traditional finish line. At the pedestals, the third male went down when a female charged it and knocked it from a plinth closest to the effigy. The remaining three slammed down the track and into the capture vehicle, to the thunderous applause of the crowd.

Smith applauded, as did Hatfield, who was now on his feet. "Wow."

"Yep!" Hatfield laughed. "A hundred and two million credits profit. One race."

A hundred million a race? Smith glanced at Hatfield. "Impressive."

Hatfield pointed behind Smith. The Jeha from before stood with a machine to take Smith's UACC. "Congratulations are in order."

Smith handed over his card, and the Jeha tapped on the screen before handing the device to him for verification. Smith studied the screen and drew in a quick breath.

"Two million and ten credits?"

Hatfield slapped him on the shoulder, and the stench of his cigar hit Smith in the nostrils. "Your bet, plus your fee for supporting our raid a few days ago. We'll hold your physical credits in the vault. You can access them at any time."

Smith smiled. "I trust there will be more opportunities in the future? I mean, you did lose three racers today." In reality, his CASPers had done nothing more than provide security for a four-hour operation. Two million credits a mission? That was the definition of easy money.

"We'll raid the camps every week, but we won't be burning them down like we did last time. We need viable subjects, you know?"

Smith nodded. "We'll be happy to assist."

"I'm gonna make it easier for you, Colonel. You, your key staff, and all your Crusaders are welcome to the upper two floors of the Omni Diamond Tower. All expenses are on me." Hatfield motioned to the Veetch, and she approached with two flutes of champagne. "Here's to the beginning of a beautiful friendship."

They touched glasses. Smith couldn't help smiling. "Pleasure doing business with you."

* * *

As the crowd, including Colonel Smith, filtered out of the arena, Hatfield remained to oversee his cleaning crews. At least that's what he told the staff, aside from Brusk. The Oogar was far from a lowly security guard, after all.

"Ensure Smith's soldiers get the best of everything. We'll separate some of our money from them, but it's far more important they take what we give them."

"I'll inform Mr. Randazzo. He and his people will keep an eye on them within the casino itself. He'll ensure some is separated, but not too much. He's good at his job."

"He should be," Hatfield remarked. "He didn't come cheap. It weren't easy luring him away from his previous job on Earth. I reckon his skills remain in demand in Vegas."

"I'm sure. Anything else, sir?"

"Pay them solely out of my coffers."

Hatfield kept his face straight. The first rule of laundering money was to find a sucker to do it. Smith would be so enamored with the millions in his accounts, he wouldn't even think twice to check the credits themselves. Nor would any of his soldiers. What was better than a sucker? A whole bunch of them.

"This might speed up the timetable, sir," Brusk said.

"Only if Kr'et'Socae comes up for air. I'm starting to think he's lost his nerve."

"You really think so? He's been known to stay hidden for long periods of time and return with a vengeance. Just recently, I might add."

Hatfield puffed on the end of his cigar and stubbed it out in the ashtray. "Until he does, we continue our plan, Brusk. Skim. A little or a lot, I don't think it's going to matter. His inaction means more credits for us."

In reality? More credits for me.

*****

Chapter Ten

Weqq

Her first trip off Earth in more than two years passed in a blur of general boredom, with the exception of her Mk 7/8 CASPer simulation package. Familiarizing herself with the systems and capabilities of a CASPer she'd never piloted was far better than planning for the future or trying to sleep in microgravity. They'd done enough planning in the last two years, and Kr'et'Socae hardly bothered her with requests to do more of it. He wanted a company to control, yet with Nigel Shirazi's Phoenix Initiative, Raley believed her mentor would wait as long as necessary to do whatever he had in mind for them. But the more time passed, the more she wondered if his pause wasn't due to something more specific, like the lack of a real target. Or even the inability to do something with nefarious consequences and risk the condemnation of the Mercenary Guild as well. Some lines weren't worth crossing.

The Phoenix Initiative was about business as usual. For the Raiders to regain their standing in the Mercenary Guild, they'd have to perform standard mercenary contracts under a high degree of scrutiny—at least for the foreseeable future. Kr'et'Socae's hesitancy seemed to lean toward a less than legitimate reason. As such, they'd need a miracle to start acquiring funds and forces. But companies would fail, and those survivors would need work. The Raiders would be there to pick up the pieces. All they had to do was wait for the right window of opportunity.

Raley noticed the return of gravity before Kr'et'Socae called from the *Dolly's* cockpit. The Equiri's interest and excitement at flying the dropship amused her. For someone so serious and focused, the exuberance on his face when he flew them from Earth's surface to the thrustcore made her laugh. He was more like a child than at any time since she'd known him.

"*Atmospheric interface. We'll land at the* Satisfaction's *crash site in twenty minutes,*" Kr'et'Socae said. "*Are you ready?*"

"I am. Think I'm gonna boot up that old Mk 6 in case we need to move something."

"*You just want actual command time.*"

All told, she only had about 100 hours as the pilot in command of an actual CASPer. Her simulations, no matter how realistic, didn't count. "Look who's talking, Mister I'm-the-Command-Pilot."

"*I never said that.*" Kr'et'Socae chuckled. "*Go ahead. It'll do you good to walk it around for a change.*"

"You're assuming it'll move off the wall."

"*It is what you call a 'hangar queen,' right?*"

"Precisely," Raley replied, and the connection dropped. She undid the sleep restraint and rolled off her bunk while reaching for a haptic suit. She tugged it on over her Raiders T-shirt and shorts and grabbed her boots. As she tightened their straps, she thought about her boot knife and decided against it. Clambering around inside the *Satisfaction's* hull would be a tight enough fit without weapons and such, and the haptic suit wasn't exactly comfortable in its own right. Dressed, she pulled her long, dark hair into a ponytail and made her way toward the *Dolly's* cargo bay.

The scarred Mk 6 hung in its maintenance rack. Try as she might, Raley couldn't remember ever seeing it off the rack and in use. A holdover from her father's time, his first CASPer, its presence made her feel as close to him as any of her memories—both good and bad. The Mk 6 was a maintenance trainer and carried no weaponry. Raley assumed it would respond to the start-up checklist and be usable. There was no telling what they were going to find at the crash site.

She climbed aboard and worked herself into the cockpit. She grabbed a ring-bound notebook from one side of the cockpit and started the power-up checklist. The Mk 6 responded to the initial commands. Batteries indicated a good charge, and the onboard command-and-control interface launched flawlessly. As the systems booted, Raley prepared to connect her haptic suit to the corded interface. The master caution light came on, and a buzzer sounded. She glanced at the caution and warning panel and saw six separate notifications appear. The master arm light illuminated with a fault, as did a light marked MAC 1. There wasn't a MAC onboard.

Another light illuminated. The master bus for the CASPer's legs showed failure. She tapped the comms panel and connected to the *Dolly's* intercom system. "I'm in the rack. How long to landing?"

"*Stay there. Three minutes.*"

"I'm not going anywhere, I think." Raley frowned. "Damned thing has a fault list as long as my arm."

With nothing better to do for the rest of the descent, Raley ran a handful of troubleshooting routines. She cleared the weapon faults, a navigation system fault, and the backup battery connection displays before the dropship touched down. There was no fixing the master bus from inside the CASPer.

Maybe Kr'et'Socae is right about CASPers, that Humans would be better off without the stupid things.

She heard the *Dolly's* engines power down and dismounted the CASPer. She jogged down the passageway and tugged at her haptic suit. Back in her cabin, she disrobed, pulled on fatigue pants with her boots, and added her boot knife and weapons belt. With the heat outside, she grabbed a fatigue shirt, but left it unbuttoned over her black shirt before opening her door. Kr'et'Socae leaned against the far bulkhead.

"You gave up on it?"

"For now," Raley replied. "We shouldn't need it, anyway."

The Equiri pointed over his wide shoulder to a large rifle. "We won't need it. Are you ready for this?"

The change in the tone of his voice caught her attention. Not a question, or the request of a mentor, it was more like that of… a father. "I'm fine."

He nodded and moved swiftly down the passageway. Raley followed a few steps behind. When they reached the bay, Kr'et'Socae wasted no time in opening the outer cargo door. The rush of rich, humid air took her breath away. She inhaled the loamy scent of the air, and it caught in her chest as the stripped hull of the *Satisfaction* came into view.

Oh, Daddy.

Memories threatened to overwhelm her. The first time she'd seen *Satisfaction* in Earth orbit, on her daddy's arm at fourteen years old. The first time she'd walked down the main passageway. Flying in microgravity for the first time. Her father's smiling face dominated all the memories. She blinked and focused on the distance.

The wreck sat a kilometer away through splotches of high green grass. Eyes on the hull, Raley walked down the ramp and heard birds squawking from the distant tree line. Insects of a size and shape she'd never seen before buzzed around her. She turned to Kr'et'Socae and tapped her wrist slate. "Biologics. Recommend jammers on."

"Agreed." The Equiri also turned on the hypersonic buzzer from his slate. The intent was to create a small field of irritation for any biological creature, enough for the wearer to be left alone.

Raley walked toward the hulk. The ship's sensors, weapons, and major components had long ago been scavenged. Even hatches and portholes stood open to Weqq's atmosphere. Rust dotted exposed surfaces on all sections of the hull. As they closed the distance, the hypersonic jammers flushed more small animals from the grasses at her feet and then the ship itself. Raley stepped up to the hull and pressed her palm against the sun-warmed metal.

It's real, Daddy. Our real ship.

That's right, Rae. We're gonna see the galaxy. Together.

Her vision blurred with tears, and her chest hitched. Her throat tightened and then released the sob she'd carried since receiving the news of her father's death. She leaned her head against the ship and let the tears come until her thoughts cleared, and her breath returned to a vestige of normal.

I'm here now, Daddy. Let's see if you left me a key.

Raley wiped her face and climbed through the open hatch to her left. The *Satisfaction* rested in the mud at about a fifteen-degree list to port. Movement inside would be difficult, but manageable, if she took her time.

"Where are you going?"

"My dad's cabin."

"Why?"

She clenched her jaw and tried to summon anger, but tears came instead. "I just need to see it. It holds my only memories of this ship, and it'll help me close this chapter. Okay?"

"I'll come with you," Kr'et'Socae said and then backed off. "If you want, that is."

Raley covered her surprise by wiping at her cheeks. "No. I need to do this."

"I'll wait out here. There are containers nearby I want to inspect. Call me if you need me."

"I will." She smiled at him and climbed into the passageway without turning back again. The angle of the deck and the mix of moisture and mud on the floor made the trek slow and arduous. She'd spent almost a year onboard with her father, doing the check-outs and tests. She knew every space from bow to stern. All of them were stripped to the bulkheads. Whoever had done—

Crusaders had been here.

Raley stared at the graffiti and clenched a hand in rage. "Motherfuckers."

It took her ten minutes to reach her father's cabin. The space had been scavenged to the walls, but the bunk itself remained folded into the wall. The controls wouldn't work, but she tried them anyway. She drew her boot knife, worked the blade into the seam between the bunk and the wall, and pushed. There was just enough space to wedge her fingers inside and pull. With her body weight on the bunk, it finally disengaged and extended on its hydraulic arms. Before it stopped moving, Raley inspected it and found the small canister intact.

Removing it took another moment with the knife, and, as she worked it loose, her hands shook. There was a tiny seam on one end. Raley twisted the cap, and it turned. As she disengaged the cap, she turned the cylinder on its end, and an antique brass key, splotched with corrosion, fell into her palm. On the clover-shaped end of the key, attached to a small metal ring, she saw letters hidden by dark spots. She rubbed at them with her thumb, and the splotches cleared enough that she could make out a single word.

Naduhli.

"What in the hell is that, Daddy?"

Raley tucked the key into an empty pouch on her weapon's belt. She looked around at the cabin, but the bare walls held no more memories for her. If anything, the cabin felt cold and empty.

Sadness washed over her, and Raley knew Kr'et'Socae had been right. Her father was dead. Almost everything he'd worked for had been sacrificed, except for what she had in her control. Building upon that would be up to her and no one else.

* * *

Daniels

Krifay System

Pete floated at a slight angle while he held on to an overhead strap and kept his right foot wedged under the pilot's seat in the operation's center of the Barnstormers' command ship. On the main screen, Cora and Jyrall were split, as the signal came in from their respective ships. Cora floated as he did. Jyrall was seated and securely strapped into the copilot's seat beside Keaton on the Peacemakers' ship.

"I think I got it all straight," Pete said. "We go ahead and make the jump to the meeting point. During the trip, I'll have Haney and a few of the others give some lessons on how to be different types of troops. I'm sure he can pull it off."

"What about you?" Jyrall asked. "Can you be something you're not?"

Pete cocked his head and grinned. "Yeah, I think so. I'll try to gather my thoughts and get in the mindset on the way as well. I think I'll be about ready when we meet up."

Keaton spoke up as he reached over and adjusted a small screen. "I'll have the identities of your ships ready when we get to the meet up. I doubt anyone in the Prestone System has ever encountered any of our ships, but there ain't no sense in taking a chance. I'll also have a series of records for folks to find, should anyone go poking into your history."

"Sounds good," Pete said. "We may just keep those disguises for when we come back and set things straight here in Krifay. See you at the meet point."

"Oh, we're going to set things straight here," Cora said. "You can bet the farm on it."

"You damn right!" Ricky added over Jyrall's shoulder before the main screen went blank as both colonels ended their call.

* * *

Night Moves

Larth looked over at Ricky with a grin. "That's funny. She said, 'bet the farm.' We're going to a gambling planet. Hilarious."

"Yeah," Ricky agreed. "That was purty good. I wonder if she knows she did it?"

"The Barnstormers' ships have made the jump," Keaton announced. "Scanners indicate the Kin's ships are preparing to do the same."

"We'll give it a few before we transition," Jyrall decided. "Just to keep a little space on reentry."

"Roger, Boss," Keaton said.

"All right," Jyrall said. He turned his huge head and looked back and up at his partner. "Larth, I know you have an idea for this. You've practically been dancing as you hang there, waiting to give me your thoughts."

"Oh, I do, Snarlyface. I do."

"I'm all ears."

"And what big ears you have, Grandmother…" Larth started to say.

"I will unstrap from this seat and actually *eat* you if you continue with that Human fairytale," Jyrall threatened.

Ricky's feet bounced off a bulkhead as he laughed. "Dang! I didn't know Jyrall had read that story. Pops read it to us when we were knee high. He did the voices. Used to scare the shit out of Keaton."

"It did," Keaton admitted. "He read from the original once. Not a good idea."

"We had to leave a light on at night for years," Ricky said. "Not that I minded." He shuddered. "Brrrrr."

"Enough of the fairytales," Jyrall said. "Tell me your thoughts on this, Little Buddy."

"Well," Larth said, "we already know Pete's going to play a merc commander with what's left of a company. He's been through hell and is disillusioned with it all. He just wants a chance to finally make some credits. The Barnstormers are all Human troops, so that shouldn't be an issue. As long as they act like down on their luck, slightly-less-than-honorable troops."

Jyrall said, "Right. They're the kind of people the Crusaders employ. He should be able to get a contract with them."

"I think we'll need to do several things at once," Larth continued. "We need to gain some intel, get someone on the inside of the casino, make our way around the various gambling areas and in the Omni Racing Arena, and we need to figure out what kind of long game Hatfield is playing."

"Hatfield!" Ricky stated with disgust. He turned and spat.

"Bastard," Keaton mumbled.

"Needs killin'," Ricky agreed.

Jyrall shook his head. "I understand how you two feel about even *hearing* the name Hatfield, but let's stay on track here. Continue, Larth. I like where this is going."

"Once we figure out what's going on, we can hit him and his people hard and fast. Use the Kin, the Barnstormers, and everything at our disposal."

"I like it," Ricky volunteered.

"How do you propose we get into the gambling areas?" Jyrall asked. "It's not like we can blend in like Cora, Pete, and the other Humans."

"Other races gamble in those places," Larth said. "I can be a gambler. I'm pretty good at it. With a little help from Keaton, I can be great."

"As Switch?" Jyrall asked.

"No. We can't go as Varkell and his crew. Those kinds of people will be able to find the info available on us. I mean, it won't show who we really are, but Varkell's business guy winning a bunch of credits will be suspicious as hell. They'll think we're cheating somehow, and security will disappear us."

"Yeah," Keaton advised. "Those security guys play all kinds of games to throw off winners. Sometimes the winners never make it off the property with the credits… or their lives, if it's determined no one will look too hard for them."

"It's serious business," Larth agreed. "You should watch some of those movies, Jyrall. They aren't just entertainment. On Earth, criminals started all the gambling in Las Vegas. There are still unmarked graves full of bones in that desert."

"True," Keaton said. He checked his screen. "Five minutes until transition."

"Noted," Jyrall said. "This mission will be dangerous on many levels. So you'll be the gambler. What will I be? Your security?"

"Yeah," Larth said. He grinned. "But you won't be head of security. That may be too obvious and lead people to think of Varkell. Keaton will be head of security, and you and Ricky work for him."

Jyrall tilted his head and thought for a moment. "I like it. It'll give me the excuse to constantly be looking all around like a good member of a security team for a rich client. All eyes will be on you and Keaton."

"Keaton?" Larth asked. "You good with that?"

"Yes, sir," Keaton said, also grinning. "I do believe I'm quite ready."

"Quite ready?" Ricky asked. "What the hell's that supposed to mean… and where did yer dang accent go? You sound like some kind of momma's boy with a fancy degree from New England or some Yankee-ass place."

"Indeed," Keaton said. "Indeed, I do."

* * *

"How does it look?" Larth asked. He blinked his eyes. "Does is look real?"

"It looks gross," Ricky said. "Like it's s'posed to, I reckon."

"I'm activating the program now," Keaton said.

"Whoa!" Larth exclaimed. "Cool. I can see everything. Seems kinda normal. Not quite, but almost."

"You should be seeing information scroll now."

"Got it."

"Okay, concentrate on the small image in the corner. It'll enlarge and show what the camera sees. Like a split screen."

"Sweet! I can see what cards Ricky and Jyrall are holding. This is perfect. What are those numbers… oh, I get it. The odds of what remains in the deck."

"Right," Keaton said. "Now, let me show you how to determine odds in the old game of Blackjack. You won't see the cards the dealer has, but you'll know the odds on what remains in the decks."

"What else have you two made?" Jyrall asked.

"I got something that'll screw with slot machines," Ricky stated. He held up a small gold ring with a blue jewel, sized for Larth's finger. "It'll play pure hell with four or five of the machines the place uses. Even the newest model. Keaton found the specs and programming on it."

"Found?" Jyrall asked with a raised eyebrow.

"Absolutely," Keaton answered. "Found it within the company's secure internal servers, buried beneath four different encrypted firewalls. I won't be held responsible for their shortcomings when they left it out in the open for an individual such as myself."

"There's that dang fancy accent again," Ricky complained.

*****

Chapter Eleven

Blue Ridge

Planet Gondlo

Trindlark System

Jyrall grinned at Cora and gestured to his right. Larth sat beside him with a patch on his right eye. Cora looked confused. She looked past Larth to Keaton. Keaton was wearing a very nice… charcoal gray suit, complete with a red tie and matching corner of a handkerchief poking out. His fur was groomed to perfection. May and Lisalle giggled and stared at Keaton.

Nileah said, "You clean up purty good."

"Thank you, my dear," Keaton said, staying in character. "How kind of you to notice."

Pete was the last to enter the conference room. Every head turned when May gasped.

Pete had shaved his head and started growing a goatee. He looked nothing like the man they knew. He carried himself with a slight stoop and favored his left leg. He wasn't wearing a Barnstormers' uniform. It was more of a generic, run-of-the-mill mercenary uniform. The patch on his shoulder said The Island Storms. His island accent and those of many of his troops would have been too much to overcome, so the unit's name was perfect.

He slumped into a seat. "What's the final plan?"

Jyrall looked around. "We'll go from here directly to Prestone. You and… the Island Storms will go ahead, so you won't be associated with us. You'll seek a contract with the Crusaders. I don't foresee any problems securing one. You and your troops are now the type of men and women they are looking for."

"Got it," Pete said. "My ships are the *Summer Squall* and *Reef Runner*. Thanks, Keaton."

"Right," Jyrall continued. "Cora will work her way into the employment of the racetrack. From what Keaton's been able to find, they're expanding and looking for help. There are VIP suites that need servers. Haney will be assigned the three new Jivool and several others. They'll find a way into the stables as labor or whatever they can use. The different races won't be an issue there.

"Lissale and Nileah will be part of Larth's socialites. Rhineder and May will be handlers, taking care of their needs and desires, including Larth's."

He continued, "Speaking of Larth, he's now Garnovel Weezik, an extraordinarily rich, self-spoiled Zuparti. He has old family credits, and credits he's earned gambling across the galaxy. He is, of course, banned from the city limits of Las Vegas now.

"Keaton is Lothar Parthkit, a private security specialist. His services are highly sought after, and he constantly turns down job offers. He's known to be neat, polite, and proper at all times, but there are hints of the violence he's capable of unleashing. He handles security only, not the other stuff. That's why we need Rhineder and May. His employees are loyal to a fault and very, very good at their jobs."

"That's you and Ricky?" Cora asked. "What are your names?"

"I'm known as Rizzit. Ricky is Trang. We won't speak much, just stay observant and be ready to move as soon as Keaton instructs us.

We'll both be obvious violence, barely restrained. We'll also have others with us. The five Lumar you recently hired. I intend for them to remain in the guest suite until they're needed."

"As long as the instructions ain't too complicated," Lissale suggested.

"They won't be," Jyrall assured her. "They'll carry all the luggage and secure the room where we'll have everything. They're not to allow anyone access to the suite."

"So how in tarnation are y'all supposed to gather information? You ain't gonna be in there long. Everyone knows places like that will get all yer money. Quick, fast, and in a hurry."

"It's designed for the house to win," Pete agreed.

"We have this," Larth said. He flipped up the eye patch to reveal a milky white eye. He was obviously blind in it.

"That's nasty," Cora said. She leaned closer. "It looks so real. Is that a contact lens?"

"More," Keaton said. "The lens doesn't just cover the cornea, it covers the entire eye. There's no lens to detect, as the edges can't be seen. He can see through it, and it can receive images from micro cameras, so he can see data on cards and odds."

"Well, dang," May said. "What cameras? You know a place like that sweeps purty regular for electronic devices."

"We'll put 'em where they won't look," Ricky said. He leaned back with his hands behind his head. "Figured that out myself."

"Where?" Cora asked.

"We'll put them on the outside of their own security cameras. They don't sweep their own systems."

"Nice," Pete said. "You know they have them set so they can see what cards folks hold to ensure they aren't switching and cheating. They probably signal dealers with the information, too."

"Or fake players they send in to disrupt winning streaks," Larth added. "We'll be one step ahead of them. Oh, and I have this." He held up his paw to show the ring. "Keaton says it's undetectable."

"Until you use it," Keaton advised. "I'd say about three uses is all we can get before their security system tracks its signal."

"Good enough," Larth said. "I'll use it on 'em last."

* * *

Cirque D'Or
Limerick, Prestone

An experienced mercenary commander always knows where the troops hang out on shore leave. Even in the midst of an entertainment complex like none he'd ever seen, Pete Brentale followed his ear as he walked past the myriad bars and nightclubs until he heard the familiar strains of country music from Earth.

While there was certainly a plethora of Human options in the species-centric hotel, there was something about country music in particular that drew the mercenary forces Pete believed would be there. Specifically, he was looking for the Crusaders. He'd been surprised that there hadn't been any in the sports bar, nor had there been any in line for two of the more popular nightclubs within the Omni.

When he heard the unmistakable voice of Patsy Cline above the din of the casino floor, he turned right and entered a bar that looked like it was taken straight from the 1870s Old West. He pushed through the swinging doors, fighting a smile, and walked into the dark establishment, the air redolent with beer and the smell of hamburgers. Pete moved through the crowd toward the bar and noted he'd definitely found the right place.

Most mercenaries on shore leave did one of two things. The more experienced mercenaries and the ones not looking for a fight before a good time would bring civilian clothes instead of wearing anything identifying them as a combat soldier. The inexperienced and those looking for a fight would wear their uniforms. The Crusaders undoubtedly fit the second example. They crowded around the bar and huddled around tables, watching the televisions showing college football. Pete gave it a look and saw that it was a Big 14 Conference matchup and fought rolling his eyes as he bellied up to the bar.

He sat at an open chair. Inlaid into the bar was a video poker machine bearing a sign that indicated to sit at the bar one had to play more than five credits. Pete withdrew his UACC and slipped it into the machine. The display came to life, and Pete selected a simple five card stud game. He drew the first hand and looked up to see an Oogar bartender wearing a bright red bow tie looking down at him with the open-mouthed approximation of a Human smile.

"I know that look," the Oogar said. "Just get down on the surface?"

Pete nodded and allowed a tired smile to play across his face. "Yeah, just in from Karma."

"Here on business?"

"Naw." Pete shook his head. "Just a little rest and relaxation."

The Oogar looked at him for a moment as if wanting to say more, but didn't. He twisted a towel in his massive hands. "What'll you have?"

Pete glanced at the taps at the bar. "I think a Budweiser, please."

The grizzly-like alien nodded, moved down the bar, and retrieved his beer in a cold glass. While Bud wasn't his favorite drink, Pete had to admit the ice cold draft was about as good as anything he'd had in a while.

He looked up at the television screen and watched for a moment before a gentle buzz from the display told him he needed to do something with his poker hand. He discarded two cards and came back with a pair of kings, which paid him exactly one credit.

After a few minutes, the Oogar returned and asked, "Can I get you a menu?"

"No, thanks." Pete shook his head again. "Just gonna watch the game and relax a little bit."

Instead of paying attention to the game, Pete used his ears and tried to eavesdrop on the conversations around him. To his right at the far end of the bar sat three Crusaders, eagerly watching the game. Judging by the stack of glasses in front of them, they'd been at the bar for quite some time. As such, their conversation grew steadily louder. Within a minute, Pete knew they were undoubtedly Crusaders, and they were here on some type of special mission for Crusader Prime.

Pete decided this had been a good place to drop into. He got a flash of movement to his right. An older man wearing a Crusader uniform sat down at the terminal beside him, slipped his card into the machine, and tapped to play a game.

The Oogar appeared in an instant. "Lieutenant Colonel Smith. Welcome back. Your usual?"

Smith laughed. "You know what I like, Wreng. Go ahead and make it a double."

"Yes, Colonel." Pete noticed the Oogar's name tag for the first time and memorized Wreng for later. The bartender moved down the bar to fetch the whiskey, and Pete felt Smith's eyes on him.

"Haven't seen you around here," Smith said.

Pete shook his head and turned to look the older man in the face. At least he assumed he was older. From what he could tell, Lieutenant Colonel Smith was younger than he was by many years, but appeared to be the same age. Multiple pinplants glinted in the light of the bar from Smith's head.

Pete stuck out his hand. "I'm Pete Connors."

"Bob Smith." They shook hands. Smith looked at Pete's clothes and asked, "I'd assumed you were a mercenary."

Pete forced a laugh and tried to make it sound as disappointed as he could. "Maybe once. Normally I'd say I'm between jobs, but in this case, the company went bankrupt. For a guy my age… well, being a mercenary is a young man's game."

Smith chuckled. "There's other ways to play the game."

"Oh, really?" Pete asked. "I got a few debts I need to settle."

Smith smiled at him. "Let me give you my sales pitch."

Pete took a long sip of beer and nodded. "Buy me another beer, and I'll listen to anything you want."

Smith grinned. "I can do that. Who were you last with?"

Pete had memorized the back data in his "Pete Connors" identity. "I was with Buckley's Bombers until a couple months ago. Before that, I spent three years on the admin side, working logistics for

Bjorn's Berserkers, and the Forresters before that. Tried my hand at running my own company, but it didn't end well. Only a few of us made it. I have an old ship and some troops still hanging around me."

Smith looked away, and Pete knew the man was checking whatever databases he had available to see if Pete was legitimate. He'd initially been worried about this part, but Jyrall and Larth had assured him that Keaton was as good as they came as far as implanting data into the network.

He relaxed, albeit a little, when Smith said, "You've got an impressive background, Pete Connors. How much debt are we talking?"

Pete shrugged and returned the man's grin. "About 60,000 credits. Full credits. Not these play toys here at the bar."

Smith nodded, and the smile on his face grew even wider. "Logistics, hmm? As in the ability to move precious cargo?"

Pete nodded. "Moved more than my fair share of it."

Smith clapped him on the back and signaled to the Oogar for another round for both of them. "Pete Connors, I'm gonna make you an offer you really don't want to refuse."

* * *

Limerick Airfield

Prestone

Pete stepped off the ramp of his command ship. The *Daniels* was now known as *Summer Squall*, and it looked to be in terrible shape. He glanced to his left and spotted who he was looking for. He limped toward the man in a Crusader's uniform fifty yards away.

"Major Sciortino?" Pete asked. He held out a hand.

Sciortino reached out. "Yes… sir. Colonel Smith sends his regards. He's indisposed at the moment."

"Pete Conners, of the Island Storms. Well, what's left of it. One merc officer to another, call me Pete."

"Sounds good. Call me Russo."

"Will do. Besides, an XO in the Crusaders is bound to make colonel sooner rather than later. We might as well get used to it."

Sciortino brightened slightly. "Yeah. It's on the horizon. Listen, the colonel says you check out so far. I agree. Besides the last bit of bad luck your unit had, your record is okay. We will be digging deeper, of course."

"Yeah. Lost some on that last one, a few on the one before. It seems the contracts just kept getting worse. It gets to where a man wonders if there's a living to be made in this line of work." Pete ran his hand over his now artificially tanned bald head. "Seems to be too many laws concerning merc work to make it profitable. I've never been very far in the black, if you know what I mean. I'm way in the red now."

"I understand," Sciortino said. "Hell, I was in several units that went bust. Shitty contracts, shitty equipment. Shitty pay… I get it."

"Well, you're a Crusader now; that's impressive, if you ask me."

"Our records indicate you have a CASPer."

"I do. It's not new, but it's not in bad shape. I hope to use it again." He rubbed his goatee. "No call for that inside a casino, though."

"You'll get a chance to use it… far from the inside of a casino."

"Sounds good to me. Say, how did you find out so much about me so fast?"

"We have our ways."

* * *

Colonel Smith leaned back and stared at the screen. He looked around the huge suite. It was the nicest accommodations he'd ever had. Hatfield had gone all out when he'd given him and his people the entire floor.

The information on the screen still checked out. The short-lived, now-defunct mercenary company the Island Storms was perfect for what he had in mind. He checked the time. Sciortino should be meeting with Pete Conners right about now.

A desperate man who's ready to take anything he can get will be one who doesn't ask a lot of questions. He and his troops can brave the swamps and gather racers for Hatfield when we leave. I'm pretty sure Prime won't just leave me here on a permanent vacation.

He stood up. There were games he wanted to try out downstairs. Maybe he could win a little more for his private account.

* * *

Blue Ridge
Emergence Zone
Prestone System

To May, Sergeant Rhineder had first looked like an opossum in a trap. Dressed in a custom-tailored suit made from Italian silk, complete with a stylish red tie and a pocket handkerchief, the grizzled old sergeant stood in front of the mirror, looking in absolute horror at his appearance. He'd stammered something about not being able to do the job before Jyrall had approached and put a large, powerful arm around the sergeant's shoulders. They'd turned around, and after a minute, Rhineder turned back to the group with a calm, serious demeanor.

"My name is Rhineder Nails," Rhineder said in a smooth, cultured tone, quite different from his normal gruff delivery. The transformation was nothing short of incredible. "I am Mister Weezik's valet and personal assistant."

They gasped collectively. May clapped a hand over her mouth until Jyrall asked her for her name. The big Besquith's eyes narrowed, and she realized it was time to play the game. To fall into her character. To become something she really wasn't and channel it.

"My name is Julie May. I am Mister Weezik's fashion consultant and aesthetician."

Jyrall shook his head. "Again."

May took a breath and tried to bring the cultured diction of a classically-trained personal assistant and beautician to life. "My name is Julie May. I am Mister Weezik's—"

"Come here, May," Jyrall said. He knelt in front of her so his face was level with hers. "Start in the middle. You must provide everything that comes before. Know Julie May as you know yourself. Where did she come from? How was she raised? You know the file like the back of your hand, May. Now become it. Slip into her skin and become her. Channel her past into your body, your voice, and your mannerisms. Channel her so deeply it feels natural. Once you're there, never let go."

"Okay," May said. "Right."

Jyrall's dark eyes twinkled at her words. "That's it. Wrap yourself in her and show us who she is."

He stood up and stepped back. May closed her eyes and took a deep breath. Jyrall was right—she'd memorized the file they'd created for the Julie May persona. Being the aesthetician was, perhaps, too close to her own name, but she knew it was done for her comfort. If things went according to plan, she would be the lead element of the incursion into the operations of the racing arena. She'd have to drop in and out of the persona at will. It needed to be her. The dates and details flashed through her mind, and she inhabited them. She saw herself as Julie May experiencing those moments. Those memories. All of it gelled together, and she fell into it.

Her eyes opened, and she turned around. The faint Liverpool accent rolled off her tongue like it hadn't before, her shoulders back and her back straight. She'd once thought of Julie May as a sort of Mary Poppins—practically perfect and all that. The image stuck and came out in her words. "Good morning. My name is Julie May, Mister Weezik's aesthetician and dietitian."

Cora laughed and shook her head. "Jyrall? How do you do that?"

The Besquith grinned. "My favorite classes at the Academy were the acting ones. They were quite useful."

"To the point you never know if a Peacemaker is around you," Larth replied. "The good ones can disappear for decades, if necessary."

Cora turned to May and let the smile evaporate from her face. "What are Mister Weezik's dietary restrictions?"

"He has an allergy to pescatarian foods and shellfish," May said in her accent. "He must also remain on a higher protein and lower carbohydrate diet to combat his blood pressure issues."

"Does Mister Weezik adhere to your recommendations?" Cora asked.

"Almost never. He is a gambler at heart," May replied.

Jyrall nodded. "You're ready, May. You, too, Sergeant Rhineder. Good luck."

"Thank you, dear Rizzit. We best be in character from now on, yes?" she asked Rhineder. The older man almost smiled.

"Quite right, Miss May," Rhineder replied.

"I think you've created a monster, Snarlyface," Larth said with a grin.

"Two of them," Jyrall replied.

"Tell me about it," Larth grumbled. "I can't have fish sticks for this whole damned operation."

Ricky whooped. "More for us!"

* * *

Owner's Suite

The Omni

Hatfield stood behind the chair at his massive desk. What he was looking at intrigued him. Prestone Control had contacted him directly, per instructions, when the ships had made entry into the system. Well, once they ran the information through GalNet. Anyone well known or well off in the gambling community was a priority. The individual on his way to Prestone was interesting. *Very interesting.*

He turned to his left and asked his security manager, "What do you mean by an 'advantage player?'"

Victor Randazzo cleared his throat and spoke. "It's a guy who wins. Wins a lot, see? When you get someone like this guy taking home far more than he leaves in the house, it's not a good thing."

"So, he's lucky?"

"Not exactly, sir. In my experience, nobody is that lucky. To win millions and millions every year is more than luck. Those kinda guys count cards or have scams worked out with others. Whatever it is they do, they always get caught in the end."

Hatfield turned back to the screen and read the name again. "This Zuparti, Garnovel Weezik. He's been caught cheating?"

"Well, no, sir. Not yet. He was banned from the Strip before they actually caught him."

"And you know this how?"

"Well, there's an internal industry site with the images and names of everyone who's been banned or is suspected of being an advantage player. It's just a matter of time. Now, I don't know this Zuparti myself—he never came into the casino I covered—but he's on the list, and I know several of the guys he got over on."

"So, you're saying I should ban him before he arrives?"

"Yes, sir. I am."

"Because he's on the list."

"Yes, sir."

Hatfield ran his hand over and back down his long hair. "I don't reckon I will. The guy is rich, and he'll bet a lot. How sure are you of the security system you had me install? You told me it's the best in the galaxy."

Randazzo bristled. "It is the best. I helped design it."

"Well, then, I reckon we'll test it. He hasn't actually been caught cheating, so we'll let him come. You do a few of the things you do and make sure he leaves more credits here than he wins. If you catch him in the act, well then, that's different. If I can get him to the track, he sure can't cheat there."

"No, sir."

Hatfield turned to the other occupant of his office. "Mr. Mink. When he gets here, I want you to make sure they roll out the red carpet."

"I'll put my best on it," Mink said.

"You do that." He waved his hand toward the door.

Dismissed, the casino manager and security manager left him to his thoughts.

*****

Chapter Twelve

Omni

Limerick, Prestone

Two long rental hovercraft with darkened windows pulled around the front of the casino. Before the drivers could race around and open the doors, the security team for the Zuparti riding in the first had them open, and the look they gave the drivers was enough to make them go back around to the driver's seats.

Mr. Mink waited with his hands behind his back. Beside him was his hospitality manager, several of his assistant managers, and staff to carry bags. He noticed a well-dressed… Pushtal. He didn't let the surprise show on his face. This was not the first Pushtal he'd seen since he worked here, but it was the first he'd seen in a Human three-piece suit, and an expensive one, at that. He patted the front of his own, feeling a little apprehensive of his own choice of suit and tie that morning.

From the same craft, another Pushtal emerged before one of the largest—if not *the* largest—Besquith he'd ever seen, who stepped out with his massive head on a swivel as he took in the entire area. The second Pushtal bared his fangs, and everyone stepped back a pace. These last two wore clothes similar to the plain-clothes suits Mr.

Randazzo and his security members wore, unbuttoned for easy access to whatever weapon was concealed beneath their jackets.

The well-dressed Pushtal opened the back door, and a small Zuparti in a garish green outfit stepped onto the walkway. He wore a dark maroon patch over one eye. Two beautiful Human females climbed out after him. One brushed long, dark hair behind an ear and adjusted her sunglasses. Both seemingly wore as few articles of clothing as possible.

From the second hovercraft, an older man with a close flattop hairstyle and a third attractive woman began directing five huge Lumars to get the luggage piled in both trunks. In less than a minute, all five had four hands full of cases and hardened bags.

Mink waved the Oogar he'd brought with him to carry the bags into the building. He expected the Pushtal to approach him. To his surprise, he didn't. He stayed close to the Zuparti, while the older man stepped over.

"Welcome to the Omni," Mink said. "I am Mr. Mink, casino manager. This is Mrs. Fletcher, the hospitality manager."

Rhineder shook his hand. "I am Rhineder Nails. I'm Garnovel Weezik's personal assistant. This is Mr. Weezik's aesthetician and dietitian, Julie May."

"Pleased," Mink said. "How may I assist your employer in his check-in?"

"He will require an entire floor. No staff. A private kitchen for Miss May to use for meal preparation. We will pay for, and inspect, all food deliveries. The cost is irrelevant. His privacy and health are of some import."

"Certainly, Mr. Nails. I've been instructed by the owner of this establishment, Mr. Hatfield, to offer the top floor of the Embassy Tower. There will be no charge, of course."

Nails looked toward the Pushtal. "Mr. Parthkit, they've offered the top floor of the Embassy Tower. Will that be sufficient?"

Keaton stepped over and ran several of his claws down the side of his face, grooming the already perfect fur. "It will indeed, Mr. Nails. I've studied the architecture of the building and the schematics of the alarm systems. The exits are well placed and easily defendable. I was not, however, able to gain access to a security camera diagram. My team will determine the locations quickly enough."

Keaton turned to Mink. "All elevators to the top floor will be disabled. No one will be allowed to access the floor. I will require the code to use one lift for Mr. Weezik. This is non-negotiable."

"I… certainly. I'll speak to Mr. Randazzo, our security manager, but I'm sure it can be arranged."

"I'm sure it can," Keaton said. He raised an eyebrow. "If you will excuse me, I'll now escort my employer and his guests to the tower."

Mink stood, lost, while the entire group passed him and went into the building. He looked around and reached for his communication device to talk to Randazzo. The Pushtal had sounded Ivy League.

Did he say "defend?"

* * *

Security Office
The Omni

Randazzo was furious. He practically screamed into his device, "What do you *mean* you didn't run the bags through the scanners?"

"He has his own staff. Personal assistant, personal assistant's assistant, head of security, security team, baggage handlers… the works," Mink explained. "My people weren't alone with the bags at any time."

"What about the floor staff? Can they get a portable scanner into the suite?"

"I'm afraid that won't be possible. The Zuparti has his own staff, including a chef. They'll be arriving shortly. His head of security insists no one else is allowed on the floor, and they're demanding to inspect all food items unless purchased and prepared themselves."

"Dammit!" Randazzo said. "Fine. I'll go talk to Mr. Hatfield."

Randazzo looked at the screen on his desk. One Lothar Parthkit, a Pushtal. The file he'd quickly amassed was impressive. The Pushtal was a sought-after commodity among the galaxy's elite. He and his security team were top notch in every sense of the word, and *very* expensive. Several investigations had been commissioned when clients had been threatened and the threats ended. The investigations were to determine whether excessive force had been used by Parthkit and his crew in the fulfillment of their contract. In every instance, the results were found to be justified… homicides.

Is this gonna be a problem?

* * *

Stable Manager's Office

"Yeah. You'll do. Standard pay rates," the Goka said.

Figgle waved a pincer in agreement. "Agreed. Squarlik and I can start anytime you wish."

"Lost all your credits, did you?" the older Goka asked.

"It was a sure thing," Squarlik complained.

"It always is," the manager said dismissively. "Your ability to understand the Human English language and utter a few phrases is commendable. We use translators, so it won't get you a bump in pay, but it did move you to the top of the list of potential employees. Go clean stables eleven through fifteen. I'll see you get a full day's pay."

Figgle ushered Squarlik out the door. When they were a safe distance away, he said, "You're cleaning. I'm scouting. The Old Lady should already be looking around. If you see her, ignore her."

"Yes, First Sergeant," Squarlik replied. "What about the Oogar?"

"I imagine the Old Lady has a plan. We should follow it."

* * *

Cirque D'Or
Limerick, Prestone

"Gods, would you look at this place?" Tara Mason shook her head in disbelief at the opulence of the suite they'd acquired. The very Human décor of the suite gravitated to marble and sleek. There were six bedrooms, a large common area, a full kitchen with an on-call chef, and a valet. They'd opted not to have the extra support, but should things change, the staff was more than ready to accommodate them.

In the New Vegas area, there were four Human-centric resorts: the Omni, Cirque D'Or, the Brooklyn, and the Palace. They'd had their choice of suites at any of them, but the Cirque gave them proximity to the Omni just across the elevated hyperway. While The Omni was the highest-rated resort for total experience by its Human patrons, the Cirque was by far the most expensive and well appointed. At the Cirque, everything truly had its price, and Tara had spared no expense to obtain the best suite and the highest level of privacy for their operation. "I've never seen anything like this."

Araceli laughed. "This might make up for leaving my suite behind, Tara."

One whole wall was made up of windows overlooking the Omni and its racing arena. They were on the top floor of the hotel, more than 70 floors up, and the view defied description. The entirety of the Limerick area was spread out beneath them. The setting sun to one side of the room gave a golden glow to everything in the richly-appointed main room. Quin'taa and Homer appeared from a hallway off the main room.

"We claimed the rooms on the end over here. Figure you'll have the main bedroom suite, Boss." Quin'taa grinned.

"King-size bed?" Tara asked. When the Oogar nodded, she laughed. "Should be just perfect for Eponil to take up two-thirds of it."

The Depik emerged from the opposite hallway. "I heard that."

"You were meant to," Tara replied. "Sleeping in a bed has spoiled you."

The Depik didn't immediately reply. "The suite is secure, but I've emplaced a few jammers to be safe. Don't turn on the Tri-Vs until Maarg can get them off the hotel's network."

Tara frowned. "They promised complete security. Are they lying?"

Eponil shrugged as much as a Depik could. "I don't trust anyone."

"Point taken." Tara looked around the room. For the moment, it looked like a suite. Soon enough, that would change. "We have access to the hover pad?"

One of the major selling points for the Cirque's penthouse suites was the private hover pad. While not a necessity, it would make moving materials into the suite easier and provide a much faster response time for movement than having to fight Limerick's legendary traffic. They'd have to rent a flyer, but there were more than enough credits to cover the expenses. Between what Tara had saved from the liquidation of Force 25 and what Intergalactic Haulers had provided, they'd be well funded. But they also didn't want to call unnecessary attention to themselves.

"Gnrra and Whirr are checking it out," Homer said. "Once it's secure, we can start ferrying stuff here from *Mako*."

"You did get them a bridal suite, yes?" Araceli asked. Though Carter and Mata had been married for more than two years, the bridal suite and its accoutrements had been the young woman's idea, and everyone had pitched in for it.

"We did," Tara replied. "They'll get the full experience. Let's not worry about getting too much moved in and around tonight. Have you located the Crusaders' assembly area?"

"Wasn't too hard," Homer said. "They've taken up residence at one of the airfields reserved for VIPs."

"Which is saying something," Quin'taa rumbled. "The Omni owns four of them, spread equidistant from the hotel. The Crusaders have taken up roughly half the northern site."

"Which means they have a full company here, and at least three ships in orbit," Homer said. "As soon as it's full dark outside, we planned to give it a walk around and see about some surveillance."

"Nike and I have already been looking at what feeds I can get into. The airfield, surprisingly, isn't as secure as you'd think. There are groups of media who attempt to track and follow the celebrities visiting the planet. Apparently, there are a lot of credits in this business." Maarg trundled over to one of the side couches and sat down heavily. The all-species-capable furniture groaned. She gazed outside. "The view is pretty nice. I bet the city is gorgeous at night."

"From afar, it will be," Tara said. "Down there isn't always so pretty, and that's where we're going. We need to go over entrance and exit plans—who goes where and when. We have backup rooms at multiple hotels. If you think you're compromised, go there. Your relays will alert us, and Nike will send the cavalry."

She glanced at Eponil, sitting at the high window, silently staring at the Omni. He rippled with quintessence, but they could still see him. Tara had seen it before, and it never ceased to amaze her. However it worked, her companion was effectively in two places at once.

The shimmer faded, and Eponil shook himself from head to toe and glanced over his shoulder. He shook again, then licked one forepaw before rubbing his face with it. Tara thought she heard a slight groan.

"You okay?"

"I am. It's actually easier to do that the farther we are away. Right across the hyperway, apparently, has too much distortion, but it works well enough for short durations." Eponil blinked a few times. "Our… friends are there and in cover. I've arranged a meeting for you and Araceli tomorrow, but I think there may have been something lost in the message."

Tara frowned. She'd been counting on the Depik communications as a primary avenue of keeping tabs on the young Peacemakers. "Walk me through it."

"Tsan said you two are supposed to go poolside, and appropriately dressed, to a private cabana, number 15, at the Omni. Any time after 1100 local." Eponil appeared to shrug. "Does that mean anything to you? I mean, I understand the time and the location, but what is a… cabana?"

Araceli laughed. "Poolside at a private cabana? Forget every bit of bitching about my suite at the Farm, Tara."

"Banana?" Homer asked with a giggle. "At a waterpark?"

"A swimming pool," Tara explained. "A cabana is a private structure, like a tent, for folks who want some privacy and private service. Exactly the kind of thing our high roller would want. We'll be meeting Lisalle and Nileah, most likely. They're playing their roles, and that means we need to."

Araceli tapped furiously on her slate. "There's a shopping district downstairs. I'm sure we can find swimsuits even at this hour."

Tara nodded. "It's been a while since I've had a makeover."

Araceli blinked and then gasped. "Really? Are you serious?"

Quin'taa exchanged a look with Homer. "What's a makeover?"

"I heard makeover." Whirr clacked forward on her claws. The MinSha extended her foreclaws and appeared to examine them for a moment. "If they do manicures, can I come, too?"

Gnrra appeared from behind the MinSha warrior. He spoke to Quin'taa and Homer. "Why are the ladies smiling, and the two of you looking confused? Isn't it usually the other way around?"

Tara laughed. "Most of the time. Everyone get settled and figure out something for dinner. Araceli and I need to go shopping."

*****

Chapter Thirteen

Employment Services
The Omni
Limerick, Prestone

When she was sixteen, Cora had spent a summer sharing a house with five other friends in Gatlinburg, Tennessee. Working at the touristy town for three months had taught her how to deal with people of all types and reinforced one of her mother's favorite lessons.

"Do the work nobody else wants, and you'll be successful," her mother used to say. She'd grown up on a dairy farm in Wisconsin and spent decades doing some of the dirtiest, physically taxing work imaginable. Working to support various mercenary companies with administration, logistics, and other critical aspects was always far easier. Yet, her mother also volunteered for the hardest things—notification of next of kin being one job nobody wanted. As such, she was financially successful but, more importantly, she'd gained the trust and confidence of more than a dozen mercenary unit commanders. Those things were far more important than money.

For Cora, building trust came easy because of her upbringing. That it would serve a purpose in a different, potentially dishonest way, bothered her. But a doorway was a doorway, and getting through it meant mission success.

The Jeha hiring manager, wearing an oval Omni badge bearing the name Streecha, peered over her slate at Cora. "I'm afraid we have no vacancies for showgirls or lounge acts, Miss Long."

Cora frowned and let her shoulders slump. "I was hoping to find something quick. I just arrived on planet day before yesterday, and my credits are gonna run out in a week, and—"

Streecha harrumphed. "Your employment history includes a year as a veterinary assistant and a livestock wrangler? As in—"

"Cattle. My family has a small farm in Tennessee. I worked it with my—"

"I have an immediate opening in our stables as part of the Racing Arena," Streecha said, "and being an employee does give you priority in the event other positions come along that you may be interested in. I'm happy to make a note in your file of your… aspirations."

Cora brightened. "You'd do that? I mean, I really want to be a showgirl or a dancer, like, as soon as possible."

Streecha's antennae bounced. "You'll have to start as a stable hand and work yourself up. Is that an issue?"

Cora beamed. "Oh, not at all. I've worked in stables and barns most of my life. I mean, I left home because I wanted to do something new, but if getting my start means doing the hard work again? Sure, sign me up."

"Excellent." Streecha tapped on her slate. "We can offer you room and board, which would come out of your salary. We also ask that you shop exclusively inside the compound. We have thousands of vendors, and the credits we'll pay you are good there."

Cora looked confused. "You don't pay standard credits?"

"We have a local currency here at the Omni. It's exchangeable for credits at any time," Streecha said. "I'm afraid that's resort policy. Is that going to be a problem?"

Her father's parents had grown up in the coal mines and the concept of the "company store" was familiar and enraging. Cora smiled. "Oh, no problem. Just asking questions to clarify."

"Certainly," Streecha said. "The first thing we want employees to do is ask questions in the interest of the paying guests and customers. Beyond that, you always have a vehicle for discussion through your immediate supervisor."

"And who will that be?"

Streecha looked at the slate. "Arun Marwok. He's the stablemaster. He'll be here in a few minutes to take you through orientation. Let me get a picture and your fingerprints for your identification badge."

"Sure."

"I must say, I love your hair color. Red is such an attractive shade."

Cora blushed and patted her hair. The dye would come out eventually. As different as it was, and the fact that Jyrall seemed to like it, didn't make it permanent. But she'd think about it. "Thank you."

Streecha turned the slate toward Cora. "Your fingerprints, please."

Cora placed her fingers in the boxes and followed the on-screen directions.

I hope you're right about this, Ricky. Manufactured prints sounds a lot like Ricky Shit.

The slate beeped and presented a green border. "You're officially approved and hired, Miss Long. Welcome to the Omni team."

* * *

Arun Marwok lumbered into the Omni Hiring Services office on a thick cane and clearly favoring his right hip. Cora knew older Oogars often dealt with hip dysplasia issues, but Arun's limp suggested trauma of some sort. The fur on his muzzle remained mostly purple, so age likely wasn't the cause of the limp. Given the position of his right foot as he walked, he'd likely seen a significant injury there, as well.

"You're Cara Long?" The Oogar stared down at her. The one letter difference in her name sounded so different, but she caught it clearly.

"I am."

Arun shook his head. "I need help, and I get a damned Human."

"I have relevant experience."

"Oh, you Humans always do, but when it's time to dig in and shovel the shit, you always quit." Arun turned toward Streecha's desk. "This is why I prefer the track staffing office to do all of our hiring. Larklin just hired two Goka. A couple of hard workers to clean stables and pens. You make me come all the way here for a *Human*."

Cora realized what was about to happen. She stood and pushed between the Oogar and the Jeha. "Please, Mister Arun, I need this job. I just moved here, and if I don't start getting paid, I'll be out of credits, and—"

"That's not my problem," he replied. "You can't handle the work I need."

"You wanna bet?" Cora squared her shoulders. "I'm guessing I've cleaned more stables, worked more animals, and overseen more veterinary procedures than *you* have. I worked on my daddy's farm from the time I could walk. Just because I'm Human doesn't mean I can't handle whatever you're going to throw at me. I need the work, and I'll do it."

Arun peered over her at Streecha, and then lowered his eyes. "We'll see, Cara Long. You can follow me."

They stepped into one of the connecting corridors and walked toward the main casino complex. The Oogar's pace was easy for Cora to match, but it was evident he'd walked with a cane for a significant amount of time.

Arun said nothing as they turned into an adjacent corridor and approached an unmarked door.

"Touch the sensor and scan your badge."

Cora did as she was told, and there was an electronic buzz from the door as it unlocked. Arun opened the door and motioned her through. When she stepped into the stark corridor beyond, Cora realized what Keaton had meant about casinos showing one thing and being something else. The immaculate resort had a dirty, workmanlike backside, and she'd just stepped into it. While not surprising after working the tourist traps in Gatlinburg, she'd somehow expected more from the Omni.

They moved deeper into the corridor and past a refuse gathering site. The room stank of trash and all kinds of biological waste. Vast pipes ran across the ceiling and the dirty floor. The stench grew worse the deeper they went into the industrial areas of the Omni.

Arun stopped suddenly and stared at her. Cora raised her chin and stared back.

The Oogar grunted. "First test passed. Most Humans can't handle the smell here."

"You've never dealt with a sick and pregnant cow," Cora replied. "Hell, even the bathrooms at Old Mining Camp Amusement Park were worse than this."

Arun turned and led her out of the area and into a nicer, but still back of the house area, before descending a long concrete corridor toward the stables. As they walked, Cora smelled hay, waste, and a variety of other scents she'd never smelled before. They entered the stables near the horses. One of them nickered as she approached. Arun reached over to the wall and grabbed a wide metal shovel.

"Start with these stalls." He pointed at the horses. "There're twenty-four of them. Use the cart. When it's full, take it around the far corner to the dump site. Somebody will give you a new cart and take the full one. Got it?"

"Got it," Cora replied. Arun turned his back on her and walked away. She turned and looked into the long face of a black thoroughbred. "You gonna be a problem?"

The horse backed away from the door, and Cora walked inside. For two hours, she shoveled manure, moved new hay into the stalls, and removed old feed bags. The hot, sweaty work didn't bother her. As she worked, she listened to snippets of conversations from other stalls. She'd seen Squarlik and Figgle at a distance, and they'd played seeing her equally cool, if not frigid.

She finished the last stall with a brown thoroughbred named Missile Alert and spun the loaded waste cart toward the loading dock. A dump truck-like vehicle backed into place just as Cora arrived. Two Humans got out of the truck. One of them was Jimmy-Ray Jerund. He stared at her.

"Good, a new girl. Can you dump that thing by yourself, honey?"

Cora positioned herself on the cart's handlebars as if doing a shoulder press and lifted. She grunted and feigned straining, but moved the cart up and over. As the other Human—a dark-haired man with crazy eyes and a wild goatee adorned with little ornaments—shoveled, Jimmy-Ray moved to her side.

"Not bad, little bit." He grinned and leaned close. She felt his hand sliding something into her back pocket.

When he withdrew, she slapped him. "Hands off, asshole."

The cart fell back, and the dark-haired man cackled. "Whoo-ee, Jimmy. Your luck with women ain't ever gonna change."

"Whatever, Lenny. Least I got all my teeth," Jimmy-Ray bantered back. Cora could see where this was going. Lenny was an easy mark.

"Just means you fight like a pussy. Probably drink like one, too."

Jimmy-Ray glanced at Cora. "He thinks I can't drink him under the table, just 'cause he drives the race hauler and all that shit."

"Drink me under the table?" Lenny laughed. "Never gonna happen."

Cora glanced at Lenny and back to Jimmy-Ray. "No way."

"And if I prove I can?" Jimmy-Ray leered. "You gonna go out with me?"

Cora smiled coyly. "Maybe. Gonna need proof, though."

"Oh, I got that, new girl." Jimmy-Ray grinned. "What's your name?"

"Cara Long."

"You're pretty for a shit shoveler." He laughed. "Tell you what. Whoever shows up for work tomorrow is the winner. Race call is at six am sharp. That good for you, Lenny?"

"If I show up, do I get the date, new girl?"

Cora beamed. "Sure."

Lenny whooped and headed back to the truck. Jimmy-Ray smiled and, through his act, she knew what he said would be true.

"No way he's here in the morning. Especially missing stuff." He winked and moved to the passenger side of the truck.

As it roared to life, Cora heard Arun's cane tap on the floor behind her. "Finished?"

"With those twelve stalls, yes," Cora replied. "Have you had anybody clean them in the past month?"

Arun snorted. "Not like you did today, and in half the time my usuals do. I'm impressed, Cara Long."

"Thanks."

Arun motioned for her to follow him. "You handled the horses well. Let's try the greyhounds next. Once you're done, you're finished for the day."

"But I thought this was a full-time gig?"

Arun nodded. "If you work like this every day, you finish in four hours, and I pay you for eight."

Cora blinked. "Nobody catches that?"

"They're too busy counting credits. I pay to *my* standards, and no one bothers me. If we don't have racers, they get concerned. Horses and dogs are good. Many others, too. They care only about the Agamydi right now. They have enough for one more race, and then they'll go capture more. Until then, keep the stables clean and enjoy your spoils. If your work slacks, though, you only get paid for what you do. Don't do it, and I fire you. Clear?"

"Clear, Mister Arun."

The Oogar grunted. "Just Arun, Cara Long. There is one other thing?"

"Whatever you need?"

"Do you type?"

Cora nodded. "A hundred words a minute."

Arun waved a hand dismissively. "My slate isn't working, and I have to submit a daily report. Would you mind?"

"Not at all. What's wrong with your slate?"

His eyes narrowed. "You fix slates, too?"

"No." She shrugged. "My roommate does, though. Won't the company sell you one?"

"For three times street value!" Arun thundered. "I've had it fixed many times, but all the technicians here want extra pay or favors for it. Your… roommate, what would they charge?"

"Let me take it to her and see what she says," Cora replied. "Would that work?"

Arun nodded. "Help me turn in these reports. I'll pay you six additional hours."

"How many for the slate?"

"Twelve," Arun answered. "It's been broken a long time."

Cora flexed her fingers. "Let me finish the dog yard, and I'll get started."

"I admire your drive, Cara Long," Arun said. "I think you're going to do very well here, if you can keep up this attitude and performance."

Cora laughed. "This ain't nothing, Arun. I can do this all day."

* * *

The Emperor Penthouse
The Omni
Limerick, Prestone

Keaton had been so in character and clearly enjoying himself that Jyrall decided to let the Pushtal arrange the security, brief the Lumar, and inspect the entire top floor with his brother. With the unexpected free time, Jyrall had tried to sit and relax, but he couldn't. Wandering the casino to gather his thoughts was out of the question, and with the sun setting outside and cooler air moving in, he didn't want to sit on the veranda overlooking the city from a hundred floors up. His options exhausted, he went to check on Larth. They'd be heading to the floor soon for a gaming session.

"Hey, Little Buddy," Jyrall said from the door. "You getting dressed?"

Larth sat on the corner of the expansive bed looking at his paws in his lap. "I'm dressed."

"But you're not ready."

Larth sighed. "This whole thing revolves around two things, Snarlyface. I have to play this part well enough to convince Hatfield to let me into his inner sanctum, and I have to get there by losing. I *hate* losing."

"I know you do," Jyrall replied. "There'll be a time for winning."

"But winning is the only surefire way to take him down." Larth sat up and turned to face his friend. "I can play Garnovel Weezik in my sleep. I'm worried about getting frustrated because I can't do any winning."

"That makes it normal, Larth. Every gambler really *believes* they can take the house. That frustration will give you more credibility than anything else. You can play the part of the loser; that's easy. I know what's really bothering you."

"Oh, yeah?"

"We grew up in similar situations, remember? The idea of dropping a hundred-credit bet scares the hell out of you because you've been in a place where a hundred credits was the difference between eating for a month and keeping your family in proper raiment."

"Clothes aren't that important for Zuparti, but I get your meaning."

"Do you?" Jyrall challenged. "You're going to walk into the high rollers' area and sit down at a table. Let's say it's poker, right? You're a good card player. You've lost good hands and bad hands before. That's not the issue. You're going to sit there, staring at all those chips, thinking it's more money than you've ever seen, and you're supposed to *lose* it. That's what's making you angry. That's why you're doubting yourself."

Larth opened his mouth and closed it. He looked at the floor for a long moment, and his shoulders slumped. "Yeah. I can't imagine having that kind of money to lose."

"Well, you really don't. It's a line of credit, remember."

"And that means at some point I'll have to win it back." Larth chuckled. "I can do that. It's losing it that chaps my ass."

"Did you really just say—"

"I did," Larth replied with a grin which faded quickly. "But I think about losing it to these assholes for even a short amount of time, and it pulls me out of character."

Jyrall put his hands on his hips. "So, don't lose it all. Keep your bets smaller than we planned at the tables, but spend the money."

"Doing what?"

"I don't know." Jyrall shrugged. "Maybe buy the house a drink. Go downstairs and rent a private cabana at the pool for the next two weeks. Tip the bartenders a hundred-credit chip apiece. If you're worried about enjoying the fall and spending a whole bunch of money you don't really have, you're the wrong Zuparti for the job. I suppose Zetchek is available."

"Oh, please," Larth sputtered. "I'm fine, okay."

"Then prove it. When we go downstairs, spend twenty thousand credits before you sit down at the table of your choice. Hit the mega slots, the sportsbook, the concierge desk, whatever you choose. Twenty thousand credits. Done."

"You make it sound easy."

Jyrall walked over to the concierge terminal and tapped a button. Immediately, the hospitality manager, Mrs. Fletcher's face appeared. Despite the hour, the older woman appeared perfectly made up and dressed for duty.

"Can I help you… it's Mister Rizzit, yes?"

Jyrall nodded, fully in character. "Mister Weezik is asking for champagne. A case of it. Specifically, Dom Perignon 2345."

"We can certainly arrange that. There's a surcharge for that particular year, if you weren't aware. Each bottle is extremely rare and carries a price tag of—"

"I don't care!" Larth shouted in Weezik's voice from behind Jyrall. "A case, chilled, within the hour."

Mrs. Fletcher appeared unruffled. "Certainly, Mister Weezik. Will there be anything else?"

Larth shoved Jyrall aside. "A private cabana for Tiffany and Crystal for the week. Massage appointments every day for the three of us, too. Ninety minutes at a time."

"I'm happy to arrange that for you. May I also suggest a private VIP suite at our nightclub, Maxim? You'll have direct access whenever you choose, along with private service."

Larth grinned. "Perfect. My thanks, Mrs. Fletcher."

"Have a good evening, Mister Weezik. If you require anything, I'm available to you at any hour." She smiled. "With Mister Hatfield's compliments, of course. I'll have the case waiting for Mister Nails or Miss May to retrieve in thirty minutes."

The connection winked out, and Larth turned to face Jyrall. "Asshole."

"You realize you just spent ten thousand credits, right? Maybe more?" Jyrall grinned. "Did you fall, Peacemaker?"

"I didn't," Larth replied. "Thanks, Snarlyface."

"Now, get in character and ready to spend. The minute the boys finish their inspection, we're heading to the floor for the night."

Larth replied, "I'm assuming it'll be a late night?"

"Late enough I asked Lisalle and Nileah to take a good nap," Jyrall replied. "I'm going down to their suite and make sure they're getting ready. I was worried they'd take longer than you, Mister Weezik."

Larth smiled but didn't take the bait. "Do I still have to spend twenty thousand credits in an hour?"

"At least," Jyrall replied. "And when you lose? Let it get to you—to a point. You're a professional gambler. There are highs and lows."

"Kinda like being partnered with you." Larth grinned and adjusted his eye patch.

"Something like that." Jyrall grinned. "We'll leave as soon as the boys get back and the girls are ready."

"I don't want to wait long," Larth replied in Weezik's voice.

"That right there? Keep that up. This is the one time you can act demanding and entitled, and I won't kick your ass." Jyrall changed his stance to a more aggressive one and put on Rizzit's voice. "You get me, Boss?"

Larth grinned. "Let's get this party started."

*****

Chapter Fourteen

The Omni
Limerick, Prestone

Tara Mason believed she was ready for anything until she entered the dressing room at the Omni. The gold-plated fixtures, opulent marble floors, and exotic facilities exemplified how different the Omni was from most places she'd visited. It was designed to appeal to Human celebrities and the insanely wealthy, and Tara felt distinctly out of place. She tugged on a blue one-piece swimsuit she'd paid an exorbitant amount of credits for and glanced down at her artificial legs. Despite being state of the art, complete with the ability to adaptively match her skin tone, Tara wondered for the first time since the incident what people around her would think.

At home, everyone knew she'd been a mercenary, and that it had cost her both legs. But here among the rich and famous? Would it alert Hatfield's security? She didn't know, and because she didn't know, her resolve faltered. Tara sat heavily on the bench for a long moment before Araceli reappeared from the shower area.

"Are you okay?" the young woman asked in a low voice. Nearby, other women dressed and showered, but no one seemed to be paying attention to them.

"I think so," Tara replied. "Wondering if we're taking a risk with me being here."

Araceli nodded, and her face was calm. She knelt down in front of Tara. "Nobody's going to know you outside that door. Even if they do, and someone looks you up, you're not a mercenary anymore. Remember? Your company is gone. Force 25 no longer exists. All you have to be is a woman on vacation. A very rich woman—that's who you are to the majority of the galaxy. It's been long enough, you're out of any spotlight, Tara."

"We can't be sure."

"We can't be sure of anything. You always say a bus could hit us tomorrow. Look, I realize this act might be pretty hard for you, so take your cues from me."

Tara's eyebrows rose. The more time she spent around Araceli, the more she recognized just how much the young woman had grown in the last few years. Not only was she a more than competent CASPer pilot, she also had the wisdom and experience of someone much older. Araceli was a soldier and much more.

Tara nodded. "Okay, I'll follow your lead."

Araceli smiled. "Good. Just do like I do, and don't enjoy the fall too much."

Tara laughed. She'd heard Jessica use the same phrase many times. She hadn't understood how Peacemakers could sometimes fall into roles and do things well outside their training until Jessica had broken it down for her. There were times Peacemakers needed to blend in, and doing so made their jobs easier. That was enough for Tara. She stood and slipped the sandals on her feet, still marveling at the ability to flex the toes of her artificial legs.

"Do you know where we're going?" she asked Araceli.

Araceli chuckled. "Something tells me we'll know exactly where we're going once we get out there."

At the exterior door, they paused. Araceli pulled down her sunglasses and winked at Tara before pushing through. Tara waited three seconds, as they'd agreed, and followed. They walked into the main pool complex under a warm sun. To Tara, the area resembled a rainforest built around several large, round and kidney-shaped pools interconnected by a lazy river and waterfalls as far as the eye could see. Humans filled lounge chairs around the pool decks she could see on the far side. To her right, she saw a line of twelve posh cabanas. As they were the only ones in sight, she figured that was where they needed to go. Araceli was already far ahead of her.

For a moment, Tara almost stopped. The young woman positively *glowed* in her sandals and sleek, one-piece black swimsuit. She walked on the heels with a roll of her hips that caught the eye of every Human male—and more than a few females—in the area. All eyes were on Araceli and not her. Tara relaxed and followed, letting her silk robe dangle open over her own swimsuit. As they walked, Tara allowed her eyes to flit around behind her sunglasses. Cameras built into the frame relayed what she saw to Nike for correlation and analysis, but Tara wanted to see what she could see.

More than a few young men, and some older ones, took more than a passing interest in Araceli as she walked. One handsome kid turned around to watch her and walked directly into a palm tree, much to the delight of his friends. Tara also noticed, to her surprise, that a few looked in her direction. The realization made her feel good and brought the hint of a smile to her face. It was one thing to hang out on the campus of the University of Nebraska, but being here in a purely social environment was something else entirely. It was something she'd missed for quite some time. She hadn't been the center of attention like this since she'd become a mercenary. It was a bit foreign and new to realize she liked the feeling. That's when she recognized exactly what Jessica had meant by "enjoying the fall." The role was tempting, and with the right motivation, she could fall into it and not return.

That's not me.

Focus, Tara.

Araceli weaved between the lounge chairs to reach the cabanas. Tara saw that about half of them remained closed. The other five or six were open, with groups of scantily-clad Humans in front of them. At the far end, Tara caught sight of two women lying in the sun wearing very revealing bikinis. Both of them had dark hair, one black and one dark brown. Tara recognized them as Lisalle and Nileah from the Blue Ridge Kin. Tara reached up to adjust her sunglasses and made sure she pressed the button to transmit information from them directly to Nike over an encrypted link. Text emerged in a window below her left eye.

Good to go, Maarg replied when they were about thirty meters away. Nileah, the dark-haired one, stood, waved, and squealed at Araceli.

Araceli waved vigorously and did the same. Amused, Tara raised both her hands and waved, but decided not to squeal. They entered the private cabana area, and Lisalle jumped up as well. There were hugs and over-the-top air kisses all around. The effect on the surrounding crowd was immediate. Tara realized they were making quite the show, and she gave in and decided to help as much as she could. As the introductions waned, Tara noticed the effect on the surrounding guests. None of them were looking in their direction anymore.

They'd entered the high rollers area, and most everyone returned to their own pieces of relaxation and paid them no mind, other than a few resigned head shakes and unspoken wishes written on smiling faces.

Amazing.

"We're so glad you're here," Nileah said. "Drop your things in here, and then let's catch some rays and have a few drinks."

Araceli beamed. "Like, sure!"

They stepped into the cabana, and the obtuse and overdone socialite act dropped immediately. Lisalle met Tara's eyes as she removed her sunglasses and placed them on top of her head. "We're really glad you're here. We're secure."

Lisalle pointed to a Jeha anti-listening device on the small table in the center of the cabana. "But we can't stay inside too long. Drop your things, and we'll go outside, get some sun, and have a drink. We can make plans and trade news throughout the morning."

"Just knowing you're here is a huge thing for us," Nileah added.

"You'll give us a full brief later?" Tara asked.

Araceli gently punched her in the shoulder. "Outside and relax, Boss. Period."

Tara grinned. "Okay, okay. It sounds like you all have a plan."

Nileah smiled. "Cora thinks you're gonna like it. She said to tell you hello."

"And the boys?" Tara asked.

Lisalle laughed. "Oh, wait until you hear how this is going so far. Tomorrow is going to be a very big day."

* * *

Greyhound Stables

"That's the last pen," Squarlik said. He attempted to twist back and forth. He waved several pincers around in small circles to get the blood flowing again. "I hate crawling into those… dog boxes to clean them out. What are they called? Greyhounds?"

"Quit complaining," Figgle said. "It's better than shoveling after the horses."

"If you say so, First Sergeant."

Figgle looked around. No one was near them. He saw Cora enter the horse stables across the way. He ignored her, according to the plan. "What did I tell you about calling me that?"

"Sorry."

"Drag that wagon around so it can be added to the other waste—what are you doing?" The last came out in a stern tone.

"I'm rubbing her ears. She likes it."

"Well, stop it. It's embarrassing. We're not here to befriend animals. She's not sapient. It's not like we can gather any information from a creature whose only lot in life is to race."

"If she could talk, she'd say she likes her ears rubbed," Squarlik protested as he rubbed the black and white dog's head and back with two small pincers.

"Get your sorry ass in gear and move that cart. We're supposed to go to the Agamydi pens next. Remember, if we finish early, we still get paid for a full day's work."

"Yeah, but we can only spend it here," Squarlik said.

"You don't need to spend it anywhere. We're here on a mission, not trying to live off what we earn."

"Peacemaker Jyrall," he whispered the name, "said we need to spend money like we are. If we save all of it, we'll look suspicious."

"True," Figgle agreed. "You can pay for dinner tonight… and cookies. Now move that damn cart."

* * *

A half hour later, Figgle stood with pincers on what might be considered his hip area. "I think you're right. There are far more empty cages than full ones. It's less for us to clean."

"I don't think it would matter," Squarlik said. "The Agamydi only mess up one corner. It's not like the horses and the dogs. They just go anywhere. These things are pretty smart."

"You have a point," Figgle agreed, "though that doesn't mean they're any smarter than the others. A lot of creatures on all kinds of planets do that by instinct."

"I don't know," Squarlik argued. "They *seem* smart. The way they watch you, following your every move. I don't know if I like it."

"You just watch them and make sure they don't try to escape," a voice behind them said.

Even with the translation coming through the small device clipped on his chest, Figgle knew it was the stable manager, Arun Marwok. He turned to face the manager. The older Oogar leaned on his cane, propping himself up to take weight off his bad hip and foot.

"Yes, sir," Figgle said. "I close it behind him when he goes in and make sure they don't make a break for it. Not that they have anywhere to go."

"True," Arun answered. "Their home is halfway around the planet. There's no chance of one making it back there, even if it managed to get out."

He stood upright and turned to go. Before he left, he said, "Still, we can't afford to lose any more before the big race. Mr. Hatfield would be furious if he had to cancel it. We'll have to go get more in a few days. It stretches the security team, but it's not so bad now, with the Crusaders helping to round them up in the swamps."

"Crusaders?" Figgle asked, though he knew more about them than the Oogar did.

"You've seen them strutting around in their uniforms. Ex-mercs, most of them. Still mercs? Whatever. They're part of the Peacemaker Guild. All I know is, on the last run, they brought more back than any other. I'm glad they're helping. I just wish we didn't need so many."

The Oogar stared at nothing for a moment. He spoke almost to himself. "The horses, the dogs… they run the race and come back to live the easy life until the next race day. They deserve it. They work hard. The Agamydi don't stand a chance. I wish…"

He didn't finish his thought and waved a paw dismissively. "Get these clean, and you two are done for the day. I'm going to go put my foot up."

As the Oogar limped away, Figgle noticed three of the small Agamydi had eased toward them. He turned and realized they were staring at the translator on his chest. They'd heard two different languages come through it.

"See!" Squarlik said. "They follow everything you do."

"Yeah," Figgle said. "I see. It's almost as if they know what a translator is. I wonder…"

Figgle reached up and unclipped his translator. He held it toward the closest one. It looked back and forth between the other of its kind and the translator. For a moment he thought it was going to reach for it. At the last moment, they turned away and moved to the far side of the cage.

Figgle looked around at the sound of the dump vehicle rumbling into the stables. Moments later, it went by. Jimmy-Ray waved casually to the two Goka. Not like he knew them, more like acknowledging that they worked in the same general area together.

Figgle turned back with the translator in his pincer, but the moment had passed, and the Agamydi ignored him. He clipped it back to his chest and pondered what it might have meant as Squarlik finished cleaning the other pens.

Whatever it meant, it was going in his nightly AAR.

* * * * *

Chapter Fifteen

The Omni
Limerick, Prestone

Race day dawned with an energy even Hatfield couldn't deny. Before the sun had risen, he woke, dressed quickly in his beige suit with burgundy ascot, and pushed his feet into handmade loafers before moving downstairs to the Omni's premier restaurant for his breakfast. As usual, he had eggs with corned beef hash, coffee, and orange juice. Pleasantly full, he decided to make a quick round of the casino and the other areas, using the old principle he'd learned as a mercenary of management by wandering around. The idea of inspections and scheduled activities for a leader always meant the dogs and ponies were properly arranged.

Management by wandering around gave him the opportunity to see things in real time. He enjoyed surprising staff—both those working tirelessly, and those working nonchalantly—and just seeing the customer experience with his own two eyes. Since purchasing the casino, he hadn't minded the daily chores, but the management aspects still seemed foreign. He'd never been much of a leader. He'd always been happiest as a follower. And then, as his mercenary career had deteriorated, he became interested in being the fixer and the fence.

His ability to find items of value and new homes for profit had served him well until his expulsion from the guild nearly a dozen years before he'd met Kr'et'Socae. Shortly thereafter, the disgraced Equiri had given him plenty of opportunities to shine using all of his abilities, with the caveat that he make them both filthy rich.

While Hatfield couldn't speak for Kr'et'Socae anymore, because the Equiri hadn't come out of hiding in almost three years, Hatfield could speak for himself, and his accounts were very well stuffed, to the point that there might even be an end to his activities in the future.

In the meantime, he enjoyed winning, and he stood to win a lot of money on the day's main event. The casino bustled with people. Not only Humans, but other species were represented, as well. He saw all kinds, and he noticed a long line across one of the areas between the table games and the slots, and it made him smile. The betting line at the sportsbook for the racing complex snaked back to the main casino. An impressive distance—he'd never seen the line that long.

As he passed the gaming pits, Hatfield stopped and waved over one of the bosses, a grizzly named Balta.

"Yes, sir?" The Oogar kept his voice low.

"A bit busy this morning."

"Sir, we haven't seen a line like this since opening day. Reports are that the stadium is 100 percent sold out, and all the standing areas will be packed."

"Any news on the current numbers?" Hatfield assumed it would be too early for a report on their expected take for the day.

"No. Would you like me to fetch Mr. Mink for you?"

Hatfield shook his head. His casino manager would be somewhere on the floor near the sportsbook at this point. He'd make his way there shortly. First, though, he just wanted to gauge a thought. With all the activity in the casino, the outdoor spaces—especially the swimming pools—had to be close to empty today. Seeing who might be outside would tell him what to expect for the day—especially his high rollers.

Hatfield grinned. "I'll catch up with him later. Keep up the good work."

Balta returned to the floor, and Hatfield made his way down the corridor and out into the sunshine. As he thought, the pools were nearly vacant. A few of the cabanas still held some of the high rollers—but mostly their entourages. There were a hundred or so around the two main pools. Most of them were guests, enjoying that it wasn't crowded at the swimming pool today.

All that would change later, and his hospitality staff would be ready. After the race, people would either be celebrating or drowning their sorrows. Hatfield would make sure to open all the different bars around the facility. Those preparations were already underway. As he made his way past the cabanas, Hatfield saw the two women he knew were accompanying the Zuparti named Garnovel Weezik. Hatfield detoured from his walk to play the gracious host and to take the opportunity to ogle two pretty young Human women.

Both were wearing their sunglasses and appeared to be studying slates. He wondered if they were reading fashion magazines or classical literature. The thought made him smile as he approached. "Good morning, ladies."

The dark-haired one looked up from her slate. "Oh, you're Mr. Hatfield. Am I right?"

The brunette next to her laughed. "Of course he is, silly. Don't you remember him from when we arrived?"

"I guess," the dark-haired one said and returned to her slate, dismissing him.

"You ladies aren't going to the race?"

The brunette said, "No. It's not something we're interested in."

He looked at the dark-haired girl. She made no response and appeared to be lost in her slate again. "Say, I haven't seen Mr. Weezik today. Is he around?"

The brunette shrugged and smiled. "I'm sure he's around somewhere. I know he was gonna go place some bets, and then he'll probably play a game or two before it starts. The race, that is. He's very excited about it. Says we're gonna win a lot of money today. I like a lot of money."

Hatfield couldn't resist smiling at the vapid comment. "I hope we all win a lot of money today."

The dark-haired girl looked up again. "But, like, don't you have a lot of money already? I mean, look at this place. I'm sure you've got money coming out your ears around here."

Hatfield laughed. "The casino does pretty well. I don't even keep my money on the same continent."

The girls laughed at the joke enough that Hatfield forgave himself for letting something slip that he shouldn't have. The two young socialites didn't care about his money, other than whether he'd spend it on them, and he knew that wasn't going to happen. Chances were they knew it, too, or they'd have been doing much more than holding their slates and sunning themselves.

"And where do you keep your money?" a familiar voice called from behind him. Hatfield turned and smiled at Garnovel Weezik as he approached. Dressed in a purple robe with a towel slung over one shoulder, the Zuparti bounded into the cabana area. "Mr. Hatfield, you're a man of secrets. I like that. You're also a man who knows his hospitality. I must say, this is quite the operation you have. We've been made to feel as if we were at home."

"And where is home?" Hatfield asked.

Weezik smiled. "Wherever we need it to be. Isn't that the story of money?"

"Indeed," Hatfield replied. "And what's your story of money today? Have you placed your bets?"

The Zuparti rubbed his hands together. "I have six of them. I might even be tempted to make a few more right before the race starts. Your Agamydi racers are very impressive. I'm hopeful to take a few million dollars out of your coffers today."

Hatfield felt his eyebrows raise involuntarily. "A few million credits?"

"Yeah, and not your pseudo-casino credits, either." Weezik grinned. "I've got a good feeling about this."

For a high roller with a great reputation, this Weezik didn't have particularly good luck. He was already down about 200,000 Galactic Union credits to the casino. No small amount. The night before at the craps table, he'd lost almost 90,000 credits alone in an epic beatdown. Hatfield wished he could have seen the smug little alien's face.

An idea came to him. "Would you like to join me in my private box today?"

Weezik grinned. "Of course I would."

* * *

Cirque D'Or
Limerick, Prestone

"Hey, boss? We've got movement at the airfield," Maarg called from across the main room of the suite.

Tara sat up from her reclined position on the sofa and set her slate aside. She yawned and rubbed her eyes. Two hours of scrolling through architectural designs for the Omni Casino and Racing Arena, secured by Tsan and Eponil, had given little insight into how Hatfield had secured the casino's financial holdings. There were vault complexes, a dozen of them, but there was no centralized main vault. The arrangement made no sense.

"What is it, Maarg?" she asked.

"Looks like the Crusaders are spinning up for some action," the TriRusk replied with a grunt. "I guess that Brentale guy was right about the capture raid in a couple days. They're preparing to go someplace, and spinning up a whole bunch of combat power from a dead stop in operations. I'd estimate they're two days out from movement."

Tara swung her artificial legs off the couch and picked up the slate. "I'll be there in a second. Engage Nike and correlate what we can see against what we don't know."

"That list is long," Araceli said from an adjacent couch. "Hatfield owns the casino, but there's not a legal record of anything. I can't see who the previous owners were—just a record of sale. Like, ever. The casino is thirty-five years old, give or take, and there's never been a record of legal ownership until Hatfield had one drawn up. It's weird."

Tara had to agree, but she didn't say anything. Instead, she stood and approached the makeshift command consoles Maarg had placed on the wide dining table. Two wide Tri-Vs connected security feeds from the Omni, Cirque D'Or, and the remote cameras they'd installed at the spaceport to track the Crusaders. Sure enough, a dropship had landed at a previously empty landing pad, and crews appeared to be offloading CASPers and their maintenance racks.

"Getting busy." Tara chuckled. "Nike? What do you see?"

<<The Crusaders are preparing at least a platoon of infantry supported by two squads of CASPers. They appear to have no flyer support as part of this plan, unless they're secured inside the dropship. By type, the *Ivanhoe* can carry two flyers in addition to the other equipment being prepared. I agree with the assessment that the Crusaders will move in two days' time. The presence of F11 containers indicates the *Ivanhoe* and other vehicles are in need of fuel. Refueling will take time.>>

"They're not taking them. The flyers I mean." Maarg pointed at the screen bearing information. "The Agamydi are native to the southern continent of Reortia. Lots of dense jungle and swamp. Flyers are about as worthless as an honest Pushtal there."

"I heard that!" Homer yelled from across the room. He and Quin'taa were cleaning weapons in a stream of sunlight coming through the wide windows.

"You were meant to!" Maarg laughed. "Doesn't mean we don't love you, Homer."

"That's exactly how I feel. Loved. Appreciated. Scorned at will."

Quin'taa slugged him in the shoulder. "If you were truly scorned, you wouldn't feel loved."

"We should totally do something about that, too." Araceli smiled.

Tara cleared her throat. "Not to break up the rhythm of our banter, but movement equals intent. And that means we—"

"Get ready," Maarg finished. "I've alerted Carter and Mata that their additional honeymoon is over. Carter says they'll be here in an hour."

Tara nodded. "We need to let the Kin know we have eyes on the Crusaders and are prepared to move. Where's Eponil?"

"Scouting," Araceli replied. "Said he'd be back by nightfall."

Tara stared at the young woman for a moment. "We promised Lisalle and Nileah to let them know the minute the Crusaders started moving. We're right in the middle of their window at the cabana."

"We're outside the agreed times," Araceli said. "We have to find another way."

"I'd go," Maarg said, "but there's that whole 'lost species creates a big scene' thing, and we don't want that."

"Homer is out, too," Tara replied. "Eventually, we'll need him to augment Ricky and Keaton as the security team. That leaves—"

"I'll go," Quin'taa said.

Everyone looked at him. Tara opened her mouth and closed it. The very idea of the Oogar playing tourist seemed absurd.

"I know what you're thinking, but hear me out. There are a ton of Oogar staff in the Omni. We've seen them in the security teams, the casino staff, and the racing complex handlers. I won't draw the eye of any customers. There have been other Oogar around the pool. Not very many, I agree, but I've seen a few on the feeds."

Tara glanced at the console. "Nike? How many Oogar are guests in the Omni?"

<<While species aren't codified on registration documents, analysis of camera feeds for the past thirty-six hours indicates there are fifty-two Oogar guests in the facility—plus or minus three.>>

Quin'taa stood. "That's enough leeway to get me in and out. Plus, they have an extreme cold-water pool out there, which sounds really good. They market it especially to Oogar visitors and sell daily use passes for it. It's a no-brainer."

"You certainly are a no-brainer." Homer shivered. "You can have your cold water, Buddy. I'll keep our steam shower."

"You can't stay in there less than thirty minutes," Quin'taa said. "Be thankful we have an endless supply of hot water, unlike on the ship. Besides, extreme cold is good for metabolic function. Wakes you up."

"That's what caffeine is for." Araceli raised a coffee mug in salute. "For us normal folks, that is."

Tara stared at Quin'taa for a long moment. "Are you sure about this?"

"Yes," Quin'taa replied. "Contrary to what you're thinking, which is written all over your face, I can act like a normal Oogar."

Maarg laughed. "That's an oxymoron."

"A what?" Quin'taa asked.

"A saying of two contrary, or seemingly contrary, terms. Like jumbo shrimp," Araceli said.

"Or military intelligence," Tara replied. She drew a deep breath and exhaled sharply through her nose. "Okay, you're on, Q. We'll be watching here. If anything happens, Carter and Mata can assist until we get there."

The Oogar grinned. "Don't worry about me, Tara. I'm ready for just about anything."

* * *

The Omni

The life of a pit boss was an exercise in constant vigilance. While the Omni was one of the most sophisticated and secure casinos ever constructed, security was a task for every staff member, from janitors and pool cleaners to the armed guards and the cashiers. Cameras followed every guest, and as good as the surveillance of the gaming areas was, nothing compared to the trained eyes of the staff. Every dealer could identify a threat in a heartbeat. The pit bosses were the link between identification of the threat and the removal of the threat. As such, they required every ounce of focus throughout their shift and beyond.

After more than ten years as a boss, Balta knew his role far better than most. He'd risen to floor boss because nothing ever escaped his senses. With the biggest race day in decades coming to the Omni, the gambling floor was overflowing with customers. He'd brought on extra staffers, including four roving bosses in addition to himself. The mood of the crowd soared with every toss of the dice at the craps tables to his left. His eyes flitted to a celebration—GenSha cavorting at the end of a *makuur* run. He'd never understood the card and stone game, but the payouts for the very infrequent winners could be great. He checked his slate and saw the winning bet was modest. Most bets were. Transient gamblers often bet a small amount and indulged in the free drinks and what hospitality they could until their money ran out. A few would delve farther into their accounts, attempting to beat the house. Some of them would learn their lesson; others would believe, until their death, that the house could be beaten.

Balta knew better. His job was to spot those willing to do anything to beat the house. To cheat. To steal. To subvert the rules. Such incidents were infrequent, but under his watch, none had been successful. He intended to keep it that way. His nose wrinkled as a scent, slight but persistent, caught his attention.

Feral.

Balta knew it wasn't a purely feral Oogar. Technically, every Oogar carried a hint of feral scent, based on their particular genetic heritage. This one, though, wasn't familiar. Something about it seemed different. Altered. He turned his head slowly, not wanting any of his staff to sense his alarm. Between the craps tables and the large banks of video slot machines, he saw the male walking toward the pool complex.

Balta turned to one of his rovers and jerked his head toward the restroom facilities, their unspoken procedure for when they needed to step away. He received a nod in response. As the Blevin took his place, Balta turned and headed for the Oogar's path, intent on following at a discreet distance. As he left the gaming area, he was aware he'd left his post. His wrist slate tingled.

He spoke softly into the microphone embedded in the name tag pinned to his vest. "Tracking something odd. Likely nothing. Will alert as needed."

"*Copy*," came the brief response. He knew their protection schemes would change and follow him. They'd see the Oogar but wouldn't understand the concern until Balta explained it. How could he explain it? The Oogar smelled funny? He'd say he had a hunch something was wrong and wanted to ensure he was wrong. He could say that without discrediting himself. He'd done it on several occasions. Reputation was important, but the security of the facility was paramount.

The target Oogar moved naturally and very much unlike a feral. Balta believed that was a good thing. He appeared to be carrying a day pass for the cryo pools, which was also a plus. What the Oogar wasn't doing kept Balta in pursuit.

Given the lights, sounds, and constant action of a casino floor, most guests and transient passersby couldn't stop looking around in all directions at once. This Oogar kept his head and eyes focused on the pool complex. Balta followed. As they exited into the pool complex, though, the Oogar's head swiveled in all directions. Balta slowed his pace, but stepped out into the sunshine. He watched the Oogar walk slower now, looking around for signage and… interestingly, Human females.

Balta felt his disgust rise. He'd seen far too many of his species chase others. It was bad enough that many Oogar pursued relationships with the Jivool, in complete disrespect to their own species, but many had become enamored with Human females in the last few years. Popular holo-movies and productions had glamorized these relationships—which could never physically work—as being fun and frivolous.

The perfect pursuit for a feral. Balta shook his head. The Oogar drifted along a pathway just outside the high roller's areas toward the cryo pool. Near the end, two Humans sunbathed in attire Balta thought pushed the boundaries of the complex's regulations. The Oogar grabbed a towel and tossed it casually over one large shoulder before ambling up to the fence and speaking to the Humans.

Balta shook his head. *Godsdamned ferals.*

"Security, Balta. Disregard."

"Copy."

He'd catch good-natured ribbing for his concern over another horny Oogar. What did so many of his species see in those thin, disgustingly hairless beings? Human females were gross and vastly inferior to just about everyone else in the galaxy.

Why them?

Balta shook off the thought and made his way to the restroom, then back to the floor. His shift was half over, and he could bemoan the state of his species later. For now, there was far more important work to do.

* * *

Cirque D'Or

"Contact made and message passed," Maarg replied. "I have to say, I'm impressed with the big guy."

Tara nodded. "He's a natural."

Just like his father, according to Hak-Chet.

"Let me know when he's out of the pool and headed back this way," Tara replied. "Especially if the ladies make additional contact."

"You think they will?"

"No. Not unless there's an emergency. I'd say we're still on our own. That means we prepare to move. We're not doing ourselves any favors by sitting here," Tara said. She felt the anticipation rising in her gut, and she welcomed it. As much as she'd tried to tell herself otherwise, she'd missed the feeling of being in the game. But it came with unease. The stakes were high, but for whom?

And who benefited the most from all of this?

* * * * *

Chapter Sixteen

The Omni Racing Complex
Limerick, Prestone

Behind custom-made sunglasses, Jyrall took in the scene and tried to remain in character. Keaton led Larth, dressed in a garish purple and gold ensemble, toward the VIP area and Hatfield's private viewing box. He knew the seating capacity of the complex was completely sold out, and it appeared just as many patrons had opted for the viewing areas in the infield and along the curves as paid for seats. There were easily a hundred thousand in the complex, and, from a security perspective, it was a total nightmare. There were way too many variables if something actually went wrong. Jyrall kept observing as they moved through the crowd until they paused. An Oogar security officer dressed in mostly symbolic body armor stopped them.

"Name of your party?" the Oogar asked.

Keaton stepped forward. "Ah, yes, Mister Brusk. Pleasure to meet you. This is Garnovel Weezik. He has an invitation from Mister Hatfield."

Brusk nodded. "Of course, we're expecting Mister Weezik, but I'm afraid the seating area cannot hold the rest of your party."

"I'm afraid that's unacceptable," Keaton replied. "Mister Weezik doesn't travel without security, and we refuse to leave his side. Certainly, an accommodation can and will be made."

Brusk shook his head and locked eyes with Jyrall as if finally registering just how large the Besquith was. "You can rest assured Mister Weezik's security is of paramount concern to my team. I will ensure he is—"

Keaton whirled and bent over to whisper in Larth's ear. Jyrall read his lips. Standard English was such an amusing language.

"This motherfucker won't let us in the box with you," Keaton said.

Larth nodded, and while Jyrall couldn't see his lips, he could imagine what his friend was saying all too well.

Keaton turned back to the Oogar. "My apologies, but Mister Weezik would like to speak with Mister Hatfield."

"He's in a conversation with another guest and is not to be disturbed."

Larth stepped forward, and the Oogar stared down at him with contempt. "Where's Hatfield? Tell him I want to speak with him. Find out why I can't bring my team, you know?"

"I do not take orders from customers," Brusk said menacingly.

Larth raised a finger. "Then you're going to reall—"

"Mister Weezik, what seems to be the trouble?" Hatfield appeared from behind the Oogar.

"Your overgrown rug of a security officer has refused entry to my team," Larth replied. "I never travel without them."

"Sure enough." Hatfield clapped the Oogar on the shoulder. "There's room along the main aisle. They'll have to stand, though. Ain't an empty seat in this whole damned place."

"And their weapons?" Brusk asked. While everything they carried was well concealed, the Oogar at least recognized the type of team he faced. One willing to do anything to protect their charge. "They should surrender them."

"It's fine for this race." Hatfield smiled at Larth. "I have your word no weapons from this point forward, Mister Weezik?"

"Agreed. My boys can handle anything without them anyway." Larth turned to Keaton. "Lothar? No weapons from now on—even inside the casino. Mister Hatfield has extended us trust, and we should do the same."

"Yes, sir," Keaton said and nodded respectfully at Brusk. "Your professionalism is most appreciated."

Brusk nodded but said nothing. He waved them into the box and glared at Jyrall as he passed.

Jyrall bared his teeth and growled slightly.

Fucker.

Jyrall used his height to his advantage and moved to the back corner of Hatfield's box. He enjoyed a good look at Hatfield's private display and could easily hear their conversation as Larth took his seat and reached for the betting slate.

"Millions of credits, huh?" Hatfield teased.

"Two," Larth replied, studying the betting board. "Depending on the walkout, I might throw down a little more."

Hatfield leaned back, smiling broadly, and fished a cigar from his jacket pocket. He puffed the vile-smelling tobacco to life and appeared to peer over Larth's shoulder.

"One piece of advice?"

"Sure," Larth replied.

"They won't all finish the race." Hatfield grinned and set his slate down on the table between them. Its screen remained lit. "Once these Agamydi see their target, they'll kill each other to get it."

Jyrall clenched his jaw to keep his mouth from dropping open. *Gods, what's going on here?*

"Oh, yeah? Ferocious, are they?" Larth grinned. Jyrall had to admit, his friend was convincing. Given the situation, and his urge to rip off Hatfield's face, he doubted he could have been.

"Just watch."

Larth cackled. "Two million in bets placed, Mister Hatfield. I look forward to depleting your coffers."

The racing trumpet call sounded, and the crowd roared. Jyrall kept watching the crowd, wondering how a hundred thousand beings of all species could be so excited for another species to kill themselves over a race.

* * *

Stables

Arun Marwok fumed. "Where in the four forests is Lenny? And Jimmy? Neither of them are here?"

The two Goka shivered. "We don't know."

"I need drivers for the cleanup truck." Arun shook his head. He looked into the converted office at Cara Long, typing away on the tardy daily reports from his scrawled handwriting. "Cara Long? Can you drive—what's it called?"

The Goka jumped.

"A standard transmission," one of them said.

"Lenny called it a stick," the other added.

Cora smiled. "Sure. First type of vehicle I learned to drive."

"Then you're my driver." Arun pointed at the Goka. "Figgle, you're with her in the truck. Squarlik, help me with these body bags."

Body bags?

Cora stood up. "I'm done for now. I can help. Why are we getting body bags?"

"The Agamydi," Arun replied. "When they race, they die."

Cora shook her head. "What are you talking about? They barely move when we clean their cages. Right?"

She directed the question to Figgle, knowing he'd play along. Squarlik seemed scared, if anything.

"That is correct," Figgle replied stiffly.

"They're scared of everything," Squarlik piped up, "but when they see their target, they… change."

Cora wanted to ask more, but Arun turned to her. "Help me. We only need six of them. Get them loaded in the rear of the truck. Squarlik? Get the other stable hands ready to clear the track of the remains. Mister Hatfield wants them removed quickly."

"Yes, sir," Squarlik replied. Arun walked away on his cane, and Cora followed.

"They kill each other for sport?" she asked.

"They kill each other for *our* sport, Cara Long. Over a little gold statue." Arun sighed. "Whatever pays the bills."

Cora was silent as they opened a box and removed six black canvas bags. She folded them under one arm and made her way to the truck. When she climbed up into the cab, Figgle sat on the passenger seat and brought a control panel to life.

"Any survivors won't be able to stop. They'll enter the truck, and the doors will fire closed," Figgle said. "I expect this to be brutal, Miss."

Cora nodded, thankful her first sergeant hadn't said "ma'am." Listening devices could be anywhere. She didn't respond. When the time came, she pulled the truck up to its entrance and put the transmission in neutral. Trumpets sounded, and the crowd roared.

She looked at Figgle for a long moment, and then brought up her wrist slate and typed a message, but didn't send it. She showed it to Figgle, who merely nodded.

"We have to end this."

* * *

VIP Area

Pete Brentale followed Smith to the VIP seating area. The Oogar guard waved them both in without a second glance. As they turned a corner and climbed the few stairs to the box, Pete swallowed. Jyrall, Larth, and the McCoy twins were in the box. It was the first time he'd seen them completely in character and costume, and while they looked different, they were still his friends.

Pull it together. Just breathe and do what you do. They'll ignore you unless something goes down.

As if on cue, Pete locked eyes for a moment with Ricky McCoy—or Trang, as he was known now. The Pushtal twitched his nose to the right and looked away.

All is well.

Okay, you can do this.

"Over here, Pete," Smith said. He gestured toward two seats. A Veetch server appeared with a fizzy water for Smith and turned to him.

"What would you like to drink, sir?"

"Budweiser."

The Veetch flitted out of the way, and he sat down. Smith passed him a slate.

"You betting today?"

"Why not?" Pete asked. "I have 5,000 hotel chips."

Smith's eyes brightened. "You're gonna go big, aren't you?"

"I don't know," Pete replied. He didn't know. As a supposedly broke and down on his luck mercenary, he shouldn't be placing any bets at all. But he also needed to show his risky side to further ingratiate himself to Smith. "What about you?"

"I have a spread. Going to try and break even before I leave tonight," Smith replied. "Recalled to a place called Krifay by Crusader Prime."

Pete nodded and pretended to study his bet sheet. He caught a glance of Smith's slate and saw a connection dialog box open, and then a torrent of scrolling data. As fast as it appeared, the window closed, and Smith sighed deeply and reached for his glass.

Pete tapped on the slate, not really paying much attention until the confirmation window opened. He'd bet the balance of his hotel chip account on Racer #5 to be the sole Agamydi to cross the line at 250 to 1 odds.

Well, that's pretty damned stupid.

"One minute to the bell," the public address announcer called.

"Here we go!" Smith slapped him on the back, and they stood. Hatfield turned around, and Smith introduced them.

"Pete Connors, this is Mister Hatfield, the Omni's owner."

"Pleasure, Pete," Hatfield said. "Colonel Smith, Mister Conners, allow me to present Garnovel Weezik, my distinguished guest."

Smith stuck out a hand, and Larth, in disguise, demurred.

"Colonel. Mister Conners." The Zuparti turned his attention to the track.

Pete saw Hatfield glance at Smith and shrug. "Y'all place your bets?"

"Good ones," Smith said. "Right, Pete?"

"There's always hope," Pete said, deadpan.

The men laughed, and the bell rang. The crowd roared, and all hell broke loose. Pete drew a breath and held it.

By the time the Agamydi reached the first turn, one male was down. The other five roared and chased what appeared to be a gold statue of some kind down the main straightaway. By the end, two more Agamydi were down from the other racers' ambitions and effort to get the effigy.

Gods, they're killing *themselves for that thing. That's why they're racing, sure, but how did Hatfield get it? And why is he doing this?*

Pete tried to follow the action on the track, but he caught sight of a container truck pulling onto the track to recover the Agamydi at the end. A familiar Goka sat in the front seat.

Pete turned back to the race to see one Agamydi round the final turn, sprint down the straightaway, and cross the finish line before slamming into the open rear doors of the truck. Explosive bolts fired the doors closed, and the truck rocked on its chassis for a moment. The crowd roared its approval. Hatfield and the rest of the box applauded heartily. Pete felt sick to his stomach. He reached for his beer, took a long pull, and shook his head as a Jeha approached.

"Mister Connors?"

"That's me."

"My congratulations," the Jeha said. "May I see your UACC for your winnings."

Pete fumbled for his card. "I won?"

"Yes. Your bet was the largest, based on the odds. A formidable win."

"How formidable?" he asked.

"Five thousand credits at 250 to 1 odds pays 12.5 million Omni credits. At the current exchange rate, that's one million standard credits," the Jeha said.

Pete felt a hard slap on his shoulder. "You bet 5,000 credits at 250 to 1 odds and *won*?" Smith cackled. "You really are a lucky man, Pete Connors."

Pete grinned, dumbstruck. "Under normal circumstances, I'd say that's good enough, but I believe your offer is still on the table?"

Smith nodded. "After winning that much money? You're in?"

"My gambling days are over." Pete clinked his beer against Smith's seltzer. "Gonna see to my debts, take care of some other business, and sock the rest away. Only sure things from here on out. If that makes me a Crusader and not a mercenary anymore, then I'm in. When do we start?"

"Day after tomorrow. That's when the real credits rain, Pete Connors." Smith laughed. "I almost hate that I'll miss it, but you and Russo won't fail to deliver. Luck favors the bold, and you, my friend, qualify on both counts."

Pete nodded. "Drinks on me in the bar."

Smith looked at his seltzer. "I think my duty day has ended. I fly in three hours, so yeah, drinks are on you, after I meet Major Sciortino and make arrangements."

Smith slapped him on the shoulder and left the box. Pete caught Jyrall looking at him before Larth slammed the betting slate down on the table and stormed out of the box. Jyrall and the boys scrambled to follow him.

Hatfield looked at him. "Not everyone got lucky today, Mister Connors. You're staying in the Omni, yes?"

"I have a nice room overlooking the pool in the Silver Tower."

"Not anymore, my friend." Hatfield waved to Brusk. "Make sure Mister Connors' belongings are moved to the Washington Suite, please? With my compliments."

Pete shook his head. "I don't know what to say."

"It's not every day a man gets lucky. You might as well enjoy the rest of your stay."

Pete smiled and nodded. "I'll be sure to."

Particularly when we wipe that smile off your face, asshole.

* * *

Lieutenant Colonel Smith met Major Sciortino at a table in the country bar. The waiter had just dropped off a plate of fried mushrooms. At least that was what the menu said it was. Smith shrugged and dug in with his subordinate. If they were something else, they were a close facsimile, but it didn't matter. The Omni wouldn't risk serving food to a Human if it wasn't something edible.

"Not bad," Smith said. "Catch the waiter's attention and see if we can get some kind of dipping sauce. Ranch if they have it."

"Yes, sir." Sciortino raised a hand. In an establishment like this, even if the waiter didn't see him, the cameras would pick up the motion and alert the staff.

"I'm glad you ordered these. I don't have time to order a meal. After I give you some marching orders, I need to meet Pete over at the bar for a round or two."

"Sir?"

"Prime has ordered me away from here. I'm leaving you in charge with a contingent to continue. I want you to supplement your troops with Pete Conners and what's left of his unit, the Island Storm."

The waiter approached, and Sciortino requested the sauce.

After the waiter walked away, Sciortino said, "Yes, sir. Can we trust him? I mean, *really* trust him?"

"Yeah. The question is, can he trust us?"

"I don't follow, sir."

"I want you to be prepared to throw all the blame on him if what I have planned doesn't go right."

"Ah, I got it." Sciortino leaned forward. "I take it there's a change to the actual plan to gather more racers?"

"Absolutely." Smith put his slate on the table and entered a code. After it accepted him, he forwarded a message to his XO. He put it face down before the approaching waiter could see it.

After the waiter dropped off two small bowls, he turned back to his subordinate. "When you go out, I want you to fabricate an issue. Whatever it needs to be for your ship to fall back and get left behind by Hatfield's team. Take a look at what I forwarded. I was able to get those coordinates from Hatfield's slate, along with some other information. Go to those locations and search the area. I'm betting they're caches."

"You want us to load up what we find?"

"Yes. Bring it to the airfield and secure it in the ship I'll leave behind for you. Don't enter it into the Crusader files. Not until I tell you to. We have to get our cut."

"Roger that, sir." Sciortino grinned. He knew he'd get a decent share. Senior command didn't need to know about everything.

The major typed in his code to his own slate. He held it close so any cameras couldn't see what he saw. He scrolled through the information. He paused and scrolled back.

"Who's the girl with Kr'et'Socae?" Sciortino asked. He looked around again to ensure no one was listening.

"I have no idea. I know Prime wants to find the Equiri bastard. Whoever she is, it's obvious she's with him. When I get to Krifay, I'll ask around. This may lead us to him. Might be a hefty bonus in it, so keep that information between you and me."

"Yes, sir. Back to Pete. If we find anything good, and it looks like we may get caught, you want me to pin it on the Island Storm, right?"

"Exactly." Smith popped the last mushroom in his mouth. He wiped his mouth and stood. "Only if you have to. I may have use for him later, so use your better judgment."

"You can count on me. I can always say he pulled rank on me."

"Good idea."

* * *

Pete took a sip of his beer. He spotted Smith approaching.

"Spending some of your luck, I see," Smith teased.

"Hey. I didn't see you. Is that Sciortino? Does he want to join us? I'm buying."

"I think he ordered a steak and wants to read his messages from home. He's fine."

"Can't blame the guy. Name your poison," Pete said.

"Just a beer. It's after the workday, but I have to check out in a few hours and head toward the airfield. Duty calls, you know how it is."

"Back to Karma, huh?"

"Uh, yeah… Karma."

Pete noticed the hesitation. *I bet Keaton could figure out the real destination.*

"I guess it's a good thing I won some credits. There goes my opportunity to join you."

"Not at all," Smith reassured him. "Major Sciortino is a good officer. He'll handle things here, including squaring you and your company away."

"What's left of us," Pete reminded him. "I've got a few of them staying down the strip in a cheaper place. I may have run into some credits, but I'm not springing for them to stay here. Left a specialist in charge of my command ship."

"A specialist? In charge of your frigate? You really *are* in bad shape."

"Haney is a good troop. He can fly one, too."

"Maybe you should promote him."

"Nah, that didn't work out in his old unit."

"Gotcha. Some people shouldn't be given the responsibility of leadership. This Haney sounds like one who doesn't need that kind of power."

"God, no." Pete visibly shuddered.

"Anyway—" Smith held up his beer "—here's to future work. We can use a good man like you."

"Sounds like a plan," Pete said and tapped his beer against Smith's.

They watched the game up on the big screen for a few minutes and chatted about old contracts and places each may have seen the other, had the timing been right. Pete made most of it up on the spot.

"Well, I need to get moving," Smith said.

He held out his hand. "Sciortino has a mission coming up. I want you to go with them and get a feel for what it is. We may need you and your crew to do it sometime. Just you on this first one. He'll let you know the specifics."

"I'll be ready."

"Is there going to be an issue, with him a major, and you technically a lieutenant colonel with your own merc company?"

"Hey, if the Crusaders hold my contract, I follow orders. Authority by position, not rank. If he's in charge, then he's in charge."

"Glad to hear it."

* * * * *

Chapter Seventeen

Earth

Serendipity struck, and Raley realized she needed to take it. They'd returned to Earth from Weqq, and she'd received a holomail from her graduate advisor at North Carolina State University. She needed to go early for her group presentation, thesis approval meeting, and exams. This wasn't an uncommon thing, especially because she'd worked so far ahead during the course of the school year. Still, she couldn't believe her luck. She'd have an opportunity to be away from the compound for a couple of weeks. Maybe she'd be able to explore what her father had left for her.

The key's etching had been simple. *Naduhli.* Raley hadn't wanted to do any type of searching for the meaning of the word for fear of Kr'et'Socae finding it. So she'd decided to wait. Now, with the fortunate opportunity at hand, she slipped the key into the front pocket of her jeans and carried the last of her bags out to her Jeep.

Kr'et'Socae was waiting. "When will you be back?"

Raley shrugged. "It'll take me a day to get there, and a couple of days to do the meetings and presentations. My thesis approval is Friday afternoon, then the weekend, and then exams. So probably by next weekend; say, two weeks. If I decide to walk at graduation, it'll be an extra day. I probably won't; it's only a bachelor's degree."

He nodded. "This is the last school requirement for this semester?"

She sighed and smiled. "Yeah, one more semester to go. Most of that will be thesis writing."

Kr'et'Socae nodded appreciatively, and she thought there was a hint of a smile on his long face. "You've done very well with this, Raley. I'm proud of you."

She flushed at his words. As much pride as she felt from him, she still recognized she couldn't trust him. But for the last two years, he'd been more of a father to her than her own father had been when he'd been alive.

"Thanks," she said. "I'll let you know when I get there. I thought about stopping to see my friend Abby in Asheville for a little bit. I might spend the night if we get to talking."

Kr'et'Socae picked up her bag and loaded it into the back of the Jeep. "You said the drive's five hours?"

"Give or take. I did tell Abby I was stopping by."

"You know, you could take the other car," he said. Hover cars were inherently faster, but she didn't necessarily want the speed. Taking her Jeep with its conventional gas power gave her the opportunity to explore the old interstates, and maybe leave the beaten path if her search turned up something.

She laughed. "I'm good with my Jeep. You know that."

He nodded. "I do. Be safe, and let me know when you get to Abby's. I know you'll end up staying there. You always do."

Rae climbed into the Jeep, started it, and left the compound without looking back. She connected across the country roads to the interstate and drove south toward Knoxville before meeting up at the junction of old Interstate 40 to head toward Asheville, North Carolina.

The drive through the mountains never ceased to amaze her. While not at the peak of fall and its array of beautiful colors, the deep greens and the lush shadows spoke to her and said more about her home state than anything she'd ever seen. She loved the mountains, and there was nothing quite like them, despite all the different places she'd managed to go.

The drive passed quickly, and, as she pulled into the outskirts of Asheville, Raley found one of her favorite places to get away. In this case, a gas station across the street from a library. She parked the Jeep at the gas station in case Kr'et'Socae was watching where it might be parked. She wouldn't put it past him.

Raley walked across to the library. Inside, she found a public AetherNet terminal and typed in the word "naduhli." The search function returned numerous hits to the southwest of her in North Georgia. There was a Nottely Lake and a Nottley Dam, among other things. Apparently, the names had been taken from the original spelling of the ancient indigenous tribe who'd lived in the area. She smiled at its translation of "daring horsemen." Her father had wanted, at one time, to be a member of one of the Four Horsemen. That was before he learned to make easier profits on the shadier side of contracts.

Her mind worked. From Asheville, it would take her a couple hours to get to Blairsville, Georgia. With the locations memorized, Raley walked back out of the library to her Jeep, and sat in it for a moment before deciding to go. If Kr'et'Socae was watching, he'd wonder what was up. She could tell him she'd wanted to visit someone, maybe a friend from college, and ride together. Or she could tell him nothing. He normally stayed out of her business. On the off chance he pried, she could come up with something; he'd know where to find her if things went awry.

Before leaving the gas station, Raley went inside, bought a prepaid slate, and typed in her destination. She would use it to navigate. She turned to the southwest with the wind in her hair. Raley couldn't help feeling a little rebellious. For the first time in two years, she felt free.

Kr'et'Socae, despite his reputation, wasn't the type of alien to restrict her privacy, or make her feel like she was being held hostage, but he clearly wanted something from her. Now, for the first time in more than a year, she had an opportunity to get away by herself for a few days. If she didn't return, there was no doubt he'd come find her. Or worse, he'd take everything and leave her with nothing. She knew she needed to play the game. She knew she needed to be aware of his wants and wishes. She knew she needed to hold on to what she had. There was nothing else for her.

The sun was high in the sky by the time she reached the outskirts of Blairsville. Following the directions, she turned onto a road outside of town toward Nottely Lake. Once she got there, she found Nottely Dam Road, turned, and dropped into the woods. Old fields sat fallow between the breaks and the trees. She drove toward the dam, which her slate told her had been closed for more than sixty years, until she reached a fence strung with a sign that read, "Private Property, Do Not Enter." It didn't look like anyone had entered for quite some time. The gate was overgrown, and the gravel path had clearly seen better days. Stringing the two pieces of the tall gate together was an old, rusted chain with a large lock. A lock that looked like it might require the key in her pocket.

It can't be that easy.

Rae stepped out of the Jeep and walked up to the gate. Around her, the forest was alive with cicadas and the call of birds. There was a hint of breeze rustling the tops of the trees, and it was getting warm now. Raley thought about taking off her jeans and putting on shorts, but decided against it, especially given the number of weeds between the fence and whatever lay on the other side. She pulled the key out of her pocket, stepped up to the lock, and slipped it inside. She turned the key, and the lock opened.

"I'll be damned."

She pushed the gates open wide enough to drive the Jeep through. She paused and thought about locking them behind her but decided not to. She drove roughly a half mile until she came to the old dam.

Another lock secured a door that led into the embankment.

"In for a penny, in for a pound." She laughed as she walked through the weeds to the door and worked the key into the lock. It sprang open, and she pushed the door ajar. Beyond, she could barely see more than a few meters. She grabbed a flashlight from her Jeep and peered inside. On the closest wall were the maintenance racks for a dozen Mk 7 CASPers. The damned things appeared brand new. Opposite them hung a wall full of weaponry, including magnetic accelerator cannons, hand cannons, and a variety of hand-to-hand implements built for the powered armor.

Raley grinned and walked deeper inside. "I got your present, Daddy. Let's see just how much there is here."

* * *

Cirque D'Or

Limerick, Prestone

No one spoke. They'd watched the entire race in silence. As the Agamydi fell and the gaming network commentators whooped and hyped, someone had shut off the sound. Tara wasn't sure who it was, but she was thankful for it. She glanced around the room. Araceli sat with her legs crossed under herself, a pillow pressed to her chest, and tears welling in her eyes. Quin'taa was silent. Homer rubbed the fur on the back of his head and shook it from side to side. Maarg appeared to have been holding her breath for the last several minutes, and she made no attempt to exhale what she was holding in her lungs. Gnrra, their newest, sat forward, leaning on the floor in front of the Tri-V console. Tara turned to Whirr and saw the big MinSha warrior had dug her claws into the leather sofa where Araceli was sitting. She'd ripped apart several of the cushions just by gripping them. By the agitated vibration of her antennae, it was clear Whirr's rage was close to eruption.

"Gods," Gnrra said. "I've never seen anything like it."

"They're fast creatures," Quin'taa said, "but something's not right. What were they chasing?"

"Not just chasing, man," Homer replied, pointing at the screen showing a replay of one Agamydi taking down another. "They're *killing* each other for it. How fucked up is that?"

No one replied. Tara tried to contain her shock and revulsion by turning her mind to what she'd seen. Cameras followed the truck and the recovery crew. Several stable hands in uniforms worked to collect the bodies of the racers and put them into bags. There were many Humans, but one redheaded female caught her eyes. "There's Cora."

"Are you sure?" Maarg asked.

"That's her," Araceli said. "Lisalle and Nileah said she'd found work in the stables. We've got at least one person on the inside."

"More than that." Quin'taa sat forward. "Those Goka? I'm willing to bet two of them are Squarlik and Figgle, just by the way they move."

"No bet," Whirr replied and released the cushions under her foreclaws. She glanced down at the ruined couch and back up at the screen. "The one on the right is Squarlik."

"You're right." Quin'taa turned to Tara. "You said Cora's plan was to bring down the race while the others crashed the casino."

"More or less," Tara said. "It's a bit more complicated, but that's the general idea. What are you thinking?"

"They can't pull this off without our assistance," Quin'taa replied. "Not from a manpower or weaponry standpoint, but we do have something they don't. We have Nike and integrated surveillance. If we can get cameras in them, or have Cora and the others plant them, we can study what's happening and coordinate the plan in real time."

Homer stood up suddenly. "The first target would be the closed-circuit security cameras. I'm sure they're watching them and will cut them the minute they initiate whatever they're planning. But that's going to leave them blind."

"In a stadium filled with a hundred thousand assholes." Araceli shrugged. "Sorry. I can't stomach what we just saw without calling everyone who enjoyed it that. If the boys hit the race, especially in the middle of one of those events?"

"Panic. Riots. Destruction," Gnrra said. "Homer's right. They'll take down what systems they can and leave themselves blind. We need them to wait and let us get connections to Nike in there somehow."

Tara nodded and turned to Maarg. The TriRusk sat tapping furiously on her slate.

"They're right about the systems," she said, looking at Tara. "The big question is, what's their endgame?"

Tara looked at Whirr. "Okay, Whirr. Your strategic objective here would be?"

"Taking down Hatfield during a profitable race while also taking down the casino with a coordinated network attack in the gaming areas," the MinSha replied. "The boys certainly have the capability for the latter. Cora and the others are laying the groundwork for the former, but without coordination, surveillance, and better intelligence, they can't hit the target yet."

"Why?"

"There are two things missing." Whirr raised a foreclaw and extended one digit. "First, why the Agamydi behave like they do underscores a much larger problem no one has addressed yet. I would imagine, given what we saw and her proximity to it, Cora McCoy will call off whatever their initial plan is, and we can augment as Quin'taa suggests."

"What's the second thing?" Homer asked.

"Where's all this money going?" Whirr replied. "Our review of documents reveal many inconsistencies. There are tens of millions of Galactic Union credits passing through this facility, and they exchange them for their own credits? They're laundering credits. Where's the money going?"

"Follow the money," Tara said softly. She noticed everyone's eyes were on her. "Graduate school, two years ago. My last semester, I had to take an elective in contracts, so I took one titled Introduction to Forensic Accounting. Basically, how you use auditing, accounting, and investigative skills to determine what's really going on with someone's money. You follow the money."

"That's what we need to do," Whirr agreed. "I'm happy to assist Maarg with the data collection here. I'd recommend we go ahead and augment Larth's security with a third Pushtal as planned."

Tara turned to Homer. "How fast can you be ready?"

"An hour, tops," Homer replied. "Let me get a shower and unpack my disguise. We'll need to get word to them."

"Leave that to me," Gnrra said. "The stable hands hang out at a bar down the way, called the Fuel Bar. I hear they've got good drink specials. I'll pop in and buy a round or two."

Tara nodded. "Let's do that instead. Augmenting Larth's security right now might tip off Hatfield's people, and there are easier ways to do this. I'm sure the pool will be bustling. I'd imagine Lisalle and Nileah will be there. Get your stuff, Araceli. We're going over."

"You think it's time we talk to Cora directly?" Araceli asked.

Impressed, Tara nodded. "I do, Little Sister. If I know her—and I like to think I do—she's going to want to take them down. We're going to help. The first step is investigation."

"Name it, boss," Maarg replied.

"Find a way to hack the track controls. Find a way for us to get the Agamydi out of the starting boxes without them seeing that damned statue. If they don't understand what we're trying to do, they'll be too busy killing each other over it for us to get them out of there," Tara said.

Quin'taa shook his head. "That's not enough. We need to prove fraud and malicious intent, that he intended to defraud the customers somehow."

Whirr spoke slowly. "If we can get them out of there after they were loaded, the buzzer would sound, and the race would officially start. By gaming regulations, at that point, the race is valid. When the Agamydi are gone and nothing leaves the starting gate, the race would default. All bets would be canceled. Hatfield would lose millions. If we find a way to lock down the betting, meaning no refunds, we could cause a riot."

"Which gets our players off the field," Gnrra agreed.

"And the Agamydi out of harm's way. We have to know more about them, Gnrra. Get whatever you can from Figgle and Squarlik," Araceli said. "Sorry, Boss. Thinking ahead."

"It's okay, Araceli. We've got a lot of work to do in a very short time. They're going after more Agamydi in a day or two at most. We need to be prepared to make the next scheduled race Hatfield's last."

Eponil appeared in front of Tara. The look on his feline features bothered her. "What's wrong, Eponil?"

"I have news, but it's incomplete. Jessica's left Khatash. Destination unknown."

*****

Chapter Eighteen

The Omni

Limerick, Prestone

At three in the morning local time, after playing his role of security for Larth in the high rollers room, two nightclubs, and a late-night snack, Jyrall made his way down the private elevator to the main floor of the casino. He hadn't removed his custom-tailored suit, only the tie, shoulder holsters, and radio equipment. He'd find a quiet bar, watch sports with a drink, and just relax. What any normal employee might do after a long shift.

The bars at the Omni operated at all hours, and the casino remained busy. He'd identified a sports bar with booths and tables built for multiple species at the far end of the table games area and made his way there. Sure enough, though the tables and booths were packed, there were seats at the bar.

He grabbed a seat. Of the dozen places, only two were occupied by a pair of Veetch cuddled close together at one end. He sat down, and the embedded Tri-V came to life.

Sitting at the bar requires you play this console. Insert chips or a UACC to play.

Jyrall took one of Larth's 10,000 credit hotel tokens and inserted it into the machine in the hopes the amount would turn off the notifications and requirements and just let him sit in peace. No such luck.

A Jivool bartender approached. His name tag read "Vlad." He tossed a towel over his shoulder and placed a coaster in front of Jyrall. "What can I get you?"

"Bourbon. Water back."

The Jivool nodded. "Long day, or just getting started?"

"A bit of both." Jyrall laughed. He pointed up to the screen. "No offense, but can we watch something else?"

Vlad turned and laughed. "Yeah, I'm with you. What's that even called?"

Jyrall knew it was something that translated as skitter ball, a Jeha favorite, and it looked like a whole bunch of thrashing, twisting, and flicking Jeha in a bowl. "No idea."

The Jivool touched the screen. Human football appeared. Not the soccer type, either, which made Jyrall happy. "This okay? Not much on this time of morning."

"That's fine," Jyrall grunted, sounding disappointed. In truth, he was interested in the game. It was recorded, but it was the Atlanta Falcons playing the New Orleans Saints. Ricky and Keaton would hate that they'd missed it.

Vlad brought his bourbon and a tall glass of water and left him alone. The console buzzed, and Jyrall resignedly tapped the screen, selected a five card draw game, and decided to play as slow as he possibly could. He won two credits with the first hand—a pair of kings—before losing the next several.

He looked up from the console and saw the Falcons kick the ball to the Saints to start the second half. Jyrall lounged in the chair and reached a long arm over the adjacent one just as he caught sight of a

Human female with blonde hair swept up on top of her head walking into the bar. She wore a tight blue dress and a simple, yet stunning necklace that matched the earrings dangling from her ears. Every move was so fluid and graceful that he barely noticed she carried a small clutch purse until she was ten steps inside the bar. Jyrall swallowed as he recognized her through the disguise and his heart skipped a beat.

Cora really is stunning for a Human. Just how many disguises does she have? Red hair? Blonde hair? What's next?

He forced a yawn, tapped the screen, and activated his wrist slate. Cora took a seat two away from Jyrall and tapped the screen in front of her. He caught a whiff of perfume, something Cora never wore, and breathed it in. For a disguise, she'd knocked it out of the park—so to speak.

Vlad approached her. "What can I get you, Miss?"

"White wine. Chablis if you have it."

"Right away." Vlad returned with her drink far faster than he had Jyrall's. "Anything else I can get you?"

"No, thank you," Cora said. She tapped the screen for a moment, sighed, then leaned against the bar and stared at the door as if waiting for someone. Jyrall kept his attention on the screen until he saw Cora pull a mini slate from her clutch purse and tap.

Jyrall felt a buzz on his wrist as his slate connected directly to Cora's via extreme shortwave radio frequency connection. From here, they'd have to be extremely careful.

On the screen, one of the Falcons' linebackers sacked the Saints' quarterback for a significant loss. Jyrall decided to play the really involved fan.

"That was a big hit right there, but not as big as the one a few plays ago."

His slate buzzed. *"The patrons might have loved it, but it was sickening. I know you want to make your move soon, but we have to get those poor things out of here."*

Jyrall studied the next play, a running play off the left tackle for no yardage, and shook his head. "Going to need more help on the line, Falcons."

"We've made contact, and we're working the problem. We need a little more time, but I think it's possible to get both targets at once. I'm sending you a data packet for the boys' special talents."

Ricky Shit. Here we go again.

They sat for a few moments as the game went to commercial. Jyrall sipped his bourbon and considered Cora's words. The Misfits were on the ground and working the problem to get the Agamydi out and find a way to take down Hatfield at the same time. Jyrall wiped his chin and fought the urge to nod. He didn't know the specifics, but he trusted Cora implicitly. If she said they had a plan, it was a solid one.

"Get you another?" Vlad asked as he approached.

"Sure," Jyrall said. He nodded in Cora's direction. "One for the lady, if she'd like."

Cora looked surprised and shook her head. "Oh, no thank you. I'm just waiting for a friend, and I'll be going."

"No harm in asking," Jyrall said and looked genuinely disappointed for a moment before lounging back in his chair.

Another buzz. *"I miss you, too."*

He kept his eyes on the screen. "Come on, Falcons. We'll stop 'em here."

"Okay, we'll work the plan."

The commentators for the game started talking about one of the star athletes not planning to return to the team after contract negotiations failed. Jyrall shook his head. "Why do the stars always do that?"

Cora spoke again, but her voice was low, and no one else caught her words. "They follow the money."

Jyrall fought the urge to suck in a breath. *Of course!* They'd been so intent on taking down Hatfield, they'd forgotten the basic investigation. Hatfield was certainly laundering Kr'et'Socae's money, but there was far more to the situation. The Omni had to be raking in credits. Where was it going? Who else was involved?

The Falcons' quarterback threw a long pass and a Saints' defender intercepted it. Jyrall groaned. "Tried to do too much. Gotta get a defensive stop here."

Cora finished her wine and cashed out of the console. As she stood and collected her clutch, she said, "I hope your team's luck changes. Have a good evening."

"You, too, Miss." Jyrall picked up his fresh bourbon and took a long sip to avoid following her with his eyes. He set the glass down, and there was a final buzz from his slate.

"We're all in, and the lady has spoken."

Her words, both spoken and transmitted, confirmed several things. Pete had integrated with the Crusaders and would participate in their next Agamydi collection mission. She and the others were working the stables and working on a way to financially destroy Hatfield through the racing operation. All he and the boys had to do was enact their plan to hit the casino. Part of that was a change in their fortunes.

Jyrall grinned at the screen. *One thing is certain, Larth is going to be very happy.*

Time we start winning.

* * *

Omni Main Casino

Pete walked slowly through the hall. He was in no hurry. He'd slept in and was looking for a spot to grab an early lunch or late breakfast. Either one would work. He stopped to watch a woman play two slot machines at once. He glanced toward the nearest exposed camera.

They were everywhere, out in the open to remind the guests not to try any shenanigans. Rocking machines or bumping them deliberately would bring security in a hurry. He also knew there were more cameras hidden from casual observation.

"Any luck?" Pete asked casually.

She glanced back quickly and went back to pushing the buttons on each machine, one after the other.

"Yeah," Sergeant First Class Wilson said. "I got a lot going on here. Looks like they're going to hit anytime."

Pete pursed his lips. He knew there'd been activity at the airfield last night with the Crusaders leaving, but she'd used the word "they," meaning more than one force. He waited to hear more.

"One of these was really paying off," she continued, "but it slowed down. I dumped credits into it twice to get it where it needs to be. When it hits, alarms are going off, I just know it."

"Nice," Pete said. *Dumped twice… Dumped twice. What rhymes with dump? Jump! Two Jumps! Does she mean?*

"When it does, I'm taking the credits and getting out of here. Maybe go to some island paradise, you know?"

Shit.

"Can't say I blame you," Pete said. "Sand between your toes, breeze in your hair, the sound of the ocean rolling in."

"Yeah." She smiled at him over her shoulder. "I'm going there no matter what it costs me."

"Fight for your dreams, I say," Pete agreed.

He nodded at a security guard as he walked by. The man wasn't in uniform, but it was obvious what he was. The guard paid them no mind. These types of conversations occurred all over the main floor, strangers who found themselves with a kindred spirit, joined in their desire to finally hit the jackpot.

"To the death," she assured him.

After a moment she said, "Now this other one is going to kick off anytime. It's not going to be as much, but it'll happen sooner. I can feel it."

Pete nodded. "Well, I hope it does. You deserve your island paradise. Good luck."

"Thanks. You, too."

Pete turned and continued toward the smells coming from the bar and grill on the other side of the hall. He didn't look back and didn't glance at the cameras.

* * *

Pete finished the last bite of his omelet. It had been cooked to perfection, loaded with everything but peppers. He didn't like them inside. He did cover it with salsa before eating it, so he did get peppers with it… in a way.

He leaned back and thought about the message she'd relayed to him. Keaton had been able to determine the destination of the Crusaders who were leaving and had sent the message to Pete's ship and his troops.

It was too risky for any of the Peacemakers' crew to break from their roles and speak to him. It was important to let him know, so SFC Wilson had actually left the ship under Specialist Haney's control to deliver the message. The rest of his troops were awaiting his summons at another hotel down the strip. He hoped he wouldn't have to call on them, but Jyrall had felt having a reaction force available was important. The Kin were waiting on their ship at the airfield. He knew they'd been informed as well.

Damn. Smith and his fleet of Crusader ships are heading to Krifay. That's not good. The numbers of Crusaders on the planet will double, plus the ships in Smith's command far outclass the older insertion frigates of the Barnstormers and the Blue Ridge Kin.

His thoughts were interrupted when he heard Sciortino call his name. Pete waved to him. Sciortino took a seat in the booth on the other side of the table.

"Mornin'," Pete said. He waved a hand over his empty plate. "If I'd known you were going to be down here, I would have waited for you."

"I'm good," Sciortino assured him, holding up his mug. "I'm just a coffee guy in the morning. I wait until lunch proper before I eat anything. I don't care for eggs. Always been that way."

"I hear ya."

"Listen," Sciortino said. "We've got a little mission tomorrow, and I'd like you to come along. You can help me coordinate things with Hatfield's security forces."

"Hatfield's?"

"Yeah. We're going to help them hit a target and gather more of those racers. They go through them pretty quick on the track."

"I saw," Pete said. He shook his head. "Never seen anything like it."

"Made you a fortune, I heard."

"Yeah, I did all right for my first time," Pete agreed. "Say, why are we coordinating with them? Hatfield's people? They're not professional soldiers. Seems like it would be easier for us to do it ourselves. Us meaning your Crusaders and some of my company."

"I agree. But it'll just be you with us on this one. We'll bring in your troops on later missions if this goes like I plan."

"Yeah?"

Sciortino pulled out his slate. "That's why you're going to help locate another target to hit after we hit theirs. If we get some racers of our own we can sell to Hatfield, we'll make a nice little profit. Side work, you understand."

"I do." Pete grinned. "Show me what you've got, and we'll figure out a spot. Mind if I load the coordinates in my slate? I don't want to be responsible for looking at a Crusader's slate. There's bound to be stuff in there I'm not authorized to see."

Sciortino nodded thoughtfully. "You're right, there is. I like the way you think. I'll forward them to you, along with the planet overlay map."

* * * * *

Chapter Nineteen

Top Floor

Embassy Tower

Larth threw his boot across the room, where it hit the desk and knocked a bucket of ice onto the floor. One of the Lumar moved to clean it up. He sighed loudly.

"This sucks!" he shouted. "I want to win!"

"Are you sure you aren't enjoying the fall?" Jyrall asked. He leaned against the wall with his arms folded. "Because you're acting exactly like Weezik would."

Larth looked to the desk. He got up to help clean up his mess. "Sorry, Private Tivlang. Let me help."

"Yes, sir," Tivlang said with a confused look on his face. "I understand get mad. I do sometimes. This sitting around is boring. Nice rooms. Lot to watch on GalNet, but get old."

"We won't be here much longer," Jyrall said. "Now that we know the Crusaders are headed to Krifay, Colonel Brentale will try to learn more from the mission he should be going on soon. You just be ready in case the security guards try to come onto this floor."

"They're going to try," Keaton said. "It's high on the list when they want to shake up anyone on a winning streak. They toss the room and blame it on attempted robbery, and then they send the same goons back to investigate, giving them a second look around. They dump luggage and everything."

Ricky looked up from the lighted magnifying glass he was working under. "Those sumbitches dump my tools, and I'm whuppin' ass, you hear me?"

"I hear you," Keaton agreed. "My computer gets cracked, I'll beat you to them."

"I'm more worried about the weapons and body armor," Nails said.

"Me, too," Jyrall agreed.

"Yeah, well, we don't have to worry about that," Larth complained. "I'm not allowed to be on a winning streak. It's bullshit!"

Jyrall grinned.

"Wait," Larth said. "You mean…? Yes!" He pumped his fist. "It's on now!"

He turned to the brothers. "Did you two figure it out?"

"We did," Keaton said. "Well, my greasy-fingered brother did. He was able to build a reader to show what's on the chip of an actual piece of hard credit. I just wrote the program to crack it."

"Whatever," Ricky said. "Without that program, we wouldn't be able to track the RF chip."

"My program would be useless without the reader you made," Keaton countered. "It let me experiment. We can now track the credits just like this casino can. That kind of information is priceless, and one of the closest guarded secrets in the galaxy among financial institutions. There are several guilds who would hire mercs and take us out if they knew that we know. I mean, that's how counterfeit credit gets made, and it would be near impossible to tell from the real thing."

"Did you forward the program?" Jyrall asked.

"Roger," Keaton said. "It's in the right hands now."

"Good."

Larth jumped up and looked for the wayward boot. "Time's wasting! It's time to win my credits back. Well, Weezik's credits. Whatever. You know what I mean."

"I'm going to enjoy watching you," Jyrall said.

"You boys get your gadgets together," Larth said, rubbing his paws together. "I'm about to rob these fuckers *blind.* Where's my ring? Grab a handful of those micro cameras. I'm going to need to see what the house sees. I just know they're going to send ringers to the tables. Hey! Where's my eyepatch?"

* * *

Two hours later, Larth was up big at the blackjack table. Jyrall watched and managed to keep a straight face. The pile of credits in front of his partner was impressive. He glanced at Keaton who, acting as Lothar, stood off to the side, keeping an eye on his employer, Ricky, and Jyrall, along with the roving security.

The pit boss walked back over and stood behind his dealer with folded arms. It was the second dealer since Larth sat down. The first had left when his shift supposedly ended. Jyrall found it amusing that no other dealer had the same timing for shift change in the hall. When the dealers changed, a new set of six decks were produced. That didn't slow Larth down. He was already a good player and able to count cards somewhat, so the data given to him in his eye lens took it to another level.

Jyrall almost lost his composure when Larth split on 10s. It was an unusual move, especially since the dealer was showing a king. In fact, it was foolish.

Larth was dealt an ace on one and a jack on the other. The dealer turned over a nine and had to stand at nineteen. Both bets were at the maximum of fifty thousand credits. Larth shouted and clapped his hands. He stepped back from the stool and danced a jig. He'd performed the dance several times so far.

"Winner! Winner!" Larth sang. "I'm cleaning the house out today!"

The pit boss spoke quietly into his cuff. His face was beet red. A few moments later, two security guards eased up behind Larth. They didn't touch him, but they let their presence be known as they crowded him.

Keaton snapped his fingers. Jyrall and Ricky forcefully stepped in front of both security guards and backed them away. They growled softly, daring the security personnel to make a move. They looked at the pit boss but didn't go for their weapons. The pit boss made another call.

Larth played for another hour, stacking up more credits. Mr. Randazzo appeared with four more security members. All had their jackets unbuttoned.

"Mr. Weezik," the security manager said. "I'm afraid I'm going to have to check your eyepatch. I'm afraid your luck is too good today."

"My what?" Larth exclaimed. "My eyepatch? Why?"

"Your eyepatch please?"

Jyrall watched Keaton for the signal. Keaton was talking quietly into his communication device. He glanced at Jyrall and Ricky, shook his head slightly, and held up a finger.

Larth saw it, sighed, and took his patch off. One of the guards ran a scanner over it. He did it again. It didn't alert.

Larth stood, blinking his bad eye. "Well? Are you satisfied?"

Randazzo looked at the Zuparti but wasn't quite able to hide his revulsion at the milky eye. "I am. I'm sorry for the inconvenience. I must be sure of these things. I'm also afraid this table is scheduled for a deep clean today. Players leaning on it, spilling drinks, general maintenance, and the like. You understand. Perhaps another game would be suitable to you. Poker, perhaps?"

Larth waved to Lissale and Nileah. They stood up from the plush couch nearby. "Come get my winnings. Put them in your bags. I'm going to go kick ass at a poker table." He rubbed his little paws together. "A 'No Limit' table."

The ladies sashayed over, shopping bags in both hands. They'd already spent some of the earlier winnings on items that weren't counterfeit like the actual credits were. That had likely added to Randazzo's anger, as he would have watched it all on the security feeds.

* * *

Larth and the ladies headed toward the poker tables, with Jyrall and Ricky escorting them. Keaton held back.

"Mr. Randazzo. A moment of your time, please."

Randazzo left his team waiting at the table. "Yes, Mr. Parthkit?"

Keaton played the part beautifully when he reached up with the tips of his claws and groomed the perfectly placed fur at the side of his face.

He straightened his expensive suit and said quietly, "Mr. Randazzo, as of right this very moment, five men are being held up on the top floor of the Embassy Tower."

Keaton stroked his chin. "When I say 'held up,' I mean precisely that. *Held up.* Their feet are dangling approximately a foot from the floor, as five very angry Lumar have them in their grasps. It would seem my instructions to this establishment have been ignored. Someone thought, because Mr. Weezik's entourage was downstairs, the rooms were unoccupied. Especially since all the cameras on the floor have been jammed by proprietary means."

Randazzo was silent.

Keaton continued without raising his voice. "Now, I'm not saying it was on your orders, but I will say that other establishments such as this one use the same type of tactics. You know what I'm referring to. Tossing the room, blaming it on an attempted burglary, and then 'investigating' the matter, all in an attempt to disrupt a player on a winning streak."

"I…"

"Say no more," Keaton said, interrupting him. "I'll order my team to escort the men to the elevator and send them down. I'll also ensure they don't kill this group—unlike the last. I cannot, however, be responsible for any bruises… or broken bones."

Keaton continued as Randazzo's eyes widened. "Let me say this: Should any more of these type of tactics continue, it will not bode well for you, personally. Your people are not to 'crowd' my employer. They are not to search him anymore. Your scanners already found nothing. Am I clear?"

"But… he could be counting cards," Randazzo protested. "I have a job to do. We can't have an advantage player here."

Keaton stared at Randazzo until the man looked away. "I can assure you, Mr. Weezik isn't smart enough to count six decks with a computer-like accuracy. He's merely lucky. It doesn't happen all the time. You've seen for yourself how much he's lost in his time here, not to mention his losses at the track."

"He's already won half back."

"Yes, he has," Keaton agreed, "and he may very well win the rest back, and more. If he does, he does. Neither you nor anyone else will interfere."

Keaton bared his teeth slightly. "I take my job *very seriously*. You've already embarrassed my employer by making him reveal his eye to the entire floor. In doing this, you've embarrassed me. I don't like it. Don't let it happen again. Oh, I'm quite sure you could call enough security forces from this establishment and the nearby casinos to eventually take me and my team, but it'll be at heavy losses."

Keaton narrowed his eyes. "It will *not*, however, stop members of my team from visiting the Hofstell Condominiums while it's happening. Do I make myself clear?"

Randazzo stood, shaking visibly. He lived in the Hofstell Condominiums with his wife and two children.

"And I wouldn't involve Mr. Hatfield in our little conversation. You should just let Mr. Weezik enjoy himself. Like those in Number 42 at Hofstell."

Keaton walked away from the ashen-faced security manager.

* * *

Cirque D'Or
Limerick, Prestone

When the connection window initialized, Maarg rubbed her big hands together. "Here we go. I've got video, and I'm connected to Ricky's slate. Lots of good data here."

Tara sat next to her at the console and watched as Larth and the boys moved from the elevator into the high rollers' area. There was no audio feed, but that didn't really matter. All they wanted to do was to watch and see how the casino handled their credits. Over the course of the next two hours, Maarg and Tara watched as Larth started to win. Tara couldn't help but smile.

"That's got to feel good," Maarg said as Larth took down a particularly large pot at a poker game.

"He's been losing for the last several days. I'm sure it's been driving him crazy," Tara replied.

"You mean more than he already is?" Maarg asked and they laughed. Though Larth might have actually been crazy, he and Jyrall were exceptional actors and operators.

"I do wish we could've heard what Keaton said to that creepy security manager, though." Tara chuckled. "Looked like the guy was about to piss himself."

"His goons are lucky the Lumar didn't rip their arms off and beat them down with them," Maarg replied. "Program is loaded. All we have to do now is wait."

Thirty minutes later, after Larth took down more than his fair share of hands, the Zuparti pushed back from the table.

"Okay, here we go," Tara said as Larth turned to Keaton, handed the Pushtal a tray of the hotel's chips, and pointed toward the cashier's window.

"What are you thinking?" Tara asked.

Maarg pointed to one of the Omni Hotel chips enclosed in a clear container sitting on the console in front of her. "These little guys are all radio markers. They have a little chip inside that the casino tracks so they know where they are at all times inside their property. The whole place is covered by these passive sensors. That's how they send ads to your slates, monitor in case of fire or emergency, and all that." Maarg took a breath. "I put this chip inside a Faraday cage, just to make sure they couldn't track it here. You know, avoiding unnecessary attention and all that. Anyway, the idea is, they track the individual chips as they pass through certain points. At some point during the chips' journey from the floor to wherever the vault is, they'll read each of the chips and make sure they're genuine. That's really all they've done it for, or so we think."

Tara nodded. "How are we going to be able to track it?"

"We're not," Maarg said. "What we're going to be looking for is in the system here."

She pointed to one of the large monitors filled with scrolling data. "From what Ricky sent me, we can track it the same way the casino does. Think of it like a test feed for the sensor network inside the casino. It's running parallel to the main network, particularly the gaming floor and the vaults."

"And you're sitting here monitoring it in real time?" Tara asked. "Isn't that dangerous?"

Maarg shrugged. "If someone else looks into the system, I'll have time to get out. I haven't found anybody better than Keaton and Ricky at penetrating these kinds of networks."

Tara knew Maarg's words were high praise. The young TriRusk had ample experience with every type of network, and she constantly learned from everything she touched. She'd become a true professional. "What are we watching for?"

"The boys sent me the identification tag information for one of Larth's thousand-credit chips. I'm going to watch for it and see if I can correlate its position with the three-dimensional map of the casino and hotel your companion got us."

Tara squinted at the screen. "I'm not tracking this beyond ones and zeros, Maarg."

"No problem, Boss," Maarg said. She raised a large finger and pointed at the screen. "These sensors listed here should be what we find at the cashiers' windows. So, when the tray goes through, we should see a few pieces of information. One, the chip's internal tag. Two, the total amount of the chip, and three, the account they'll go to. Keaton already knows what the account is, so we're not concerned about that. Our new program is now looking only for the chip. Their sensors are looking for everything they can—a flood of data. Our program, looking for one thing? Needle in a haystack. All we have to do is match Larth's number up with what comes through the different sensors. Once we do that, we can follow it."

"Okay."

On the screen, the image didn't change from Larth sitting at the table, but Jyrall turned his head left and right with a fairly constant rhythm, enabling them to see Keaton approach the cashier and deposit the tray of chips. As the chips went through the window, there was a spike of data with the search parameters.

"There it is," Maarg said. "Now we get to watch and see where it goes from there."

"Won't they just hold it in the cashiers' room?" Tara asked.

"They might," the TriRusk admitted, "but our theory is, since this is the high rollers' area, and the Omni takes care of its customers, this will pass from the cashier to the counting rooms, then to vault control."

Sure enough, as they watched, the chip pinged out a series of sensors Keaton had marked as the counting room. Thirty minutes later, the search pinged again from vault control.

"Interesting," Maarg said. "According to what I'm seeing, there are two main destinations for the chips. One is the casino's operations vault, which they have to stock at a certain level to cover all players."

"Like a bank."

"Yep." Maarg reached for a drink container with a straw and slurped for a long moment. "Then there's a supplementary vault, which is privately coded. I'm going to assume that's Hatfield's, and, while the doors are opened on a daily basis, nothing's entered the vault in six months."

"There's the counterfeit diamonds Jyrall thought would be nearby," Tara said. "He's laundering them, without a doubt."

"Yep. Makes sense, too," Maarg replied. "He can take them through vault control and get them to the cashiers and into the hands of unknowing customers. It's pretty brilliant."

Tara didn't want to admit her friend was right. This Hatfield was a scumbag who'd suddenly come into ownership of a hotel? Something wasn't right. "So, where's the money going? Both the casino's legitimate credits and what Hatfield's taking for himself?"

"There might be an electronic transfer process, but I can't find it. Either it's going back to the operational vault, or it's being moved to another location," Maarg said. "We're going to need to find out where these credits are going."

Tara took a deep breath. "Too risky with all the other stuff going on. We need to do this the hard way."

"Meaning?"

"If the credits are headed off site, someone else has a vested interest in things here. We have to know who that is, and that means going through the documents again. We'll need to use our eyes and ears. All of us," Tara replied. "I think we'll get a lot more answers, too."

*****

Chapter Twenty

The Omni Racing Complex

Limerick, Prestone

At the midpoint of her shift, Cora walked from the Omni's Human-centric food court with a less-than-passable cinnamon roll and a cup of coffee. She'd reported to the stables early to get a jump on the day. Arun had told her they were expecting some new horses, greyhounds, and Agamydi, and the stables needed to be ready to receive all of them. When she'd asked the Oogar if that meant business was booming, he'd merely grunted and walked away. She'd earned his trust, though, and he'd even allowed her to come in earlier than normal to get things moving. After setting the horse stables right, she'd grabbed breakfast as the sun rose and headed back to the office to work on Arun's paperwork and look around a bit.

Arun's filing system was a series of piles of paperwork, receipts, and other detritus in a seemingly erratic mess. However, when asked to produce a particular item, Arun could reach into any of the piles, dig a bit with his thick fingers, and withdraw precisely what had been asked for. Cora had only seen something like that once before. During her time with Ridgerunners, she'd had a maintenance sergeant named Waits who'd had a similar system. Cora had happened into the maintenance office when the company's executive officer, Major

Smith, stood with his hands on his hips demanding Sergeant Waits clean her office.

"You couldn't find last year's comprehensive detail of what the crews did with… oh, let's say it was Copper Three-One, in less than an hour and—"

Cora had had to cover her mouth because Smith had frozen in place as Sergeant Waits held the maintenance file for the Mk 7 CASPer in her hand. Somehow, the career maintainer kept her face straight. "You want anything else, sir?"

Smith had stormed out of the office, and Cora had learned a valuable lesson. If something ain't broke, don't fix it. Like Sergeant Waits, Arun had a system, and while she hadn't had time to learn everything, she knew what he wanted her to work on and where to find it. Plus, she also knew where the keyring was stored. She'd been able to see almost everything in the stables and racing areas, except the supply cage and the racing equipment room. Arun wasn't expected in for another two hours. The window was open. It was time to crawl through.

A brown and black Zuul wearing Omni service coveralls approached her from an adjacent corridor. She glanced at the newcomer and smiled. She'd met him only by video, but she knew him on sight and by reputation. "Hey, good morning."

"Good morning," Gnrra replied. "How's it going?"

"So far, so good." Cora raised her coffee cup. "Got some life juice; I reckon I'll make it."

Gnrra had a matching cup. "Me, too."

"Yep." Cora took a sip as they turned down the empty corridor to the racing complex. The lone security guard barely acknowledged them as they passed through the turnstiles and headed for the stables. When they were out of the corridor and through the doors to the less refined spaces, she turned to the Zuul.

"We're headed to get the keys and then the supply room." Cora pointed down the hallway to a door near Arun's office. "What are we looking for?"

Gnrra kept his voice low. "Following up on your AAR. You think the Agamydi might be able to communicate, right?"

She nodded. "Figgle and Squarlik think so. I haven't had a chance to get close to them yet."

They retrieved the keys and walked down the long corridor under the track to the main supply room. After fifteen minutes searching the racks, Cora shook her head. "There's nothing really here. Just feed and tack."

Gnrra stared at the main door. "Where's the race starter's equipment stored?"

"Down the hall. What are you thinking?"

"The thing they're racing for. What is it?"

Cora shrugged. "Let's go find out."

In the starter's area, they searched through five crates of mechanical hares before they found it. Attached to a pole for mounting into the racing slot, the small effigy appeared to resemble a fat alligator and was crudely made.

Cora lifted the effigy. "This is what they're killing each other for? It's lighter than I thought it would be."

She handed it to Gnrra. "There's no way this is real. Hatfield probably has the real one hidden someplace, and he's tricking them with it. Gods, he's a sonuvabitch."

"Yeah," Cora said. With her slate, Cora took a picture of the effigy on its racing rig, and then put it back where she'd found it. She was about to say more, when they heard yelling coming from down the corridor near the waste collection area. "Come on. We've got to get out of here."

They quickly moved to the key storage and replaced the keys. Gnrra followed Cora to the office, where they found Arun standing menacingly over the regular driver Lenny and her friend Jimmy-Ray.

Oh, shit. He's early.

"You were drunk and unable to come to work on a *race day*?" Arun roared.

Lenny and Jimmy-Ray laughed. "Yeah, sorry, Arun," Lenny said. "Just couldn't make it in."

"Then you're fired. Both of you. Get out of here now." The Oogar stepped forward, raised his cane, and jabbed it in Lenny's face. "I should never have trusted you."

Lenny tried to square his shoulders, but the Oogar stood up as tall as he could.

"Come on, man," Jimmy-Ray said. "Let's get outta here. Cirque D'Or is hiring."

"Fuck that. Let's go get a drink!" The two men laughed and walked up the concrete ramp from the waste collector to the street above. Arun watched them for a moment before turning to Cora.

"I couldn't sleep." The Oogar shrugged his massive shoulders. "Guess it was worth it to fire those assholes. Cara Long, you're my senior driver now."

"Wow. Thanks," Cora replied.

Arun turned to Gnrra. "What's broken?"

Cora opened her mouth, but Gnrra was faster. "Just a couple lights out. I'll have them done in half an hour."

Arun didn't respond for a moment. He appeared confused but shook his head. "I put that request in six weeks ago, and you're just getting to it?"

Gnrra shrugged. "I just got it this morning from the front office."

Arun harrumphed. "Say no more. I'll go work on the paperwork—you two get to work."

As they walked to the holding pens, Cora whispered, "We don't have much time. Ready?"

"Yeah," Gnrra replied and handed her the extra translation pendant. "Maarg says this'll work if they're actually talking."

"She's sure?"

Gnrra shrugged. "Your guess is as good as mine."

Cora took the pendant. Gnrra opened the pen, and they walked inside. The Agamydi cowered on one side of the pen. Cora knelt in the center and held out the pendant in her left hand. She motioned with her right hand but didn't speak. A male closest to her turned toward her and received a hiss from a female in the center of the pack. The group shuffled, and Cora turned her attention to the female. Several anxious sets of eyes glanced at her, and she heard a series of coos and grunts, as well as particular sounds like the rolling of an R.

They can talk. Figgle and Squarlik were convinced. Gotta say I am, too.

She cleared her throat, and the Agamydi's eyes all locked on her. Cora touched her own pendant and raised the other as she spoke softly. "You can speak. I know you can. Please talk to me."

The pack shifted and one female, the one who'd hissed, nudged her way to the outside. More coos and growls, some seemingly urgent, erupted, but the female walked forward. She stared at the pendant.

She knows what it is.

With surprising dexterity, the Agamydi took the pendant and placed it around her neck. With a jolt of panic, Cora wondered if the Agamydi had ever contacted the Galactic Union. Would the devices work? Was this all a—

"What are you?"

Cora blinked at the Agamydi. It pointed at her. "What are you?"

"Human," Cora replied.

"Why Human hurt us?" The Agamydi gestured roughly at her. "Why hurt?"

"Not hurt. I don't want to hurt you."

"Other Human."

Hatfield. Other Human. Cora brought up her arm and tapped on her slate. She brought up the picture even as butterflies rose in her stomach. *They wouldn't attack a picture, would they?*

"What is this?" she asked.

"Other Human stole our gods."

* * *

Airfield
Limerick, Prestone

"All right, get this thing off the ground," Major Sciortino said. "We don't need to fall back from the rest just yet."

"Yes, sir," the pilot said.

The lieutenant kept his hand on the controls and pushed a button with his thumb. "This is *Ivanhoe,* moving into formation now. Be advised, I'm seeing fluctuations on the main engine's readings. It doesn't seem to be running different, so it may be a sensor issue and not an actual engine problem."

"Ivanhoe, *this is Hatfield. Y'all got all the financial backing of the Peacemaker Guild, and you have sensor problems in a dropship? Who runs the maintenance in your outfit, anyway?*"

The pilot didn't answer. Maintenance fell under the unit XO's domain. The last thing he wanted to say was Major Sciortino's name with the man sitting behind him, even if the planned engine problems weren't real.

"Asshole," Sciortino muttered.

He looked across at Pete. Pete pursed his lips, tilted his head, and nodded in agreement. The major grinned. Pete knew the Crusader was glad to have met a confidant, or what he thought was one, anyway.

Later, Sciortino advised Pete, "Check your harness. We're going to drop the ramp here in a few."

Pete ensured he was strapped in tight. He glanced back and watched the six CASPers at the far end of the troop bay. It was standing room only for them, as two hoverskiffs had been loaded behind the troop seats. They stood silent, waiting for the order to jump. He turned back and listened.

Finally, "Ivanhoe, *this is Hatfield. Y'all can spit them things out now. We've landed and offloaded the boats. We'll hit the shore on the north side about the time they land on the south side. There's an open field, so y'all don't have to get 'em muddy this time.*"

The ramp dropped, the light above it showed green, and the CASPers moved off the ramp in pairs. Sciortino pulled up the map overlay, and they watched the symbols and numbers as the elevation decreased for the Archangels.

Sciortino switched the view to the sergeant in charge of the team. For a moment, the view of the approaching ground was disorienting. It changed to the horizon as the CASPer rotated until its boots pointed downward, and the rockets fired, slowing the freefall into a controlled flight.

"Ivanhoe, *this is Archangel One. We're on the ground with no issues. Be advised, it may be an open field, but there are knee-deep bogs in several places. I've marked an area for you to land. Break. Angel 3 through 5, move to the east side. We'll cover the west. Don't let any of them get past you. Hatfield's people should be reaching shore and catching some at any time.*"

Sciortino switched the view to one of Hatfield's crew. Pete felt the change in G forces as the craft veered around and began its descent. He leaned forward to watch the screen closely. The view was from a Gtandan named Rorkr. It took a moment for Pete to get used to the difference in height and angle the Gtandan had in viewing everything around him.

Several flat-bottomed boats were ahead of them as the shoreline approached. Hatfield's boat slid onto shore first. The huts were in view, and Pete knew instantly they hadn't been built by savages, by any stretch of the imagination. Figgle and Squarlik had been right in their reports. The Agamydi were intelligent. *Probably sapient.*

Suddenly the boat on the far left lifted amid an eruption of white foam and water spray. The long snout of a huge creature, light green in color, appeared briefly. There were none on Krifay, but Pete knew a giant crocodile when he saw it. This thing looked eerily similar.

"Move, move, move!" Rorkr ordered. "Get over there so we can pick them up."

The boat veered, and several of the team members in the water reached up and grabbed the side. All but one scrambled onto the boat. Tren didn't make it.

As the dropship flared to land, Sciortino played back the moment the Jivool went under. His shoulders and head disappeared much faster than even someone who couldn't swim would. Something had pulled him under. The large green creature wasn't seen again.

"Shit," Pete said.

"Yeah," Sciortino agreed. "That's the second time those things have shown up in the water. You'd think Hatfield and his boys would figure out a better way."

They exited the craft wearing light battle armor, along with twenty Crusaders geared up as infantry soldiers. Avoiding the obvious bogs, they made their way toward the village. When they got to the edge, flanked by the CASPers, Pete watched the roundup of the scrambling Agamydi.

Like many beings across the galaxy, the adults tried to protect the young. The young were batted aside as Hatfield's crew netted the adults and dropped them into cages. Once the cages were filled, they went from hut to hut, looking for anything valuable. They burned them afterward, with no regard to the young ones running about wailing. Elderly Agamydi hissed and tried to corral the screaming young. It turned Pete's stomach.

This is a real shit show.

Pete did his best not to raise his rifle and end the evil he was witnessing. As he was struggling to remain in character, Hatfield's voice came over the comms.

"*All right. I reckon we got all we can get from this one. Y'all get 'em on the boats, and go slow across the bay. Follow my lead so we don't stir up them damn gators. Hey, Sciortino, we 'preciate y'all, but it looks like y'all came out just to watch the show. Ain't none of 'em tried to escape in y'all's direction. We got us a dozen this time. We'll see y'all back at the airfield.*"

"Affirmative," Sciortino answered. He winked at Pete. "But we may be a while. I want my pilot to run a full diagnostic. I don't like the gauge fluctuations, and I want to be sure we don't fall out of the sky. Not everyone has a CASPer to let them land safely."

"*Well, all right, if you're scared of a little free falling, just say so.*" He sang the words "free falling" like it was the song from well over a hundred years ago. "*We'll see y'all there.*"

* * *

They waited a full twenty minutes before Sciortino ordered the pilot to lift off. He pulled up the overlay map and looked at the sites he and Pete had selected. He scratched the side of his face as he thought.

"We're going to hit this one. It's the closest. We'll be all right, because we're not coming in on boats, so we don't have to worry about whatever that was in the water."

"Good plan," Pete agreed. "I don't plan on being anything's meal."

"Agreed," Sciortino said. He spoke over the team's internal net. "Ten minutes, people. Get it together. Sergeant Avery? What's the status of everyone's jump juice?"

"*We should be good for one more, sir. Just to be sure, I suggest we drop from half the normal combat height.*"

"Granted. Better safe than sorry. I don't plan on losing any of our team. Not like Hatfield seems to do every time. I'll inform the pilot."

"*Roger, sir.*"

"Not losing any of your team is always a good plan," Pete said.

"I know, right?"

Ten minutes later, the ramp was coming down as the dropship banked. A few minutes after that, Angel 1 reported the Angels on the ground, and a landing area was marked.

"*The village looks to be on the edge of the water, but it's dry here. No bogs to speak of, sir.*"

"Good," Sciortino answered. He checked the screen. "We'll be on the ground in three minutes. Wait for us."

Like the village before, the CASPers flanked the platoon of infantry soldiers. It was eerily quiet. There was no movement in the village.

"This is strange," Sciortino said.

"I've only seen one raid on a village, but this is definitely not like the last one," Pete remarked. He adjusted his rifle and made sure it was ready as they passed several empty huts and moved toward the water. He was serious about not being dinner for a twenty-foot creature.

"*Sir,*" Sergeant Avery said, "*I magnified my view to see what that is just off the shore. It looks like a temple of sorts.*"

"Let's move to the shore, people," Sciortino ordered. He removed his helmet and scratched his head. "Maybe I should be in my CASPer. These damn bugs, or whatever they are, drive me crazy."

"*Granth, Perkle, move into the water and test the depth,*" Avery ordered.

"*Yes, Sergeant.*"

"Moving, Sergeant."

Pete had to nod his head in approval. The Crusaders might be his enemy at the moment, but he appreciated the discipline. He stepped slightly to the side, so he had a better view. His boot hit something. He looked down, and to his surprise, he saw a red diamond. He put his boot over it and bent down to adjust the strap on it. He shifted his foot, palmed the diamond, and slid it deep into the top of his boot.

He looked up in time to see all hell break loose. Fifteen feet away, Granth's CASPer went sideways in a blast of frothy water as a huge mouth closed around the machine's waist. Granth screamed into the comms. He went silent as the CASPer slid beneath the water.

Perkle's machine blasted out of the water with his jump jets at full power, and a huge mouth snapped closed below the emerging legs, missing them by mere inches. The CASPer turned in the air, flew over them, and landed fifty feet from the shore. At least eight weapons fired into the dark water toward where Granth was last seen.

"Cease fire!" Sciortino ordered. "Cease fire!"

Minutes later, Sciortino conferred with Pete, away from the others. "I'm screwed if we don't find something. There's nothing of value here. We damn sure can't get to the temple. We can't even send the Mk 8s over. They're out of jump juice. Perkle is lucky he managed that little bit of boost. We need to capture some of the racers or something. Fucking crocodiles or alligators or whatever they are." He shook his head. "I can't go back empty handed and make this report. Shit."

"Why don't we make camp near the dropship and hit another spot in the morning? We get in and get out with a half dozen or more of them, and Hatfield won't know what we're up to until we offer them for sale. He'll think we're still having engine problems."

"True," Sciortino agreed. He turned toward his troops. "Head back to the ship. We're making camp for the night. Some of you are, anyway. The colonel and I will sleep on the ship. Let's move, people!"

*****

Chapter Twenty-One

Cirque D'Or
Limerick, Prestone

"Hey, have you ever heard of the Rmaska Corporation?" Araceli asked Quin'taa. "I have that they're an Oogar-founded entertainment company, and that's about it."

"What have you found?"

"The casino's documentations and licensing. Since Hatfield took over, it was like everything on the casino's ownership prior disappeared. Well, I found this one transfer of licensure from Rmaska Corporation to Hatfield about eighteen months ago."

Quin'taa frowned. "They're an entertainment company only in name, Little Sister. This is organized crime. The mafia from your Human movies, except these are Oogar with a vicious streak."

"You've heard of them, then." Araceli smiled. Her friend didn't return the gesture.

"My father made enemies of them a very long time ago. They fled from Uuwato, and he lost track of them. I should have expected they'd turn up eventually."

Araceli saw her friend struggle with the news. Whoever these Oogar were, they troubled him. "You think they're involved somehow?"

"Almost certainly. They're financially backing the casino. It makes sense now. The cold pools and security teams should have alerted me to the possibility."

"What does that mean for Hatfield?"

"If he really is laundering forged credits through the casino, they're not going to be happy with him." Quin'taa shook his head. "We should expect them to become involved when we terminate the race."

"They'll be looking for targets?"

"Oh, I'm reasonably sure they have their targets. It would be best if we were completely evacuated when the operation kicks off."

Araceli nodded. "Let's go talk to the boss."

"About what?" Tara walked into the room, carrying a bowl of yogurt and oatmeal. "What have you found?"

Araceli recapped their conversation, and Tara studied their faces for a moment before turning to Quin'taa. "Your father knew these folks?"

"From when he was fresh out of the Academy. His... ex-girlfriend is what I think you'd call her. Anyway, she wasn't a very pleasant being from the get-go, and she married the Oogar who started running Rmaska a couple years later. Father avoided them like the plague. He didn't want them coming after family."

Tara nodded. "Then we'll be prepared to evacuate this place. As a matter of fact, let's make it look like we're leaving today. We can bunk aboard *Mako 15* prior to the race tomorrow. Araceli, have Carter file the flight plans to pick us up here and depart."

"Depart for orbit? Or make a run to another place?" Araceli asked.

Tara grinned. "Yes. I'll leave that up to Carter. I also know if we pay enough, no one at traffic control will remember a thing about us."

She turned to Quin'taa. "Your safety from them is paramount. When the time comes, we'll deal with them. If they come for you, they'll have to get through us first."

Quin'taa nodded solemnly. "Thank you, Tara. I'll get the others moving."

Tara watched him as he left. Araceli wanted to say something, but Eponil climbed into her lap and sat down, expecting affection.

"Hey there," she said lightly stroking the Depik's head between the ears.

"I'm guessing I'll need to talk to Tsan?" he asked Tara.

For a moment, Araceli saw indecisiveness in Tara's face, and she wondered what it could be. But then it was gone, and she was herself again.

"Yes, set up a meeting tonight. I'll need to talk to Cora, and we can't be anywhere near here."

"I'll let them know," Eponil replied. "Anything else?

"No. Just make sure there's nothing here that'll allow anyone to track us. I don't want any surprises in a year when they figure out what went down."

Eponil growled. "Leave that to me."

"Okay, then, we stay on Hatfield and take him down tomorrow," Tara said.

"With pleasure," Araceli said. "Maybe the Crusaders, too, if all goes well."

* * *

Tennessee

Earth

From everything Raley could tell, the equipment was brand new but hadn't been used or maintained in years. A thick layer of dust had settled on everything in the room. Plastic encased most of the components. A few items were covered by tarpaulins, also caked with dust. The weapons, CASPers, and the consoles appeared to be without power connections. She found light fixtures and traced the power conduits, with no luck. Everything was shut down. Raley found the command console and saw that it had been modified to receive an emergency backup power source, and she grinned. The handiwork was her father's. He'd done similar work on many things around the compound, probably prior to his last missions. He told her he'd learned it from an old drill instructor and had decided to adopt it for the Raiders' own standard operating procedures. As such, Rae carried one of the small battery packs with its unique five-pronged adapter in the survival kit in her Jeep.

Her curiosity completely overwhelmed, Raley headed back toward the main door and her Jeep in the overgrown courtyard outside. As she broke into the sunlight, she froze. Five white utility vehicles with their engines running sat before her. Each of the vehicles' doors were open, and armed guards pointed assault weapons at her. Two CASPers stood atop the old dam with their MACs trained on her. In the center of the assembled force, a woman with dark brown hair tied back in a ponytail, dark sunglasses, and a tactical vest leveled a pistol at her chest.

"Slowly step out the door. Get your hands up where I can see them. Drop the flashlight." Rae did as she was told. Heart racing and wondering why she'd been stupid enough to leave her weapon in the Jeep, she walked forward and let the flashlight fall from her hand.

"That's far enough," the woman said. For a long moment, they stared at each other. Raley was about to ask what she was supposed to do next when a car door to her right opened. An older man wearing a light-colored suit stepped out into the high weeds and walked toward her. He wore a trimmed beard, and, despite the heat, he didn't appear heated or concerned. If anything, he seemed unbelievably calm, almost serene. He smiled at her and made his way forward, leaning slightly on a cane.

Bad hip. Kr'et'Socae's training instinctively bubbled up in her mind. *Gunshot wound. Been a while, and he's still hurting.*

"I think you can put your weapons down, Sarah," he said to the dark-haired woman. "She's unarmed."

"We can't be sure of that, sir."

He laughed. "I am. Somebody's curiosity got the better of them, didn't it?" He directed the last part to Raley, and she nodded.

"Guess so."

The man stepped closer. "You can put your hands down."

Raley did and tried to stand relaxed, despite the adrenaline pumping through her system. Getting to her Jeep and escaping was out of the question. When she dropped the flashlight, her only possible weapon was gone. Though she felt threatened, the older gentleman seemed almost friendly.

That means he wants something. She knew her father's advice as well as she knew her own. Raley swallowed and found her voice. She locked eyes with the man. "I've got a key. If this is your place, I'm sorry, but my father—"

"Your father pissed away everything he had."

The words stopped Raley cold. "What do you mean?"

The old man shook his head. "I expected your father to come and steal all this, maybe sell it to pay off debt, or to buy another year's worth of liquor. When he died, I wasn't sure he'd ever told you about this place. He couldn't have been sober enough to tell you in the last couple of years. Maybe before then, but I wasn't sure you'd come for it. But I had to be prepared for this day. I'm glad it's here."

"Be prepared for what?" Raley asked.

He laughed. "For you to steal it. For you to be just like your father. That you're here without the supplies to take it tells me you didn't know this cache was here."

Raley shook her head. "All I knew about was the key. Daddy hid it on his ship, the *Satisfaction.* He showed me where it was when I was a kid. I remembered it, so I had to go and get it."

"Resourceful." The man smiled. "In the short time I've known you, Raley Shae Reilly, I'm more inclined to say you're like your grandfather, not your father."

"You knew my grandfather?" Raley asked. Her father hadn't spoken much about his family, just that he'd once had them, and that they weren't appreciative of what he'd done with his life. Even when he'd purchased the *Satisfaction* and attempted to go legitimate as a mercenary commander, his family hadn't responded well. She'd never known her grandparents.

"Your grandfather was my best friend when we were growing up. The kind of friend I'd have done anything for. He and I took our VOWS together. He was part of a group here that was set up to be some of the best mercenaries the universe has ever seen." The man snorted and shook his head.

"My daddy said my grandfather died on his first mission. That he was a loser."

"He served more than fifteen years as a mercenary, Raley. Commanded his own unit, too, before the Science Guild came for him. Like they came for all my friends. I found out too late to save your grandfather and the rest of our friends, but when I learned who was responsible? I'm happy to say that son of a bitch is dead, but it doesn't change the past. It doesn't take back the fact that my friend is gone, and you never got a chance to meet him."

"Who are you?" she asked.

The man stepped closer to her and smiled. "Now I need to know something, all right? I need to know what your intentions are with what you just found."

"I don't know," she said. "I've never seen anything like it, and I don't have the ability to take it with me. I'd figured on leaving it here until I'm ready to launch the Raiders again."

"You're assuming it's yours to take."

"My daddy left me the key."

"That doesn't matter, honey. This is private property, and it belongs to me and Harold Riley's legitimate heir."

The breeze freshened, and she caught a whiff of the man's Old Spice cologne. She'd smelled it before, but when? "What do you mean by legitimate?"

"Someone who's not going to use it to lie, cheat, and steal from others." The man smiled, and his bright blue eyes twinkled in the light. "Is that going to be you?"

Raley nodded. "I'm legitimate."

The man smiled again and shook his head. "That remains to be seen, young lady. I'll take that key."

"You can't have it. It's mine." The security personnel shuffled uneasily behind their vehicles.

"Honey," he said and reached out a hand, palm up to receive it, "I'm going to need that key. When the time comes, and I'm sure you are who you say you're going to be, I'll give it to you. There might even be a time real soon when I need you to take what's here and do something for the good of others. But I need to know that's who you truly are, and not just who you say you are."

Anger rose in Raley's chest. "Who the hell do you think you are? My daddy left me that key. I searched for it, and I found this place. All this belongs to me."

"I didn't say it doesn't belong to you, but your grandfather helped me secure this a long time ago, and he entrusted that particular key to your father, knowing full well that if your father came here and took this, I'd be waiting, because it wasn't your father's to have to pay his debts or to use against others. There's going to come a time when this is needed by good people to do something for the good of our entire species, Raley. Until that time, I'm its custodian, and yours is the last key I need to make sure what's here stays here."

Raley realized in a flash there was far more to this cache than the powered armor, the weapons, and the consoles she'd found. There was likely much more buried deeper than her father's secrets.

"Why should you be the custodian of this key?" she asked. "Why can't it be me?"

"Because you're not in a position to defend it." The man's smile disappeared. "Where are you even living? Since your daddy died, I'm guessing the only thing you had left was the compound up on Holston Lake."

Raley shivered. "How do you even know that?"

"Your grandfather and I used to go there all the time. We'd fish out on that little point under the big cliff. You know it? You can get some pretty good bluegill out there."

Raley could only nod. She'd caught bluegill at that same spot. "It's all I have, but there's enough there to get started again. I'm going to, once I'm done with my schooling. My daddy didn't leave me with much, but it's enough to know what I've got here is valuable. You still haven't told me who you are. Once I know who you are, maybe I'll give you this key."

"You're going to give me the key, honey. I told your grandfather I'd protect this even before we finished it. He never got a chance to know you, but I told him that when the time came, I'd make sure his legitimate heir got what was left. It's enough to start a company, and more, but I need to know if that company is going to be on my side."

"And who's *your* side, mister?"

"My name is James Francis," he replied with a slight smile. "My friends call me Snowman."

Raley felt her knees quiver. "You're Jessica Francis' father. Our first Peacemaker."

"I am," he said. "Pretty damned proud of it, too. But I own a business, and that business has interests, including what's here at Nottely Lake. Now I need you to hand me that key, Raley Reilly. When the time comes, this is yours. But I think you have to prove it, and if you do something your grandfather wouldn't have liked, you might as well forget this is here, because I'll clean it out faster than shit through a goose."

"But it's mine." Raley licked her lips. "You just said it was."

"It is yours, but until you prove me wrong, it's mine," Francis said.

Raley reached into her pocket and withdrew the key. "What's here at Nottely Lake? More than what I've seen in that first room, right?"

Francis shook his head. "No secrets until you show me who you are, Raley. I need to know I can trust you when the fight comes here."

"Here? To Earth?"

Francis nodded. "I have a feeling it's already here, and I think you know that, too."

Raley slowly placed the key in his palm. Her hand shook slightly, and she knew he'd seen it. Whatever was below ground level was enough to bring out an armed security force in a matter of minutes. She could start a company with it, but she wondered what would happen if Kr'et'Socae found it. Giving Francis the key felt right, even as her stomach twisted upon itself. Not knowing something, especially what her father had known and never told her, even in his decline, stung.

"It's time to grow up, honey," Francis said. "You have a place in this galaxy, Raley. When the time comes, I know you're gonna find it. You best run on up to Raleigh and get your schoolwork done."

Raley felt frozen in place. "How do you know so much about me?"

Francis smiled. "Trade secrets, Raley. You'll learn soon enough."

*****

Chapter Twenty-Two

Crusader Campsite

Reortia

Pete walked past the fire and stood beside Sciortino. "Hey, I was looking at the overlay and the coordinates we have on other villages. There's one inland. Well, there are several, but this one is far from any water. We won't have to worry about losing anyone else, especially you or me."

"I like the way you think, Pete," Sciortino said.

"How about I sit down with my slate and figure out the best landing area and approach to the village?"

"Do it," Sciortino said. "I'll make sure you're not disturbed as you plan it."

"Appreciate it. I'll speak a few notes, too. We can use them later, as we catch more and more. We're going to make a lot of credits, my friend."

"I really like the way you think."

Pete moved away from the rest with his slate. He sat down and scrolled through his files. He entered the code Keaton had given him. He entered another and then wrote his message. He fired it off to his troops, Cora's, and to the team he had yet to meet. He included a verbal message on what he thought the temple may have been. He knew everyone trusted Keaton's encryptions, but his own voice on it would help to verify. They would undoubtedly run it through a program to ensure it wasn't a forced message.

Later, he explained the plan to Sciortino.

"I have a platoon of my own troops. I can have them at the location where we offload the skiffs and have them link up with your platoon. All I have is a shuttle to bring them, but if I give the order now, they can be at the coordinates waiting for us. With the CASPers and two platoons, we won't have any issues."

Sciortino looked hesitant. Pete continued, "Look, it's going to take longer because I want to be cautious, and we have to get everyone in place. We don't have the water to block them from escaping on one side. It's going to be up to us."

"We'll miss the race," Sciortino said. "I don't know if we can take that kind of time. Hatfield may suspect something."

"I don't think it matters. He'll be caught up in all the excitement as he counts his credits before he has them in hand. Besides, I saw the race once. I don't need to see it again."

"True," Sciortino agreed. "I already placed my bet. I just bet on number three. I hope it's not a scratch."

"Me, too, only I bet on one, three, and six. I figure the inside and outside lanes are good choices to go with three."

"A trifecta?"

"Exactly. I got lucky once, why not again?"

"I mean, it could happen," Sciortino said. "What if there are more than six racing this time?"

"The bet's already in. Can't change it now."

"True. Now show me why you think we should separate the six Mk 8s again?"

"So they can keep the racers corralled. I know they won't be able to see each other because of the trees and huts, but it shouldn't matter. Look how small they are. The big machines will scare them back into the village. The rest of us, along with the pilot and copilot, will at least catch one each. I bet Hatfield never captured that many. Credits in the bank, my friend. Easy credits."

"The copilot will be operating my Mk 8 since we lost one today. I want the pilot in the air on overwatch."

"We can do that. I'll add that to my notes. We're getting paid tomorrow."

"Say, have I told you I like the way you think?" Sciortino asked.

* * *

The Omni
Main Casino

Larth grinned as he laid down four threes and a jack. Everyone at the table groaned. A couple decided they'd had enough, gathered what few credits they had left, and walked away, hand in hand. Larth felt sorry for them, but there wasn't much he could do. He had to stay in character and stick with the plan. Win. Win at everything. He rolled his shoulders and waited on the next hand. While he waited, he studied the numbers in his lens. He was on a big streak today.

Larth clapped his paws, and then raked in the pot. The last player at the table with him had gone all in on three queens. Larth suspected he was a ringer working for the casino. Larth had beaten him with a full house, kings high. The last king was the river card. He was now far ahead for the week. He looked around. There were no empty seats at the other poker tables.

"I wonder if I should go back to the blackjack table?" Larth wondered aloud. "Maybe play some slots? I like slots."

He turned to the head of his security. "What do you think?"

"I don't know, sir. It would seem you've already proven yourself against the house at blackjack. Perhaps some roulette?"

"Yeah?" Larth glanced toward Ricky. Ricky nodded slightly.

"You think I have a good shot there?"

"I read that the corner wheels are best this time of night. I'm not sure where I read it, mind you, but I do remember that I read it."

"Good enough for me," Larth said, playing up his part. "I'd ask the ladies for their opinion, but they seem to have disappeared. Probably off spending some of the credits I won." He shrugged. "Oh, well, I can win more."

Larth walked into the area where the roulette wheels were located. He saw the one in the corner and made a straight line for it. Jyrall and Ricky made sure no one was in his way, as they created a wide path for him. Keaton followed behind as usual. Once they made it to the wheel, Ricky stood right beside it, and Jyrall stood at the end of the table.

Larth put every credit he had with him on… red. It was stacked high, and he had to ensure the operator knew it was all on only red, as some of them were beyond the edges of the box. Nails, who'd remained with Larth when the women had wandered off, called the closest roving pit boss over to verify the entire amount was on red. Once it was agreed, the operator spun the ball in the opposite direction the wheel was going. The ball landed on red 23.

"Again!" Larth shouted. "All on red again."

"I'm afraid the credits won't fit, sir," the pit boss said.

"Then bring me a bigger denomination," Larth demanded. "Call the cart over. I saw it going back to the cashier."

Reluctantly, the pit boss spoke into his cuff. Minutes later, the cart was at the table, flanked by two security guards. All of Larth's hard credits, including what they owed him for the last spin, were exchanged for ridiculously large amounts per card.

"All on red!" Larth shouted. He moved the much smaller but higher valued stack to the box for red.

Hatfield and Mr. Randazzo walked up, having been alerted by the office about the credit exchange, as the ball stopped on red 11.

"Winner!" shouted Larth. He gathered his winnings and consolidated them again. "Again! All on red."

For the third time, the ball stopped in a red slot. This time it was red 16. A pair of Zuul at the table celebrated. They'd decided to bet whatever the one-eyed Zuparti bet. For the first time all night, they were up.

As Larth celebrated, Hatfield gave Randazzo a look. Randazzo nodded at the wheel operator. The man shifted and pushed a spot on the back of the table with his knee.

"One more time on red?" Hatfield suggested. "Looks like you're on a hot streak."

Larth gathered up his credits and put them in the bag Nails was holding. "No, I don't think so. I'm bored of winning every time on the wheel. I think I'll call it an afternoon."

"Perhaps you should call it a trip," Hatfield suggested. "I mean, this is the time when most high rollers tend to leave. Especially when they're up as much as you are. I wouldn't want you to get bored of our little establishment. I want you to come back and give us a chance to win it back from you."

"I think I'll stay a while longer," Larth said. "I'm putting it all on the race tomorrow, along with ten million of my own credits. You think you can give me a good race tomorrow? I want the best. Only the best."

"For ten million?" Hatfield answered. "You're on. It'll be the best race we've ever had. I've been planning for it, anyway."

"Good. I plan on breaking the house."

"We'll see about that, Mr. Weezik." Hatfield smiled, but it didn't reach his eyes. "We will see about that."

* * *

Top Floor
Embassy Tower

Larth flopped down on the bed and giggled like a child. "Three times in a row! That was great!"

"I hoped you got my message," Keaton said.

"Me, too," Jyrall admitted. "I heard the word *red* three times when you suggested the wheel to him."

"I caught it," Larth said. "It was obvious."

"It's a dang good thing," Ricky said. "The pseudo-magnetic device in my belt was only set to work three times. I saw the looks the dealer got and watched him shift so his knee hit the table. Probably a pressure plate. You can guaran-damn-tee that next spin was landing on black."

"Agreed," Jyrall said. "I saw the subtle shift, as well."

"Cheaters!" Larth exclaimed. "I hate a cheater."

At this, Jyrall guffawed, and then broke into full-fledged laughter. The entire room joined in, even Private Tivlang, though he had no clue what was so funny.

* * *

The Omni Racing Complex
Limerick, Prestone

"You needed from the jamb of Arun's office door. She'd hauled a final load of waste from the horse stables and taken a moment to clean herself up a little.

The Oogar waved her inside. "We're to clear space for more Agamydi. Their entire main pen and the staging pen."

"Are they racing all of them?" Cora knew the answer before the question left her lips. "Oh, no."

"All twelve, three times the distance, four levels of track, and everything we can throw at the Agamydi, short of shooting them." Arun sighed. "Supposedly, Hatfield has turned over collection from his security forces to a unit connected with the Peacemakers."

"The Crusaders," Cora said. "They're in it for the money. It's not a Peacemaker thing."

Arun grunted in acknowledgment. "I would have guessed, but I know nothing about them."

"They were supposed to help. At least, that's what the last guild master said." Cora shrugged. "I think it went really wrong, and no one's capable of fixing it."

"Someone's always capable of fixing things. Doing so is a matter of time and effort," Arun replied. "Until such someone stands up, though, the wrongs continue unabated."

Cora heard the change in his voice. He'd gone from gruff and serious, his usual self, to a resigned, almost wistful tone. "What is it, Arun?"

"Hmm? Nothing." He cocked his head to one side as he looked at her, a confused look on his face. The trouble was, his countenance didn't match his eyes. There was something there. Something far greater there.

"Is it something here?"

He snorted. "What are you asking, Cara Long?"

"Why are you here?" She pulled out a stool from the far side of the desk and sat down. "A wrong?"

Arun said nothing. "I'm here to do the work I do to the best of my ability. If you ask, thinking of debts and such, I have no financial concerns. I make more than enough for sustenance."

"Then why are you here? Working?" Cora glanced at the cane against the wall.

"Because this is the only place I can work." Arun huffed. "Because what I owe cannot be paid for with credits, Cara Long. My loyalty was bought and paid for long ago."

Cora's mind worked. "I don't understand."

"I came with this racing complex. My previous employers have a vested interest in what happens here. As such, I was chosen to remain to ensure profitability. Now, I'm about to oversee the ruin of what they worked to build, because Mister Hatfield wishes to capitalize on a quick return without thinking of consequences. We have one of the finest racing tracks in the galaxy, and he's risking too much."

Cora shook her head. "He's going to kill all these racers, and then just go out and get more and more. Until what?"

"They're exhausted, or he breeds them," Arun said. "They're simply animals to him."

Cora muttered. "It's not right."

"It's what we're paid for. Please prepare the Agamydi. Have the Goka move them to the staging area, and ensure the greyhounds are prepared. They're the first two races. Then we go to the Agamydi," Arun said, turning his attention back to the mountains of paperwork strewn across his desk.

"We're giving the horses a rest?"

Arun shook his head. "Hatfield has arranged the sale of the entire stable. I'm making plans to convert it to Agamydi and greyhounds only. The horses will be gone in a week."

That sonuvabitch. He is *going to breed them.*

"This is wrong, Arun."

"And it can't be helped, Cara Long. Get things done. I know I can count on you."

"Yeah. Sure," Cora replied. "I'll get it done. But, Arun, what can you do? Isn't there something?"

"I stayed up all night thinking about this. Short of Hatfield selling the casino, or something catastrophic, there's nothing I can do for myself or my former employers and their investment. Now, please, go and let me finish this work."

"Okay." She turned to leave and heard him sigh heavily behind her.

"Cara Long?"

She turned around and saw the tiny hint of a smile on his maw.

"You have earned my trust far faster than any being I've ever known. Please keep my words between us."

"I will, Arun."

Cora went to find Figgle and Squarlik working the greyhound cages. Her mind sped through their plan, and what the Misfits intended. Arun wanted something catastrophic? They could certainly give him that. She fought her emotions and pushed the anger down. She and the others needed clear heads to do what needed to be done.

She waved the Goka to the gate. "Hey, Arun says we need to clear the Agamydi to the staging area and be prepared to convert stable spaces for more."

Squarlik ambled to the fence first. "I saw teams working on the horses for transport."

"They're being sold. Hatfield wants to bring in more Agamydi and breed them."

Figgle moved closer. "We're not going to let that happen, are we?"

"No. We're going to make our move tomorrow. If we don't, this whole thing is going to balloon into something we can't stop."

"We'll relay the word," Figgle said. "I'll have everyone ready."

"I have to get word to our friends, too," Cora said. "Do whatever you have to do. Complete the mission."

"Always," Figgle replied. He glanced at Squarlik. "What are you still standing there for? Let's get to work."

* * * * *

Chapter Twenty-Three

Giovanni's Pizza
Outskirts of Limerick, Prestone

The sign on the simple glass doors read "CLOSED," but from what Tara could see as their autocar pulled up in front, the lights inside were on. The onboard computer chimed a warning that the establishment was closed and asked if they wished for a different destination. Tara tapped the screen to send the autocar away and followed Araceli into the darkening entrance. As the autocar accelerated away, Araceli tapped on the door. Curtains hung on the inside of the glass, but Tara saw a figure unlock the door and push it open. While arranged and said to be a safe place, Tara kept her hand on the pistol in her handbag. A man with a large mustache wearing a chef's hat looked them over. The nametag on his apron read "Giuseppe."

"We're closed."

Tara fought not to clench her jaw and let the words come out. "Stand Victoria."

Giuseppe removed his hat and pushed the door open wider. "Colonel Mason. My family owes you and Force 25 for our survival. We departed Victoria Bravo after the second attack. Please, come inside. You honor us with your presence."

Araceli gasped and pointed at the script on the door. "Wait. You had a restaurant downtown in Lovell City. I remember it. Red leather-covered booths and red and white checkerboard tablecloths."

Giuseppe smiled and nodded. As he opened the door, the inside of the restaurant matched exactly what Araceli had said. She heard the younger woman choke back a sob.

"Oh. Oh, Tara. My family used to come… go to this place. It smells the same. The name is different, but, gods, it's the same place."

Giuseppe clasped his hands in front of him, still holding his hat. "On Victoria Bravo, my father called our restaurant Giordano's."

"Yes!" Araceli yelped. She pressed her face into her hands. There were tears streaming down her cheeks, but she smiled. "I'm Araceli Cignes. Growing up, I loved Giordano's pizza."

Giuseppe nodded. "We knew the Cignes family well. I'm so sorry for your loss."

"Thank you," Araceli managed to say.

"If I may, what can I make for you?"

"Pepperoni. Extra sauce and cheese." Araceli grinned.

"The Don Special." Giuseppe grinned. "Coming right up. Please, your friends are in the back room. Your food and drinks are with my most sincere compliments."

Giuseppe swept them into the back room. Lisalle, Nileah, and Cora McCoy sat at the round table, chatting in quiet voices. They looked up as Tara and Araceli entered the room.

"Hey," Cora McCoy said as she stood and walked up to Tara. The pretty, dark-haired woman opened her arms, and they embraced quickly, as friends do. "Thanks for coming."

Tara smiled. "Like we had any other choice."

The group traded hugs and sat down as Giuseppe brought in two bottles of Chianti and quickly filled their glasses before returning to the kitchen.

"I propose a toast," Lisalle said. They all raised their glasses. "Absent friends."

"Absent friends." They touched glasses and sipped their wine. Tara thought the Chianti might have been the best wine she'd ever had.

Cora smiled. "Before our food comes, I think we should update each other. If you don't mind, I'll start."

"Go right ahead," Tara said.

"Okay, from our side, we're going to get the Agamydi out of the arena immediately after the trumpet sounds the call to racing. At that point, the gaming commission's rule is that all bets must be forfeited. I'll be driving the truck, and we'll get them offsite. We have a couple of potential rally points selected, and we'll make that decision later."

"Once you're clear?" Tara asked. Cora nodded.

"Phase two is the casino. Larth and the boys have a whole bunch of toys," Lisalle said. "They've found a way to cheat the casino, and they're going to basically hijack every game so patrons start winning. As that happens, all the slots will simultaneously spew credits. It'll cause a free-for-all on the casino floor."

"Which happens," Nileah added, "as a riot is going to start in the racing complex. Forfeited bets and well-lubricated patrons won't mix well. Hatfield's security will be overwhelmed, and that should allow us to get out. We'll rendezvous with Cora and be ready to make our way to you."

Tara nodded. "As soon as we're done here, Araceli and I will head back to *Mako 15* at the spaceport and depart. We'll get to the target area Pete's selected and find an attack position. When the Crusaders come in, we have the plan Pete's briefed them. We'll hit them fast and make it look like the operation went bad. Once the field is clear, we'll meet up with you and return the Agamydi. You know where we're going?"

Cora nodded. "We'll rendezvous there once we clear the casino."

"What about Lisalle and Nileah? The boys?" Tara asked.

"There's a really good chance the casino'll get locked down, and we'll be forced to remain in character," Lisalle said. "We're prepared for that, if it happens."

"But Jyrall and Larth are prepared to fight their way out, too," Cora replied. "It all depends on what happens when the race defaults and the casino systems go crazy."

"If there's an avenue where Larth can throw a tantrum and just leave, he's prepared to do that," Nileah said. "We've been kicking around the possibilities since we got here."

Tara nodded. "So, we're not going to have Jyrall and Larth when we take the Agamydi back to Pete's target?"

"It's just going to be y'all, Pete, and the Barnstormers he has on the Crusader mission, and my team," Cora said. "Figgle, Squarlik, and me. Hopefully, by the time we get back here, things will have cleared up enough to get our folks out without breaking character. Then we'll figure out our next move."

"Pete said the temporary Crusader commander has a copy of Hatfield's slate," Lisalle said. "That might help us figure out anything we're missing here before we go after that asshole. Smith, not Hatfield."

"They're both assholes." Nileah grinned.

"We're sure Smith went to Krifay?" Araceli asked.

"Oh, he did," Lisalle said.

"We're going to give him everything he'll ever want in a fight, too," Nileah added.

Tara met Cora's eyes. "We'll be with you when you head back."

"I didn't want to assume anything," Cora replied. "You have your priorities, too."

"We take care of our friends." Tara smiled.

"Sounds like something Jessica Francis would say." Cora laughed.

"She's so nice and positive," Nileah said, "but what she says and what she does don't rightly match up."

Tara laughed. "I learned pretty early that Jessica can make friends in unusual places, and because she's nice, a lot of beings think she's a pushover. Let me tell you something, ladies. Those friends she makes? She'll kill for them. In a fight, there are very few people I've ever felt had my back like she did."

"Almost literally," Araceli added. "You know that whole you owe her your life thing, right?"

Cora sat forward. "I haven't heard this story."

"Settle in, ladies." Araceli laughed.

"Bring it!" Lisalle grinned. "And damned if that pizza don't smell amazing."

"You have no idea how much of a treat y'all are in for," Araceli said. "Now. The story, Tara."

Tara took a long sip of wine. "I met Jessica Francis on her second commissioning mission."

"Second?" Cora asked. "I thought there was only one for a Peacemaker."

"Not for Jessica," Araceli replied. "That would have been too easy."

"This is my story, Little Sister." Tara raised her eyebrows. "Selector Hak-Chet approached me to assist Jessica on this planet called Araf…"

* * *

The Omni Racing Complex
Limerick, Prestone

Cora moved quickly through the bustling stables. Race day was a seemingly chaotic experience in logistics. Handlers moved their animals to their respective areas. Costumers ensured the racing bibs and blankets for each animal sat perfectly. Closed circuit television camera crews moved though every area, seemingly at once. As such, she knew her time would be limited with the Agamydi. As long as the female alpha had kept the pendant, Cora believed she could get her message through.

She approached the holding pen and found no crews and no handlers within earshot. Cora strode up to the meter-high wall topped with tight fencing and looked into the pen. A hoot and a hiss greeted her, and then the larger female rose up and stared at her for a moment before producing the pendant and slipping it over her head.

"We're going to keep you from racing," Cora said.

"How?"

"In the starting boxes, there's a way out through the bottom. We'll get you out that way."

"But our gods?"

"You know it's false. Not the real one, yes?"

"False?"

"There's no time to explain. You can't go crazy when it appears. It's not real," Cora explained. "We have one chance to get you out."

"We must find the gods. Return them to the Narrith."

Cora drew a breath, searching for her words, and a shadow fell over her. The Agamydi fell back from the fence as she turned and looked up into the face of Arun Marwok.

"What are you doing, Cara Long?"

She turned toward the Oogar. "Getting them out of here."

"Why?"

"They're sapient, Arun. They can speak. Hatfield's taken something of great value to them. Their gods."

Arun grunted. "Their gods."

"That's how it translates, Arun." Cora pointed to her pendant. "I gave them a pendant. They can communicate. They think. They feel. They hurt."

"They kill each other for something they want," Arun replied.

"So do Humans and Oogar," Cora shot back.

The Oogar blinked and looked away for a long moment. "And we make each other suffer needlessly."

"We're getting them out, Arun," Cora said.

The Oogar turned away and motioned for her to follow him. After a pause, she did. She fell into step next to him, and he looked at her. "I wanted to be a Peacemaker when I was young. I wanted to do the right things. When I couldn't, I fell in with lower companions. I paid the price with my survival. My friends died stupidly, and, while I live, I cannot escape this life."

He stopped at the edge of the stables overlooking the first and second curves of the track. His mighty hands on the fence, he gripped it tightly enough she expected to see purple blood oozing between his fingers.

Slowly, he said, "But I *can* do the right thing."

"What do you mean?"

He reached into the always-full pockets of his vest and dug for a moment. He kept his hand closed and brought it up between them, close to the fence, before opening it. In his palm sat the Agamydi's effigy, clearly the genuine article, gold and undoubtedly heavy. He passed it to her. As she lifted the five-pound idol, he said, "You're going to need this."

Cora stared up at him. "I don't know what happened, Arun, but you're good people."

"I'm not people—" he chuckled with a rumble in his throat like a distant storm "—but I believe I understand."

"Thank you, Arun," Cora cradled the effigy with one hand as she adjusted the pack she wore under her vest and slipped it inside. "We'll get you out, too."

Arun shook his head in a very Human gesture. "No, Cara Long. It's best I don't. I'll land on my feet. Just get them to safety."

"I will," Cora replied. "You're a good boss, but an even better friend."

"Then I'm right to trust you. I know there are more of you, but I only know you. For that, I'm honored," Arun said softly. "Now, go. When you act, there will be chaos. Find your path, Cara Long, and travel it fast."

* * *

Reortia
Prestone

"All systems in warm shutdown. As long as they come in from the north, they won't even sniff us." Mike Carter turned in his seat to look at Tara. "We can deploy countermeasures if you want."

"I'm more worried about infrared than anything," Tara replied.

"I'll go verify," Irene Mata said, unbuckling from her copilot's seat, "but I'm thinking we parked close enough to the water's edge that we'll be okay."

Tara stared at the dense, pine-like forest in front of *Mako 15*. The mountain lake was much higher than the Agamydi compound twenty kilometers to the north. Tucked between mountains with traces of snow on their peaks, the lake's bowl was significantly colder than the lower terrain and, in theory, it would cool down their engine signatures enough to avoid a passive sensor detection.

"How cold is it outside?"

"Minus 10 Celsius," Carter replied. "Sure you don't want me to go instead, honey?"

"I've got it," Mata said and disappeared. Tara watched the two of them with the hint of a smile on her face. She admired the young couple's dedication to each other.

Maybe I'll have something like that someday. There's always hope, right?

She shook off the thought. "We've got comms with Homer and the others?"

"HF only. They should've had time to set up the repeater on the hill behind the compound by now," Carter said. Before Tara could respond, the command console dinged. "Contact 080 at fifty kilometers. Angels ten and climbing. No, leveling off. Looks like our friends have arrived."

"They've dropped their surface elements," Tara mused. She'd been on enough operations as a tank commander; she knew the drill. The Crusaders didn't field armor units unless it was with battalion-sized elements, so it was safe to assume it would be multiple skiffs carrying their infantry and some CASPers. A common, if overused, practice was to land outside enemy sensor range and offload surface elements. With a head start for the slower platforms, the dropship could arrange arrival over the objective at about the same time. The ground units were far closer and advancing. That was where Pete Brentale would be, too.

Homer's voice crackled through the cockpit speakers. "*Misfit 6, this is Misfit 1. Radio check. Over.*"

Tara tapped her headset. "Misfit 1, read you five by five. Radio silent. Contact northeast and close. Good hunting. Out."

Maarg climbed into the cockpit, and her size immediately made the normally open space feel cramped. "I'm ready, Boss."

Carter spun in his seat. "We're waiting until they drop?"

"When they do, and the Agamydi don't fight back when the Crusaders burst through those mud walls, that constitutes a hostile action. That's when we hit them," Tara replied.

"We're not carrying a ship killer, Boss," Carter said. "How am I going to shoot them down?"

Maarg chuckled. "Back on Snowmass, who took down a dropship? I did. I've got this."

"Can I ask how?"

"As soon as we start jamming them, they'll get a little surprise. I have the command system linkage software for their dropships. I'm going to land it, and Gnrra and Whirr will leave Homer in his sniper nest and clear the ship," Maarg replied. "We can then do whatever we want with it."

"No shit?" Carter replied. "Contact is twenty kilometers out, slowing and descending."

"As soon as they're low enough to mask our position, get us in the air. Maarg? Be ready to hit them as soon as we do."

The TriRusk produced her custom slate and tapped on the screen. "Ready to roll and rock."

Carter laughed. "You mean rock and roll."

Maarg chuckled. "Whatever. You know what I meant. And, yeah, Carter. No shit."

"Contact altitude is Angels five. We've masked, Boss," Carter replied as Mata re-entered the cockpit and moved to her seat. Tara saw her briefly touch her husband's shoulder before she sat down.

"Ready?" she asked.

"Uppa we go." Carter started the engines, and *Mako 15* rose into the sky.

Tara touched her headset. "Hey, E? Tell Tsan we're a go."

The Depik, currently in the bay readying weapons, replied a few seconds later. "*Message sent and received. They're go, and we're committed. Are you coming down here or not? I've almost finished your... preparations.*"

Tara took a deep breath and let it out. "Araceli? Are the girls ready to play?"

"Deathangel and Thumper are ready, boss."

Tara stood. "Here we go again."

Maarg laughed. "And we love it. Good hunting."

* * *

The Omni Racing Complex
Limerick, Prestone

Cora made her way through the stables with one hand in the pocket of her jeans. Inside, she felt two different ribbons. One was gold, meaning the mission was on. The other was red, meaning the mission was off, and they'd have to do something else. The responsibility of relaying the news to Jyrall and Larth was hers alone, and it unnerved her. As a commander, she'd become used to people relaying messages to her from different sensors and networks. This time, there would be no network, nothing in the electromagnetic spectrum. Only something she still struggled to understand.

She stood at the retaining wall near the now-empty staging area for the thoroughbreds and watched the stands fill with patrons. On the track, a single tractor dragged a large rake over the dirt of the final straightway in slow, careful paths.

Figgle and Squarlik really liked that damned tractor. She smiled. *We'll have to find them something like that on Krifay.*

Her stomach knotted on itself. *Presuming we can take it back from Smith and his band of assholes.*

Not now, Cora.

In the shadow cast over the wall and holding area by the temporary grandstands, a familiar shape appeared.

"Cora?"

"Hi, Tsan." Cora kept her eyes focused outside the area to avoid calling attention to the Depik. "Are we a go?"

"Yes, the Misfits have initiated. The Crusaders are preparing to hit the target."

Thank heavens.

With a deep sigh, Cora pushed back from the wall. "You might want to get out of here."

"I'll ensure your safe escape first," Tsan replied. "I believe you Humans like the phrase 'good luck' in these situations."

"Some do," Cora said. "I don't. There's nothing lucky about this business."

"I would agree," Tsan replied and started to fade away. "I prefer good hunting."

Cora pulled out the ribbons and selected the gold. She pulled her long, dark hair back and secured it with the ribbon. She stood there a moment longer until the tractor approached before turning into the stables. As she did, she saw Figgle adjust an armband to ensure the gold side was out.

Okay, Jyrall. There's your signal.

I hope this works, and I get to see you again.

* * * * *

Chapter Twenty-Four

The Omni Racing Complex

Limerick, Prestone

Larth, in his full Weezik regalia, made his way into the VIP box and immediately chatted up Hatfield with a series of loud, inane questions. Keaton, as his security team leader, spoke briefly with the Oogar named Brusk, which left Jyrall and Ricky to assume their normal positions in the rear of the box and scan the crowd. Around them, the stands filled with patrons. Alcohol and other substances flowed freely, and the atmosphere inside the racing complex surpassed electric. To Jyrall, it was perfect.

All they need is a strike on the match.

He turned his attention to the tractor dragging the dirt section of the track. Trying not to stare, he followed it for a long—

There! Figgle's armband.

Gold.

We're go.

His heart thudded in his chest a little more, knowing the operation on both continents was about to happen.

He turned to Ricky and pressed close. "Armband."

Ricky's head snapped to the track, and then back to a scanning motion. He nodded solemnly but said nothing. Instead, he raised his slate and tapped it once. Jyrall's slate buzzed twice, as he knew both Keaton and Larth's had done. Everyone now knew the operation was on.

As soon as the casino shut down all bets, a series of commands would stream through the casino's network, or, if they didn't for some reason, and more confusion reigned, then Ricky would activate it. The slot machines would cash out immediately, whether they were in use or not. Roulette wheels would seize. Across the casino, chip counters would immediately add between 100 and 5,000 percent to every active account. The presence of machines spouting credits would create pandemonium, and security would react to that distraction, while the computers chewed through the casino's funds and paid out to every customer with the adjusted percentages. For Ricky Shit, it was a whole new level. While he worried it wouldn't work, he also knew his friends were the best in the business. And they'd had a little help along the way.

Jyrall went through their exit strategy in his head. Getting from the VIP booth to their suite would be difficult if a full-fledged riot broke out. To that end, they'd arranged for a private vehicle to be staged at the valet parking area for the complex. The five Lumar would be imposing enough to keep away interested aggressors, but the real protection between them and the vehicle would be Nails and May. The two of them had disguised themselves as patrons and would be a critical link in getting them to the vehicles and out of the complex.

If all goes well, I'll see you in a few hours, Cora.

Things are about to get very interesting.

* * *

Reortia

Prestone

Pete looked over his troops. Sergeant First Class Wilson and the rest wore mottled green and brown uniforms and pieces of light battle armor. They had the same protection as the Crusaders, but didn't look as pristine.

"Staff Sergeant Jerund, are you sure you can operate this model?" Pete asked.

"Yes, sir. Normally Haney does the driving, but we'll get there in one piece."

Major Sciortino shook his head. "One piece? That's the latest model. We haven't had any issues with them. It had better be in one piece." He looked skeptically at the mercs on the skiff. "Are you sure they're up to the task?"

"They're good troops," Pete reassured him. "It's not like we'll take fire. It'll be fine. We'll follow your skiff."

"Well, let's move, then," Sciortino said. "As soon as I board our skiff, we're going. The Angels will be ready to jump any minute. I appreciate the tank of jump juice your people brought."

"I only have my machine and a few others left. It's not like we were going to use it anytime soon." Pete stroked his beard. "I guess I could have jumped with your troops."

"No, I think having you with your platoon works best. You and I will keep a tight rein on our troops. That's the best way to ensure no one opens fire on them. We want every adult in a cage, not dead."

"I hear you."

Minutes later, Pete heard the command as they raced toward the village compound. "*Ivanhoe*, you are clear to make the drop."

The pilot answered, "*Roger, sir. Light is green.*"

Moments later. "*This Angel 1. All CASPers in the green. We'll be boots down in ninety seconds.*"

"As soon as you touch down, get them into position," Sciortino ordered.

There was no resistance from the Agamydi—not that any had been expected. To everyone's surprise, the racers ran with their young ones in tow. They slipped into the trees on the east hillside before the perimeter was fully closed.

"Dammit!" Sciortino shouted. "They heard the rockets on the CASPers as they descended."

"They can't go far," Pete said. "This valley narrows on both ends."

"True," Sciortino said. He engaged his comms. "All right, people, we're not chasing them down yet. Set the perimeter."

He turned to one of the Crusaders. "Sergeant Barlon, grab your team and follow me. We're going to see if we can find anything. Colonel, are you with me?"

"Affirmative."

As they moved toward the closest hut, Pete said, "I guess I should have planned for the Agamydi to run like they did." He looked around and made a mental note of how the Crusaders set up security when they stopped moving. "Maybe we should have slipped in from our side and put troops in place."

"Nothing we can do about it now," Sciortino said. He ducked into the hut. Pete followed.

Minutes later, Sciortino shouted, "Pete! Take a look at this." He held a basket woven from grasses. It held a handful of precious stones and several quarter-inch-sized gold nuggets.

"Now *this* is what I'm talking about! I knew we'd find something." He grinned like a child. Sciortino spoke over the command net again. "Search the huts! Forget the perimeter. I want everyone searching the huts. Now!"

* * *

Reortia

Prestone

"Misfit 6, we've got hostiles out the door. Two skiffs approaching from the north," Homer reported over the radio. They were risking detection, but it would be too late for the Crusaders.

"Pull us up, Carter!" Tara ordered. *Mako 15* shot into the sky. "Maarg?"

"Jammers are on. They've got nothing in the spectrum. Launching control software on the dropship," Maarg replied. "I've got it. The *Ivanhoe*? What in the hell is that supposed to be?"

"Old Human novel about a knight returning from the Crusades," Tara replied.

"Figures." Maarg's digits flew on the slate. "I've got them. Emergency engine shutdown in progress. Knocked out a pivot thruster—they'll spin back into our landing spot."

As *Mako 15* cleared the trees and shot down slope from the higher terrain, Tara saw the *Ivanhoe* lurch wildly to the right and spin backward away from the Agamydi village. The ship never departed controlled flight, with Maarg guiding it down. It was quite a sight, and Tara had to tear her eyes from it.

"Whirr? Gnrra? Go," she called into the radio.

"Boss, we've gotta go!" Araceli called from the drop bay.

Carter turned over his shoulder. "We've got this, ma'am."

Tara dropped through the cockpit hatch and ran down the length of *Mako 15's* main hull to the drop bay. Eponil scowled at her as she climbed up into the Mk 8.

"Twenty seconds from drop," Eponil said. "You wouldn't be able to do this without her."

"I know," Tara replied as she dropped, legs first, into the cockpit. "Nike, we're go for operations."

<<Affirmative. CASPer mode engaged on Deathangel and Thumper.>> Nike's interface would work with both CASPers as they dropped, to feed information much like Lucille had done. While Nike was more than capable, Tara realized the void Lucille's absence brought.

There has to be another way to get her here. Or we turn Nike loose.

She closed the cockpit and walked Deathangel off its maintenance rack as she'd done a hundred times, but she hesitated. During her last combat operation, she'd lost her legs. Her unit had been all but eradicated by the Crusaders. Friends had died. The mix of emotions rose, and she quelled them and used them to focus.

"Ten seconds," Carter called.

"Q?" Tara called to Quin'taa at the door. With his railgun, ammunition pack, and parachute, the Oogar seemed twice his massive size. "You're first. Full melee. Take them all down, and watch out for the Barnstormers."

"Go!"

Quin'taa stepped forward and fell through the open bay door. He'd HALD to the ground. Given their rapidly decreasing altitude, she and Araceli wouldn't bother with parachutes—only the upgraded jump jets.

Araceli walked Thumper out the door, and Tara followed.

<<Whirr and Gnrra are aboard the *Ivanhoe* and are clearing the ship. Homer has identified and painted all Barnstormer targets with no-shoot markers,>> Nike reported.

Tara drew a breath and activated the command frequency. "All right, Misfits, weapons free. Take them down."

* * *

The Omni Racing Complex
Limerick, Prestone

Cora climbed into the driver's seat of the recovery truck. Figgle sat on the passenger seat of the two-being compartment. Squarlik rode in the open back of the truck. All of them had weapons on their persons, as well as stored in the van itself. As the truck rolled slowly through the support corridor toward the ramp down to the maintenance level and their target, they saw the passage blocked by two armed K'kng guards.

"Shit," Cora muttered. One of the guards started toward her with a scowl on its face, and then froze. She caught sight of Arun hobbling toward the rear of the van, waving at the guards.

"Let them pass!" Arun called waving a radio. "Didn't you hear me?"

The K'kng shook his head. "What's the problem?"

"Bad circuit in the starter box! They have to go now!" Arun roared. The K'kng stepped aside, and Cora edged forward. "No, Cara Long! Go! You've got three minutes to fix it!"

Three minutes. Gods, he gave us the timeline and got us through.

Thank you, Arun.

Cora pushed the accelerator, and the truck raced down the ramp.

"Is three minutes enough time to get the box open?" Cora asked Figgle.

In one of his claws was a small torch. "Squarlik and I practiced yesterday. We opened a hole large enough in just over two minutes."

Cora blew out her breath in a burst. "Going to be tight."

Figgle moved to the middle of the compartment and slid open the hatch separating them from the cargo area. "Squarlik has the ladder in place. I'll tell you when to stop, ma'am, and then we'll get started."

Cora nodded. "You've got it, Top. Good luck."

The Goka disappeared, and Cora drove into the maintenance level under the track, toward the marked starting line and the connected port where the starter's gate mounted into the concrete and steel ceiling. Without additional brackets or support, the metal would be accessible. Provided it was similar to what Figgle and Squarlik had practiced on, they'd have enough time.

Let's hope.

She snorted. Hope wasn't a method, after all. There were only a handful of beings she trusted like her first sergeant. Goka or not, he was a professional. They'd get the job done. The next part was up to Cora.

She reached into the center console and ensured her pistol was there. Along with the slim, curved Goka rifle Figgle had loaded into his side of the compartment and whatever Squarlik had brought along in the rear compartment and would use through the roof hatch, it would have to be enough.

The target came into view. She slowed and lined the truck up with the side of the box closest to the stands.

Here we go.

"Forward," Figgle called. Cora worked the brake pedal carefully as the truck idled forward. "Another half meter. Slow now. Slow. Stop!"

She heard the pop of their torches lighting and took a deep breath to calm her racing heart.

* * *

Omni Main Casino

May walked down the wide hallway. She was conscious of the looks she received. She knew the dress was tight, probably a little too tight, but it was all part of the disguise. As she walked, she felt for the ring on her pinky. It wasn't one she normally wore. In fact, she never had.

When she got to the bank of slot machines Ricky had described, she sat down at one, and fed it a dozen credits. She glanced around to ensure no one was nearby. It wouldn't do for the machines near her to be in use. They might get the same results. She turned her body slightly to keep the obvious cameras from seeing her hand.

She hit the button, and, as the screen showed spinning symbols, she twisted the jewelry on the ring counterclockwise one and a half turns. When the symbols quit spinning, the alarm went off, and colors flashed from the light on top. She had three bars across the center line, and several more on the screen, giving her multiple wins. The credits available kept climbing so fast, she couldn't see the numbers.

She twisted the stone twice more before the roving pit boss was close enough to see her do it.

"Congratulations, ma'am."

"Thanks!" May beamed. "I've never won this much before! I could buy a house with this! I'm cashing out right now, so I don't lose a single credit of it." She pushed the button to get her printout.

The pit boss pursed his lips. This wasn't how it was supposed to go. He, like everyone working the floor, wanted anyone who won to be so excited and into the moment that they didn't think straight and kept gambling to see if they could win more. Greed was a powerful tool the casino relied upon.

May knew this and grinned even more. She slipped her arm in his, reached over, and patted him on the stomach. "Would you be a darling and show me to the teller so I can get my credits for this ticket?"

* * *

Omni Racing Complex

Hatfield looked around. Something seemed… off. *Someone?* He ran his hand over his head, pulling his dirty blond hair back away from his face. It fell back into place, long on each side. *The Crusaders. Where are the Crusaders? Sciortino and the mercenary?*

He pulled a small slate out of a pocket and searched by name for Major Sciortino. It was on the list with a bet of 500 credits on number three. The fool had bet on a lane without knowing anything at all about the racer slotted in it. Granted, it wasn't like horse or dog racing, where you could look at the past performances, but the idiot didn't even know whether it was a male or female running in the slot.

Hell, he doesn't know if it'll be a scratch with no racer at all in the lane.

He figured Sciortino was watching on one of the screens inside the casino with his new friend. Out of curiosity, he looked for another name. It was there, along with the twelve million credits bet on lane six. True to his word, Weezik had added ten million to his winnings to make his bet.

"Problems?" Larth asked.

Hatfield looked to his left as the one-eyed Zuparti settled back into his seat with a fresh drink in hand. It took him a minute to get his bright orange, waist-length cape into place.

"Not at all. I was just admiring the zeros on your bet."

"I'm going to win. Just watch," Larth said, staying in character.

"I reckon you might. You've been tearing it up all over the place the last day or so."

"I'm a winner," Larth said with an air of arrogance. "Winners win."

"Right now you are," Hatfield admitted, "but that might change when the big female in lane one wins this dang thing. Either way, you ain't breaking the house. Take a look at this."

He held his slate so Larth could see the tallies rise from all the bets. The numbers were astronomical. Hatfield and the Omni were in no danger of losing credits, even though there would be winners. The odds of every single bet being on the right racer was beyond comprehension, and even with the odds, it wasn't happening today. The tallies showed bets across all the lanes. Hundreds of millions would be made today.

"Impressive," Larth admitted.

"Yep."

Hatfield watched the tallies and the time. When the bets tailed off, he knew it was because the windows had closed, and the online wagers were stopped. It was time for the race.

He spoke into the same device. "Get them in there and let's get this thing started."

"Yes, sir," a voice answered. Hatfield settled back and waited.

The crowd broke into a deafening roar when they realized the race was about to begin. The effigy came up, and the crazed crowd got even louder. Hatfield squinted slightly. *Wait… the Agamydi should be loud enough to hear, even with all this ruckus.*

Hatfield stood and turned toward Brusk. One of Weezik's security guards was in the way. It was the big Besquith. He leaned to one side and caught a glimpse of the Oogar beyond the big guard. Hatfield opened his mouth to shout past him.

The bell went off, and all hell *didn't* break loose.

*****

Chapter Twenty-Five

Mako 15

Reortia

Araceli stepped off *Mako 15's* ramp and oriented her Mk 7 CASPer, Thumper, with its feet toward the ground. Her own feet flexed against the jump jet pedals, ready to counter gravity and decelerate her fall toward the Agamydi compound below. She marked the location of the approaching skiffs and the Crusader CASPers on the ground. Infantry and what looked like support personnel moved from hovel to hovel, searching. There were no Agamydi to be seen, which gave her a little solace. From Tara's briefing, Pete Brentale of the Barnstormers was on the ground and had selected this site for several reasons—one of the primary ones being that, without walls to keep out other, more aggressive fauna, they had a fast avenue of retreat.

"*Eyes on*," Tara called over the radio.

Araceli saw the quick opening of a parachute at the lower edge of her limited peripheral vision as Quin'taa activated his parachute, and then just as quickly cut it away. The Oogar appeared to drop, quite literally, on top of a Crusader Mk 8 CASPer, driving it into the ground before disabling it with a blast from his railgun. Two nearby CASPers turned slowly, as if shocked by his appearance. They brought up their weapons, but Araceli was far ahead of them. She'd selected the MAC on Thumper's left shoulder and tracked both CASPers using Nike's passive targeting systems. As soon as the second reticle locked, she squeezed her left hand into a fist, and the MAC thumped out two quick rounds at each Crusader. Both went down without firing a shot.

Quin'taa was moving now, cutting through the infantry like a hot knife through Jeha waste. Had she not seen it before, the ferocity and speed would have taken her breath away. Her friend and "big brother" was a natural killing machine.

<<Altitude. Altitude.>>

Araceli pressed down on Thumper's pedals, and the CASPer steadied and thrust against gravity. At three meters off the surface, she cut the thrusters and let the CASPer fall to the ground. She barely registered the impact as she identified, targeted, and engaged two more CASPers. Neither went down, but she had their attention. They moved between the hovels as if trying to counterattack. One leapt into the air, and she tracked it for a half second before a stream of MAC fire almost tore it in half. Deathangel landed, and then bounced again into the air above the compound.

"*Bounce, Araceli! Hit them from above.*"

Araceli stomped on the pedals, and Thumper shot into the sky.

<<Targeting upload. Active targets are marked.>>

Red icons overlaid on her viewscreens. All the Crusader CASPers were marked, and so were…

"All the infantry," Araceli said. "What in the hell?"

<<All Crusaders have been targeted by internal protected linkages.>>

"*You've got targeting, Misfits. Light them up!*" Tara called over their frequency. "*Maarg? What are you doing? How did you get active targeting up? Nike can't do that yet.*"

"*Ricky Shit.*" Maarg laughed. "*His chip following program is a passive sensor system. I left it on, I guess, and Nike used it to pinpoint their positions.*"

"*We'll figure it out later,*" Tara called. "*Nike? Mark all non-tracked as friendlies. Withhold targeting on them.*"

<<Acknowledged.>>

Blue icons came on the screen. Araceli bounced again and centered her MAC on another CASPer. It raised hand cannons toward her, and she shot them out of the Mk 8's hands before sending another volley through the cockpit section. She turned back to scan for Quin'taa and saw him drop the railgun, its ammunition expended against the Crusader's infantry, and charge headlong into the back of an unsuspecting CASPer.

"Nike?" Araceli asked. "Are there any more CASPers?"

<<Negative.>>

"Does anyone have eyes on Pete?" Tara called. "Nike? Can you pick him out?"

<<Negative.>>

"*I had him a second ago,*" Homer called. "*Hang on a second.*"

"*Boss, permission to land?*" Carter radioed.

"Negative. Let's secure the objective and put down the resistance," Tara replied. "Homer? Find Pete!"

* * *

Village Compound

Reortia

Prestone

Everything had fallen apart too fast. There was no communication. No command and control. No ability to move his troops. The CASPers went one way, and the infantry went another. The only people who looked and acted like they had a clue were the remnants of the Island Storms and Brentale. His eyes locked on Brentale's men, and he saw them maneuvering from hovel to hovel like a well-coordinated and trained unit, but they didn't fire on the enemy raining death from the sky.

Sciortino's blood boiled. He darted out of a hovel, leaving behind a lifetime's fortune in gold nuggets, to charge right at Brentale.

"You! You sonuvabitch! You're one of them!" He broke into a sprint. Brentale was fifty meters away with his back turned. More cannon fire sounded behind him. He spun and saw two black-painted CASPers jumping across the compound, firing a stream of MAC rounds and hand cannon fire. He turned back toward Brentale and saw an Oogar roaring and charging through second squad, leaving nothing but corpses in its wake.

What the fuck?

He drew a breath. "Pete! You're one of them!"

Brentale turned toward him. The man's face was calm and stern. He didn't raise a weapon.

His mistake.

Sciortino brought up his pistol. Ten meters away, and moving closer, all he had to do was center the sight on the traitor's chest. There was no way he could—

* * *

Homer pulled the trigger and dropped the Crusader major with one shot through his left temple.

"*Gotcha.*"

"*Nice shot, Homer,*" Tara called. "*I've got no more targets. Confirm?*"

No one responded by their SOP. With nothing in sight and all resistance quelled there was no reason to reply.

"*Everybody up?*" Tara asked.

"*Up,*" Quin'taa called.

"*Up,*" Homer replied. "*Moving your direction from the east.*"

"*Up,*" Araceli responded.

"*Up,*" Whirr replied. "*Gnrra is with me, and we have total control of the* Ivanhoe."

"*Stand by,*" Tara called. "*I've patched in the Barnstormers. You there, Pete?*"

"*Roger, Tara. Nice work,*" Pete replied. "*Which one of you got Sciortino before he got me?*"

"*That would be me,*" Homer said. "*Homer, sir.*"

"*What do you drink?*" Pete asked.

Homer laughed. "*I like dark beers, sir.*"

Pete chuckled. "*That's a case on me. Tara? Recommend we transition to phase three.*"

Araceli squinted. *What does that mean? We only talked about actions on the objective.*

"*Confirmed, Pete,*" Tara replied. "*Maarg? Get ready to crash that drop-ship into one of the swamps as soon as we get what's left of the Crusaders aboard.*"

There was a pause, and she heard Quin'taa quietly ask, "*What about survivors?*"

"*Check. If you find any, we'll treat them,*" Tara replied. "*I'm not sure I left any. After Snowmass, none of these assholes deserve to live.*"

* * *

Omni Racetrack

The crowd was silent. When the chutes sprang open, nothing happened. The crazed racers they expected to see didn't come tearing out of the box in a mad dash. The effigy zipped along on its track, but nothing chased it. The murmurs started to build.

Larth stood up and shouted, "Hey! What the... I demand my credits back!" He pointed at Hatfield. "There's no race, and I want them all right now. Give. Me. My. Credits!"

Those around them joined in with their own demands. Across the entire crowd, the outrage exploded. Attendees screamed in anger. Servers and staff were accosted. Seats were ripped from their brackets by some of the stronger patrons. Windows were smashed in the private booths. Security all around the stands found themselves facing beings of multiple races, all demanding the same thing.

It got even worse when the track announcer called the race a default. He didn't say bets would be refunded. That detail didn't go unnoticed.

* * *

Keaton winked at his brother and input a short code into his handheld computer. It sent a signal to the ring May had tested, which was now in the front coat pocket of the unsuspecting slot machine pit boss. The final twists to the stone had increased its range. He was standing among the biggest cluster, keeping an eye on things, when alarms, bells, whistles, and flashing lights went off all over the large room. Everyone was winning mega-jackpots.

The same signal reached a dozen pseudo-magnets on the roulette wheels. Earlier, Private Tivlang had followed his instructions without deviation. He'd blundered his way around all of them, placing a small bet and losing every time. He'd slammed the table with three of his fists in frustration while the fourth stuck one of the magnets out of sight as the backing matched the table. The pit boss had him removed from the room after seeing enough of his antics. She never once suspected a dimwitted Lumar of attempting to influence the wheels with a sophisticated device.

All the balls landed on red. The next two spins were red. Noticing this, several patrons bet on red. Soon, everyone was putting credit on red at every table. It came up every time. The dealers attempted to manipulate the wheels with and without directions from their pit boss, but the pressure points wouldn't work. It was red, red, red, like the profit loss in the room.

Sure of his brother's Ricky Shit and his own programming, Keaton slipped the small computer into his inside jacket pocket in time to dodge a flying bottle. The arena was chaos.

* * *

Jyrall stepped closer to Larth as fights broke out among the attendees in their box. Track security attempted to break them up and found themselves fighting for their own survival. He saw Larth grab Hatfield by his shirt, look up, and demand his credits. Two men fighting stumbled into them. Hatfield used it to break Larth's hold, slip past the two men, and head for the exit.

Keaton and Ricky pushed and shoved to create a hole of sorts for Larth to follow Hatfield. Jyrall made his way behind them, occasionally knocking someone out of the way. He'd almost made it to the exit to follow when Brusk stepped in front of him.

Finally.

Jyrall felt his rage build. Part of it was because he knew it was bound to happen, and he'd prepared himself mentally every time he saw him. The other part was instinct among his race. A challenge must be answered.

The big Oogar growled and tensed, ready to attack. Jyrall never gave him the chance. He caught Hatfield's personal security guard with a right hook and dropped him on the spot. Jyrall felt the jaw crack when he hit him. He stepped over the unconscious Oogar and made his way to the exit.

* * *

Maintenance Level
The Omni Racing Complex
Limerick, Prestone

"They're in!" Squarlik called from the rear of the truck.

"Doors," Cora ordered.

The van had been modified with a type of pocket door that fired closed with a small explosive charge. Designed to trap the enraged Agamydi at the end of a race, it might have been overkill with them calmly loaded against the cab wall of the truck, but it saved time. Figgle fired the doors closed as Cora slammed the ancient standard transmission truck into first gear and mashed the accelerator to the floor.

"Squarlik, get up in the hatch with that weapon," Figgle commanded. "Watch for the upper—"

"Gate!" Squarlik yelped as red lights flashed along the maintenance tunnel's walls.

Cora saw the inner security gate sliding closed. She worked the clutch, slammed the truck into third gear, and pushed the gas pedal to the floorboard. "Hang on!"

The black-painted, chain-link fence shot across its roller system in front of the truck from both sides. Cora saw it nearly close as the truck's front end slammed into the fence. Metal screeched as the fence rode up the hood. Cora saw sparks flash as the gate was ripped apart and fell away to either side. The truck hardly decelerated as they raced up the ramp into the curving tunnel under the racetrack's first turn.

"Exciting," Figgle said, deadpan. He reached with two appendages to the floorboard, pulled up a rifle, and worked the action. "Where are we going?"

Cora shifted into fourth gear. The speedometer in the truck, like most of its systems, no longer worked. It had served a simple, slow mission over its long life. Tires squealed against the concrete ramp as they raced toward the main entrance. Around the curving wall, the two K'kng security guards appeared with their weapons raised. They opened fire.

"Now, Squarlik!" Figgle maneuvered his rifle out the truck's passenger window. He fired, but with little accuracy. Squarlik didn't appear to have much luck until she saw the K'kng on the left stagger after being hit in its tactical vest. Two rounds punched through the glass between her and Figgle and embedded in the wall. Cora lowered her head to where her eyes were slightly above the ratty dashboard. For the briefest second, she thought the staggering K'kng locked eyes with her. In seemingly slow motion, its weapon came up and sighted directly at her. Cora squeezed the steering wheel so tight she thought it might break. And then a purple blur tore into the K'kng and threw it across the tunnel.

Arun!

The Oogar roared, and the second K'kng turned and fired its rifle multiple times into Arun's chest. He staggered, but swung a powerful clawed hand at the K'kng's head as their bodies crashed together. Dark blood sprayed from the K'kng's neck across the tunnel wall as it fell. Arun toppled over and rolled, his face looking at the truck. He tried to prop himself up on one arm, but couldn't. As they passed, Cora let off the accelerator.

Arun waved an arm, and she heard him scream, "Go!"

Cora accelerated again, and her eyes shifted to the side mirror. Arun's head fell to the concrete floor behind them. Her chest tightened, and fresh anger surfaced. Her friend had sacrificed himself. There was no way they could fail now. They raced up through the tunnel into the main concourse.

"Hang on!" Cora called as she yanked the wheel into a tight right turn. Beings scattered around them. She saw several security officers rush into the complex itself as they raced through the backlot and onto the main road. "Figgle, navigate us to the airfield."

"First turn in three lights," Figgle replied as they barreled through an intersection with a green light.

"Squarlik, is anyone hurt?"

The response took a few seconds. "No, ma'am. All twelve are okay."

Cora's mind raced. Any Crusaders at the airfield presented a threat they needed to avoid. Likewise, they'd need to avoid their own ship to allow Jyrall and Larth a way out of the city, while not casting any scrutiny on them. "Is Haney ready?"

Figgle tapped on the slate resting between them on the seat. "*Specialist Haney*," a sleepy voice drawled.

"Haney, are you at the airfield?" Cora asked. "We're gonna need a ship. Fast. One with range. Weapons ain't important."

The perennial specialist laughed. "*I got you, ma'am. Y'all just get to the southeast FBO. I got us a ship.*"

"We'll be there in six minutes," Cora replied. Figgle and Squarlik had driven the route a dozen times and timed it. All they had to do was get there.

"*I'll need three, ma'am. Out here.*"

"FBO?" Figgle asked. "An acronym. I'm assuming the F is for—"

"Fixed." Cora laughed. "Fixed base operations, where civilians park their aircraft. There's no telling what that guy's found."

"Or how much it's going to cost us," Figgle replied. After a moment he said, "Again."

* * * * *

Chapter Twenty-Six

Management Offices

Omni Casino

Hatfield threw his slate across the room, and it shattered a vase on a shelf. The Miderall vase was over three thousand years old, and extremely rare. The dull grays and muted browns were indicators of its age. One of the main reasons it was so rare was because the Unified Government of Miderall had enacted a task force to scour the known galaxy and buy back the ugly products of its past. The entire race was horrified at the thought of colorless items representing their artwork, even if it had been made centuries ago.

Hatfield slowly shook his head. What was another million credits? The casino had lost hundreds so far today. He turned back to Randazzo.

"Do we have a total yet?" he asked.

"No, sir," Randazzo answered. He ran his hand down his face and cupped his chin for a moment. "It's in the hundreds of millions of potential winnings from the race, but it was never run, so it can't really be claimed. Somewhere between eight to ten million actual credits, before I could fully shut down everything."

"Damn. You couldn't stop them before it got that high?"

"They were racing to the various windows to cash in slot machine receipts. Hard credits were given on the roulette wheels."

"Fucking red," Hatfield said. "That's the same color that damned Weezik won on."

"Do you think he had anything to do with it?" Randazzo asked.

"How the hell would I know?" Hatfield asked. "He was in the executive box with me when everything went to shit. You're the expert. You tell me."

"My people are looking into it. It takes time to investigate."

"Well, you'd better make it fast," Hatfield said. "As in our-jobs-depend-on-it fast."

"The security programs have to run. We'll figure out what happened." He sat down in one of the chairs in front of Hatfield's desk. "Speaking of fast, you should have seen some of the guests. I've never seen a Jeha move that fast. Its legs were a blur. What I did see was the receipt it waved in a front pincer as it ran by, chittering about 500,000 credits."

The hospitality manager knocked on the door jamb. "Mr. Hatfield, we've started checking out guests. They aren't happy about it. We had several walk right past the reception counter without bothering to check out, much less pay their bill."

"Fuck."

"That's not the biggest issue I have," she said.

"Make sure you keep a spreadsheet of them," Randazzo suggested before she could continue. "If we don't get our credits, they'll be banned from here, and all the other casinos. That's the kind of thing we all work together on."

"Well, the reason I came down here myself is to let you know we don't have a list of the guests this week. It's been erased from our system *and* the backup system. It's even gone from the secure files we pay a company to maintain offsite."

"No list?" Hatfield asked. "Not one?"

"Everyone's listed as Mr. or Ms. Smith, even those who aren't Human. I mean, some of my staff remember names, and we're compiling that list, but we have no proof they were here this week. Not even the regulars. All records of payments received for rooms are gone as well."

"Well, match them with security footage, facial recognition, or whatever."

Randazzo stood. "The security footage has been erased," he admitted. His people were supposed to keep the system from getting hacked. "I need to go see about this and add it to the list."

The lead pit boss stepped into the office before he could leave. "Mr. Randazzo, we think we have something."

"Show me." He turned back to Hatfield. "I'll let you know."

Hatfield watched them leave his office. He put his hands behind his head and slowly leaned back. He was staring at the ceiling when he felt a presence. He leaned forward to see Brusk standing in his doorway. The big Oogar was holding his jaw and leaning on the opposite doorjamb.

"You owe Rmaska Corporation fifteen million credits," Brusk said through clenched teeth.

"I got that," Hatfield said.

"Beyond what is in our vaults."

"I said, I got that," Hatfield answered again. He let his exasperation come through in his voice.

"And that's just to start," Brusk warned. "There'll be a tally later for physical damages to the property beyond the loss of gambling profit."

"I got it!" Hatfield said. "Give me twelve hours."

Brusk glared at him. For a moment, Hatfield feared he'd cross the room in a couple of long strides, slam his body against the wall, and pin it there to ensure the demands of the Rmaska Cooperation were understood. They'd sold him the casino, as far as the regulators knew, but their pockets were deep, and their leashes were short. Kr'et'Socae had kept them at bay out of abject fear. Since he'd disappeared—or lost his nerve, whatever the case—they'd become more involved. Now, Hatfield knew the score. They wouldn't stop until they got their credits. Thankfully, he had plenty.

Instead, the Oogar turned and walked away, still holding his jaw. Hatfield let out the breath he hadn't realized he was holding.

Twelve hours.

* * *

Front Entrance

Omni Resort

Larth glanced sideways and saw Randazzo come through the front doors. Keaton stepped closer to Larth. Jyrall and Ricky were busy ensuring the security guards escorting them from the Embassy Tower and out of the building didn't lay a hand on any of the luggage or the ladies.

"You can just step aside," Randazzo said to Keaton. "I'd like a word with Mr. Weezik. A *private* word."

Keaton started to speak, but Randazzo interrupted him. "And before you say anything, my family is somewhere safe. Somewhere you don't know about."

Larth unbuttoned his vest, turned to Keaton, and indicated the two long hovercraft being loaded. Keaton glanced at where Larth kept his backup pistols, nodded once, and walked away.

"Something on your mind?" Larth asked. "Besides the substandard service this place provides, of course. My assistant had to locate rides for us. One was not provided."

"Yeah, something is on my mind," Randazzo said. "This."

He held a ring in the palm of his hand. The edges of the stone looked charred. The Ricky Shit built into the ring included self-destruction. The hardware inside had been destroyed, taking the programming with it.

"Hey," Larth said. "That looks like my ring." He held up his hand and showed the security manager the ring on his hand. It had an actual stone in it. "This is preposterous. I was told my ring was unique. If you have one, then any riff-raff in the galaxy can get one."

Randazzo stiffened. "I think you had something to do with this, Weezik. You'll hear from us regarding damages."

"Oh, it's Weezik now, is it?" Larth asked. "Not *Mister* Weezik?"

Randazzo continued, "If you ever step into one of our casinos again, we'll take decisive and final action. You've been warned. *Mister* Weezik."

Larth stepped close to the security manager and reached into his vest.

"The next time I walk into your casino, Mr. Randazzo, I'm coming directly for *you*."

Larth flashed the Peacemaker's badge in the palm of his hand. He held it so no one else could see and out of the line of sight of any cameras. He didn't think the technicians inside had managed to get them working again after Keaton's program bomb destroyed all electronic systems in the building, but it was better to be safe than sorry.

The badge disappeared as quickly as it came out. "I don't think you're stuck here. I think you *chose* this job, and that was a mistake. Call it professional courtesy, but if I were you, I'd get my family and take a freighter back to Earth to rethink my life."

Larth left Randazzo staring, his face ashen white, as he climbed into the back seat of the hovercraft. He grinned at Jyrall and reached up to take his eyepatch off. Larth heard a familiar voice come from the driver's seat over the intercom.

"Welcome to Conner's Getaway Service. Where to?"

"Specialist Conner?" Larth said. "Who's driving the other hovercraft?"

"Specialist Anderson."

"Where did you get two… Never mind. Something tells me Haney was involved. Take us to the airfield. We have a rendezvous to make."

They were thrown back slightly as Conner whipped the craft around the half-moon-shaped drive and into the main street traffic. Larth removed the lens from his eye. He blinked a few times and continued to take off pieces of clothing.

Jyrall lifted his brow when Larth carefully folded the orange cape. Larth caught him watching. "Hey, don't say a word, Snarlyface. I'm not keeping any of this gaudy shit. Stew and Monty asked if they could have it when the mission was over. There's no way you'd catch me willfully wearing orange and blue together ever again."

* * *

Reortia

Cora approached the cockpit of the Airmaster private exocraft Specialist Haney had… procured from the airfield. The young man had sworn everything was on the up and up, but hadn't told her what the actual cost was. They could settle the balance sheets later. There were far more important things to get done.

She'd managed an hour nap on the intercontinental flight. The Airmaster could operate hypersonically, but Prestone's air traffic control would only let them get away with Mach 4.5. While the speed cut down their travel time considerably, there had still been a chance to rest and, more importantly, to get her thoughts together. When she'd woken, though, her thoughts were front and center.

The Agamydi were clustered in the rear of the exocraft's cabin. They'd boarded in a very agitated state. Whether it was the movement or the slight amount of white noise from the Airmaster's plush cabin, they'd calmed down. Many appeared to be sleeping. The big female, though, was staring at Cora when she opened her eyes.

"Do you have a name?" the Agamydi said. "The Oogar called you Caralong."

"Cora," she replied. "Cora McCoy."

"A lie?" The Agamydi blinked.

Cora licked her lips and drew a breath before answering. "A deception. You knew Arun was an Oogar, and you know what a translator is, and it worked for you. I believe you know as much about deception as we do."

"Fair point." The Agamydi considered the cluster of her people for a moment. "My name is Rarkanta. Our people know and understand the Galactic Union, even as we have shunned it. The loss of our gods caused a war across our lands. We vowed, with our enemies, not to enter the Union until our conflict was resolved."

"You've fought for how long?"

"Two hundred years."

"Both sides agreed not to join the Union?" Cora asked. "Who is your enemy?"

Rarkanta replied slowly. "They are the Narrith. I am hopeful we can have peace so our peoples can become far more than we are."

"Two hundred years is a long time."

Rarkanta purred. "It is. We believed the Narrith stole our gods. They believed we stole it back. No one knew where it was. How the Yellow Human found it is a mystery."

Cora smiled. "You have it now. Let's hope for peace."

"You are a most curious Human, Cora McCoy. Are you a Peacemaker?"

She laughed. "No, but you're going to meet a couple very soon."

"They will help us settle the war. This is a good thing," Rarkanta replied before turning back to her group. Cora went forward with a smile on her face.

"How close are we?"

"Ten minutes," Haney replied. "We're descending, but I'm taking it easy. Running sensor sweeps. You know, that whole SOP thing."

Cora grinned. "I'm impressed you're following it."

"I'm flying the colonel. Even though you don't command my unit, it makes me behave a little."

"You might have to be my permanent pilot, Haney."

"Oh, let's not go that far, ma'am. Besides, I don't think Colonel Brentale will let me go anywhere. I'm just on temporary assignment."

Cora tapped the radio controls and dialed up the frequency Pete had provided. "Lindbergh, this is Earhart. Do you read?"

"*Got you, Earhart. I have our mutual friends on the line. We're in position and will rendezvous with you on the objective. We're expecting hostile contact as soon as you touch down. We'll be overhead and ready to drop.*"

Cora nodded. "Understand. Set weapons tight and towed. I think we're going to be okay."

"*There's these croc things, Earhart. Watched them eat through CASPers pretty easily.*" Pete Brentale sounded spooked.

"Roger, Lindbergh. Y'all are gonna have to trust me."

"*I was afraid you were going to say that,*" Pete replied. "*Good luck. Lindbergh, out.*"

* * *

To Cora's amazement, Haney found a tight landing zone near the temple, expertly guided the Airmaster into the space, and set it down without a thump. She'd known he was a good pilot, especially after his antics inside a space station, but Pete really should consider promoting him—if he could stay out of trouble.

Cora headed for the door. Figgle and Squarlik were already there, opening the hatch and deploying the stairs. Both carried their weapons in the ready position with the barrels down.

"Rarkanta?" Cora called to the stirring Agamydi. "It's time."

The Agamydi female joined her, and Cora wondered whether she was a leader of her people or just someone who'd assumed the mantle of leadership to get them through a terrible time. Would she have gone after the effigy as crazily as the others? Cora knew the answer even before she'd given Rarkanta the idol as they'd boarded the Airmaster in Limerick. The quiet reverence and immediate reaction in her demeanor had been evident. The Agamydi were ferocious when provoked, but decent and honorable. Cora wondered how bright their future within the Union would be.

Cora bounded down the stairs with Figgle and Squarlik close behind. *Mako 15*, the Misfits' dropship, hung some fifty meters above the swamp. Her drop bays were open, and she saw CASPers waiting. The captured *Ivanhoe*, and all the Crusaders' remains, both personnel and equipment, had been remotely piloted into the swamp about 800 kilometers away.

A new voice crackled over the radio. "*Cora? We're almost there.*"

Her heart leapt when she heard Jyrall's voice. "We're on the ground. I've got the Agamydi moving out of the—"

A primordial scream filled the swamp. Out from the shore, a formation of Narrith erupted through the still water's surface and charged up the shore. Tails thrashed. Jaws snapped. The massive crocodile-like beings stomped forward and then charged. They roared as one…

And froze. Some skidded to a stop in the mud. A few fell. The rest stared at Cora. No. Past her. She spun and saw Rarkanta holding the effigy over her head.

One of the Narrith, a large white and brown mottled one, stomped forward. Rarkanta let it approach and then walked toward it. Cora realized she'd been holding her breath and let it out as the two beings touched the effigy together.

The Narrith rumbled, and Rarkanta hissed and clicked in their native tongues. She bowed her head, and the Narrith turned to the others. They fell to their knees. For the first time, Cora realized the other Agamydi had also knelt.

The stunned Narrith turned to Rarkanta, and they again held the effigy together for a long moment. Rarkanta pressed the effigy into the Narrith's hands and turned to Cora, slipping her translator on as she did.

"Our war is over, Cora McCoy. Are your friends in the sky things?"

"Yes."

"Please bring them down. They frighten the Narrith, and we have business to discuss."

"Business?"

The Narrith rumbled and snarled. Rarkanta turned her head and listened before translating. "The Yellow Human told them to guard his treasure until our gods were returned. It is yours."

"Treasure?" Cora asked.

The Narrith pointed at the temple, and she heard Pete in her earpiece. "*I found a red diamond here, Cora. That's got to be what they're talking about.*"

Cora swallowed, and she turned to Figgle. "Stand everything down. Everybody land, and we'll rendezvous here."

"Security, ma'am?"

Cora shook her head and looked at Rarkanta. "We're among friends."

*****

Chapter Twenty-Seven

Reortia

Upon landing, Jyrall and Larth made their way from the inland clearing toward the temple, along with the McCoy brothers and the rest of their party. The three-kilometer walk took about half an hour, but the sun was still high in the sky, and it felt good to be outside and working up a sweat.

When they reached the temple, they found Barnstormers manning a small perimeter, watching for incoming aircraft. The Misfits' dropship, *Mako 15*, remained in position above the trees, but a discrete distance inland, recovering hover skiffs loaded with green boxes.

What have we found?

Jyrall saw Cora standing with Tara Mason and went to join them. Figgle was there, tapping on a slate, and as he closed the distance, he heard the first sergeant reporting.

"There's more to load, ma'am, but we're looking at more than 2,000 kilograms of red diamonds. We haven't had time to check them all, but there are no forgeries in what we have."

"Hatfield's treasure?" Jyrall asked.

Cora didn't reply as she wrapped him in a tight embrace. "I'm so glad to see you."

"It's good to see you, too," he whispered. "Catch me up?"

"You know it." She released him, having caught his suggestion to keep it in work mode.

He stepped over and shook hands with Tara Mason. "Good to see you again, Colonel."

"Not a colonel anymore, Peacemaker. We're private contractors. And thanks. It's good to be back in action."

For the next hour, Cora and Tara filled him and Larth in on the mission. As they did, he watched the Agamydi and the Narrith sitting together, working out two hundred years of issues. The recovery operation in the temple was nearly complete when they finished the story. Jyrall rubbed his chin as his plan of action formed.

"There's something I need to do before we leave," Jyrall said. "If you'll excuse me?"

Cora and Tara nodded, and he saw the question on Cora's face, so he elaborated. "Our new friends need to be welcomed into the Galactic Union. It may be a while before a legitimate representative from the Peacemaker Guild can be located."

"Aren't you a legitimate Peacemaker?" Tara asked.

Jyrall nodded. "I am. My apologies for any confusion. The ranking Peacemaker in a given region usually handles this. Because of our situation, I don't know if the current representative is legitimate. It's our duty to make sure contact is made. I'll just be a moment."

He made his way through the area of bustling activity, nodding to several of the Misfits and Kin. Larth was busy with Ricky and Keaton, and they appeared to be in an animated conversation with Maarg and Araceli Cignes.

Guess I'll hear about that soon. He sighed. *Captain Dreel, I wish you were here. How do I do this?*

Unsurprisingly, he knew what his mentor would have said. *"Like a Peacemaker does, pup."*

The Agamydi and the Narrith rose as he approached. He withdrew his badge and held it in one open palm.

"On behalf of the Peacemaker Guild, I greet you. I am Peacemaker Jyrall. Well met."

The Narrith spoke first. "Well met, Peacemaker. I am called Untarragg. You and your friends have brought us stillness, Peacemaker. For that, you have our gratitude."

Jyrall nodded, and the Agamydi spoke. "Well met, Peacemaker. I am Rarkanta. What we can give you pales in comparison to what you have given us. We have much to do, but we would not without Cora McCoy, you, and your friends."

"We're thankful to end your conflict and stand ready to do whatever it is you need," Jyrall replied. "A representative from the Peacemaker Guild will come soon and meet with you. I would expect other guilds as well."

"We are aware, Peacemaker," the Narrith said. "You're not the first Peacemaker we've met."

Jyrall blinked. "I don't understand."

"Two decades ago, a Jivool brought us translators and slates in the hopes we could solve our differences without our gods," Rarkanta said. She tilted her head slightly. "We could not. This Peacemaker said he would return if we could fund his travel with our gold. He disappeared into the forests of the north, and we have not seen him again."

"Ten years ago, an Oogar came searching for the Jivool," Untarragg said. "He defeated one of our warriors, and we gave him his space."

"What was his name?" Jyrall asked.

"Hr'ent Golramm," the Narrith said. "Do you know him?"

"I know of him. He passed away a few years ago, serving our guild," Jyrall said. "If he was here, I wonder why your existence wasn't reported?"

"We do not know," Rarkanta said. "We have given up hope of finding the Jivool and what we gave him for his lies."

"Did the Jivool have a name?"

"Hasnerk Tungai," Untarragg replied.

Oh, gods.

I guess that saying is true. You never need Bureau 42 until you need *Bureau 42.*

* * *

Night Moves

Orbiting Prestone

Ricky and Keaton positioned the ship abeam of the Barnstormers' ship *Daniels* and the *Albany* from Intergalactic Haulers. Jump coordinates were set for Krifay, and everyone was ready.

"*Albany, Night Moves,*" Cora said into the radio from her seat next to Jyrall. "We're ready for jump and on schedule."

"*Copy,*" Tara Mason replied. "*We're six hours behind you and will clean up any Crusaders coming in behind you.*"

Jyrall looked at Cora. "We can't be certain the Crusaders won't come in behind the Misfits."

"We'll deal with that when we need to," Cora replied. She turned to Keaton. "While everyone's on the line, Keaton? You and Maarg walk us through what you found and how it might work."

"Without being technical," Keaton said, "the program we built to track them chips in the casino and pinpoint sensors and cameras locked onto a signal common to the Crusaders. Nike found it and used it as a sensor, allowing precise targeting, which was pretty cool. But when we dug a little deeper, we found out it wasn't a normal signal in the electromagnetic spectrum. Not radio or microwave, but something else."

Maarg continued from the *Albany*. "*Simply put, we think the signal was meant to interface their pinplants. We didn't track anything inbound on the signal. I've got the slate of their commander and the copy of Hatfield's slate you have, but I haven't been through it. I'm going to dig into this and see if that signal is really what it is.*"

"We're gonna do the same," Keaton said. "If this really does identify how them pinplants are connected to control the Crusaders, it'll be the Ricky-est Shit ever."

"That ain't far," Ricky yelped from his seat looking hurt. Then he grinned. "Well, yeah, it might be that."

Jyrall grinned and shook his head. He looked at Larth. "You ready to go, big spender?"

"You realize we lost ten million credits?" Larth grumbled. "Now, I know it was house money, and between us all, we've now got like 300 million, but still. I hate losing."

"*You keep that going, Peacemaker,*" Tara Mason said over the connection. "*When you get to Krifay, you can take a little more out of their hides.*"

Larth grinned. "As long as the Crusaders are around, that's not gonna be a problem. Let's go kick some ass."

Jyrall looked at Cora. "Complete the mission."

"We'll see you on Krifay, Tara," Cora said. "Jump to hyperspace, Ricky."

"Damned right," Ricky replied.

"*Good hunting, Cora.* Albany*, out.*"

"Counting down," Ricky said. Jyrall closed his eyes against the sensation and felt Cora slip her hand into his and squeeze.

"Three, two, one—"

* * *

Hatfield checked his readings one more time. The craft he was piloting was a personal shuttle and was small by most standards, but it had the latest in technology. He'd purchased it on a whim months ago. It was more of a rich man's toy than anything else. Well, Human, Jeha, whatever race it could be configured comfortably to be purchased by. Toy or not, crossing the planet at ridiculous speeds was handy.

He flipped back to the image relayed by the external cameras. It looked like there'd been activity near the village compound, but he couldn't be sure. He knew the tramped grasses could have been caused by the Narrith. When several moved on land, they disturbed the ground and bushes.

Taking advantage of one of the features of the small craft, he banked around and came in over the water. He cut the thrust and eased it down until it was skimming. One more nudge, and it was gliding across the water like an expensive boat.

It wasn't the first time he'd visited the temple. The craft had a large stowage area for its size, and he'd brought several loads of red diamonds to be stored and guarded by the Narrith. He wasn't surprised he hadn't seen any yet. The shuttle was fairly quiet. They were usually attracted to the noise and water disturbance from the engine vibrations of the flat-bottomed boats his team used, coming in by water to other villages, and capturing the Agamydi.

The nose of the craft slid up the bank far enough that he could open the hatch. He stepped onto the island and turned toward the temple entrance. He looked around again. There were no Narrith in sight. Usually there was one near the temple entrance. He reached into his ship and retrieved his rifle.

Hatfield slipped an arm through the sling, pulled it over his head, and shifted it so he could have one hand free and still use it. As he walked to the entry, he saw the prints. Someone… someone in boots had tracked mud into the entry and foyer of the temple. He walked faster.

He rounded the bend into the great hall and stopped in his tracks. There were *dozens* of the huge Narrith surrounding the pedestal in the center of the room. Sitting on top, in the place it had been when Hatfield had slipped in and stolen it, was the effigy. A large Agamydi he knew as Rarkanta turned to face him.

"Why are you here, yellow one?" she hissed. The translator Hatfield had on him allowed her lack of surprise to come through.

He looked at the effigy, then back to her. "Who brought it back here?" he demanded.

The other Narrith moved to the side of the large room. Hatfield realized they were trying to surround him. He backed up several paces, still keeping his weapon trained on Rarkanta. When they stopped, he stopped.

"Who does not matter. What matters is that it is back, and the water is stilled between the Narrith and Agamydi. We are now ready to join the Galactic Union."

"Oh, hell no," Hatfield said. He waved the end of the rifle for emphasis. "Y'all are not fixing to do any such thing. You do that, and I can't make them race. There are too many credits at stake. Them crazy things hauling ass around the track makes me rich."

"They will no longer do your bidding. Nor will we."

Hearing this, Hatfield took careful aim… but he didn't squeeze the trigger. He was startled when more Narrith emerged from the pools on the far end of the room. There were now more of them than rounds in his rifle. He couldn't fire. It would be suicide.

"Fine," Hatfield said as he lowered his weapon. "Y'all just give me the diamonds you've been guarding, and I'm outta here."

"We cannot give you what we do not have, just as you cannot threaten us with something you no longer have."

"Who took it?" Hatfield demanded.

"It does not matter. We are at peace, and we are free of you."

Hatfield backed away. "Free? We'll just see about that. I'll bring enough folks here to snatch more of my racers and some of you. Might just have me a double header every night and make it all back real quick like."

He slipped around the bend and ran for his craft.

* * *

Gahloong waited. He was always waiting. Silent, he lay in the mud, deep in the water, waiting for prey.

He hungered.

He always hungered. He took a deep breath and inhaled gallons of water through his nostrils. It flowed to the side of his long face and out the gills near his great neck. Water or air, it didn't matter. Both brought oxygen to his body.

Quickly he snapped his mouth on one of the many denizens of the deep. A mere snack. It didn't taste of the snacks he craved. He wanted more of the two-legged kind. The shell was stronger than the flesh within, but it didn't keep him from feasting.

Untarragg had been angered when he ate those times. He didn't know why. He didn't know many things. He knew to wait patiently for his prey… for food. He knew to fight other males if they ventured into his territory. It was his. The females were his, or he theirs. He didn't concern himself with the difference. He ate, he guarded, he mated, and he obeyed the alpha female, Untarragg. There was nothing else.

He… paused, listening. He pushed up from the mud, rising. He felt her call.

He obeyed.

* * *

Untarragg stood at the entrance of the temple. The yellow one, inside his floating flyer, moved away from shore. She raised her head and rumbled. The muscles in her neck quivered faster than the eye could see. The vibration created a humming sound that carried far into the distance. It disturbed the water near her, sending the signal deep. Gahloong would hear her call. He always heard.

She lowered her large head and watched the craft pick up speed. Suddenly the water around it exploded, and she saw the familiar light green of her mate… of her tribe's mate. A third of his massive body exploded out of the water, the white craft within his jaws. He fell back into the water, taking the craft and the yellow one inside with him.

She watched and she waited. The water settled. When pieces of the craft floated to the surface, she rumbled her pleasure to her mate. The snack was well deserved. Perhaps later she would let him mate with several of the tribe. Until then, she knew, he waited patiently.

Hungry.

*****

Chapter Twenty-Eight

Commercial Terminal

Prestone

Amongst the stacks of shipping containers, a dark figure crept out of sight of the security cameras and waited. Tsan possessed enough food and water to wait several days in her hiding spot, but she enjoyed peering into what containers she could while she awaited transport. Getting to Khatash would take more than a little luck, as well as quite a bit of time, but she understood, and it didn't bother her. As it was, she'd needed to ensure a final message home made its way there before she did. Her clan knew the situation, but there were others who needed to know what she'd found.

From her supplies, she withdrew a slate she could easily operate. Once she turned it on, she inserted a tiny chip card into the customized slot for uploads. The slate *beeped* and registered the information and encrypted itself. Satisfied it was ready, Tsan tapped the screen and let the device connect to the GalNet from one of the mobile towers in the vicinity of the airfield. After thirty seconds, the connection was private, and a series of dialog boxes opened, allowing her access to a network hidden beneath the data feeds from the spaceport to the gate and the higher gain antennae there.

While information couldn't travel faster than the speed of light in the traditional sense, there were two ways now, where there had only been one. Reaching out to her clan and the others gifted like her served one purpose. The clan must be informed. But there were other friends who needed to understand the situation. While a tenuous peace had fallen over most of the galaxy, there were still enemies lurking.

A final series of windows opened, and more than once Tsan had to place her paw over a box and let the slate read it for encryption. After a long moment, the screen faded to a pleasant bluish color, and several slash marks appeared in one corner, along with a flashing cursor.

//Connection established. Tap for voice connection.//

Tsan tapped the screen and waited.

<<Honored Tsan, this is Lucille. What can I do for you?>>

"The Crusaders have moved against Krifay. The young Peacemakers and their friends are headed there. I've arranged for reinforcements, but I worry they may not be enough."

<<Understood. I have relayed a priority request for assistance to Intergalactic Haulers. They will send a complement of ships and personnel.>>

"Will you alert Jessica?"

<<Of course, but there is little she can do in our present situation. Please trust that I will get this done. The Haulers will be there.>>

"Thank you, Lucille."

<<You are welcome, Honored Tsan. Terminating the connection now.>>

* * *

Location: Undisclosed

Earth

"Lucille, has Dad answered?" Jessica toweled her hair dry as she crossed the suite and sat down. While she'd had more than adequate facilities on Khatash, her first real Human shower in more than two years had been nothing short of *glorious.*

<<Affirmative. He is sending a complement of ten ships. Five will be mercenary ships with a full load of ground forces. The *Brunswick* and the *Athens* will be the primary combat load carriers, and he has released the *Currahee* from dock and ordered it fully loaded. They will be ready to jump in six hours.>>

"*Currahee?* That's a new one." Jessica took a deep breath and sighed. Since he'd returned to Earth and reinvigorated the Intergalactic Haulers, she'd lost track of his acquisitions. His progress, though, was phenomenal. "Okay, there's nothing more we can do with that right now. Have you completed the analysis on the Crusaders' logistical movements?"

<<I have. I have concluded that the Crusaders are stockpiling their stolen goods at a location on Marian Seven.>>

"Really? That's kind of hiding it in plain sight."

<<I would agree. The regional Peacemaker barracks there, though, has more than ample storage facilities. It was constructed to guard the guild's major supply of F11, which makes it a perfect location.>>

"As all the Crusader traffic is going to have to use one of those supply depots, why not store what they've stolen from others there?"

Jessica mused and shook her head. "I really can't believe Marc would do something like this."

<<The possibility that he is being manipulated by Counselor is still statistically relevant,>> Lucille said.

Jessica nodded. "I get that, Lucille, but there's more to it. Marc is doing this for personal gain. So there's some part of him that understands that his mission with the Crusaders is only going to last for so long. This is the kind of redundancy plan he's used for years. Now he just has a bigger organization to do the skimming for him."

<<And you are not the only one watching the accounting this time. I agree, this fits his *modus operandi*,>> Lucille replied. <<I will begin pulling information on the depot at Marian Seven.>>

"Good," Jessica said. "That's one part of this. If they're keeping these treasures and stolen funds there, we'll need the right folks to do this. We'll need to notify the Kin, the Barnstormers, and the Misfits once their mission at Krifay is over."

<<Are you worried about them?>>

Jessica chewed the inside of her lip for a moment. Lucille understood nuances of data and Human expression, and with every conversation, she grew in ways Jessica hadn't expected. Bull had warned her about that, but it still often caught her by surprise. "I am worried about them, but I have faith they're going to be successful."

<<May I ask why? To corroborate my data?>>

"They're well trained, well equipped, and fighting for the Kin's home. Plus, Marc and his cronies aren't going to fight to the death or anything. When challenged, I think he'll run. Especially if the Kin have a numerical advantage."

<<I agree with your assessment. If they are successful, that ought to provide a statistical advantage for us to attack the depot at Marian Seven.>>

"That's not enough," Jessica said. "The numbers are good, but we're going to need something else. An intangible I don't necessarily want, but one I believe we have to act upon. It might make a difference."

<<You are speaking of your father's message.>>

"I am," Jessica replied. "We're going to need to pay a visit to this Raley Reilly. If Dad's hunch is right, and she's in danger, I have a feeling I know who it might be with."

<<My data does not corroborate your suspicion, Jessica,>> Lucille noted. <<From a data perspective, I understand feelings are important to being a Peacemaker, and to being a Human, but I cannot help but think you might be wrong here. There is no proof that Kr'et'Socae knew Raleigh Reilly. Nor is there proof he is on this planet.>>

"He didn't have to know him, Lucille. He had to know *of* him and believe that Raleigh Riley was capable of hiding things and operating semi-legitimately in plain sight."

<<You say that as if he wasn't a bad man,>> Lucille replied. <<Everything I have seen says differently.>>

"Reilly was a good commander, to a point. Even Tara said so. Chances are very good he taught his daughter well. According to Dad's folks, Raley Reilly was using a burner slate. *Naduhli* was the only search she made on it. Her other slate was encrypted and protected with an Equiri-derived algorithm. We've traced Hatfield to Tennessee in the last two years. I have to believe Raley Reilly is the missing piece of information—our missing link."

<<And you believe she's worthy of what you're giving her?>>

"Dad seems to think so. I trust his judgment."

<<At times like these, I understand the nuances of the Human phrase 'I wish.'>>

Jessica laughed. "Why do you say that?"

<<Because I am incapable of wishing, but I would want you to choose another course of action.>>

"I don't think we have a choice, Lucille. If we're going to do this, we're going to have to have the mind of someone who's done this sort of thing before. Our friends are good, but they're not criminals. They aren't going to see all the angles."

<<What do you possibly have that could persuade Kr'et'Socae to help you?>>

Jessica paused. While Lucille was as much a friend as anyone, there were certain things that ran through her mind that Jessica didn't want to share—at least not yet. There would be time in the future, maybe even after this mission, but for the moment, Lucille couldn't know what Jessica had planned… or what she feared.

"He's the best opportunity we have to pull this off, Lucille. If we can steal what Marc's stolen and return all of it to its rightful owners, we'll undermine the Crusaders. If we do this right, we catch Marc, and maybe even the guild master, red-handed. We can destroy the Crusaders' mission and the guild's relationship with the Galactic Union. We might even create a situation where they can be taken down."

<<That's where I come in,>> Lucille said, <<when it's time to release intelligence. Collecting the reports they've restricted about their conduct across the galaxy.>>

"That's right," Jessica said. "We'll make our move soon. Right now, we have to get all the pieces on the board, and that includes Raley Reilly and Kr'et'Socae."

Azho entered the room after a quick sweep of the area. He sat on the floor looking dourly at Jessica. "I know, I know. I can't kill him, either."

Jessica smiled. "If he makes a move on me or my friends, he's fair game, Azho."

"Good." Azho flicked an ear. "I haven't forgotten Diam, and when I'm through with him, he won't, either."

* * *

Trindlark System
Blue Ridge

Cora leaned back in her seat and looked around the crowded conference room. "If they haven't moved their headquarters, they'll be in Sandy Bay. Snapper Isle is home to many of the export companies. Also, they can maintain their control of the planet administration if they remain based in the capital."

"The bay on one side, and rolling hills on the other," Pete remarked. On cue, Specialist Conner put a map on the large screen covering one bulkhead. "It's definitely defensible. But… it leaves some avenues of approach they can't cover. Visibility is limited in some places due to the terrain."

"Is it possible they have enough troops to cover them?" May asked. "I mean, we know that bastard Smith is there, or will be by the time we get there. What we don't know is the size of his forces."

"We know he'll have Mk 8s," Pete said. "His pilots know how to use them, too. If it wasn't for the surprise attack by the Misfits, the six in the village would've been more than enough for the platoon of infantry I had with me."

"Speaking of CASPers," Cora said. "Nileah, how many machines do we have mission capable?"

Nileah sighed. "We have sixteen, including the four Mk 4s. Of the rest, four are Mk 6s. Corporal Kylont and his guys have been working nonstop on the last two 7s we have, but he can't guarantee they'll be up by the time we need them."

Cora ran her hand down her face. "All right. Command decision time. Have them cannibalize the one in worst shape and get the other mission capable."

"Will do."

She turned to Nails. "Your platoon's up?"

"Yes, ma'am," Nails said. "I have 1st Platoon. I'll feel a little strange going into battle outside of my CASPer, but with Top leading 2nd Platoon, we should be all right."

"Hey, ma'am," First Sergeant Figgle said, "don't even think of pinning a bar on me."

Sergeant First Class Wilson looked to her own commander. "Me, either. I'm not officer material."

"Same," Figgle said. "Fuck that noise."

"We have fourteen Mk 6s and my Mk 7," Pete said. "One platoon of regular infantry and another platoon for the gliders. Once they touch down, there's no difference between the two."

Cora nodded. "Between us, thirty-one CASPers, maybe thirty-two, and eighty infantry troops—against who knows how many."

"We have the armored hovercraft and the skiffs," Nileah said.

"You have us," Jyrall added. "I'm sure we'll be able to inflict more damage than four individuals should be capable of."

"A little sneaking around behind the lines," Larth agreed. He rubbed his paws together. "They won't know what hit them."

"Especially when we get our asses into their HQ," Ricky said. "I got an idea for a whoopie-cushion that should damn near launch someone."

"You make sure you don't put it in place until after I get into their system," Keaton said. "I'm not going to sit down in front of a computer and get blown the hell up by some of your Ricky Shit."

* * *

Hours later, everyone was back on their ships. Cora, her officers—except for Lieutenant Rhineder—and the CASPer platoon were on *Blue Ridge*. The newest officer in the company commanded those on *Kellie's Last Stand*. The Barnstormers were split between their two ships, *Daniels* and the large shuttle converted to dropship, *Prized Catch*. All were equipped with their own shunts.

Cora sat in the extra seat in the operations center. She tightened the straps on the harness and looked around. Both Mideralls wore capes, along with the rest of their brightly-colored outfits. It was enough to make one squint.

"Mr. Monty," Cora asked, "are we prepared to make the jump?"

"Yes, ma'am. Ma'am, I say," Monty answered. He moved his wings and flared the orange cape Larth had given him. "Two minutes. That's two, don't you know."

Specialist Conner sat at the communication console. "Ma'am, Colonel Brentale and the others report all ships are prepared to make the transition, including *Night Moves.*"

"Thanks, Conner," Cora said. "Gentlemen, one more jump. Take us home."

She'd said it without realizing it. *Home.* They were going home. Against whatever odds stood in front of them, they were going home to Krifay. Home to fight for it.

Or die trying.

* * * * *

Chapter Twenty-Nine

Emergence Zone
Krifay System

Marc Lemieux woke when the *Warrior Apostle* transitioned, then lay strapped into his bunk for another thirty minutes, downloading and reviewing intelligence reports via GalNet. His multiple sets of pinplants helped process the data faster, which made reviewing 14 days of messages and requests easier. In reality, there were few messages that required his personal attention. His staff, mainly the officers overseeing the fundamental areas of maneuver, logistics, intelligence, and command and control, handled most matters. They did an overall admirable job, and there was nothing to concern him in their performance or interactions. What bothered him was he hadn't heard from Counselor as expected at their six-month check in.

After the debacle on Uluru, as Counselor had called it in his first message afterward to Lemieux, the SI had withdrawn. From what Lemieux had seen of the Peacemaker Guild, Counselor's focus was on the guild master and the re-establishment of a Council. However, that wasn't going well, either. Around the galaxy, Peacemakers were rebelling against the guild. Their primary reason for dissent was his Crusaders. Their pursuit of credits and stolen goods to finance operations and "ensure Galactic peace" had triggered the moral code of idealistic Peacemakers, and they increasingly attempted to take action. At least until his forces put them down like the rabid animals they'd become.

Doing so, though, was another matter. The logistical needs of his forces were greater than the typically meager resources under the control of the Peacemaker Guild. To truly perform their mission, stores of F11, ammunition, and food sources were critical. Based on his staff's recommendations, believing the ocean world of Krifay to be virtually defenseless and one of the galaxy's major providers of food, he'd sent Lieutenant Colonel Smith and a small force to scout the target. They'd found everything they were looking for, save the remnants of a few mercenary companies. Smith and his force had laid waste to their meager, individualistic resistance. Now, occupation would commence.

Lemieux unstrapped from his bunk and floated across his stateroom. He grabbed his uniform coveralls, which were secured to the bulkhead, and slipped them on, whistling a tune he realized he hadn't heard since—

* * *

"Hammer, I'm on the way," Maven called from her flyer. "You've got a platoon of Jivool at your three o'clock in a ravine."

He frowned and kept his focus on the targets to his front. "I'm not seeing them."

<<Confirm high confidence of ambush probability,>> Lucille said.

Fine. He turned the tank's gun tube to the right and, sure enough, he caught a thermal signature.

"I see them, Maven. Take them out."

She laughed. "You know I always bring the thunder."

The music, all electric guitars and drums, came over the frequency. He smiled and settled into the battle. When all the pieces came together, and he had the intelligence to make good decisions, everything—

* * *

"Clicked," Lemieux said to no one. He ran his electric razor over his face while a bulb of coffee brewed. He took his time getting ready. The staff knew he'd want a briefing the moment he hit the bridge, and he knew they'd be ready. All he needed was a plan.

Look for the ambush.

Lemieux grinned. He knew exactly what he was going to do. Smith would take the full complement of his ground forces and root out any other targets, then secure the production plants. His fleet would remain spread around the planet in groups of three. They'd orbit at a geosynchronous distance and have line of sight with each other. It would take some time to set up, and it would leave the polar approaches open, but it was viable. Once the fleet was positioned, sensor packages could protect the poles, and they could scan every square centimeter of the planet. Resistance would truly be futile. In twelve hours, he'd have a complete picture of all traffic in and out of the Krifay system. The first time anything out of the ordinary happened, they'd pounce.

From there, taking the planet would be easier than stealing candy from a baby.

* * *

Emergence Zone

Krifay System

Jyrall closed his eyes before Keaton completed his countdown. A moment later, his body let him know they'd emerged into the Krifay system. He swallowed hard, determined to gain control of himself quickly. Now was not the time to slowly acclimate to normal space.

His eyes snapped open at Keaton's shout. "Shit!"

"Tell me," Jyrall demanded, the nausea gone faster than it ever had before.

Ricky peered over his brother's shoulder at the screens, his body angled as he gripped the handhold above him. "Hell fahr! They's a bunch of 'em. We been bushwhacked!"

Keaton's paws were a blur as he changed settings and increased velocity. "I count twelve ships. From what I can tell, they're all squawking Crusader. Damn, look at those two. They got more firepower than us and the four merc ships combined."

"How close?" Jyrall asked. "Are we within their range?"

"No," Keaton said, "not yet, but if we don't change our heading, we will be. We ain't the only ones who see 'em. The Kin and Barnstormers' ships are banking with us."

"Good," Jyrall said as he slumped, momentarily relieved. He sat back up. "Open a channel to all four."

"Roger. I'm also running a probability program I designed. It should show the projected maneuvers they'll have to make to intercept us. It'll also give us options… if there are any."

Larth swung into the operations center. "What's going on around here? You made me spill the last of the ketchup. Well, not spill it exactly, but I did squirt it across the galley, and now it's floating around in little globs. It's going straight to the deck when we hit atmosphere."

"The Crusaders were waiting for us," Jyrall answered.

"Well, yeah, Snarlyface. We knew Smith was here. He has ships."

Jyrall shook his head and looked back. "We didn't know he had this many. There are twelve Crusaders ships in the system now."

"Shit!"

"That's what I said!" Keaton remarked. He tapped a button. "Everyone's on the command net, Boss."

The large screen in the center was split four ways. It showed all four of the operations centers.

"It would appear the Crusaders have reinforcements," Jyrall said. "For right now, continue to mirror our course adjustments."

"If we can see them on our sensors, you know they can see us," Cora said. "This is not good."

"No," Jyrall agreed, "it's not." He turned to Keaton. "What have you found after running your probability program?"

"It's still running."

"What's the plan?" Cora asked.

"We can't possibly hope to defeat them," Jyrall said. "We're outclassed as far as warships, and hopelessly outnumbered."

"We can't just turn and run," Cora said. "It's our home." The frustration was obvious in her voice.

"I have family on Krifay," Pete said. "Many of us do. I, we… can't leave them under the rule of the Crusaders."

"We're not running," Jyrall said. "We're maneuvering. Keaton?"

"From the readings, only the ships we know Smith came with are near orbit. The others haven't made it to the planet."

"Good," Pete said. "At least they haven't put reinforcements on the ground."

After a moment, Keaton said, "It shows a trajectory that'll keep us beyond their reach. We go the long way around and come in on the backside of the planet. We can stay low and get to Snapper Isle. We won't be close to Sandy Bay, but then again, we'll also be out of range of any anti-ship weapons they may have deployed."

"I like it," Larth said. "If we can take out Smith, whoever's commanding their fleet may decide to leave. Especially if we can defeat the forces on the surface."

"Speaking of the Crusader fleet," Jyrall said. "Once all troops and equipment are offloaded, the ships need to get back into space. They'll need to play a—what's the term? Cat and mice game. Stay close enough the Crusader ships try to engage, but far enough away they can't."

"Lead them away," Pete said.

"Exactly," Jyrall agreed. "We don't want them sending reinforcements to the surface. We want them worried our frigates will destroy their transport craft before they reach the surface."

"Who'll we leave in command?" Pete said. "We need every single body we can muster on the surface with weapons in hand."

"The pilots and copilots can handle the ships and weapons systems," Cora said, "but we need someone with experience in command." She blew a puff of air in frustration. "Hell, *I* don't have that kind of experience."

"Me, either," Pete admitted. "Having my own ships is still new to me. But we do have an option."

"Which is?" Jyrall asked.

"Ward Pintair. He's a retired ship commander. He had years running a ship twice the size of our frigates. It was a warship, too, a Jivool ship. His last years were with the Slow Killers. He was the only Human ship commander in the company. That was unusual, but Nahgrod gave him a contract on my word. He and my father knew each other for decades. He's been retired about ten years now. He has a place on the side of Snapper Isle where we have to land. He's a good man."

"I wish we had their ships here," Cora said.

"So do I," Pete said. "Even if I'd sent a message before our last jump, they wouldn't get here in time."

"It's up to us," Jyrall said. "Colonel Brentale, as soon as we're in range, attempt to reach your friend. We'll need him."

"Understood."

"Now," Jyrall said. "Troop movement when we reach the surface."

"We can move the infantry with the skiffs. Multiple trips should get them close enough so the road march won't wear them out before we engage with the Crusaders," Cora suggested.

"Ma'am?" Specialist Haney said over Pete's shoulder. "If we get to the surface, I can get us a ride close to Sandy Bay."

"Can you?" Then she realized she was talking to Haney. "Of course you can. How?"

"I know a guy. He has a friend, and she knows a girl whose father owns a transportation company. Freezer rigs. They move fresh seafood from the other side of Snapper Isle to the processing plants. We can get closer."

"You're sure?"

"Absolutely. The guy owes another friend of mine a favor. I'll call in two of them with my friend, and he'll call his in. Nothing to it."

"He makes my head hurt," First Sergeant Figgle said. "I'm glad he's not my headache."

"I heard that," Sergeant First Class Wilson said. "Thanks for the sympathy. I thought us senior NCOs were supposed to stick together."

"I can't help you with that one," Figgle admitted. "I could show you some one-handed choking techniques while using the knife hand to enforce your directives."

"We'll get to the surface first," Jyrall said. "From there, we'll finalize troop movements." He bared his teeth slightly. "We'll get there. There's no other option. Ending transmission." The screen went blank.

"Locking in the trajectory," Keaton said. "Sending it to the others now."

"Hey." Larth looked around. "Where did Ricky go?"

"If I know that greasy-fingered brother of mine, he's working on something dangerous. More of those shock plugs or whatever," Keaton said.

"I might go see what he's doing," Larth said. He let go with one paw and reached for another strap.

"You know, he could be in the galley eating whatever you fixed before we emerged," Jyrall suggested.

"Shit! Hey! If there's any more ketchup, it's mine!"

*****

Chapter Thirty

Snapper Isle

Krifay

Larth stood with his hands on his hips. "It sure is crowded."

"Yes," Jyrall agreed. "This airfield was never designed for this many ships capable of leaving the atmosphere."

"Not the size of these, anyway," Keaton added. "Maybe small freighters and shuttles."

"Well, hell," Ricky said, "we may have taken the whole dang airfield and most of the old-fashioned runway, but the locals don't seem to mind. Looks like some of them moved their craft before we touched down."

"Pete's message to his friend," Larth said. "Had to be where that came from."

"Yes," Jyrall said. "Keaton, it would appear your encryption program allows us to communicate without fear of the Crusaders intercepting and unscrambling our calls. Excellent job."

Keaton shrugged. "Thanks. I had time before we left for Prestone to get the data I needed to work on it. I finished it during the last jump."

"The best part is, when we get close enough, we'll be able to listen to them sumbitches' command network," Ricky said. "Well, Cora and Pete will. We just need the frequencies from their communications center."

Jyrall winked. "We'll get them. Or should I say, *Larth* will get them. I'm just the lookout for our little mission."

"As long as I don't have to climb through a window into a waste relief room," Larth said. He held his nose. "I'm tired of that."

"Better you than me, Little Buddy."

* * *

"Ward, meet Colonel Cora McCoy and Peacemakers Jyrall and Larth," Pete said. "This is Ship Commander Ward Pintair."

"*Retired* ship commander," Ward corrected him, "of the Slow Killers. I was in several units throughout my career, but I still consider myself a Slow Killer."

"The Jivool mercenary company," Jyrall said. "An honorable company, by all accounts. It's unusual for them to let a non-Jivool command one of their ships."

"Yeah," Ward agreed. "It is. Was. If I hadn't got old, I'd still be with them." He ran his fingers through his silver hair. "It got to where I couldn't keep up during emergency action drills. I couldn't preach safety if I couldn't do it myself, you know."

"Admirable," Jyrall said. "You realized a deficiency in your ship crew, and you corrected it, even though it forced retirement on you. I'm impressed."

Ward shrugged. "Had to. It was the right thing to do. My old XO took over command of the *Slow Slasher*. Good man, he is." He grinned, the wrinkles deepening on his face. "Well, not really a man.

Hell of a Jivool, I should say. His name is Lengoot. He's the nephew of the commander of the Slow Killers."

Pete nodded. "I know Nargrod's nephew. I agree."

Cora smiled. "You're not retired as of today. Thank you for doing this."

"No need to thank me," Ward said. "Krifay is my home. I'd have to be dead and buried not to fight for her. I'm not there yet. Thank *you* for giving me the opportunity."

He turned toward the ships filling the tarmac and beyond. "Two old Zuul insertion frigates, a converted freighter, and a hopped-up shuttle, huh?"

"It's what we have," Pete said.

Ward nodded. "We work with what we've got. I think I can threaten any troop transports they may think to send down. At least I can make them think I can. We'll stay out of reach… until we can't."

First Sergeant Figgle and Sergeant First Class Wilson approached them. "Ma'am, that's the last of it. We got the racks off for diagnostics and charging the CASPers, too."

Ward raised an eyebrow at the sight of a Goka wearing Human first sergeant rank. Figgle turned to him and said, "You have some of the best pilots I've ever worked with. A little flashy, but damn good at their jobs. We want them back when you're done. Oh, and keep an eye on Conner. She runs with a bad crowd."

"Speaking of that, where the hell is Haney?" SFC Wilson said. She looked around.

"That fuckwinkle better be with the truck drivers," Figgle said. "Come on. Let's go see."

"What's a fuckwinkle?" Ward asked.

"Who knows?" Cora answered. "My first sergeant has a colorful list of names to call the troops, but he would die for each and every one of them."

"Sounds like a good man—Goka. You know what I mean," the unretired ship commander said.

"Yeah, he's good people."

* * *

Cora and Pete stood with the Peacemakers. "All the equipment and the CASPers are loaded. We have the skiffs and the hovercraft on flatbeds. All we need to do is load the troops and get the convoy moving."

They heard Figgle scream, "Haney! You frozen turd! If you don't tell these damn drivers to turn off the refrigeration units, you won't arrive alive with the rest of us!"

Even Jyrall laughed aloud.

Larth pointed at two trucks. "That looks like boats under those tarps."

"Ricky and my technicians built the frames in less than thirty minutes," Cora said.

"Make sure the transport vehicles are spaced. The route shouldn't cause concern. These same vehicles make the trip regularly," Jyrall said. "Still, be wary… and take care."

He looked right at Cora when he said it. She knew he meant so much more than he seemed to convey to the others. "We will. *You* be careful. You're going right into the hornet's nest."

Larth broke the mood. "I'm not getting stung; you can bet on that. We'd better go. The brothers are waiting. We're going to fly so low, we'll scrape the hillsides. It's going to be great!"

"Yeah… great," Jyrall intoned.

* * *

Two Miles from Sandy Bay

"That's the last of them," Nileah said. "The racks and spare parts are in that warehouse with the technicians." She shook her head. "I had to order Corporal Kylont and the other three Makis to stay with it and be ready to quick-charge and repair damage. They wanted to put on battle armor and go with the infantry platoons."

"They're feisty," May said. "I hope the Crusaders don't attempt to gain entry to the building. They set out micro cameras. I think they have their own version of Ricky Shit."

"Lord help us," Lissale said.

"Well, let's move out while it's still dark. I don't want to give the warehouse away by being near it until we have to. Pete is in place two clicks west of here. His trucks split off four hours ago and took a longer route. He says he's entrenched in a forest in the valley. He can follow the creek in the valley right to the edge of Sandy Bay, so we can give them two fronts."

* * *

Crusader Command Center
Loading Docks
Sandy Bay, Snapper Isle
Krifay

"Say that again." Smith's eyes were closed, and he felt heat coursing up his neck and into his face. Everything he'd taken precautions against, planned for, and staged his forces to prevent had happened. Not one of his people had seen it. "Say that again. Slowly."

He opened his eyes and stared at his once promising—and newly promoted—operations officer, Major Thornton. For a brief instant, Smith wondered if he'd promoted the man too soon.

"Sir, a routine patrol determined movement in a sector near Fuller's Crossroads. On closer inspection, we discovered the CASPers and infantry must have been delivered by… refrigeration trucks. Once we discovered them, we checked the highways. Multiple trucks are headed back east, but we can find no proof they came into Sandy Bay to deliver anything. The trucks are now hours from Fuller's Crossroads."

He paused a moment before continuing as the bearer of bad news. "Imagery confirms the unit to be the Blue Ridge Kin. They've returned to Krifay."

"Obviously," Smith said. "What's their strength?"

"We've counted sixteen Mk 4 to Mk 6 CASPers and around fifty infantry personnel," Thornton replied. "We've doubled patrols in the area, but we've found nothing to indicate a greater force. We don't know where they're commanded from. We can assume their commander is forward with this element."

Damn you, Cora McCoy.

Smith considered the imagery for a moment. His forces were more than twice the Kin's force, so the numerical advantage was his. They undoubtedly knew the terrain and surrounding coastline better than his forces did. Sensors, after all, only did so much in a combat environment. He studied the CASPers and the leg infantry on the ground.

This is a feint. Nice try, Cora. I know you've got more out there, and you're not going to sucker us into an unfair fight.

"Unlikely," Smith said. "Their commander is too sneaky for that. There are more CASPers out there. Your first priority is to find them."

"Yes, sir," Thornton replied. "We've upped our security to 75 percent in response." He stood waiting for any other orders.

"What are you up to?" Smith said aloud to himself. "That other unit. The Barn something…" He snapped his fingers and pointed at Thornton. "Barnstormers!"

He paused. "Barnstormers…Stormers…Storm? Where have I heard that?"

"You had me look into the merc company the Island Storm, sir," Thornton suggested, "and their commander, if that's what you are referring to."

"Maybe."

Trying to be helpful, the major added, "This planet is full of islands. Snapper Isle is the size of a small continent, but they still call it an island."

Smith stared at his subordinate.

Surely not.

Smith grunted. "Set security to 100 percent. I want everyone ready for orders. Notify Prime of our situation."

"Yes, sir," Thornton said. The major turned to the staff and sent the command through voice and data channels to all the units.

As he expected, Prime didn't respond. With the orbital blockade in place, Prime was watching the big picture as it unfolded. The likelihood this was one small part of Cora McCoy's plan was very real. Smith was determined to stop her.

He examined a digital map of the command center and the surrounding complex. Backed up against the ocean as it was, there were a few potential avenues of approach the CASPers could use through the city itself. Granted, they could attempt to jump over his defenses, but there were answers for that eventuality, too.

"What do you think their intention is?" Smith asked. He knew the answer. This planet was the Blue Ridge Kin's homeworld now. With any luck, it would be their graveyard. "What have you and your staff determined?"

Thornton caught the subtle change in his voice. He recognized his newly-won promotion and contract were on the line. "They're going to attack. We've prepared first battalion for deployment forward to battle positions on the outskirts of the city. We were about to notify the citizens and prepare them to evacuate on—"

"Leave them. The presence of civilians on the battlefield will slow down the Kin. If they attack and get past 1st Battalion, have 2nd Battalion ready to support by fire. If the Kin push through them, we'll bring up the tanks and give Captain Strauss a chance to prove his armor can take out CASPers in close quarters."

Two battalions of CASPer-led infantry backed up by two platoons of tanks in a door-to-door urban environment. Smith couldn't help but smile. He had the advantage now. All he needed to do was press the knife to the throat of the populace, and the Kin and their perverted sense of family honor would take over.

"Send the orders and deploy our forces in response to their movement. They think they have the advantage," Smith replied. "We're going to show them."

He turned to leave the command center. "I'm headed to 1st Battalion and will be with them until I need to jump back to 2nd Battalion. Chain of command is by SOP. If the Kin attack us, we'll hit them."

"If they attack our rear positions? The headquarters?" Thornton asked.

Smith grinned. "Highly unlikely, unless they've grown gills and can attack from the water. I don't expect them to attack us, much less you, but it could happen. If it does, take as many of them with you as you can. We'll clean up what's left."

"Yes, sir."

* * *

Night Moves
Fifty Feet above the Sea
West of Snapper Isle

"*They've agreed*," Keaton said. "*I'm maneuvering into place. Tell Ricky to lower the ramp and get the hoist he rigged ready.*"

"Good job," Jyrall said. He tapped the small microphone on his neck to turn it off.

"Lower the ramp," Jyrall said. He shifted his backpack.

"It's gonna get loud as hell," Ricky warned, "and windy in here."

"Our earpieces will dampen it," Jyrall said. "We're ready."

The wind whipped around the small cargo hold as the ramp descended. Jyrall leaned near the edge and looked down at the fishing boat below them. It was loaded with crab pots, with room for maybe a dozen more near the back where they were stored.

"You go first," Larth said. He pulled on a set of gloves, shifted his holsters, and made sure his pistols were secure.

Jyrall nodded, clipped the cable to his harness, and stepped to the edge of the ramp. Ricky swung the arm over so the end was off the side of the ramp. Jyrall stepped out, and Ricky worked the controls, lowering him to the boat's deck.

When his feet hit the deck, he bent his knees and waited a moment, getting a feel for the rolling motion. He felt the cable move in his hands as he started to unhook. He looked up to see Larth sliding down toward him. He ducked reflexively, but Larth stopped just above him. He shook his head when Larth climbed down his back using the backpack to hang on to.

"That was great!" Larth exclaimed. "I thought about waiting, but then I thought I might never get a chance to do that again, so I went for it."

Jyrall tapped his collar. "We're on deck; retract the cable, and good luck. Don't fly high enough to be picked up on sensors and wait for our call."

"*Roger that*," Keaton answered. "*Good luck, Boss*."

They moved across the deck to the three men looking out the hatch to the wheelhouse. Jyrall produced his badge. The older man grinned and shook his head.

"No need for that, Peacemaker. I know who you are." He held up a communication slate. "We all talk among ourselves. Not where those damned Crusaders can hear us, but we talk. Come on in, and let me fix you a cup of coffee. We've got one more string of pots to pick up, then we're headed back to port. It'll be near dark when we get there."

* * *

Sandy Bay Docks

When it was dark enough, Jyrall and Larth slipped out of the wheelhouse. Staying low, they eased onto the dock. It was dark where the captain tied his boat after offloading the crabs from the ship's live well. One of the deck-hands made sure of it when he broke a lightbulb with one of the long gaffs. He winked through the porthole as he put it back in its hooks on the side of the wheelhouse.

"Keaton says the majority of the signals are coming from that building," Jyrall said. His voice was barely a whisper picked up by the sensitive mic.

"Looks like some kind of government office," Larth answered. "Maybe an inspection or regulations enforcement office."

"Probably. It all has to be regulated to keep the industry viable. Let's get close and find a way in. We can't just use the front door. Looks like they have two on sentry."

Minutes later, they were against the back wall of the building. Above them on the second floor was a small window, partially open. Jyrall laced his fingers together and bent down.

"Ready?" he asked.

"Yep. Lift me up."

Then, "Shit!" Larth said.

"What?"

"It's a damned waste relief room. What the hell is the deal with it always being a stinking waste room? Lift me higher, I need to open the window a little more."

Moments later, the back door opened a crack. Jyrall slipped inside the darkened hallway. "What's the layout?"

"The stairwell is in this back hall, nothing else. No one was upstairs. Smith's office is up there. Doesn't look like he's been there in a while, probably all day. There's a coffee cup with a dry ring in the bottom. I think it's from yesterday."

"How many are in the building?"

"Two. They're asleep."

"What?"

"Yeah. For real. One on a couch, he has major rank on his collar, and a sergeant's nodded off at the front desk. There are several other desks. Probably for the day crew."

"Incredible," Jyrall said. "Figgle would have someone's head for that."

"Yep. Come on, let's get what we came for and play with some of that stuff in your backpack." He rubbed his paws together in anticipation.

Jyrall stood ready between the two sleeping men while Larth inserted a small drive into the communications tablet open beside the comms equipment. While it was downloading, he tapped the screen to see if there were any messages displayed. Jyrall heard him inhale sharply. He wanted to know what Larth had found, but neither could risk whispering.

Larth pulled the drive out and slipped it into his pocket. He eased toward Jyrall and held out his paws. Jyrall grinned and handed him the cushion. Larth carefully set it in the chair in front of the computer and secured it like it belonged there. He pulled a small tab, and three inches of padded material slid out. Larth pocketed it, and they eased into the hallway and out the back door.

Near the dock, they stopped deep in the shadows. "That was too easy," Larth said.

"Sometimes a mission goes according to plan," Jyrall argued. "What did you find out from the communications computer?"

"Prime's called for reinforcements. The message I saw was dated this evening, but it refers to a decision made days ago. A lot more ships are coming to the Krifay system."

"*That's* not according to our plan," Jyrall said. "Not at all."

* * *

Currahee
Intergalactic Haulers
Hyperspace

"Emergence in one hour, twenty-five minutes. Marek," the officer of the watch called across *Currahee's* bridge.

Captain Reginald Washburn released the five-point harness holding him into the seat. "Commander Hesse? I'm heading to inspect the weapons bays. I'll be back fifteen minutes prior to emergence. Set the watch to 100 percent. I want everyone manning their stations and conducting final combat checks."

"Aye, aye, sir," Hesse replied with a curt nod. The German operations officer, the *Currahee*'s third in command, was the picture of effective leadership. Washburn had no doubt Lieutenant Commander Marek Hesse would have the bridge, and the rest of the ship, ready for its first combat action. Washburn had grown up in East Lake, Georgia, and spent his formative years in a state of constant vigilance. He'd been raised by his mercenary parents to be ready for any eventuality. Having Hesse, and his executive officer Sandra Jones, on the same proverbial sheet of music was critical in combat. Especially with an unproven ship.

"Captain leaving the bridge," the officer of the watch, Lieutenant Sparks, called as Washburn made his way into the central passageway and propelled himself with his hands down the length of the *Currahee.*

Originally a Besquith long-duration freighter, it had been purchased by Intergalactic Haulers twelve months before and immediately put it into the docking facilities at Luna for refit. A sturdy and reliable freighter had gone into the facility. A weapons-heavy, thoroughly shielded dreadnought emerged just eleven months later. Washburn had been one of the Haulers' senior search and rescue mission commanders for more than a decade. When the company's CEO, James Francis, went missing, Washburn and the other captains merely continued operations until the Board of Directors ordered them to cease and desist all operations. Like his friends, Washburn had done no such thing.

When Francis returned a changed man, Washburn was among the first of the captains brought up to speed on new mission requirements and capabilities. Refitting the *Currahee* and having it ready to support operations by fire was Washburn's responsibility. His undergraduate engineering degree from Tuskegee and multiple graduate degrees from Georgia Tech set Washburn apart from the other captains. All of them could pilot the behemoth interstellar ships, but few of them could build from the keel up.

At the junction of the main passageway and the first set of fuselage-mounted weapon pylons, he saw Commander Jones tapping on her slate after speaking with Lieutenant Fenn, the forward weapons control officer.

"Sir, Lieutenant Fenn says the forward pylons are loading with no issues. The port feed mechanism has been cleared, lubricated, and is ready for action."

"Good to hear," Washburn replied. "The stern?"

"Also in the process of loading," Jones replied. She smiled at him and slipped the stylus for her slate into her pinned up blonde hair. She lowered her voice. They were the only people in the passageway for a moment. "Everything okay?"

Washburn felt his tension ebb slightly. While Sandra had never been a mercenary, she knew *Currahee's* systems as well as she knew him. They'd been married a decade. "I'm fine, Sandy. Just making my rounds."

She grinned. "*Currahee's* going to be fine, Reg. She's a good ship with a great crew. If we emerge into a fight, she'll take as much as she gives."

Washburn nodded. "We stand alone."

"We stand alone—together," Jones replied and broke decorum to kiss him on the cheek. She touched his cheek. "I think you need to grow your beard again."

He laughed. "Now you tell me."

"Gives you a dignified look. I miss it." She quickly grabbed his hand. "Now, get back to work, Skipper. I'll see you on the bridge."

Washburn smiled and turned toward the forward starboard pylon. Sandy always knew how to calm him down and focus him. All he needed to do was trust in his crew and his ship. They'd be there when he needed them… but it wouldn't hurt to finish his rounds.

*****

Chapter Thirty-One

Blue Ridge Kin

One Mile from Sandy Bay

Cora toggled through her screens. She felt comfortable, her Mk 6 surrounding her and responding like her own limbs. She also felt the nervous pressure of command. Lives were at stake—the lives of the Kin—her family. Her whole planet. She checked again for the message she was waiting for.

There! "All right, people, this is Blue 6. I just received the download. Sending it now."

Every CASPer in the company received it, and symbols appeared over all the map overlays. There were many more than they had hoped to see. Cora closed her eyes for a second in frustration.

"*Blue 6, Stormer 6,*" came the direct call on a private channel.

Cora answered, "I got you, Pete."

"*Did you take a quick count? 'Cause I sure did.*"

"Yeah. I see them. The program Keaton and Ricky came up with shows us every Crusader. There are a lot of little symbols… and eighty larger ones."

"*Eighty Mk 8s,*" Pete said. "*Damn.*"

"I know. Knowing precise locations helps, though."

"*Does it help enough?*"

Cora paused before answering. "I don't know. I just don't know."

* * *

Seventy Feet above the Surface
Eastern Sea

"*Do you see that, Lieutenant?*" Haney asked.

"I see it," Lieutenant Jaslien said. She, like the others, had a translucent screen on the visor of her helmet. "Break. Jonesy, you're drifting too far. Tighten it up!"

"*Yes, ma'am,*" the private answered.

"*There's a lot of them,*" Haney remarked. "*Hey, look! There's the symbols for tanks. Cool, they used the old-fashioned ones. Anyway, after we take care of the radar system for their anti-air, I have an idea.*"

"Fuck."

"*No. It's a good one, I swear.*"

"*I've heard this before,*" Staff Sergeant Tyner said. "*Ma'am… you know how he is.*"

The lieutenant knew her platoon sergeant was right. "Haney… I… fine. Once we complete our mission—God help me, 'cause my cousin is going to kill me—you can break free and do what you do."

"*Nah. Colonel Brentale wouldn't kill a family member. Me, maybe, but not you. Besides, it's a good idea.*"

"Cut power," Jaslien ordered.

Twenty powered hang gliders went silent moments later. The last of them touched down on the beach as the sun broke over the horizon behind them. The pre-dawn had given them what they needed to see the light-colored beach sand and perform the landings.

"Get the wings off and drag them up here. Move it!" Tyner ordered.

They pulled the gliders to a long dune. Two troops pulled sand-colored tarps out of their packs and covered them. A few handfuls of sand kept the edges down. A close inspection would find them, but one wasn't expected. The majority of the Crusader forces were oriented to the other side of the city Sandy Bay and not toward the actual bay and sea beyond.

By squads, they leapfrogged into the city itself. It was eerily quiet. The normal early morning traffic was nowhere to be seen. In a large city park, they located their target. Four large antennae spun slowly on their mobile towers. On the edge of the western side sat three tracked vehicles. The lasers atop two of them looked impressive. They'd slice into any craft within range, and from the looks of them, their range was vast.

Four Crusaders in light battle armor stood near one. Its rear hatch was open, the light bright as it shone out in the early morning. Laughter echoed across the park. One of the men took off his helmet and ran a hand over his short hair. He was the first to die.

When the lieutenant's rifle fired, it was the signal to the rest of the platoon. The three other men never fired a shot. The hatch opened on the command-and-control vehicle, only to be filled with kinetic rounds bouncing around the interior. There was no escape for the troops inside.

Sergeant Tyner pounded on the rear hatch of the last vehicle, its weapon useless. The turret wouldn't depress low enough to shoot toward the ground, and safety protocols would prevent it even if it could. Finally, the two men inside opened the hatch and held their hands up.

"Get out," the lieutenant ordered.

The look of hatred on both men's faces made her consider dispatching them, but she restrained herself. She put one of Ricky's smaller plugs against their pinplants and activated it. They both flinched. The shock was painful.

Unable to help himself, one said, "We already called this in. You'll be surrounded in minutes."

"I know," Jaslien said. "I heard." Their eyes widened. "Why do you think the rest of my platoon is already out of sight? That's how ambushes work, you know." She turned to the squad with her. "Secure their hands and feet, gag them, and roll them under the command vehicle."

She switched from her platoon's internal frequency to another. "*Night Moves*, Glider 6. Air defense is down. I say again, air defense is down."

She looked around. "Where is Haney? He's supposed to be here, not prepping the ambush… or has he snuck off already?"

* * *

Crusader HQ

Dock Area

Sandy Bay

Major Thornton sat up quickly and blinked in the early morning light. He heard the call from the anti-air unit in his earpiece while he was half-asleep and didn't know if he'd dreamed it or if they were actually under attack.

They didn't answer when he attempted to contact them to repeat the message. He looked toward the sergeant on duty and saw he was sleeping.

Damn!

"Get up, Combs!" he said as he walked by. He kicked the leg of the chair for emphasis. Thornton pulled out the chair at the communications desk and sat down.

I'll run the call back on audio replay, he thought.

That was his last thought.

The connectors touched in the seat cushion, and the explosives went off in a horrific blast that destroyed everything in the room, knocked down all the inner walls, shredded the sergeant's desk, and killed him as well. All the windows on the first floor blew out from the overpressure, and part of the second floor collapsed. One sentry out front was killed when the door slammed into him and threw him into the street. The other went tumbling. He sat up, dazed, his ears bleeding.

* * *

Night Moves

Eastern Sea

"That's what we were waiting for," Jyrall said. "Take us up. We need to let Ward know more ships are inbound."

"Roger," Keaton said. They all felt the G forces from the rapid ascent. "Sensors show an explosion near the docks."

"Hell, yeah!" Ricky said. "Blew them sumbitches into orbit!"

Larth looked to his partner. "You're all right with that?"

Jyrall nodded once. "The ends justify the means. Espionage may seem less than honorable, but it can be honorable when it saves many lives. I think I'm good with it."

"Me, too, Snarlyface. Fuck the Crusaders."

"What's the plan?" Keaton asked as he made course adjustments. "We gonna get the word to the other ships and come back for the battle?"

"We can sic Frank and Stein on them bastards," Ricky suggested.

"We may have to join the battle in near space," Jyrall said, "at least until we exhaust our missile supply. They're out-massed and outgunned. The Kin and Barnstormers now have a better chance. They can make jumps without fear of being cut out of the sky, and we've severed much of their communications."

"Speaking of which," Keaton said, "we're close enough to the satellite I designated. You want me to send the signal to disrupt their pinplants?"

"Will it work?" Larth asked.

"We think so," Keaton said. "Maarg thought it would. She looked it over after Ricky and I built it."

Jyrall tightened his harness to prepare himself for the lack of gravity. "Do it."

* * *

Blue Ridge Kin
CASPer Platoon

"You heard the call," Cora said. "Fifty meters, on the bounce. Go!"

Teams of three Mk 6 CASPers lifted off and

moved toward the Crusader lines, led by the officers. The Mk 4s followed shortly after, prepared to deploy their mortar tubes when they landed. Their job was to prep the battlefield for the ground troops in the center. They no longer had to fear the slow-moving rounds being cut from the air.

The Crusader pilots within range countered the move with small bounds of their own. MAC rounds and rockets flew back and forth as the CASPers cut into each other's armor. Each found cover of sorts in the uneven terrain as, by squads, they tried to exploit each other's lines.

* * *

1st INF Platoon

Blue Ridge Kin

Lieutenant Nails Rhineder moved his platoon forward forty yards before the return fire was too much to continue. The Crusaders had them vastly outnumbered. The only saving grace was that Nails could hear the commands given on the enemy's own network. He called back to Specialist Anderson and the other Mk 4 pilots.

"Shift fire! Shift fire! One hundred meters right, add fifty!"

"Roger, sir," Anderson answered.

The explosions moved closer to the entrenched Crusaders, some landing directly without inflicting many casualties. The enemy was dug in deeply. Smith had been given ample opportunity to prepare. It was a stalemate.

* * *

2nd INF Platoon

Blue Ridge Kin

"Fuck!" First Sergeant Figgle exclaimed. He keyed his comms. "We can't risk half the platoon just to take a hundred yards of friggin' dirt. We'll lose too many trying to get to that draw."

"It's bad, First Sergeant," Sergeant Gallyind agreed. "I can come around with the hovercar, but they've already taken out one of the skiffs with portable rockets." He paused a moment. "They got Bweenkit, Top."

"Dammit! When I get close enough, I'm killing one with my bare pincers. He was a good troop, even if he only had one eye and claimed he was a pirate."

"They're embedded in those bunkers, and the colonel and the CASPer platoon can't make their way to us," Gallyind said.

"I know," Figgle agreed, "and the damned Crusaders are calling for reinforcements. If those tanks move forward, we're all fucked. Squarlik, see if you can make your way back behind us and get to high ground. Maybe you can pick a few off with that .50 you've been carrying around."

"Roger, First Sergeant. Who'll take my squad?"

"I got 'em. Hey, you four-armed knuckle draggers. Bring those rocket launchers over here. Can you arch one and have it come down and blow when it hits?"

"Arch?" Private Tivlang asked. "What is arch?"

Figgle sighed. "Fuck me."

* * *

Barnstormers

"*Sir, we're pinned down. We can't go any farther. They have crew-served weapons trained on the end of this ravine. We can't get out of the creek bed. If we round the bend, we're exposed to the Mk 8s they have supporting them.*"

"Roger, Jerund," Pete answered. "Stay put. I don't like the traffic I'm hearing on the Crusaders' net. I'm going to talk to Blue 6. Hold what ya got."

"*Roger, sir.*"

* * *

Blue Ridge Kin

CASPer Platoon

"We're in the same predicament, Pete. They had too much time to prepare, and they used their Mk 8s to help dig the fortifications. They dug deep, and they did it in a hurry."

She paused and said, "I think it's time."

"*I agree,*" he answered. "*If we don't use it, I think they'll bring the other battalion forward, and there'll be nothing we can do. The numbers alone will take us out. I can't even send anyone back for a reload. I have empty racks on several troops.*"

"If we could get to one of our caches, it would go a long way," Cora agreed.

"*If,*" Pete said. "*If is a helluva word out here.*"

* * *

1st Battalion

Crusader Temporary Command Post

Colonel Smith pinched his nose and grimaced. Like everyone around him, he had a headache and an empty feeling. After a few minutes, he discovered the cause. His pinplants wouldn't work. They could neither receive nor send data. He shook his head and put his helmet back on.

"We've stopped their movement," he said. "Get on the comms and tell Major Cranter to prepare to move 2nd Battalion forward… and tell Captain Clarkson to swing his tanks around the southern end and sweep across the creek bed. Tell them to load sabot rounds only. A Mk 6 doesn't stand a chance against them."

"Yes, sir," the corporal said.

"This stalemate ends now. We'll see how they like being pinched between CASPers and good old-fashioned armor."

* * *

Sandy Bay

Crusader Armor Company

1st Platoon Holding Area

Specialist Haney walked up to the last tank in the courtyard. He raised a finger and waved his hand slightly. The tank commander looked at him, puzzled.

The staff sergeant removed his helmet and shouted, "What?"

Haney pointed to where pinplants would be on his head. The man gave him a knowing look and grimaced. He shook his head as if he were trying shake cobwebs out. Haney nodded.

Haney climbed the tank and stood beside the turret. He leaned close so the man could hear him over the noise of the turbine fan running at the rear of the tank. The idling tanks didn't help with the noise, either.

"Hey!" Haney yelled in his ear. "They sent me from HQ. I'm supposed to clear your pins and reboot them."

"HQ?" the staff sergeant yelled. He looked Haney up and down. "Why are you wearing an air defense designator, Corporal?"

"Who do you think deals with all the connection and computer issues with the radars and lasers?" Haney grinned with his best conspirator smile. "Not some officer, you can bet your ass."

"True," the tanker agreed. He nodded and pursed his lips as if a profound statement had been made. He looked at the items in Haney's hand. "How are you going to do that?"

"Let me come inside, and I'll show you the gear."

Once Haney was inside, the tank commander closed the top hatch. Inside, normal conversation could resume. Haney nodded to the other two occupants, the driver and the gunner.

"You boys got a headache?"

"Yeah," the gunner answered. "What the hell is going on with our pinplants?"

"Those damned mercs and their Jeha electronics," Haney explained. "I'm here to reboot your pins, so you guys will be good to go."

He handed all three of them one of Ricky's large shock plugs. They were as wide as his palm, and a half inch thick. The staff sergeant stared at it for a moment and looked expectantly at Haney.

"Hold it against your pins. Make sure it's firm, you want good contact. All right? Good. Let me scoot back away from you so the signal gets them all."

He looked them over. "Could you move out of the gunner's seat? That's right, scoot near the driver. All right. Looks good. It might sting a bit at first, but then the headache will be gone, and then you won't feel a thing."

Haney took out a sender Ricky had made for the plugs. "Let me just check the frequency. We're set. On my countdown. Three, two, one."

Haney pressed the trigger, and all three tankers' bodies went rigid. Eyes rolled back, and bodies spasmed. They were dead in moments.

Haney shook his head. "That's a bad way to go," he said to the bodies, "but it beats how the rest are going."

He slipped into the gunner's seat, checked to ensure the autoloader was in the green, armed the main gun, and sighted in on the rear of the farthest tank in the platoon. He fired, then aimed and repeated when the gun was loaded. Each target was closer than the last. By the time one of the turrets had finally started to turn his way, it exploded like the other four tanks had when hit directly in the thinnest part of its armor. The last turret went spinning away when the rounds in the ammo rack blew.

Haney heard the call for the tanks to move forward. He shrugged. This platoon wasn't going anywhere. He eyed the driver slumped in the driver's compartment. *Unless…*

* * *

Daniels

Orbit of Krifay

"Emergence warning at L2."

Ward Pintair turned to the operations screen in the *Daniels'* Combat Information Center. "What have we got out there?"

His intelligence officer, a SleSha named Wootrax, moved a box icon over LaGrange point L2 on the far side of Krifay. The sensor relays processed the image and enhanced the resolution. "Looks like another eight ships, all squawking Crusader codes. Detecting movement signatures. They're heading to the group in our sector, by the looks of it."

Right over Snapper Isle. Great.

Pintair frowned. The *Daniels* and her small fleet were orbiting Krifay at about two thousand kilometers. The Crusaders had four groups of ships in geosynchronous orbit above them. Two groups of Crusader ships were always in view. There was no doubt in his mind that if they warmed up weapons or displayed any hostile intent, the Crusaders would rain missiles down on them.

We're fish in a damned barrel. Us and everybody on the ground, apparently.

"Where's the *Blue Ridge*?" Pintair asked.

"Approaching from astern, sir. She's eight thousand kilometers away and slowing down to meet our altitude," Wootrax replied. "We have secure comms."

Pintair nodded. As usual, Wootrax was thinking ahead of him, which was precisely why he'd hired the SleSha all those years ago. The ex-intelligence officer, like his former ship commander, had been enjoying retirement on Krifay. It hadn't taken much of a nudge to get his old friend to join him in one last excursion off planet. It hadn't hurt matters that the SleSha was already the friend of two of the pilots in Blue Ridge Kin. Those two were assigned to the frigate, *Kellie's Last Stand.*

"Let me talk to them. Not the pilots, either."

Wootrax laughed but didn't reply. Cora McCoy had hired the Mideralls as pilots, and they were damned good ones, but communicating with them was anything but easy. "I have Specialist Conner, sir. There's video, too."

Pintair saw Wootrax's approximation of a smile and head shake. He snorted. "Put it on screen."

"Sir, Specialist Conner." He saw the young woman, busy at her console. She didn't bother to look at the camera, and he took no offense. He hated interrupting her duties, but they needed a plan. Behind her, he saw the Mideralls in their command chairs. The parrot-like aliens, known for their audacious fashion choices, appeared to be decked out in gold, orange, and purple robes covered with ornate designs.

"Conner, you've got eyes on our friends up there?"

"Affirmative, sir," Conner replied. "We're maintaining a standard approach and rendezvous. Our sister ship is mirroring us off our bow. When we join up, we'll perform a gate injection burn alongside you and move that direction. We're going to have extremely limited engagement windows."

Pintair nodded. "We're going to go ahead and burn, *Blue Ridge*. If we maintain our distance, we can maybe keep up the ruse a bit longer."

"Roger. Understand, sir," Conner replied.

There was a click on the channel. "We'll burn in six. Six minutes, that is," the Miderall named Monty squawked.

"Nominal burns. Burns, don't you know," Stew replied. "Weapons at the ready. Ready, you understand. All hands, set battle, I say, battle stations."

Pintair saw a red light bathe the *Blue Ridge's* bridge. The hideous ensemble worn by the Miderall appeared to almost… glow.

"What in the hell are they wearing?" he muttered.

Monty squawked. "We are dressed, dressed in our best, I say!"

"Prepared to die, looking our finest. Finest, that is," Stew replied.

"We must be. Must, that is," Monty explained. "It would not do to be any less for eternity. That's eternity, you understand."

Pintair saw Conner roll her eyes and try not to smile. He wiped his nose and mouth with one hand to cover his own smile. "Roger, *Blue Ridge*, we're going to—"

Alarms went off on the *Blue Ridge's* bridge, followed closely by his own. He glanced at Wootrax.

"Emergence warning. I've got twelve… no sixteen ships at L2 behind the Crusaders. They've opened fire!"

Pintair stabbed his radio controls. "Blue 6, this is *Daniels*, in the clear. We're engaged at L2. Friendlies unknown. As soon as we make contact, I'll update. *Daniels*, out."

He worked the controls for the *Daniels'* communication suite himself and initiated a scan using the two polar inclined satellites the Fishing Wardens used for planet-wide communications. The scan locked on a signal high in the S band. "…Killers. Crusader vessels, you are ordered to stand down or face the consequences!"

Killers?

"Sir, I've got Jivool cruisers and Bakulu missile frigates in that formation," Wootrax said.

The radio erupted again. "Any friendly station, this is the Slow Killers in the vicinity of emergence zone L2. We are engaging Crusader vessels and request assistance. Over."

Time to fight.

Pintair turned to his helm officer. "Escape velocity burn. Set battle stations and prepare weapons. Relay to the *Blue Ridge* and all our ships."

Alarms sounded throughout the ship. The helm replied and lit the *Daniels'* engines in a sustained burn at just over half a G. Pintair studied the screen and watched the Crusader vessels above them. They didn't fire. After about thirty seconds, the radio connected.

"*Captain of the* Daniels, *this is Crusader Prime. We have the high ground and have locked missiles on your ships. More missiles than you can hope to stop. State your intentions. Any act of aggression will be treated as a hostile action, and you will be fired upon. I will not warn you again. State your intentions.*"

Pintair clenched his jaw and reached for the radio button. His hand hovered over it for a second as he tried to think of something to say. Something for the history books. Something that could—

<<PROXIMITY WARNING ON ASCENT PATH. EMERGENCE DETECTED,>> the *Daniels'* automated caution and warning system blared as it cut the thrust from the main engines and applied reaction control thrusters on the bow to start deceleration.

A ship appeared in the blackness above them. Based on its albedo, it was much larger than the *Daniels* or the *Blue Ridge*, and likely dwarfed the Crusader vessels as well. Pintair scanned it and saw its bow oriented on the Crusaders at geo. At an altitude of roughly 15,000 kilometers, it was well within a standard weapons envelope.

Who in the—

"*Crusader Prime, this is the* Currahee. *You'll do no such thing.*"

"*Who do you think you are? You're just one more ship, and I have the numerical advantage,*" Prime responded.

"*This is Captain Reginald Washburn, and I think you're going to be sorely mistaken in three, two, one...*"

* * *

Warrior Apostle

Lemieux mashed the transmit button to tell his ships to open fire when another twelve ships, including familiar hulls from the Intergalactic Haulers, emerged in the space between his ship and the planet.

They're not in the emergence zone! How in the hell did they do that?

Lemieux hesitated. These mercenaries were well connected, to the point they'd gotten Jessica and her father's business into it. He was tempted, so very tempted, to fire everything in his arsenal from all of his ships, but they had the advantage now. They had—

"Sir, the *Currahee* appears to be a Besquith design, but it's bristling with weapons pods like nothing I've ever seen," his weapons officer, Lieutenant Commander Felix, replied. "It's like a dreadnought."

Lemieux pulled his hand back from the radio control. He locked eyes with his helm officer. "Prepare the shunts and execute jump to the nearest safe harbor. Advise all ships to do the same and rendezvous at Marian Seven."

"Sir?" Commander Farrell, the *Apostle's* executive officer, asked. "Full retreat? We have mission objectives that—"

"Don't lecture me on objectives, Farrell!" Lemieux roared. "Surviving the day and executing the plan takes precedence. They want this water world so bad? They can keep it. But the first time any of them leave here, every Crusader unit is ordered to kill them on sight. Is that clear?"

"Yes, sir," the XO replied. "Will transmit."

"Shunts ready for jump in one minute," the helm called.

"*What's it going to be,* Warrior Apostle*?*" Washburn's deep voice mocked him. "*We're ready to trade blows anytime you want.*"

Lemieux reached for the transmit button. "You'll get your chance someday, *Currahee.* Tell Snowman, the next time I see a Haulers' ship perform a hostile act, they're dead."

"*We haven't performed any hostile acts, merely warned you of the consequences,*" Washburn replied. Lemieux could hear the smile in his voice. "*I'd imagine you're going to hear a whole lot of that from all the citizens and species your Crusaders have fucked over. There's a storm coming, friend.*"

"I'm not your friend, *Currahee,*" Lemieux growled. "Next time."

"*Count on it,*" Washburn replied.

"Shunts at full power," the helmsman reported.

He waited for ten seconds, hoping Counselor would connect. It didn't happen. Instead, he tapped a button for Smith.

"*Prime?*" his ground commander called.

"You're on your own, Smith. Prime, out." Lemieux turned to his XO. "Necessary sacrifice. Jump."

"Yes, sir."

Lemieux squeezed his eyelids shut and grabbed the armrests.

Gods damn you, Jessica, but you just became public enemy number one. Lemieux grinned as the *Warrior Apostle* transitioned into hyperspace.

* * * * *

Chapter Thirty-Two

1st Battalion

Crusader Temporary Command Post

Colonel Smith threw his helmet against the dirt embankment making up the wall in the bunker. "Bastard!" He turned to the 1st Battalion commander. "I hear nothing from him since this shit kicked off, and he finally contacts me to tell me we're on our own. I don't give a fuck if he *is* Prime. After we handle this bullshit, he better have a good reason. Like our fleet destroyed the merc ships, and he didn't see the need to deploy additional troops—something!"

"Yes, sir," Major Darvin said. He managed to keep the look of shock off his face at his commander's blatant disrespect of Crusader Prime. He waited for instructions, careful not to make Smith any angrier.

"Call 2nd Battalion. Tell them to hold their movement for three hours. Distribute the spare ammunition. Ensure the men eat something, and be prepared to attack. I've had enough of this stalemate. We'll time it for when they arrive, and they can occupy our positions when we go forward. Find out what's holding up the armor company. I want them to cross that creek when we kick off."

"Yes, sir."

"Fuckin' Prime. I'd better not find out he's a coward," Smith said as he snatched up his helmet and ducked out the rear of the bunker.

Major Darvin didn't try to hide the shock on his face this time. He turned to his operation's officer. "See if you can reach Prime's ship. If not, any of the ships in the fleet. Search all communications bands."

"Yes, sir."

* * *

Blue Ridge Kin

CASPer Platoon

"All right, Kin, Barnstormers, this is Colonel McCoy… I'm calling for the secret weapon."

Every member of both companies heard her through various comms. Earpieces, helmets, from within the cockpit of their CASPer, everyone listened intently, because she used her name and not her call sign. There was silence on the frequency.

"From this point on, I want you to be vigilant in identifying your target before firing. Do not, I say again, *do not* engage any target other than Crusaders or Crusader machines."

Pete cut in. "*For verification, this is Colonel Brentale. You heard her. There can be no mistakes here.*"

A lone voice was heard. "*Uh, what secret weapon?*"

"*Dammit Private Tivlang!*" Figgle shouted. "*Get off the net. It's REDACTED!*"

Cora couldn't help but smile, despite the situation they were in. "Yes. It's a Redacted Weapon."

* * *

Snapper Isle

When the call came, it was answered.

They eased out of hurricane shelters, basements, and apartments in twos and threes, meeting at designated places in the city until their numbers grew into squads and platoons. They wore old equipment, battle armor, and mismatched helmets. All were armed with rifles or pistols, some with shoulder-fired rockets, others with pieces of crew-served weapons they hastily put together. Still more eased vehicles from locked sheds with darkened windows, metal affixed to them, and most had extra rounds, rockets, and missiles loaded for distribution.

From the docks, fishing vessels threw off mooring lines and took to the intercoastal waters or approached the shore at best speed. Tarps were pulled from makeshift mortars. Crab pots, with floats for retrieval, were pushed overboard, revealing crates with a CASPer, sometimes two, stored and waiting at the center of the stacks. They were older models, but all were topped off with jump juice and fully armed.

From large caves near Sandy Bay, barges were moved, loaded with equipment. Some old, some newer, purchased from the Slow Killers. From the largest cave, its entry below the water level, twenty CASPers exploded from the sea, rockets firing at full thrust. They landed on the edge of the cliff above them and moved toward the city.

From the rural areas, farmers and others gathered with rifles in hand. Some had never fired a weapon at another sapient being, while others were long retired from merc life. None of that mattered now.

All manner of races gathered, every one of them prepared to fight for their home.

Krifay had answered the call, its inhabitants *were* the Redacted Weapon.

* * *

1st Battalion

Crusader Temporary Command Post

The major ran out of the bunker searching for Colonel Smith. He found him seated behind the next bunker eating a protein bar. He wasted no time reporting.

"What?" Smith demanded.

"Sir, the Crusader fleet jumped. They left the system."

"I guess he finally realized I have it under control."

"No, sir. There are over thirty ships near orbit. They belong to mercenary companies. My ops officer heard the traffic between them. The Blue Ridge Kin and Barnstormer ships haven't been destroyed. We've identified the Slow Killers, which is a Jivool company, other Jivool ships, a Bakulu fleet, and… the Intergalactic Haulers. Sir, we don't have any reinforcements coming."

"Shit! We've got to end this now. If we take care of these merc units, we can take over the leadership of this planet and threaten the source of protein. They'll play ball."

"What if they send down reinforcements to the enemy?"

"They won't," Smith decided. "If someone has a valid contract with merc fleets, I doubt it includes troops on the ground. We'll be fine down here until Prime comes back with a big enough fleet to crush them. Crusader pockets are deep, and two can play the 'contract a mercenary fleet' game. What's the word on those tanks?"

* * *

Downtown Sandy Bay

Haney stood in the hatch of the tank with his hands up. "Hey! I'm not one of them! I'm only wearing this uniform so I could snag a tank."

Mike stepped forward. "Haney? You crazy bastard. Get down here. Let me put some of these boys in there. Who brought the paint? Cover that damn cross. Somebody paint Krifay on both sides."

The owner of Sandy Bay's most popular bar and grill shook Haney's hand. "You might want to get out of that uniform. Krifay's Volunteers are moving toward the edge of the city to hit the Crusaders. I'd hate for some teenage girl to pick you off from the top of a building with her daddy's spare rifle."

"Me, too," Haney agreed as he took off the jacket. "I want this tank back after the battle. It's mine; I acquired it myself. We can negotiate later if the Volunteers want to buy it, or better, trade for it. Now, let me tell you how to take out their last platoon of tanks. You ease up behind and…"

* * *

Crusaders

2nd INF Battalion

Mortar rounds came screaming in from several directions… including behind them. Multiple shots rained down into the assembly area. Soldiers scrambled and were caught in the open by the residents of Krifay. For many, their battle armor saved them from the initial onslaught. That didn't last, as it was chipped away while they scrambled for cover.

The CASPers assigned to the unit turned and moved in pairs toward the city. They were met by rockets from both shoulder-fired weapons and from Mk 5s and Mk 6s. Occasionally a Mk 4 showed on their sensors. The pilots of the Crusader Mk 8s gave more than they received, but fighting in pairs was no match for the MAC rounds, missiles, and rockets engaged against them.

The battalion commander was screaming into his comms for support from 1st Battalion when he saw a tank round the building nearest to him. His eyes widened when he realized the gun was trained on the utility vehicle he was standing next to.

* * *

1st Battalion

Crusader Temporary Command Post

"Get him back!" Colonel Smith demanded. "Now!"

"Sir, Major Cranter isn't answering. His XO claims they're being attacked by overwhelming numbers from the city."

"Overwhelming?" Smith asked. "How the hell are they being overwhelmed? There are no enemy units back there. What? A few civilians with rifles? We encountered very few weapons in our spot checks. These people aren't armed like that."

"He claims they're facing artillery and crew-served weapons. Tanks have fired on them."

"That's bullshit. The anti-air would burn them from the sky. Call HQ."

"HQ has been off the net all day, sir."

"What the fuck is going…"

He didn't finish the sentence. A call came in directly to him.

"*Smith. This is Colonel Cora McCoy of the Blue Ridge Kin. Surrender now, and you can stop the loss of life among your troops.*"

"What?" he screamed. "Surrender? I have you outnumbered and unable to advance. Why would I surrender to you?"

"*Because we have* you *surrounded and outnumbered. The residents of Krifay have had enough. They hold our contract. If you don't surrender, we'll be forced to complete the terms of that contract. We'll rid this planet… and system of Crusaders.*"

"Residents? They're fishermen and farmers… easily put down. You can go to hell."

"*I gave you a choice. That's all I'm obligated to do. McCoy, out.*"

Smith looked at the major. "This ends now. Get the troops ready to advance. 2nd Battalion can catch up when they finish with the rabble they're dealing with."

"Yes, sir."

Smith tightened the strap on his helmet and pulled up the map overlay in his visor.

Fucking bitch.

* * *

Blue Ridge Kin
CASPer Platoon

"Here they come!" Cora said. "Conserve your shots, and be sure of them. I know we've reloaded and topped off, but we'll need every round. Left side, move up!"

The Mk 8s were heavily armored and dealt damage to the Kin's Mk 6s and Mk 7s. Cora watched as several went offline, Kin who would never fight again for their family. She pushed them to the back of her mind and fought on, directing her officers and their teams as they met the Crusaders head on.

From the flank, friendly rockets hammered the Crusaders.

* * *

2nd INF Platoon
Blue Ridge Kin

"Son of a bitch!" Figgle screamed. "Dammit, Squarlik. Can you get this four-armed dumbass to drag me any easier? Fuck, this hurts!"

"Sorry, First Sergeant, but we have to get you to cover. You've been hit bad."

"Fine, but give me my rifle, and prop me up. This is bullshit." He shifted, trying to get comfortable. Tivlang moved to help. "Now, get out there and help Gallyind. Move 'em up to the ridge and get the drop on those bastards. I can guarantee they'll regroup and try it again. Shit!"

Figgle flinched. "Fucking Tivlang! Sorry, Private. Thanks."

He took a deep breath. "Squarlik, if you see any-damn-body with officer rank, you take him out with that .50. Now move, you two!"

* * *

1st INF Platoon

Blue Ridge Kin

"Anderson, hit 'em with everything. They're in the open. Fire for effect!"

"*Roger, sir.*"

Nails Rhineder watched the dirt fly and bodies fall until Anderson called to let him know they'd exhausted their rounds.

"Roger, get back with the colonel, and get ready to do real CASPer shit. Out here."

He turned to his platoon. "By squads! Let's move out!"

* * *

Barnstormers

"There's our cue," Pete said. "Get up that bank, and give them everything we've got!"

"Look, sir!" Sergeant First Class Wilson said. "There's our gliders. They're dropping mines and impact grenades. That's going to get ugly."

"I see them. They better stay high and out of range. Wait. Who's that on a dive run?"

"I bet you a week's pay it's fucking Haney," Wilson said.

"No bet."

* * *

Sandy Bay

Travis Gannon rolled his neck. It was a tighter fit in his CASPer than he remembered. Of course, it hadn't been used for more than moving it since he'd last strapped into her years ago. Clamming and running a few crab pots hadn't done much for his expanding waistline in his retirement years. He checked his readings. Everything was in the green, with the occasional flicker of orange. She wasn't in perfect shape, but she was in fighting shape.

He checked the squad he was assigned to support. They moved ahead of him from doorway to doorway, hiding in the shadows. He couldn't do the same.

Kids. They're just kids. Early twenties, most of them. He knew they could move faster if they didn't play leapfrog with doorways. After all, with a CASPer trailing them, they weren't hidden. Moments later, he realized hiding was what had saved most of them.

A pair of Mk 8s came around the corner. The one on the left fired at a man running for a doorway, killing him. The other fired at Gannon. Armor peeled from the shoulder, and the machine stumbled. Without thinking, Gannon hit the ground and rolled his CASPer. It was an impressive move most pilots couldn't achieve, and he'd done it instinctively. He came up on one knee and discharged all the rockets in his pod. Most hit. The Crusader's Mk 8 toppled, smoking, with its cockpit partially exposed.

The radio filled with whoops and cheers. He turned it off. The fight wasn't over. Breathing heavily, Gannon toggled to his MAC and fired at the same time the remaining Crusader did. Their MAC rounds tore through each other's armor. Gannon could no longer move his left arm. Red lights flashed on his cracked screens. He got off one last shot and finished the Crusader before he felt his machine topple.

Retired Master Sergeant Travis Gannon felt numb. And cold. So cold. He panted in rapid, shallow breaths and watched his remaining panel flash red until his blurred vision slowly tunneled and went black. The ringing in his ears faded.

He blinked several times, and his vision cleared, better than it had been for years. He stared up into the face of a beautiful woman. She smiled and reached for him.

He took his Emma's hand.

*****

Chapter Thirty-Three

Front Lines
Sandy Bay
Krifay

"Yes!" Larth exclaimed. "Dropped them right in their laps! This thing is great, Ricky."

"It's not a thing. Its name is Scar. I had to rebuild it after Squarlik shot it."

"Whatever its name is, it's great." Larth ran his finger over the screen of the tablet controlling one of Ricky's drones. "I'm bringing it back so we can attach more grenades."

Behind them, Jyrall hurried down the ramp, carrying a large heavy crate. "Here are the last of the missiles for Frank and Stein. Belts for the .50 and the last two drums of .45 rounds are in it, too."

"I'll load Frank, you load Stein," Keaton said to his brother.

"Let me put them on safe," Ricky said. "There." He looked around the edge of the battlefield near them. "They dang sure ain't tryin' to slip around the flank anymore, are they?"

"No," Jyrall agreed, "they're not. After all this, I'd like a weapons option on the ship to engage ground forces." He leaned against Frank and steadied his pistol with two paws. The huge hand cannon went off. Two hundred meters away, a Crusader dropped.

"Hell, yeah, we can figure somethin' out," Ricky assured him as he worked. "Damn! That barrel is hot!"

"Don't let the grease on your fingers catch fire," Keaton teased.

"Funny! Ow! Shit! Shit! Shit!"

* * *

CASPer Platoon
Blue Ridge Kin

Cora tried a system reboot. It was useless. Her Mk 6 had taken more damage than its operating system could handle. Armor was missing from its left shoulder, right thigh, and hip area. She hit the emergency eject and dismounted. She rolled to her left and looked toward the last two standing Crusader Mk 8s.

She heard the external speaker on one crackle. "Now you'll get what you've had coming to you since you punched me years ago." She recognized Smith's voice.

The MAC on its shoulder shifted slightly and was blown off by a MAC round fired from behind her. Cora ducked her head and stayed low. Several more shots were exchanged by the Crusader CASPers and those behind her. The Mk 8s went down smoking.

"Cora!" Nileah shouted as she climbed down from the open cockpit, the knee joint glowing red hot on her Mk 6. In a similar CASPer slightly behind hers, May's boots appeared as she forced her cockpit open with her legs. It was damaged extensively.

"I'm good," Cora reassured them. She felt the ground shake as Lissale's CASPer landed between her and Smith's downed machine.

There was no movement from the Crusaders, so Lissale cracked her cockpit and stood in the opening. She was looking back when Smith crawled from his Mk 8 on his knees and raised a pistol.

To Cora, it all happened in slow motion. The pistol swung toward her and... Smith's head exploded. The body toppled over. Time resumed its normal flow, and she heard a call in her earpiece.

"Blue 6, this is Squarlik. He's down. First sergeant said to shoot any Crusader officer I saw. I hope you didn't want him captured or anything, because he's kind of dead."

Mako 15
Near Orbit
Krifay

"Go, Carter!" Tara ordered from inside Deathangel's cockpit. As soon as they'd emerged, tucked safely along the hull of the Haulers' freighter *Bringing The Goods*, the plan was a fast, powered descent to the top of Krifay's atmosphere and then good, old-fashioned hypersonic curves to null their speed. Tara and Araceli had mounted their CASPers and were ready to drop as soon as *Mako 15* shed enough speed. "Maarg, get me comms!"

"Mako 15, *this is* Currahee. *Your skies are clear.*"

Tara blinked. "Carter? Get that clarified."

"*Currahee, Mako 15*. Say again?"

The deep voice chuckled. "Mako 15, *we have air and near-space superiority. You're clear to Snapper Isle.*"

"What?" Tara gasped. "Nike, connect me to the *Currahee.*"

<<Enabled.>>

"*Currahee*, this is Misfit 6. Where are the Crusaders?"

"*Facing negative odds, they jumped. Destination unknown*," the man said. "*This is Captain Reginald Washburn. We're standing by and at your service. Snowman sends his compliments.*"

No school like the old school. Tara grinned. "Copy, *Currahee.* I'll get back with you as soon as we establish comms with the ground units."

"Already scanning, Boss," Maarg replied. "I can't reach the Peacemakers, but I've got the Kin's command frequency. Button one."

Tara tapped the button inside Deathangel. "Blue 6, this is Misfit 6, over."

"*Misfit 6!*" Cora yelped. "*Going to private connection.*"

Tara heard a series of digital tones, and she knew Nike would interpret them and make the private connection viable. She waited five seconds. "Cora? You there?"

"*Roger. We've got the Crusaders either on the run or surrendering. Would've been much worse without our secret weapon.*"

"Glad to hear everything went pretty much to plan. Casualties?"

Cora's voice changed slightly. "*We're still getting word in. My forces got hit pretty hard. Same for the Barnstormers. Krifay's Volunteers had many who gave their all, as well.*"

"The cost of freedom," Tara said reverently. "It's never free."

"*Yeah.*" Cora sighed. "*It sure ain't.*"

There was silence on the call for a moment, then Tara said, "We're on our way and will be there in thirty-six minutes."

"*We'll be glad to have you,*" Cora replied. The edge was back in her voice. "*We're rounding up the Crusaders, but Krifay doesn't have any place to hold them. There are quite a few residents who've suggested a 'one shot per and a big ol' hole' solution.*"

Tara thought quickly. "We'll get them off planet. If they want to transfer, don't let them. Their pinplants might have been disrupted, but they're still tainted. You don't want Counselor knowing what you're doing from here on out."

"*Yeah, I copy. Tell Maarg thank you from me, will you? Her insight really helped us with Ricky and Keaton's frequency match and signal interrupter.*"

"Roger, will do. Is the transmitter off? Recommend you all turn it off. Anybody could still be listening," Tara said.

"*Copy. Stand by one,*" Cora replied. "*It's off. Need to get a few things done before y'all get here. Anything else?*"

"We brought a present for the boys," Tara replied. "One they're gonna love."

The connection broke down with a series of digital tones. Tara tapped the radio and went back to the *Currahee*'s frequency. "*Currahee*, Misfit 6. We've got a mission for y'all. We're gonna exile the Crusaders."

"*Roger. They're Humans, so back to Earth?*"

"No. Take them to Karma. They can fend for themselves on that shithole," Tara replied. With any luck, they'd be unable to find work. The rest of the galaxy had had enough of their act. The coming days would be interesting on many levels, especially once the boys saw what Maarg had found in Hatfield's files.

* * *

Blue Ridge Kin
Temporary Headquarters
Sandy Bay

Tara listened to the conversation from a few meters away as she prepared Deathangel to reload into its rack aboard *Mako 15*. Maarg, Gnrra, and the two Pushtal brothers stood in a circle around a terminal set up atop its carrying case.

"I wanted to show you guys," Maarg said. "The pinplant connection might not work again on that same frequency. Especially now that Counselor has undoubtedly seen the data from our jamming signature, it'll adapt and overcome. But there's some good news."

"It's still in the same relative band." Keaton rubbed the fur on his face with one hand. "Unless Counselor figures out a different way or changes frequency bands."

"Yeah, but the program can find that shit right fast and in a hurry," Ricky replied. "Collectin' it ain't a problem."

"It's hiding it that we had to be careful of," Gnrra said. "Just because we have it doesn't mean we can collect it all the time without something to manage all the data."

"I can whip up something purty damned fast," Keaton replied, "but you've got an idea, don't you?"

Maarg turned toward Tara. "Can we give them Nike?"

"Shoes?" Ricky guffawed. "What they—"

"Shut up, Ricky." Keaton hit him in the shoulder. "What's Nike?"

Maarg motioned with her big arms, and the group tightened around the console. They reminded Tara of a group of kids in a football huddle, and it made her laugh. She turned to see Peacemakers Jyrall and Larth walking toward her. Cora McCoy was there, too, walking hand in hand with the Besquith.

Tara couldn't help but smile. *Good for them. However they can manage it.*

"Tara!" Cora called as they approached.

She stood, wiped her hands on her coveralls, and returned Cora's wave. Araceli and Whirr also waved as they came together in a loose circle around Deathangel. The mood was light, but remained serious. Around them, the Blue Ridge Kin, Barnstormers, and a host of other units and civilians began the long clean up after a conflict.

"We've got the Crusaders loading aboard shuttles for the ships *Bringing The Goods* and the *Yargo* now. *Currahee* is going to escort them to Karma," Cora said.

"Great suggestion," Jyrall said. "They'll likely have an interesting welcome."

"Who cares?" Larth cackled. "Fuckers!"

Tara laughed and shook her head. "I know you have a lot to do here, but we found something the two of you are going to want to see."

Jyrall released Cora's hand and shook hands with Tara. "Well met, Tara."

"Well met, Peacemaker." She repeated the gesture with Larth, and then offered her hand to Cora. "Thanks for everything. You and your Kin are amazing, Cora."

"That's high praise, coming from you." Cora blushed. "Working with you and the Misfits has been amazing. I'm sure our paths will cross again."

Tara reached for a large slate and held it up so she could tap a series of access commands on the screen. "If this is right, I'm sure we will. Maarg found this picture in Hatfield's files."

Tara watched the young Peacemakers immediately lock eyes on Kr'et'Socae. Their emotional reactions were muted, but Tara felt the anger, especially from Jyrall. He studied the picture for a long moment and pointed at the Human.

"Who's the woman?"

"Her name is Raley Shea Reilly. Raleigh Reilly was her father," Tara replied.

"And I'm guessing the apple didn't roll far from the tree, huh?" Larth asked. "She's involved on the wrong side now."

"The picture had a geo-tag. We know precisely where and when it was taken." Tara pulled up the application. "Six months ago. Earth."

"Dammit! We coulda had him there!" Larth exclaimed.

Jyrall shook his head. "No, Little Buddy. What matters is, we've found him now. What's the location?"

"Near a lake in eastern Tennessee." Tara handed over the slate again with the location marked. "This slate has all of Hatfield's information decoded and sorted, thanks to Maarg. You have the location you've been searching for. Good luck."

Jyrall nodded. He turned to look at Cora for a moment. "We're going to have to leave, Cora. We have a mission—"

Cora reached up with both hands and grabbed the sides of the Besquith's head. She pulled him down to her level and planted a kiss on his maw. Jyrall shook visibly, and then grabbed her shoulders lightly before the short kiss was over. Tara saw a crowd had gathered around them, including Nileah, Lisalle, and May. All of them whooped, and Cora blushed. Jyrall looked as embarrassed as a Besquith could, which turned out to be pretty embarrassed. There was little doubt they were more than friends, and no one around the little group minded. They'd figure something out.

Larth wrinkled his nose. "Eww. I might actually have lost my appetite." He rubbed his stomach.

"Unlikely," Cora and Jyrall replied at the same time.

"Hey, Jyrall?" Ricky called. "Iffin you're gonna be some kinda Kin and all, ya gotta do somethin' for us, all right?"

"What, Ricky?" He squeezed Cora's shoulder and shook his head at the Pushtal.

"Ya ever say Hatfield's name again, ya gotta learn to spit after it," Ricky said. He turned and spat. "Get that shit outa yer mouth."

"Them rotten sumbitches," Keaton agreed.

"Snake bellies," Ricky added.

"Egg sucking dogs?" Jyrall asked.

The group gasped.

"Jyrall? Honey? That might not be the best thing, comin' outta your mouth." Cora nudged him in the shoulder. "I mean..."

*****

Chapter Thirty-Four

Vicinity of Bean Station, Tennessee
Earth

Cool rain drummed onto the roof of Raley Reilly's cabin as daylight broke. A quick look outside confirmed the clouds weren't breaking in the near future. Based on the rate and intensity, the rain would hang around until lunch, and maybe after. Raley rolled out of bed and dressed quickly in clothes she'd laid out the night before.

She'd promised Kr'et'Socae she would zero and get her new XR43 smooth-bore sniper rifle mission ready. The graduation present, especially coming from the Equiri, had surprised her. She'd trained with him for the bulk of two years, while also working on dual college degrees at his urging. She didn't fully trust him, which he likely knew and understood, but she appreciated what he'd done for her after the death of her father.

His intentions and motivations, though, were still unclear. He wanted her to restart the Raiders and fully outfit a mercenary company, and she'd agreed without knowing what his endgame was. As smart as she was, and as skeptical as her father had taught her to be, she couldn't see what he was doing, other than biding his time. One of the galaxy's most wanted, he'd only left the Reilly's Raiders compound once in the last two and half years, to go to Weqq with her.

He either didn't know what she'd found there or her subsequent discovery at Nottely Dam, or he didn't care. His mind was elsewhere, and that bothered her.

Dressed in boots and fatigue pants, Raley pulled on a black hooded sweatshirt and a rainproof combat jacket while she waited for the coffee maker. With a stainless-steel mug in her gloved hands, Raley walked out into the rain and turned east toward the rifle range a half mile away. Between the raindrops, she saw a faint cloud of steam with every exhale. Walking the road would have soaked her from head-to-toe without her gear.

As she neared the forest, where the trail to the range emerged into the wide clearing she'd crossed, the rain turned into a heavy mist. Under the cover of the forest, only a few drops fell from the saturated leaves above. Raley pushed back her hood and sipped her coffee as she walked.

The trail ended at another freshly-mown field. A small herd of deer wandered out of the trees to her left and watched her walk for a moment before returning to their idle grazing. Raley smiled. As she watched them, she remembered her father doing the same with a serene look on his face. He'd loved nature, and he'd loved their refuge. She also knew he would've appreciated everything she'd done. Her twenty-first birthday was two weeks away and, per her father's trust, the bulk of his holdings would finally be completely hers. Then, she believed, they could get to work.

At the top of a knoll at one end of the field was the rifle range. She walked up to the covered concrete porch and shook the rain off her jacket before taking it off. She laid it on a wooden picnic table with her coffee cup and turned to the heavy steel door built into a small room at the end of the range. She tapped the electronic combination lock, and the door opened to the training vault. With the press of a button, she turned on a light, just as she heard the faint scuff of a boot on the concrete behind her. She turned, already well into the open-handed strike toward the throat of the attacker she believed to be her mentor and one of his—

She caught a glimpse of red hair before her strike was knocked away, and the attacker pushed her shoulder hard enough to force her off the concrete pad and send her sprawling on the gravel apron. Through the mist, Raley looked up to see a Human female standing over her. The redhead didn't appear to have a weapon, nor was she in a fighting stance. There was a hint of a smile on her face.

"Who are you?" Raley asked even as she recognized the stranger.

"Jessica Francis," the redhead said.

Raley felt an icy bolt of fear shoot down her spine. "What do you want?"

"I'm not here for you, Raley. My father sends his regards." She reached out a hand. After considering a possible counterattack, Raley took her hand, and the former Peacemaker pulled her to her feet.

"How did you find us?"

"My father told you he thought you might be here. He and your grandfather used to come here as kids. You didn't leave here after he called you out. That means you heard what he was saying. That's a good thing."

"I got nowhere else to go," Raley said.

Jessica nodded and motioned her back under the cover of the porch. "Let's get out of the rain. When's he going to be here?"

"Any minute," Raley said. "You're here to arrest him?"

"No," Jessica replied. "I'm not here to kill him, either. I need his help. Yours, too."

"Mine?" Raley blurted. "How?"

Jessica pointed at the table. "First, I need to borrow your jacket and have you wait inside the weapons vault. I need you to trust me."

"He doesn't like surprises."

"That's the point. But he's probably not carrying a weapon, is he? Being here in relative safety, he's grown a little soft. That gives me the opening I need to broach something with the two of you."

"An operation?"

"Of sorts." Jessica smiled. "Can I borrow your jacket?"

* * *

What are you doing? Raley paced in the vault. *What if she lied and she tries to kill him?*

She said she wasn't going to.

Her father's voice said, *"Can you trust her?"*

Raley knew the answer should have been no, but she couldn't bring herself to think it, much less say it. Something about the woman—and her father, too—told Raley otherwise.

You should at least get a weapon in your hand and be ready in case things between the two of them go bad.

"Yeah," she whispered to herself. "That's a good idea."

She reached up to open a cabinet. There was a shimmer, and a large black and white cat appeared atop the cabinet and reached a paw down—with a thumb, she noted—to press against the door.

"You really don't want to do that, Raley."

She gasped. "You can talk?"

"Among other things. My name is Azho, and I am a Depik."

Raley nodded. "I've heard of you. Don't you say things like 'Welcome to our negotiation' a lot?"

"Not as much as you'd think," Azho replied. "This isn't a negotiation, after all. You keep your hands off the weapons in here, and trust Jessica to do her thing, and I'll do the same."

Raley's brow furrowed. "You're not watching her back?"

"No. I'm watching you."

* * *

Kr'et'Socae hadn't made his way directly to the range. He'd gone for a long run in the early morning rain for the first time in weeks. Exercise cleared his thoughts and made him more present. The time had almost come to make his move, but Hatfield had gone quiet. Operations on Prestone were under a communications blackout, as was the SOP when trouble arose. He wasn't concerned. Yet. If the blackout continued another fortnight, he'd be forced to go. Fortunately, Raley was ready. They wouldn't have the full complement of forces he would have liked, but he and Raley could surely defeat a few Crusaders.

The very idea of the guild getting involved and creating these pseudo-mercenary units to enforce martial law on civilians angered him. For all they'd done to him, the Peacemakers had forgotten their charter and their very reason for existing. The time he'd spent with Hr'ent Golramm and served with honor seemed so long ago. The way so many of the current Peacemakers had swallowed the leadership's ploy without question nagged at him. The Crusaders were a pall on the guild, beyond getting between him and his fortune. If he needed to hurt them to get what he wanted, so be it.

At a jog, he turned into the southern end of the field and made his way toward the range. He hadn't heard any rounds being fired, or their echoes off the nearby trees. With a glance toward the horizon, he wondered if she'd slept in, until he caught sight of her sitting at one of the firing tables in her parka with the hood pulled tight about her head. She'd waited for him after all.

He slowed to a walk. "I thought you might be firing already."

Her head was down, studying her slate, and he couldn't see her face. She shook her head but didn't reply. He'd known her long enough to know something must have upset her. They'd made so much progress after the trip to Weqq and her semester trips to Raleigh, but Raley clearly had to find closure on her own.

"I'm flattered you waited on me," he said, stepping onto the porch.

Her head came up. It wasn't Raley.

He froze.

"Kr'et'Socae," the woman said.

"Francis."

The Peacemaker didn't move. Both of her hands remained on the edges of the slate. There was no weapon present that he could see. He had no weapon. There was little doubt he was faster, stronger, and more powerful than Jessica Francis was, but she appeared relaxed and confident, nonetheless. He sniffed the air and thought there might have been a hint of Depik, but there wasn't anything else on the breeze. If she'd brought assistance, they were very well hidden.

"You're not here alone, are you?"

She shook her head. "My companion is with Raley in the vault behind you. I asked them to stay out of the way while we talked."

Impressed, he nodded. "Why are you here, Peacemaker?"

"I'm not a Peacemaker, Kr'et'Socae. At least not right now," Francis replied. "You've undoubtedly heard that, and you're already thinking this through. You know I'm here because your time here is at an end."

"I'm not going with you. Arresting me isn't going to get you reinstated to the guild or anything—"

"My friends are coming here, today, with kill orders from Guild Master Rsach, to which they're bound." Francis stood. He still towered over her, but her demeanor never faltered. "They took down your friend Hatfield on Prestone. You're the last piece of their business, and they were prepared to take you in, dead or alive. The Rmaska Corporation wants you, too, but I'm not going to let that happen. I'm here with a proposition for you and for Miss Reilly."

"And what would that be?"

"The Crusaders are in possession of your fortune, both the legitimate credits you've collected and earned over time, as well as the remainder of the counterfeits you had Hatfield launder into the economy from Prestone. It's a sizable sum. An amount that facilitates your next phase of operations. You've been training Raley and making improvements here for the last two years with the intent of raising a company, yes?"

He didn't reply. Undaunted, the Human continued.

"Only now, you don't have the time. You'd likely be moving to Prestone in a couple of weeks, a month at the most, if you lost contact with Hatfield. Well, we know he's dead, and we know the Crusaders have moved your fortune to Marian Seven. You'd need a full mercenary company or some serious hired help to get it. I'm prepared to do that. Work with me and my friends. We take down the Crusaders, and you get your fortune. If we live through it, you walk away."

"You can't speak for the guild, Francis."

"Let's be clear about this. I'm not speaking for anyone but me and my friends. The same ones coming to kill you today. I'm bringing them into this, too," Francis replied. "The Crusaders are killing civilians, taking what doesn't belong to them, and running amok across the galaxy. They need to be stopped. Doing so is going to require a lot of credits. I help you get your credits, you pay me and my friends a fee, and then you walk away."

He laughed. "You can't think me that naïve, Francis. What's to keep me from killing you?"

"You want your credits. I want to take down the Crusaders. Your credits have been added to their treasure horde on Marian Seven. We're not only talking billions of credits, but priceless artifacts taken from civilians and the other guilds. I'm taking that to bankrupt them before we hit them with every unit I can contract to take them down," Francis replied. "You play a role in that, and when the Peacemaker Guild leadership goes down, your charges disappear."

"You think the guild is going down. I met Counselor. He—"

"He was a puppet. Counselor is an SI. They've been taking control of anyone with pinplants, especially those with multiple sets. That includes almost all the Peacemakers commissioned between you and me. That they didn't initially trust Humans with them used to annoy the hell out of me. I'm thankful for it now. They disconnected yours in prison. That gives us an advantage."

"Indeed," Kr'et'Socae replied. "I noticed the Goltar's pinplants when it recruited me. I didn't think much of it then, but I see it now. All of it."

Francis said nothing. She watched him as circuits connected in his mind. For all his maneuvering and careful planning, he'd allowed himself to be used by a being he'd thought was an ally. Now, an enemy stood before him asking for his help. He wouldn't be used again. There would be a way out of this.

Keep your ears up, and the right breeze will blow your way.

Marian Seven had its merits, too, if it was the same as he remembered. "You want my help to hit this target. I'm familiar with the extensive facilities there. Hr'ent and I spent a year on that planet. We both enjoyed it."

Francis nodded. "You're in?"

"Yes." He nodded solemnly and kept his face still.

Until such time as I can walk away, even if I have to kill you to do it.

Francis extended a hand to him, which he shook, dwarfing the Human's. "You have my word, Kr'et'Socae. Well met."

His throat tightened inexplicably. The words rang in his ears as if Francis had struck a tuning fork. He hadn't said those words in decades. "Well met."

Hands still clasped, she stared up at him. "Your past doesn't matter to me. Help me take down the Crusaders, and I'll fight for your future."

"Forgive me if I don't believe you."

"I don't expect you to, but I'm going to believe you as long as you keep my trust. I simply ask that you trust me to do the same. Fair enough?"

"That's fair," he rumbled and relaxed his grip.

May we live in interesting times.

"Rae? Come on out, honey. It's okay, Azho," Francis said. The vault door opened, and he saw Raley looking at him with concern in her eyes. The Depik stared at him. He held its gaze and nodded respectfully. To his surprise, the catlike being did the same.

"Y'all gonna tell me what's goin' on?" she asked.

"It's fine, Rae. We have a common interest and an opportunity we cannot allow to pass," Kr'et'Socae said. "When will they be here, Francis? Your friends. I'm assuming the Besquith and his friends, yes?"

"Jessica," she said. "Their strike package is planning for a raid around sunset. I have something else arriving before them."

"Something else?" Raley asked. "Why all this now?"

Jessica Francis smiled at her and then turned to stare up into Kr'et'Socae's eyes. "Because your friend knows the target, and I know the enemy. Where I'm from, they call that 'high cotton.'"

Kr'et'Socae shook his head. "I don't understand."

"Good times. Easy money," Raley said. "What do you need from us?"

"As much gear as you can spare from your stores here," Jessica said. "I'll cover transportation. Aside from that, I'll need your utmost performance and your trust. I'll give you mine in return."

"Your friends aren't going to kill us on sight?" Kr'et'Socae asked.

"Leave that to me," Azho said. "It's going to take a lot more than words to make this work. It's going to take trust. They trust Jessica as much as I do. If you know what's good for you both, you'll do the same."

*****

Chapter Thirty-Five

Blue Ridge Kin Headquarters

Sandy Bay Starport

Snapper Isle, Krifay

Pete sat down at the end of the conference table, a cup of coffee in his hand. "Thirty percent KIA. Twenty of my troops." He shook his head. "I've got another fifteen out of action for the near future. My cousin will need a prosthetic. She swears it won't matter, and you won't be able to see it in a boot. I expect her back in uniform faster than the doc thinks it will be."

"She's a good woman, even if she does give in to Haney's insanity," Cora said. "Then again, he took care of the tanks for us."

"Yeah, I suppose." He took a sip. "Do you still want to plan on a joint ceremony?" Pete asked.

"Yes. We lost twenty-two good troops, men, women, Jivool, Goka, and two Lumar among them. Half the rest deserve commendations for major injuries sustained. To a being, they swear they'll attend the funeral ceremony."

"I think there'll be one big one for the Krifay Volunteers," Pete said. "They really took a pounding."

"They made the difference," Cora said. "There's no doubt in my mind, they were the turning point and reason for our victory."

"Agreed. They've been collecting Crusader weapons and gear, so some of them will be better equipped in the future. I also introduced the Planetary Leadership to the Slow Killers. I think orders for modern stuff are being put together. Everyone… and I mean everyone, says never again."

"Can you blame them? Us?" Cora asked. "This is our home. We'll never let it be taken. Besides, I heard other systems are sending aid packages, including military gear. They don't want an important source of protein captured by any who would use it as a threat. They want it the way it's always been. So do I."

"I hear you," Pete said. He held up his cup in salute and flinched. "Damn, my shoulder."

"Speaking of shoulders," Cora said, "did Haney really dislocate both of his?"

"Hell yes, he did," Pete answered. "He plowed in on a crazy-ass strafing run with a crew-served auto rifle tied to the control bar on his glider. They shot a wing off. He's lucky he wasn't killed."

"I saw Conner helping him eat earlier. She was spoon-feeding him clam chowder."

"That's love," Pete said. "Speaking of which, I heard…"

"Yeah," Cora said. She blushed. "Yeah."

"Congratulations. As you'd say, he's good people."

"Thanks."

Her grin stretched across her face. She was happy, despite the sadness at the loss of so many of her beloved Kin. Nails, in the wisdom he'd gained over his many years as a merc, had told her it was okay to be both at the same time. Every unit, everyone, paid a price in this line of work. You had to mourn and move on. The next contract was always looming.

"Let me ask you," Pete said. "Have you found yourself with stacks of messages and inquiries to fill your ranks like I have?"

"Yeah," Cora answered. "Residents of Krifay looking for more than voluntary service. Some are ex-mercs who realized they have a few years left in them. The ranks are filling already. We'll expand, too. My technicians say they can put together some Mk 8s from our spoils. My XO is overseeing it."

"Jerund tells me the same. Modern CASPers. Go figure."

"I know, right? Anyway, Top is interviewing potential recruits with May and Lisalle, so we'll see what shakes out."

"Is he getting around yet?" Pete asked. "He was injured pretty bad, I hear."

"Not really, but Private First Class Tivlang hovers over him and makes sure he takes it easy. He ignores Figgle's complaints and demands that he leave him alone. Tivlang has a one-track mind. There's no way he'll disobey his commander's orders, not even for the first sergeant."

"Nice."

"It has its advantages," she agreed. "Newly promoted Staff Sergeant Squarlik has been taking up the slack. He has the makings of a good NCO."

"I believe it," Pete agreed. "He's a hell of shot, that's for sure. That was 800 yards if it was one."

"I know."

Pete stood up. "Well, I need to get back to my side of the tarmac. I need to help Wilson with the potential recruits, myself. Something tells me we need to fill the ranks and grow our units ASAP. There are still Crusaders out there."

"That's my plan, too. Tell the family I said hello."

"Will do."

* * *

60,000 ft. AGL
Vicinity of Bean Station, Tennessee
Earth

Jyrall held onto a handhold in the drop bay and leaned over the ramp as he watched the Misfits fall toward the darkened planet below. They'd planned to perform a water insertion on the far western edge of Holston Lake and make their way, slowly, toward Raley Reilly's compound on the far southeastern side. Traveling by boat and by foot would take them roughly fifteen hours. They'd infiltrate the western edge of the compound and conduct reconnaissance while Jyrall, Larth, and the McCoy brothers infiltrated by land from the east. *Mako 15* held a steady course at altitude on a filed flight plan toward Raleigh-Durham International Spaceport. At their speed, the drop zone for part two of the operation was seconds away.

"Ready, Snarlyface." Larth grinned. Wearing oversized goggles and a Zuparti protective helmet, not to mention his parachute, reserve parachute, combat assault pack, and weapons case, his partner looked like a bloated insect, but Jyrall didn't have the heart to say it.

Jyrall turned to the McCoy brothers. Both of them were uncharacteristically quiet. "You guys ready?"

"Yeah," Keaton replied as he finished checking his brother's parachute and harness. "You're good, Ricky."

"The hell I am," Ricky said. "I can't jump outta this thing."

"Come on!" Larth laughed. "All the shit you pull, and you can't handle a little freefall? This is the best thing ever!" Larth rubbed his hands together and waddled to the ramp.

Keaton followed, but Ricky didn't move. Jyrall made his way over to the Pushtal, grabbed him by the upper arm, and pulled him toward the ramp. "Listen to me, Ricky. Eyes on me. I'm the only thing you need to focus on right now. Got it?"

"I ain't doin' this, Jyrall. I cain't." Jyrall felt the Pushtal tremble.

"Yes, you can." Jyrall pulled him closer to the ramp. "I've done this a thousand times. There's nothing to it. You step out, and we fly for a few minutes, pull the parachute, and let it bring you down."

"What if I cain't pull the chute?"

"It does it for you, Ricky." Jyrall kept his voice low and calm. "All you have to do is step off the plane."

Ricky locked his legs two steps from the edge. He shook his head violently but said nothing. The jump light turned green, and Keaton and Larth waddled to the edge of the ramp and stepped off.

"You can do this, Ricky."

Ricky shook his head and mumbled incoherently. From his own parachute training at the Academy—one of the easiest three week periods he'd had during training—Jyrall and the other candidates knew their jumpmasters could do anything necessary to get a candidate out of an aircraft on their first jump. Overcoming the fear once often proved enough to help them through the rest of the course. Jyrall pulled, but Ricky didn't budge.

Jyrall shifted his weight, grabbed the front of Ricky's parachute harness with his left hand, and brought his right fist up for a quick, hopefully not too painful, jab to the nose. Ricky flinched and snarled, but his legs unlocked, and before he could take a step back, Jyrall picked him up with both arms, spun to the ramp, and leapt into the air.

Ricky screamed all the way down.

* * *

Tara and the Misfits landed exactly on target a half mile inland of the private marina. They moved silently and swiftly through the early morning and reached their first target as the horizon appeared out of the dawn. They boarded a pontoon boat equipped with a gasoline engine and an electronic trolling motor and pushed off. Using the motor, they glided silently away from the marina and into the expansive lake. Only then, with the dock behind them and the sky brightening, did they relax.

"I could get used to this," Quin'taa said from the captain's chair. He steered the boat with casual ease and spent his time looking around for other boats.

"We can engage the engine whenever you're ready, Boss." Homer pointed to Araceli. "Go ahead and lower it into the water."

Araceli stepped behind Quin'taa and used the throttle to lower the engine into the water. "Set."

"Go ahead and start it," Tara ordered. "Keep it to a dull roar, Q."

"Yes, ma'am." The Oogar actually sounded a little hurt as he turned the engine to idle. He pushed the throttle forward slightly, and the boat accelerated to the east.

Tara walked forward to where Whirr maintained forward security. "Everything clear?"

"This is a regular Human activity? Boating?" Whirr's antennae bobbled in the light breeze. "I find it relaxing, despite maintaining security."

Tara nodded and let a small smile crease her face. "We're on the boat for an hour. Enjoy it. I don't think we're going to find anything to worry about out here."

"Vigilance must be constant," Whirr replied and tapped her carapace with respect. "I won't let my family down."

Tara felt her throat tighten. She'd often felt the same way, and she recognized their closeness was both their greatest strength and their most glaring weakness. For the millionth time, she closed her eyes and prayed to anyone listening that she wouldn't have to bury her team. She thought of her former soldiers, of the young officers Howl and Kirkland, and Hex Allison. There had been so much death, but the fight wasn't over. There would be more, and she knew it was her responsibility to keep it from happening to her team. Fate couldn't be stopped, she knew. It was a mighty hunter that preyed on the unprepared. They could've sashayed into Reilly's compound, but instead, they took their time. They would do it right.

"Me either, Whirr." Tara patted the MinSha warrior on her shoulder. "Me, either. Make sure you get some chow before we hit the shore. It's a long walk."

Whirr didn't reply, nor did she need to. She was a Misfit like the rest of them. Everything they would do would be done together, and Tara wouldn't have it any other way.

* * *

Jyrall and Larth led the McCoys through the deep, dark woods until they reached a series of freshly mown clearings. They passed an obstacle course, a rifle range, and what looked to be a series of small shacks for billeting before they reached a much larger clearing. Across the meter-high grass, roughly two hundred meters away, was a maintenance barn large enough for a battalion of CASPers.

It was far larger than Jyrall had expected to find. Based on Jessica Francis' mission reports, Raleigh Reilly was a terrible commander. The compound said otherwise, but Jyrall also realized that could easily be the work of his daughter and the coal-black Equiri he saw working outside the building in the midday sun.

"Eyes on Kr'et'Socae." Jyrall felt his heartbeat accelerate. Since Diam and their last fight, he'd wanted another shot at the disgraced Enforcer. Kr'et'Socae had very nearly taken Jyrall's eye with his explosive vest. There would be no such advantage now. All he had to do was—

"Hey, check it out. Two CASPers," Larth called. "I've got eyes on a… yeah that's a Besquith."

Jyrall's head snapped toward the targets moving out of the maintenance shed. He found the older Gamma easily. She wore elaborate braces on her legs, and still barely kept up with the CASPers. She leaned on a cane, and the white on the end of her maw glistened in the sun. Jyrall's rage calmed. An elder Gamma, by her presence alone, commanded respect.

What's going on here?

The two CASPers were carrying a crate between them. One was a scarred, barely functional Mk 6 without any weaponry at all. The other was a sleek, black Mk 8 that looked brand new and carried a MAC cannon in a stored position on both shoulders. A formidable machine in the hands of a competent pilot. They walked forward, and Jyrall studied the crate they carried. It was devoid of logos and markings. The Mk 8 CASPer's cockpit appeared to be marked with nose art—a typical Human display of affection for their equipment. He'd noted several amongst the recordings and files from Force 25 and other unit histories. The Mk 6 CASPer's cockpit opened, and the dark-haired girl climbed out.

"Eyes on Raley Reilly," Larth whispered. "I'm letting the Misfits know we've identified the targets and are waiting for their arrival."

"How long?"

"No more than an hour," Larth replied.

Jyrall looked past him to Ricky and Keaton. "Any network you can take down?"

"I've got a strong signal, but it's well encrypted. I'm not getting in without a direct connection," Keaton replied. "Get me close enough, and I'll take it down."

"Shoulda dropped Frank and Stein," Ricky lamented. He'd gradually warmed up into almost his usual self after his first HALD.

The Mk 8 stepped back into the maintenance shed as the dark-haired girl and Kr'et'Socae worked on the top of the crate with power drills.

"Wonder what's in the box?" Larth asked.

Jyrall didn't answer. Instead, he turned his attention again to the Besquith. The female's mechanical brace appeared to be the only thing enabling the older one to even walk. She carried herself with a quiet dignity. Jyrall wondered if she'd overseen the delivery of this particular crate herself. If so, what did it mean?

"What d'ya reckon that is?" Keaton whispered. Jyrall shrugged but didn't reply. He hadn't been looking at the crate, so he turned the viewer back to his original target.

"It's big enough for a CASPer. You think it's that missing Mk 9?" Larth wondered aloud.

"That's what concerns me," Jyrall growled.

"What's that dadgum symbol on it? The silver thing," Ricky whispered.

"Looks like a lion's—"

The Mk 8 returned and blocked their view. Its cockpit opened, and Jyrall turned the viewer in its direction to identify the pilot and froze. "What in the hell?"

Larth bumped his shoulder. "Who is it, Snarlyface?"

Jyrall's mouth fell open. He turned to his friend and tried to find his voice.

"Jessica."

There was a rustle in the grass in front of them, and a familiar black and white form appeared from nothing.

"Peacemakers. If you recall, my name is Azho. Welcome to our negotiation. Jessica is expecting you. Please have the Misfits stand down and rendezvous here immediately. We have a situation."

# # # # #

About Kevin Ikenberry

Kevin's head has been in the clouds since he was old enough to read. Ask him and he'll tell you that he still wants to be an astronaut. A retired Army officer, Kevin has a diverse background in space and space science education. A former manager of the world-renowned U.S. Space Camp program in Huntsville, Alabama and a former executive of two Challenger Learning Centers, Kevin works with space every day and lives in Colorado with his family.

Kevin's bestselling debut science fiction novel, ***Sleeper Protocol***, was released by Red Adept Publishing in January 2016 and was a Finalist for the 2017 Colorado Book Award. Publisher's Weekly called it "an emotionally powerful debut." His military science fiction novel ***Runs In The Family*** was released by Strigidae Publishing in January 2016 and re-released by Theogony books in 2018. ***Peacemaker***, Book 6 of the Revelations Cycle, was released in 2017, spawning its own line of books in the Four Horsemen Universe.

Kevin is an Active Member of the Science Fiction Writers of America and he is member of Pikes Peak Writers and the Rocky Mountain Fiction Writers. He is an alumna of the Superstars Writing Seminar.

* * *

About Kevin Steverson

Kevin Steverson is a retired veteran of the U.S. Army. Among other works, he is the author of the Amazon bestselling science fiction novels, the Salvage Title Trilogy, now optioned for feature film. He is a published songwriter as well as an author. When he is not on the road as the Tour Manager for the band Cypress Spring, he can be found in the foothills of the NE Georgia mountains, writing in one fashion or another.

* * * * *

The following is an

Excerpt from Book One of the Lunar Free State:

The Moon and Beyond

John E. Siers

Available from Theogony Books

eBook, Audio, and Paperback

Excerpt from "The Moon and Beyond:"

"So, what have we got?" The chief had no patience for inter-agency squabbles.

The FBI man turned to him with a scowl. "We've got some abandoned buildings, a lot of abandoned stuff—none of which has anything to do with spaceships—and about a hundred and sixty scientists, maintenance people, and dependents left behind, all of whom claim they knew nothing at all about what was really going on until today. Oh, yeah, and we have some stripped computer hardware with all memory and processor sections removed. I mean physically taken out, not a chip left, nothing for the techies to work with. And not a scrap of paper around that will give us any more information…at least, not that we've found so far. My people are still looking."

"What about that underground complex on the other side of the hill?"

"That place is wiped out. It looks like somebody set off a *nuke* in there. The concrete walls are partly fused! The floor is still too hot to walk on. Our people say they aren't sure how you could even *do* something like that. They're working on it, but I doubt they're going to find anything."

"What about our man inside, the guy who set up the computer tap?"

"Not a trace, chief," one of the NSA men said. "Either he managed to keep his cover and stayed with them, or they're holding him prisoner, or else…" The agent shrugged.

"You think they terminated him?" The chief lifted an eyebrow. "A bunch of rocket scientists?"

"Wouldn't put it past them. Look at what Homeland Security ran into. Those motion-sensing chain guns are *nasty*, and the area between the inner and outer perimeter fence is mined! Of course, they posted warning signs, even marked the fire zones for the guns. Nobody would have gotten hurt if the troops had taken the signs seriously."

The Homeland Security colonel favored the NSA man with an icy look. "That's bullshit. How did we know they weren't bluffing? You'd feel pretty stupid if we'd played it safe and then found out there were no defenses, just a bunch of signs!"

"Forget it!" snarled the chief. "Their whole purpose was to delay us, and it worked. What about the Air Force?"

"It might as well have been a UFO sighting as far as they're concerned. Two of their F-25s went after that spaceship, or whatever it was we saw leaving. The damned thing went straight up, over eighty thousand meters per minute, they say. That's nearly Mach Two, in a *vertical climb*. No aircraft in *anybody's* arsenal can sustain a climb like that. Thirty seconds after they picked it up, it was well above their service ceiling and still accelerating. Ordinary ground radar couldn't find it, but NORAD *thinks* they might have caught a short glimpse with one of their satellite-watch systems, a hundred miles up and still going."

"So where did they go?"

"Well, chief, if we believe what those leftover scientists are telling us, I guess they went to the Moon."

*****

Get "The Moon and Beyond" here:
https://www.amazon.com/dp/B097QMN7PJ.

Find out more about John E. Siers at:
https://chriskennedypublishing.com.

*****

The following is an

Excerpt from Book One of Abner Fortis, ISMC:

Cherry Drop

P.A. Piatt

Available from Theogony Books

eBook, Audio, and Paperback

Excerpt from "Cherry Drop:"

"Here they come!"

A low, throbbing buzz rose from the trees and the undergrowth shook. Thousands of bugs exploded out of the jungle, and Fortis' breath caught in his throat. The insects tumbled over each other in a rolling, skittering mass that engulfed everything in its path.

The Space Marines didn't need an order to open fire. Rifles cracked and the grenade launcher thumped over and over as they tried to stem the tide of bugs. Grenades tore holes in the ranks of the bugs and well-aimed rifle fire dropped many more. Still, the bugs advanced.

Hawkins' voice boomed in Fortis' ear. "LT, fall back behind the fighting position, clear the way for the heavy weapons."

Fortis looked over his shoulder and saw the fighting holes bristling with Marines who couldn't fire for fear of hitting their own comrades. He thumped Thorsen on the shoulder.

"Fall back!" he ordered. "Take up positions behind the fighting holes."

Thorsen stopped firing and moved among the other Marines, relaying Fortis' order. One by one, the Marines stopped firing and made for the rear. As the gunfire slacked off, the bugs closed ranks and continued forward.

After the last Marine had fallen back, Fortis motioned to Thorsen.

"Let's go!"

Thorsen turned and let out a blood-chilling scream. A bug had approached unnoticed and buried its stinger deep in Thorsen's calf. The stricken Marine fell to the ground and began to convulse as the neurotoxin entered his bloodstream.

"Holy shit!" Fortis drew his kukri, ran over, and chopped at the insect stinger. The injured bug made a high-pitched shrieking noise, which Fortis cut short with another stroke of his knife.

Viscous, black goo oozed from the hole in Thorsen's armor and his convulsions ceased.

"Get the hell out of there!"

Hawkins was shouting in his ear, and Abner looked up. The line of bugs was ten meters away. For a split second he almost turned and ran, but the urge vanished as quickly as it appeared. He grabbed Thorsen under the arms and dragged the injured Marine along with him, pursued by the inexorable tide of gaping pincers and dripping stingers.

Fortis pulled Thorsen as fast as he could, straining with all his might against the substantial Pada-Pada gravity. Thorsen convulsed and slipped from Abner's grip and the young officer fell backward. When he sat up, he saw the bugs were almost on them.

* * * * *

* * * * *

The following is an

Excerpt from Book One of This Fine Crew:

The Signal Out of Space

Mike Jack Stoumbos

Now Available from Theogony Books

eBook and Paperback

Excerpt from "The Signal Out of Space:"

Day 4 of Training, Olympus Mons Academy

I want to make something clear from square one: we were winning.

More importantly, *I* was winning. Sure, the whole thing was meant to be a "team effort," and I'd never say this to an academy instructor, but the fact of the matter is this: it was a race and I was in the driver's seat. Like hell I was going to let any other team beat us, experimental squad or not.

At our velocity, even the low planetary grav didn't temper the impact of each ice mogul on the glistening red terrain. We rocketed up, plummeted down, and cut new trails in the geo-formations, spraying orange ice and surface rust in our wake. So much of the red planet was still like a fresh sheet of snow, and I was eager to carve every inch of it.

Checking on the rest of the crew, I thought our tactical cadet was going to lose her lunch. I had no idea how the rest of the group was managing, different species being what they are.

Of our complement of five souls, sans AI-assist or anything else that cadets should learn to live without, Shin and I were the only Humans. The communications cadet was a Teek—all exoskeleton and antennae, but the closest to familiar. He sat in the copilot seat, ready to take the controls if I had to tap out. His two primary arms were busy with the scanning equipment, but one of his secondary hands hovered over the E-brake, which made me more anxious than assured.

I could hear the reptile humming in the seat behind me, in what I registered as "thrill," each time I overcame a terrain obstacle with even greater speed, rather than erring on the side of caution.

Rushing along the ice hills of Mars on six beautifully balanced wheels was a giant step up from the simulator. The design of the Red Terrain Vehicle was pristine, but academy-contrived obstacles mixed with natural formations bumped up the challenge factor. The dummy fire sounds from our sensors and our mounted cannon only added to the sense of adventure. The whole thing was like fulfilling a fantasy, greater than my first jet around good ol' Luna. If the camera evidence had survived, I bet I would have been grinning like an idiot right up until the Teek got the bogey signal.

"Cadet Lidstrom," the Teek said, fast but formal through his clicking mandibles, "unidentified signal fifteen degrees right of heading." His large eyes pulsed with green luminescence, bright enough for me to see in the corner of my vision. It was an eerie way to express emotion, which I imagined would make them terrible at poker.

I hardly had a chance to look at the data while maintaining breakneck KPH, but in the distance, it appeared to be one of our surface vehicles, all six wheels turned up to the stars.

The lizard hummed a different note and spoke in strongly accented English, "Do we have time to check?"

The big furry one at the rear gruffed in reply, but not in any language I could understand.

"Maybe it's part of the test," I suggested. "Like a bonus. Paul, was it hard to find?"

The Teek, who went by Paul, clicked to himself and considered the question. His exoskeletal fingers worked furiously for maybe a second before he informed us, "It is obscured by interference."

"Sounds like a bonus to me," Shin said. Then she asked me just the right question: "Lidstrom, can you get us close without losing our lead?"

The Arteevee would have answered for me if it could, casting an arc of red debris as I swerved. I admit, I did not run any mental calculations, but a quick glance at my rear sensors assured me. "Hell yeah! I got this."

In the mirror, I saw our large, hairy squadmate, the P'rukktah, transitioning to the grappler interface, in case we needed to pick something up when we got there. Shin, on tactical, laid down some cannon fire behind us—tiny, non-lethal silicon scattershot—to kick up enough dust that even the closest pursuer would lose our visual heading for a few seconds at least. I did not get a chance to find out what the reptile was doing as we neared the overturned vehicle.

I had maybe another half-k to go when Paul's eyes suddenly shifted to shallow blue and his jaw clicked wildly. He only managed one English word: "Peculiar!"

Before I could ask, I was overcome with a sound, a voice, a shrill screech. I shut my eyes for an instant, then opened them to see where I was driving and the rest of my squad, but everything was awash in some kind of blue light. If I thought it would do any good, I might have tried to plug my ears.

Paul didn't have the luxury of closing his compound eyes, but his primary arms tried to block them. His hands instinctively guarded his antennae.

Shin half fell from the pivoting cannon rig, both palms cupping her ears, which told me the sound wasn't just in my head.

The reptile bared teeth in a manner too predatory to be a smile and a rattling hum escaped her throat, dissonant to the sound.

Only the P'rukktah weathered this unexpected cacophony with grace. She stretched out clearly muscled arms and grabbed anchor points on either side of the vehicle. In blocky computer-generated words, her translator pulsed out, "What—Is—That?"

Facing forward again, I was able to see the signs of wreckage ahead and of distressed ground. I think I was about to ask if I should turn away when the choice was taken from me.

An explosion beneath our vehicle heaved us upward, nose first. Though nearly bucked out of my seat, I was prepared to recover our heading or even to stop and assess what had felt like a bomb.

A second blast, larger than the first, pushed us from behind, probably just off my right rear wheel, spraying more particulates and lifting us again.

One screech was replaced with another. Where the first had been almost organic, this new one was clearly the sound of tearing metal.

The safety belt caught my collarbone hard as my body tried to torque out of the seat. Keeping my eyes open, I saw one of our tires—maybe two thirds of a tire—whip off into the distance on a strange trajectory, made even stranger by the fact that the horizon was spinning.

The red planet came at the windshield and the vehicle was wrenched enough to break a seal. I barely noticed the sudden escape of air; I was too busy trying, futilely, to drive the now upside-down craft…

*****

*****

Made in the USA
Las Vegas, NV
29 March 2025